The Reviewers Rave Over Kat Martin

"Kat Martin is pure entertainment from page one!"
—Jill Marie Landis

"Kat Martin shimmers like a bright diamond in the genre."
—*Romantic Times*

"Kat Martin keeps on getting better and better . . . A premier historical writer."
—*Affaire de Coeur*

"Kat Martin dishes up sizzling passion and true love, then she serves it with savoir faire."
—*Los Angeles Daily News*

Wicked Promise

"Conflict dogs the steps of the protagonists while tension keeps the reader alert. Humor is like icing on a cake in this delightful tale."
—*Rendezvous*

"This is a fast-paced and passionate story; as always, Ms. Martin is wonderful."
—*Bell, Book and Candle*

"A mistress of the genre, Kat Martin delivers what readers desire: an exciting, sensual, engrossing romance whose characters use the power of their love to give them strength."
—*Romantic Times* (4½ Stars, Top Pick)

more . . .

Dangerous Passions

"Ms. Martin has an excitement and edge to all the books that bring the readers back time after time."

—*Bell, Book and Candle*

"War, lust, deception, and seduction make this thrilling historical come alive as this intense romance unfolds. Graphic war passages, sensuous romantic encounters, and the quest to find an unknown traitor make this historical masterpiece unforgettable. Kat Martin has once again given us an inspiring tale of love, hope, and promise."

—*Rendezvous*

"Kat Martin weaves a tale as compelling as any she has written. This novel is un-put-downable—a non-stop read filled with excitement, tempestuous passion, betrayal, mystery, and everything romance readers have come to expect from a top-notch writer."

—*Romantic Times* (4½ Stars)

"The irresistible but scarred lead protagonists add the needed romantic element that turn a fabulous novel into a tremendous reading experience that will captivate readers."

—*Affaire de Coeur* (Five Stars)

"You'll enjoy every fast-paced minute!"

—*Interludes*

The Reviewers Rave Over Kat Martin

"Kat Martin is pure entertainment from page one!"
—Jill Marie Landis

"Kat Martin shimmers like a bright diamond in the genre."
—*Romantic Times*

"Kat Martin keeps on getting better and better . . . A premier historical writer."
—*Affaire de Coeur*

"Kat Martin dishes up sizzling passion and true love, then she serves it with savoir faire."
—*Los Angeles Daily News*

Wicked Promise

"Conflict dogs the steps of the protagonists while tension keeps the reader alert. Humor is like icing on a cake in this delightful tale."
—*Rendezvous*

"This is a fast-paced and passionate story; as always, Ms. Martin is wonderful."
—*Bell, Book and Candle*

"A mistress of the genre, Kat Martin delivers what readers desire: an exciting, sensual, engrossing romance whose characters use the power of their love to give them strength."
—*Romantic Times* (4½ Stars, Top Pick)

more . . .

DANGEROUS PASSIONS

''Ms. Martin has an excitement and edge to all the books that bring the readers back time after time.''

—*Bell, Book and Candle*

''War, lust, deception, and seduction make this thrilling historical come alive as this intense romance unfolds. Graphic war passages, sensuous romantic encounters, and the quest to find an unknown traitor make this historical masterpiece unforgettable. Kat Martin has once again given us an inspiring tale of love, hope, and promise.''

—*Rendezvous*

''Kat Martin weaves a tale as compelling as any she has written. This novel is un-put-downable—a non-stop read filled with excitement, tempestuous passion, betrayal, mystery, and everything romance readers have come to expect from a top-notch writer.''

—*Romantic Times* (4½ Stars)

''The irresistible but scarred lead protagonists add the needed romantic element that turn a fabulous novel into a tremendous reading experience that will captivate readers.''

—*Affaire de Coeur* (Five Stars)

''You'll enjoy every fast-paced minute!''

—*Interludes*

"Steamy, sensual, magnificent, and exciting describe the scintillating new novel by Kat Martin as she takes fans on a perilous journey through the tempestuous Napoleonic war. Ms. Martin weaves history into her story creating a tapestry rich and elegant with romance hot enough to singe the fingers, curl the toes, and scorch the pages as we turn them ever fast. Destined to shoot to the top of the charts, DANGEROUS PASSIONS leaves the reader breathless, exhilarated, clamoring for more. A keeper!"

—*Romancing the Web*

NOTHING BUT VELVET

"Kat Martin draws the reader into Regency England and the lives of wealth and privilege, with the assurance of a master . . . A writer of renown who thrills us."

—*Under the Covers Book Reviews*

"NOTHING BUT VELVET is nothing but brilliant. The lead characters are super, and the villain as vile as they come. The story line is fast-paced and extremely interesting."

—*Affaire de Coeur*

"What more could a romance reader want? . . . [NOTHING BUT VELVET] is a boisterous carriage ride in which Martin shows herself to have a firm grasp on the reins."

—*Publishers Weekly*

MIDNIGHT RIDER

"Kat Martin weaves a marvelous western romance that sizzles with unbridled passion and a heated battle of wills. Readers will be enraptured by the heart-pounding adventure and warmed to their toes of the sensuality of MIDNIGHT RIDER."

—*Romantic Times*

"Another winner . . . Kat Martin keeps on getting better and better."

—*Affaire de Coeur*

"What an outlaw! Dark, daring, dangerous and delicious! MIDNIGHT RIDER is a rich panorama of old California. I couldn't put it down!"

—Georgina Gentry

DEVIL'S PRIZE

"Tempting, alluring, sensual and irresistible—destined to be a soaring success."

—*Romantic Times*

"Kat Martin is a premier historical romance author . . . and DEVIL'S PRIZE enhances her first-class reputation."

—*Affaire de Coeur*

BOLD ANGEL

''This medieval romance is a real pleasure . . . the romance is paramount.''

—*Publishers Weekly*

''BOLD ANGEL moves quickly through a bold and exciting period of history. As usual, Kat has written an excellent and entertaining novel of days gone by.''

—Heather Graham

''An excellent medieval romance . . . Readers will not only love this novel but clamor for a sequel.''

—*Affaire de Coeur*

ST. MARTIN'S PAPERBACKS TITLES BY
KAT MARTIN

Gypsy Lord
Sweet Vengeance
Bold Angel
Devil's Prize
Midnight Rider
Innocence Undone
Nothing But Velvet
Dangerous Passions
Wicked Promise
Night Secrets

St. Martin's Paperbacks

NIGHT SECRETS

ISBN: 0-312-97002-1

Printed in the United States of America

St. Martin's Paperbacks edition/May 1999

St. Martin's Paperbacks are published by St. Martin's Press, 175 Fifth Avenue, New York, NY 10010.

10 9 8 7 6 5 4 3 2 1

To my husband, Larry, on the release of his first big contemporary novel, *Sounding Drum*. Good luck, honey. Hope it's a huge bestseller!

Night Secrets

CHAPTER 1

MARCH 1803

Night was always the worst. Brandy stared out through the wavy glass panes that distorted the darkness, saw only her weary reflection, and wondered how much longer she could stand it.

As far back as she could remember, every day of her nineteen years, Brianne Winters had worked from the first gray hint of dawn till blackness curtained the mullioned windows of the White Horse Tavern.

"Brandy, girl, you had better stop daydreamin' and get back to work. Your papa will be back any minute and there's customers with empty tankards out there." Her best friend, Florence Moody, a slender, dark-haired woman six years older than Brandy, stood at the kitchen door, her thin face nearly obscured by steam. They had worked together so long, Flo seemed more a mother or an older sister than merely a friend.

Brandy smiled. "Sorry. I didn't mean to be gone so long. Old Salty Johnson is back in port. He was telling me about his trip down from Halifax. I guess they ran into some weather and one of the masts went down. Nearly sank the blasted ship."

Flo wiped her hands on the apron tied over her skirt. "Old Salty always could tell a tale. Don't worry yourself about it. We just now started getting busy. The *Fairwind*'s dropped anchor and the crew has begun driftin' in. They'll be a handful tonight, seein' as they been at sea for nigh on two months."

Brandy groaned as she walked out of the kitchen and into the smoky, dimly lit taproom. "I swear Dalton's crew is the worst of the lot. I don't look forward to their arrival." The tavern was nearly a hundred years old, with heavy oak beams and flagstone floors. Pewter sconces lined the walls, casting shadowy candlelight against the smoke-darkened wood. Though her father loved the old place, Brandy hated it. It was dingy, she thought, smelled of stale beer, and the walls were cold and dank.

"They're a rowdy lot," Flo said, "and no mistake. We'll be sportin' bruises from our backsides to our knees come mornin'."

"Not me. I'm sick unto death of these damnable sailors and their pinching and pawing ways. The first man who lays a hand on me will be feeling the weight of a tankard against the side of his head."

Flo just laughed. "Your papa won't much like that. Bad for business. He likes you to keep the sailors happy."

But Brandy didn't really care what her father liked. He certainly didn't care what she liked or wanted. All he cared about was his wretched tavern and making more money.

"I'm Big Jake Winters," he would say, "owner of the White Horse, finest tavern on the Charleston quay." He was always so proud of the place, a legacy he was building for his son. Only Big Jake never had a son.

In truth, his wife had died giving him his one and only heir, a petite daughter, with Ellen Winters's same red-gold hair. Nothing at all like the big strapping boy Jake had so desperately wanted. A second wife had birthed another girl, smaller even than Brandy, and so frail she hadn't lasted through the first Charleston cold. Frances Winters died of the yellow fever when Brandy was ten years old, and Big Jake finally resigned himself to what he saw as God's will.

The bitter fact was he would never have a son. A daughter would have to suffice, but Jake's resentment of the fact hovered like a huge, dark cloud over Brandy's head every minute of every day.

"You went to market this morning, didn't you?" she

asked Flo. In a simple brown skirt that showed a bit too much ankle, a lace-up stomacher, and a scoop-necked white peasant blouse that exposed the tops of her breasts—the attire of the White Horse serving maids—Brandy leaned over a scarred wooden table to mop up a spilled tankard of ale, her single long braid sliding over one shoulder.

"Matter of fact, I just got back," Flo said. "We ran short of eggs. Picked some up along with some side pork for your papa's breakfast."

"So what interesting tidbits of gossip did you hear?"

"Bless me—I nearly forgot. I did hear a bit of news you'll want to hear."

"Good news, I hope. I could stand a little of that for a change."

Flo moved behind the wide plank bar to tighten the loose bung on a cask that had started dripping brandy. "Word is *Seahawk*'s comin' in. Should be docking anytime now. Cap Ogden down to the lighthouse spotted her off the point, sailin' in toward the harbor."

Brandy's heart began thudding uncomfortably. *Seahawk.* Surely not. But her pulse inched up several notches just the same. "I thought Captain Delaine was headed back to England. I didn't expect we'd be seeing him again for at least a couple more months."

Flo shrugged her shoulders. She was a slender woman with broad hips and a wide, welcoming smile. "Wouldn't know about that. Cap sounded pretty sure, though. He don't make many mistakes."

Brandy's hand shook faintly. "No . . . no he doesn't make many mistakes." Absently, she walked away, her mind on the big, full-rigged ship *Seahawk* and its handsome owner, Captain Marcus Delaine. Or more accurately, Captain Delaine, Lord Hawksmoor, his newly inherited title as much a surprise to him as it was to everyone else.

Recalling his lean, dark, slightly arrogant profile, she thought that it probably shouldn't have been. He had always had a presence about him. His aristocratic blood was apparent in every gesture, every self-assured movement. He was born to command and it showed in every line of his darkly attractive face, from the high-carved cheekbones to the firm set of his well-formed lips.

He was tall and broad-shouldered, with narrow hips and not an ounce of spare flesh over his bones. He was solid and sinewy, his hair coal-black and slightly curly, always a little too long, feathering over the collar of his perfectly tailored navy blue coat. Marcus Delaine was a man among men. His crew knew it and so did Brandy Winters.

Which was why, for as long as she could remember, she had been a little in love with him.

''Better get movin', girl.'' Flo nudged her toward the bar. ''Big Jake's comin' down the stairs.''

Brandy sighed and nodded, pasted on a smile, and set to work. The afternoon slid past and evening crept in. The taproom had begun to fill up, mostly with *Fairwind* sailors. Smoke hung in patches above the wide plank bar, burning her lungs with the harsh smell of tobacco. Raucous laughter drifted into the heavy, age-darkened rafters.

The hours moved sluggishly past, a blur of bawdy jokes and fending off the sailors' roaming hands. God, she hated this place. If the Lord would grant her a single wish, it would be escape from the mindless drudgery and endless hours of boredom at the White Horse Tavern.

Someday, she thought wistfully. Someday, I'll find a way to leave.

The evening wore on. She waited on a table of British seamen and found herself enthralled by a story told by a sailor named Boggs. He'd been forced into service by an English press gang when he was just a boy. Oddly, over the years, the boy had become a man who loved the sea and its many adventures. Brandy listened with a sharp pang of envy, wishing as she had a hundred times that she had been born a lad who could run away to sea and seek a life of adventure, instead of being shackled like a prisoner to a dreary future in the White Horse Tavern.

The hour grew late. It was nearly midnight when Cole Proctor, first mate aboard the *Fairwind,* shoved through the swinging doors with some of his men and walked into the taproom. Brandy had been up since dawn. Her feet hurt, her eyes burned, and a dull ache stabbed into her lower back. Now, big, burly, loudmouthed Cole Proctor was here. Brandy wondered if the night could possibly get any worse.

Hoping he would take a seat on Flo's side of the taproom, she slipped silently into the kitchen and peered through a crack in the door.

"What the devil do you think you're doin'?" Big Jake strolled up, his bushy salt and pepper brows drawn together in a scowl. "We've help enough in the kitchen. Get back out there where yer needed. There's customers a-waitin'. Get yerself back to work, or I'll be takin' a switch to yer fanny."

She started to argue, to ask him to let her stay hidden for a minute or two so she might avoid Cole Proctor and his too-friendly hands, but she knew it would do her no good. Big Jake was a strict disciplinarian and to him the customer always came first. His daughter was only a woman. A little mauling never hurt her and it was good for business. At times Brandy wondered just how far her father would go to ensure the success of the White Horse Tavern.

"Get along with ye, now." He gripped her arm so tight she winced, and dragged her back toward the door.

"I'm going, Papa." Unconsciously rubbing the red spot on her arm, she walked back into the room, heading straight for the table in the corner Cole Proctor had chosen, a place he had purposely selected on her side of the taproom.

"Good evening, Mr. Proctor." She forced herself to smile, being careful to stand just out of his reach. "What'll it be for you and your men tonight?"

"Well, now, look what we have here, mates." His eyes raked downward from the top of her head to the soles of her sturdy brown shoes. They lingered for a moment on her ankles, then crept upward to settle on her breasts. "What ya say, mates? Ain't she the prettiest bit of baggage this side of the Atlantic?"

She colored a little and her chin went up. Compliments from women-hungry sailors were hardly new, but Proctor's were always slightly crude. And none of them looked at her with the same naked lust the big first mate always did.

"I asked what it was you would like to have."

He laughed, long and lewdly. "Did you hear that, lads? The lady wants to know what it is that we'd like to have." A meaty hand snaked out and grabbed her wrist. She tried to pull away, but he was more than twice her size and his hold was unbreakable. With little effort, he dragged her down on his lap and wrapped a beefy arm around her waist.

"What we'd like, my little dove, is a big piece of you."

"Let me go—I have work to do." Brandy started to struggle but he merely laughed in that vulgar way of his. Clamping both her wrists together in one of his big hands, he settled her more squarely on his knees.

"No, sir, I can't think of a thing that would please me more than spreading those pretty white thighs of yours and burying my big, hard—"

"That's enough, Proctor." Brandy's eyes slashed upward to the tall dark figure with the deep, forbidding voice. "Let the girl go."

Her cheeks were flaming. She felt embarrassed and humiliated, yet she had never been so relieved as she was to see Marcus Delaine.

"The girl asked me a question. I was only just giving her an answer. I'd advise you, Captain, to trim your own sails and stay the devil out of this."

Brandy squirmed but she couldn't break free. The captain watched her struggle and the hand at his side balled into a fist.

"I told you to let her go. I won't say it again."

Brandy bit her lip. Her father would be furious if she were the cause of a fight in the tavern. She forced her eyes to the captain's face, hoping she looked more composed than she felt. "It's all right, Captain Delaine. Mr. Proctor was only teasing. Weren't you . . . Cole?" She said with what she hoped was a soft, cajoling voice that disguised the anger bubbling up inside her.

The big first mate cracked a lustful smile. "That's right,

Captain. We was just bein' friendly-like. Nothin' for you to get all worked up about.''

Eyes an intense midnight blue so dark they looked black speared into her. ''Is that right, Miss Winters? Mr. Proctor is just being friendly?''

She nearly choked on the word. ''Yes.'' The thought of Marcus Delaine believing she actually enjoyed the pawing attentions of a man like Cole Proctor made her stomach turn in disgust. But fear of her father's wrath was far worse.

He straightened, drawing himself up to his full, imposing height. ''Then I shall have to beg your pardon.'' He made a slight bow, but his smile was hard-edged and cold. He started to turn away and she might have survived the moment with only a bit of humiliation. She might have been able to discreetly extricate herself from Cole's octopus-tentacled embrace if the beefy sailor hadn't chosen that moment to crudely pinch her bottom.

Fury swept her like a gale-force wind and all her good intentions flew right out the window. With a shriek, Brandy leaped to her feet, moving so swiftly the first mate lost his hold. She slapped him hard across the face.

''You are the most despicable, foulest creature I have every had the misfortune to meet. If you ever touch me that way again I swear I'll find a pistol and shoot you!''

She whirled away from him and smack into Marcus Delaine's broad chest. A corner of his mouth quirked upward in the barest hint of a smile. ''I thought he was just being friendly.''

Brandy flushed and backed a step away. ''Cole Proctor wouldn't know the first thing about being friendly. I just didn't want to cause any trouble.''

''The fault was hardly yours.''

''True, but that's the way my father would see it.'' She started to say something else, to thank him for his effort to intervene, when she heard Cole Proctor's chair scraping backward and turned to see him coming to his feet.

His thick fingers rubbed a reddened cheek. ''You little hellcat, you hit me. I'll teach you what happens when you raise a hand against Cole Proctor.'' He reached for her but the captain pulled her out of harm's way and stepped between them.

''You had that slap coming, Proctor, and you know it. You want to teach someone a lesson, why don't you start with me?''

Big teeth flashed in a feral grin. ''Now, there's a good idea. I'll take care of you, then haul the girl out back and deal with her.''

''Her father might have something to say about that.''

Proctor scoffed. ''Big Jake don't give a damn about her. Odds are, if he thought she'd bring a high enough price, he'd sell her off for the night to the highest bidder.''

Brandy's face went pale, and a muscle tightened in the captain's lean cheek. ''Why don't we go outside?'' he said softly. ''Perhaps we can discuss the subject more fully.''

But the beefy first mate had no intention of leaving the safety of his men. Instead he swung a roundhouse punch that Marcus Delaine neatly sidestepped, then a second powerful blow that would have sent a strong man to his knees. The captain dodged them both, avoided the chair the first mate tossed at his head, stepped in, and landed a crushing blow to Proctor's stomach that doubled him over.

A second hard punch, neatly delivered to the side of Proctor's jaw, sent him sprawling into a corner, his head thudding loudly against the wall. With a grunt of pain his eyes rolled back and the fight was over.

Unfortunately, by now every *Fairwind* crewman in the tavern was on his feet and itching to take up the gauntlet against the men in the crew of the *Seahawk* who had come in behind their captain. Someone swore, another curse followed, and the tavern erupted in chaos. Chairs flew through the air. Tankards of ale crashed against men's skulls. Brandy dodged an upended table and squeaked out a warning to Flo, who ducked a flying pewter mug and crawled to safety behind the bar.

By the time Big Jake Winters had the fighting under control, the inside of the tavern looked as if it had been through a hurricane. Though his men were only partly to blame, Captain Delaine offered to pay for the damage. Brandy's father eyed the small leather purse the captain set on the bar.

"I'll take yer coin for what's been done, but the payment for me trouble will come from me daughter's hide." Gripping her wrist, he started dragging her toward the stairs. " 'Tis past the time she learned the price of her high and mighty ways."

"This wasn't my fault," Brandy argued, setting her heels and pulling against him. "I didn't start this—Cole Proctor did."

"Your daughter is right. She was a victim, not the cause. It would be unjust for you to make her pay for something she had no control over."

Big Jake's jaw firmed up. His grip tightened painfully on her wrist. "She's trouble, just like her mother and every other woman I ever knew. Never should have paid for that fancy tutor. Thinks she's too good for the rest of us just 'cause she's got a little schoolin'."

"That isn't true. I—"

His palm cracked hard across her cheek. "Ye need to learn yer place, girl. I mean to see that ye do."

The captain's dark eyes locked on her face, which stung and had begun to turn red. The only sign of his anger was the muscle that throbbed in his cheek. Very slowly he shoved the pouch of coins on the bar in front of Jake Winters.

"The fault was mine and my crew's. If the girl is made to pay, it won't sit well with the men." He smiled but his lips were tight with warning. "Everyone knows the White Horse is the finest tavern on the quay. It would certainly be a shame if my men no longer felt welcome."

Jake Winters heard the words and the underlying threat that went with them. Marcus Delaine was a wealthy, powerful man. He was an earl and the owner of Hawksmoor Shipping. It wouldn't be simply the crew of the *Seahawk* Jake would be losing as customers but five other ships' crews as well—and anyone else under the captain's influence.

Her father clamped hard on his temper, but the ruddy color of his skin told Brandy how difficult a task it was. "Perhaps ye be right, Captain. Perhaps I was a bit too hasty." He flashed Brandy a menacing look and shoved her toward the stairs leading up to her room. "You've the captain to thank for sparing ye the beatin' ye deserve. The next time yer uppity ways bring trouble down on yer head, I promise ye won't be so lucky."

Brandy nodded, embarrassment colliding with relief. She gave the captain a grateful, trembling smile, and started up the stairs, her long copper braid bobbing against her back all the way. She wasn't a child anymore but her father treated her as if she were, and Marcus saw her that way as well. Why was it only men like Cole Proctor saw her for the woman she had become?

And how much longer would she put up with her father's tyranny before she decided to do something about it?

Not much longer, Brandy vowed. Not much longer at all.

Her chance came far sooner than she had imagined. It was fate, she thought, God's answer to one of her thousands of prayers. It happened the following morning as she was walking past an inn called the Pines, just a few doors down from the tavern. She had just stepped into the street when Marcus Delaine appeared through the carved front doors of the inn, striding off toward the spot where the *Seahawk* was docked.

Brandy watched his tall, leanly muscled frame moving with brusque authority and felt the same thread of warmth she always felt when she saw him. She hurried her steps, catching up to him as he crossed the street and began to walk along the quay.

"Good morning, Captain." She gave him a bright, sunny smile. "I saw you come out of the inn. I wanted to thank you for what you did for me last night in the tavern."

He slowed his long strides so she didn't have to run to keep pace with him. "I assure you, Miss Winters, it was my pleasure. Proctor has had that beating coming for a very long time." He smiled faintly. She noticed a slight bruise darkened the skin over one of his high cheekbones.

"I thought you were off to England. I didn't think to see you back in port for some time."

Black brows drew together above a fine, straight nose. "We had some problems with the rudder on our way back from Virginia. Had to have it replaced before we set sail for home."

He was so tall she had to crane her neck to look up at him. When she did, sunlight glinted on his wavy black hair. Brandy felt the oddest urge to run her fingers through it. "As I recall, you were having trouble with your ship the last time you were in port."

A hint of displeasure roughened his voice. "Bad luck seems to be dogging us lately. I hope that's going to change. In the meantime, we've contracted for a short sail to the Bahamas, a load of flour we took on in Alexandria, some timber, and a few other trade goods. We'll be returning here to pick up a load of cargo before we head back home."

Her pulse kicked up with a sudden thread of interest. "How long will you be gone?"

"If all goes well, less than a month. It isn't far to the islands. We'll off-load and return as quickly as we can."

Her pulse began beating even faster as an idea took root in her head. "You'll be traveling to the Bahamas, then coming straight back here?"

"That's right. We hadn't planned to make the run, but the money is good and with the setbacks we've suffered of late, we can certainly use it."

"When will you be leaving?"

"As soon as the rudder is put right. If all goes well, that should be the day after the morrow."

They had reached the landing where his ship was moored and the captain turned to face her. "Should I not see you again before the *Seahawk* sets sail, take care of yourself, Miss Winters." He smiled, a flash of white against his sun-darkened skin. "With luck the *Fairwind* will be leaving Charleston as well."

Brandy grinned, seeing in her mind's eye the captain's fist connecting with the first mate's jaw. "With luck."

He reached out and touched her cheek, ran his hand lightly over her hair. "How long have we known each other, Miss Winters?"

"The better part of ten years, I would say." She remembered the exact moment she had first seen him, a handsome young lieutenant in a British Navy uniform walking through the tavern's front doors. She was little more than a child back then, but still, he had intrigued her.

"You're growing up, lass. You'll be needing a husband soon, wanting a home and family of your own."

Brandy shook her head. "I don't want a husband—at least not yet. I want to see things, go places. I want a chance to live my own life before I settle down."

The captain looked at her with what might have been a trace of pity. He had heard her say those words at least a dozen times. "Independence is not an easy thing for a woman."

"I'll make it happen. You'll see."

He glanced toward the harbor, to the tall ship rocking gently, its huge spruce masts swaying in the wind. A seagull screeched high above his head. "You're a good girl, Brandy. You deserve to find whatever it is you want."

In that moment, Brandy knew exactly what it was that she wanted. She wanted to sail the seas with Marcus Delaine. She wanted the chance for adventure. And for the first time in her life, she was going to get what she wanted.

Brandy smiled. "Have a good trip, Captain."

He merely nodded and waved, his thoughts already drifting toward the tall ship and his men. Brandy watched his broad-shouldered frame disappear in that direction, then turned and raced back toward the tavern. Two days was all she had. Two days. It was scarcely enough time to make plans for a journey that could change the course of her life. It was a thrill just to think of it.

Brandy grinned and stepped up her pace.

"Well, Cap'n, what ye think?"

It was late in the afternoon. Standing on the dock next to

the ship, Marcus studied the broken rudder that had been removed from the *Seahawk* and replaced.

"I don't know. If you look at the crack in the wood, the line seems a little too clean. There's a chance it could have been sawed, but there's no way to tell for sure. And these dents . . . as if it might have been struck by a sledge. It's possible someone wanted the rudder to split. By weakening the wood, they could have helped it along."

Hamish Bass, first mate aboard *Seahawk* and Marcus's longtime friend, surveyed the huge piece of wood, cracked clear through, broken and totally useless. "Aye, that could be, Cap'n." He scratched his craggy gray beard. "In truth, with all that water passin' over it, workin' against the edges, it's hard to say. Could be it just looks that way."

Marcus raked a hand through his hair. "You're probably right. But this makes the third problem we've had in the past two months and I don't like it. I suppose I'm groping for anything that might pose an answer."

"Ain't many who'd have reason to do such a thing."

"No. A disgruntled crewman, perhaps. Someone with a grudge."

"You've a loyal crew, Cap'n. They know you're a fair man, and far more lenient than most. They're lucky to have a berth aboard *Seahawk* and most of 'em are more than grateful for it."

He nodded, pleased at the words. "It's cost us a little time, but with the extra load we'll be carrying to the Bahamas, we'll actually come out ahead."

Hamish grinned crookedly. "See? Things is lookin' up already."

Marcus smiled. "Perhaps you're right. I presume we'll be ready to sail with the tide."

"Aye, Cap'n. She'll be shipshape by then."

Marcus nodded once more and they turned and walked back to the gangway leading up onto the deck. *Seahawk* was a triple-masted, full-rigged ship, her hull sleek and fast, the flagship of the Hawksmoor Shipping fleet and the best vessel Marcus had ever sailed. He had owned her for the past two years. He was proud to own her, proud of the success he had achieved that allowed him to purchase such a beautiful ship.

When they reached the quarterdeck, he clapped the older man on the shoulder. "You had better get some rest, Hamish. You've the watch tonight, and tomorrow will be here before you know it."

The older man nodded and waved as he sauntered away. Leaning against the rail, Marcus smiled at his slightly bow-legged, rolling seaman's gait. Perhaps Hamish was right and their bad luck was behind them. Marcus hoped so. He'd turned thirty last month. For the past six years, since he'd been shot in the shoulder in a battle against the French and finally left the Navy, he had worked with single-minded purpose to build Hawksmoor Shipping into the successful enterprise it was.

A year ago, his older brother Geoffrey had drowned when a bridge collapsed and his carriage went into the river. Marcus inherited the family title and a good deal of money, but it hadn't been that way in the beginning. He had built Hawksmoor Shipping from a shoestring inheritance he had received from his maternal grandmother. He had worked sixteen-hour days to make the company a success and he meant to keep it that way.

He stared out at the quay, feeling the slight chop of waves against the hull, enjoying the salty tang of the air, the smell of damp hemp and tar, the feel of the mist against his skin. He loved everything about his life at sea, the life he had so determinedly forged for himself. He had loved the ocean since he was a boy living in Hawksmoor House, high on the cliffs of Cornwall above the windswept water.

It was a life he would never leave, never give up, not for love nor money, nor even to satisfy his responsibilities as earl. His younger brother could see to that, could provide for the needed Hawksmoor heir as well. Marcus would never marry. There was no woman on earth who could possibly compete with the lure of the mistress he loved above all others.

Marcus thought of the sea as a beautiful woman who had captured his soul entirely, and he smiled.

CHAPTER 2

"You're going to what?"

Brandy grinned. "I told you—I'm sailing to the Bahamas. We leave on the morning tide."

Flo sank down on the narrow bed in Brandy's small attic bedchamber above the tavern. "You're insane. If you even think about runnin' away, your father will kill you."

"I'm not running away. I'm going on a trip. I'll be back in less than thirty days. If my father wishes to kill me, he will have to wait until then."

"You're smilin'. I can't believe you think this is funny. What do you think Big Jake is gonna do when he finds out what you've done?"

"Perhaps he'll never find out . . . at least not exactly. I'm leaving him a note. I'm telling him I've gone to visit Cousin Myra in Savannah. He'll be furious, of course, but I don't care. By the time I get back, I'll have figured out what I'm going to do with the rest of my life, and it won't be working my fingers to the bone for the next thirty years at the White Horse Tavern. I'm not throwing my life away so my father can squirrel away more money. Sweet God, I swear it is some kind of sickness. He's never satisfied. He never has enough, and I, for one, am through with it."

Brandy walked over to her friend. "The only thing I'm going to miss about this place is you, Flo." She grinned. "Are you sure you don't want to come with me?"

Flo sniffed her disapproval, a single dark brow arching up.

"If I have to dress like that, there isn't a snowball's chance in Hades."

Brandy glanced down at the cabin boy's clothes she had finagled from Old Salty Johnson, a pair of course brown breeches and a full-sleeved homespun shirt. "I thought I looked rather dashing."

"Dashin'? You look like a street urchin. If it wasn't for those big cat eyes of yours—"

"I don't care what I look like as long as it gets me aboard that ship." She reached out and caught Flo's hand. "I wish you were coming, but I never really thought you would. I'm just praying I don't get caught while I'm trying to sneak aboard. Or that no one finds me until we're far enough out to sea that the captain can't bring me back."

Flo squeezed her hand. "He'll be furious, you know. Underneath that cool exterior, he's a harder man even than your father. God knows what he might do."

Brandy unconsciously shivered. Marcus Delaine had been kind to her over the years, but there was a ruthless side to his nature she had glimpsed more than once. He was a man who didn't like to be thwarted. Clearly she would be doing so when she boarded his ship without permission and stowed away below.

She wondered what he would do to her once they were at sea and she made an appearance on deck. It wasn't a moment she looked forward to, yet whatever the consequences she would not be deterred.

"I have to do this, Flo. I've been waiting all my life for a chance like this. I have to find out what it's like in the world outside the White Horse Tavern. I have to discover what I really want to do with my life."

"Why can't you just want a husband and children like every other girl?"

"Why can't you?" Brandy asked.

"You think that isn't what I want?" Flo stood up from the bed. "There's nothin' in this world I want more than a husband and home of my own."

"You never said so—not in all these years. You've never

shown an interest in any of the men who come into the tavern. I thought you weren't interested in marriage."

"Oh, I'm interested, all right." Flo glanced away. "Unfortunately, the man I want is already married."

"What?"

"That's right. I'm not proud of it. That's why I never said. But I been in love with William Brewster for years. He's the only man for me even if I can't never have him."

"But surely you could find someone else, someone who—"

"There *is* no one else. Not for me. Some people love only once. For me there's only Willie. You had best pray to God, you ever do fall in love, it'll be with a man who'll love you back."

Brandy said nothing more, but Marcus Delaine's handsome face rose into her mind. With it came an odd chill of apprehension. The journey ahead would be fraught with peril. Marcus Delaine and the fierce attraction she had always felt for him would surely be among them.

"I have to go." She plucked up the tattered woolen coat lying on the bed and crammed her arms into the sleeves. "I've got to find a way to board the ship without anyone seeing me. The crew will be returning sometime before midnight. I want to be safely hidden away before they get there."

Flo leaned over and hugged her. "Are you sure I can't talk you out of this?"

Brandy smiled. "What do you think?"

"I think you're crazy, but I told you that before."

"Wish me luck, Flo. Luck and a grand adventure."

"I wish you Godspeed and a safe journey home."

Brandy hugged her one last time. "Thank you, Flo. I'll see you in thirty days. With luck my father will be so glad to have me back he'll forgo whatever punishment he's come up with by then."

"Fat chance of that." Flo walked her down the back stairs, then stood waving as Brandy tossed her small bundle of clothes, her few days' supply of food and water, over her shoulder and crossed the street, heading off toward the docks.

Brandy turned to see her friend disappear inside the tavern, then continued on her way, her sturdy leather shoes thumping along the wooden dock. Most of the crew would be on shore leave for a couple more hours. She imagined Captain Delaine was already aboard and perhaps Hamish Bass, the first mate.

Her plan was simple. Dressed in her cabin boy's clothes, her hair tucked up under a brown woolen cap, she would simply board the ship in the darkness as if she were one of the more than forty crewmen returning aboard. She would make her way below without being seen and find a safe place to hide.

Standing at the bottom of the gangway, she took a deep breath, pulled the cap down low across her forehead, and started up the wide wooden plank, praying the rapid flutter of her heart wasn't really loud enough to hear. A sailor stood on deck at the opposite rail, but his back was turned in her direction. A pair of men played whist by the light of a lantern. In the distance she could hear a sailor trilling notes on a flute.

Brandy ignored them and kept on walking, heading for the passage that led down to the cargo hold in the center of the ship.

She had been aboard the *Seahawk* only once, when Hamish Bass had volunteered a tour. She'd been enthralled, of course, and even now she remembered the layout and nearly every passage.

Finding her way was easier than she had expected, and with so few crewmen aboard, no one paid her the least attention. The ladders were steep, the passageways dim. The hold was dank and colder than she remembered, but it was piled high with crates and boxes, kegs and hundreds of sacks of flour, and finding a comfortable hiding place wasn't really all that hard. She made a den for herself behind some wooden crates and lined it with bags of flour to insulate against the chill.

Most of the cargo was well secured, lines and ricking pulled and pounded tight to keep it from shifting. It was lit only by a lamp at each end, providing a meager barrier against the impinging darkness.

Brandy shivered and pulled her tattered coat a little closer around her. A rat skittered along the hull, chattering noisily as it ran. Seconds later, an insect crawled across her hand. Brandy suppressed another shiver.

Nothing worth doing is ever easy, she told herself. She was safely hidden and ready to begin her great adventure. Still, she hoped she wouldn't have to stay in the hold too terribly long.

The winds kicked up the first day out of port and the seas turned rough. Marcus stood at the helm, his legs splayed against the roll of the ship, staring off toward the horizon. Flat gray clouds hovered above a whitecapped sea. Distant lightning flashed, but the thunder remained elusive, too far away to hear.

"Looks as if she might blow up a bad one," Marcus said to Hamish.

"Aye, Cap'n, that she could."

"Send one of the men down to check the cargo, make sure the lines are secure."

"Aye, that I'll do." Hamish shuffled off in that rolling gait of his, his long gray hair fluttering beneath the bottom of a woolen cap. He disappeared out of sight and Marcus returned his attention to the sea.

Like a beautiful woman, he thought as he had before, untamed, passionate, and willful. Strangely enough the notion brought a different image to mind, a sweetly smiling face and thick red-gold hair, full red lips, and amber eyes, slightly tilted up at the corners.

He scoffed at himself. Not a woman, merely a girl. True, she had the body of a woman, a tiny waist and high round breasts, a trim pair of ankles, and, he imagined, a tight little derriere. But Brianne Winters was young yet, innocent and incredibly naive. He was surprised he had thought of her at all, surprised it was her face he had imagined instead of the dark-haired woman he had slept with when he had arrived in port, a lusty widow who had skillfully satisfied his baser needs.

Perhaps it was Brandy's spirit, for in truth he admired her, found himself smiling at the memory of her clash with the *Fairwind*'s first mate. She was a fiery little thing—not yet a woman, he reminded himself once again.

Still, her image lingered softly in his mind as he stared out over the water.

The ship rolled sideways, rose on a wave, poised there for an instant, then dropped away. Brandy's stomach dropped with it, turned over, and lurched upward. She barely made it to her knees in time to heave into the bucket she had scavenged when she realized she was going to be sick. That was two days ago—or was it three? It felt more like twenty. She couldn't remember the last time she had eaten, yet she continued to wretch into the bucket as if there were actually still something left in her stomach.

Trembling, she lay back on her makeshift pallet, resting her head against the hull. Her cap was long gone, her braid hanging limply against her shoulder. She was so weak she could barely lift the flagon of water she had brought. She took a few tentative sips, felt the cold water hit her empty stomach, and immediately regretted it.

She groaned as she leaned toward the bucket and forced up another dry heave. In the back of her mind, a slight noise registered, then grew louder, but she was too sick to put the signals together.

"Jesus, Mary, and Joseph!" The short man jerked off his cap and scratched his thinning gray-brown hair. "A stowaway. Ain't seen the like in years. What the bloody devil is ye doin' down here?"

Brandy groaned again, this time with disgust at herself for not being more careful. She knew the little man standing over her, recognized his pork-chop side-whiskers and thin, mouse-brown hair. Joshua Dobbs, one of the *Seahawk* crewmen who came into the tavern.

She turned her head to look up at him. "How many . . . how many days have we been at sea?"

The little man sucked in a breath. "Why, I know you!

You're Miss Brandy—from down to the White Horse Tavern!''

''How many days, Mr. Dobbs?''

He scratched his head. ''Three days, miss.''

Brandy groaned. She was sure it had been at least five.

''Cap'n Delaine, he's gonna be real unhappy when he finds out what you gone and done.''

Brandy reached out a shaky hand and caught the little man's arm. ''You can't tell him, Mr. Dobbs. Please . . . you mustn't tell him yet. In two more days we'll be too far out to sea to go back. I want to go with you to the islands. I have to.''

Joshua Dobbs just shook his head. ''Couldn't do that, miss. Cap'n would be real put out with me, I didn't tell him you was down here.''

''Please, Mr. Dobbs, couldn't you just pretend you didn't see me . . . just for a couple more days?'' She tightened her hold on his arm. ''I could pay you. I've saved a little money. I could—''

''It ain't the money, miss. It's just that the cap'n—''

She broke away from him then, leaning over the bucket, retching miserably in front of Joshua Dobbs.

''You don't look so good.'' He left her a moment and returned with a tin cup of water. He dampened his handkerchief in the cup and handed it to her.

Brandy accepted it gratefully. ''Thank you.'' She washed her face with a trembling hand and lay back in her pallet. ''Just one more day, Mr. Dobbs. Please . . . just give me one more day.'' The ship rose on a wave and Brandy's eyes drifted closed. She was so tired . . . so unbearably tired.

Joshua Dobbs stood over her. Poor little thing. So small. So pale. He remembered her well. Brandy Winters had served him many a time at the tavern. She always had a smile for him, always made time to listen to one of his stories. He remembered how her eyes would light up whenever he talked about his adventures, the prettiest light brown, they were, so shiny they almost looked golden.

He'd always felt sorry for her, the way her father treated

her, like she was no better than a servant. He'd whipped her, Josh recalled, just for standin' outside too long, listening to one of his tales.

Poor little thing. What would it hurt if he helped her just this once? What would it hurt?

Josh glanced around. No one was near. If he got her a little broth and some crackers she'd feel better. She could face the captain then, and like she said—maybe it would be too late to take her back home. He wondered if she was running away from her father. If she was, Josh didn't blame her. And he decided he would help her as long as he could.

Brandy mustered a weak smile for the little man who had helped her through another miserable day. The storm had worsened, but thanks to him, she felt a little better. The crackers Josh Dobbs brought had helped to settle her stomach, though she still didn't dare try to eat.

He waved at her as he scurried away, staying only minutes for fear someone would see him. For his sake, she had tried to hold down a bit of broth, but it had come right back up. Surely by tomorrow the storm would abate and she would be able to eat, get back a little of her strength. She propped herself against the hull, huddled beneath the blanket Josh had brought her. She couldn't remember when she had ever been so cold.

Still, the prospect of going on deck, of facing the captain's fury, had begun to hold little more appeal than staying below.

The ship creaked and moaned. It rose on a wave and dropped into a trough, and she heard the unexpected sound of splintering wood. A jolt of alarm slid through her and she braced herself against the hull. The ship leaned sideways, more wood snapped, and alarm swelled into a sharp stab of fear. One of the ropes that held a stack of boxes in place just a few feet away began to groan, and she looked upward, gasping as the heavy boxes shifted, stretching the line so taut it started to quiver.

Sweet God, something was happening to the ship, and whatever it was, it wasn't good. As weak and unsteady as she felt, Brandy drew herself up and peered into the darkness, trying to discover the problem and decide what she should do. Her heart was hammering, pounding out a warning, yet she forced herself to stay calm. She trusted Marcus Delaine to captain the ship and keep them safe. She had nothing to fear, she told herself, yet her pulse beat wildly just the same.

She was wishing Josh Dobbs would return when the ship lurched downward again and she heard the distinct, eerie snapping of wood. Sweet God, it was the ricking that kept the cargo in place! Crates and boxes began to move, sliding toward her along the hull. Brandy screamed as they started crashing around her.

She tried to dodge the heavy crate that tumbled from the stack above her head, but she was so weak her movements were slow and clumsy. The edge of the box tipped downward, bounced against the hull, and smashed into the side of her head. Josh Dobbs's worried voice hurrying toward her was the last thing that she saw.

"Cap'n! Cap'n Delaine, ye've gotta come quick!"

Marcus heard Josh Dobbs's frantic cry and alarm bells went off in his head. "Take the wheel, Hamish. Something's amiss. I'll be back as soon as I find out what it is." Pulling up the collar of his heavy oiled slicker against the wind, Marcus stepped out from beneath the cover of the wheelhouse and into the driving rain.

"What is it, Dobbs?" he yelled above the storm. "What's happened?"

"Cargo's shifting, Cap'n. The ricking musta been faulty. Started snappin' like matchsticks when this last big swell hit the ship."

Marcus whirled away and began shouting orders. "Mr. Butler!"

The big, powerfully built young sailor appeared through the salty spray like a ghost in the mist. "Aye, Captain?"

"There's a problem below. Take half a dozen men and as much line as you can carry. Follow Mr. Dobbs and make fast the cargo as quickly as you can."

"Aye, sir!" Butler raced off, gathering crewmen as he ran. Shifting cargo could breach a ship, even one the size of the *Seahawk,* putting her to the bottom in a matter of minutes. Marcus strode toward the ladder leading down to the hold, then realized Josh Dobbs still dogged his heels. He was hopping from one foot to the other in an effort to regain his attention.

"What is it, Dobbs? I thought I told you to go below with Butler."

"There's somethin' else, sir. A stowaway, Cap'n. She's down in the hold, sir. Trapped beneath a stack of boxes that come down when the cargo shifted."

Marcus froze midstride. "She? There is a woman stowaway aboard this ship?"

Dobbs flushed to the roots of his thinning brown hair. "Aye, sir. Miss Brandy, sir. From down to the White Horse Tavern. She's in trouble, sir. Please—ye've got ta come quick."

Marcus thought surely his hearing must be wrong. Brianne Winters would have more sense than to stow away aboard his ship. Still, he started moving, striding even faster toward the ladder. It wasn't possible. Surely it wasn't. But when he reached the bottom of the ladder and Josh rushed past him, guiding him into a darkened corner of the hold, he saw that it was true.

There was no mistaking the thick copper braid beside the pale female face, and a knot of fear tightened in his chest.

"Miss Winters—can you hear me? It's Captain Delaine."

Her eyes cracked open, searched and found his face. "Captain . . ."

"Don't move, do you hear? Just stay where you are and remain very still." At the slight nod of her head, he turned his attention to Dobbs. "Get me something to brace that stack of boxes. They're hanging by a thread. If they fall, it's likely going to kill her."

Dobbs's face turned ghost-white. He nodded and backed away, racing off toward the other men working to secure the shifting cargo. Marcus looked up at the heavy boxes tilted precariously above Brianne's head, his nerves stretched taut. Little fool. What the devil was she playing at? Whatever it was, it was a dangerous game.

He reached down and brushed back her hair. "Where are you injured?"

She tried to smile, but it came out wobbly. "My head hurts. My legs are caught and I can't get out, but other than that I think I'm all right."

But she didn't look all right. Her face was as pale as glass and her lips faintly trembled. He caught a glimpse of the bucket next to her pallet, caught the unpleasant smell, and realized she had been seasick—and that Joshua Dobbs must have known for some time that she was here.

Marcus cursed softly, surveying her pale face again, furious and worried all at once. He wanted to rail at her, to shake some sense into her reckless little head. Mostly he just wanted her out of danger.

Dobbs raced up with several of the men, a sturdy pole, and some line. They used the rope to secure the boxes, then used the pole as a lever to hoist the crates that imprisoned her legs.

"On the count of three, I want you men to lift those boxes and hold them steady so that I can pull her free."

"Aye, sir!" Brig Butler and the other sailors snapped to the task.

Marcus slid his hands beneath Brandy's arms and began to count. On three, the men threw their full weight on the pole and, inch by inch, began raising the heavy boxes off her legs. The minute the load was high enough, Marcus dragged her free. At the same instant, the ship lurched into a trough and above his head the boxes tilted precariously.

Brandy shrieked and closed her eyes as he lifted her into his arms, hauling her out of the way just seconds before the stack of heavy boxes came crashing down onto the the hull of the ship.

"Little fool," he whispered, striding away from the others toward the ladder. Now that she was safe and apparently unharmed, he wanted to wring her neck. He could feel her trembling, but it only pricked his temper. They were four days out of port. For four damnable days she had been hiding in the hold. Anything could have happened. In truth, she had nearly been killed! Good Christ, didn't she have a lick of sense?

By the time they reached his cabin, he was so furious he could barely speak. He strode straight to his berth and settled her there more roughly than he had meant to, stripped off his water-soaked slicker and turned to face her. She was wearing men's clothes, he noticed for the first time, breeches that hugged her bottom and a shirt that outlined her high, full breasts.

"Captain, I—"

"Don't! I'm not ready to listen to any of your cockeyed explanations. Just tell me where it is that you are injured."

She bit down on her lip. He noticed that it quivered beneath her small white teeth. "Nothing is broken. My leg is bruised and a box hit my head."

He turned her chin with his hand to study the dark blood near her temple. A lump had risen as well, he saw, and he cursed beneath his breath.

"You're lucky you weren't killed. Do you have any idea what a foolish, dangerous thing that was to do? What the devil possessed you?" She opened her mouth to answer but he cut her off. "Never mind. You can tell me later. Perhaps, if you are lucky, I'll be in a better frame of mind."

Moving toward the teakwood bureau built into the wall of the master's cabin, he poured water from the pitcher into a porcelain bowl, dipped in a cloth, and wrung it out. Returning to the bed, he carefully cleansed the gash on the side of her head.

"Look at me."

She looked up at him and he studied her eyes. They didn't appear to be dilated. She blinked several times, but he saw no sign of disorientation. "How is your vision? Do I look clear or fuzzy?"

"My vision is fine."

"Hopefully nothing serious has occurred, but it's a bit hard to tell. You'll probably have a headache for a while, but I would rather not give you a powder until we are certain nothing is seriously wrong. As to your leg, you'll have to disrobe so that I can have a look at it."

"What?"

"I said you'll have to—" He paused at the look on her face. "Dammit, you're little more than a child. I'm not going to ravish you. We haven't a surgeon aboard on such a short trip. All I want to do is tend your leg."

"I'm not a child," she said with a stubborn lift of her chin. "I'm a woman. And my leg is fine—a bruise, nothing more."

The anger he'd been fighting rose up. "I'm in command here, Miss Winters, not you. I'll decide for myself what is fine and what is not." He unfurled the blanket folded across the foot of his bed and tossed it roughly in her direction. "Now you will kindly remove those breeches or I shall remove them for you."

Her pale face went even paler, but her chin never wavered. "As you wish, Captain Delaine. If you will be so good as to turn around."

He swore a silent oath, but did as she asked, standing with his legs splayed, his hands clasped behind him, listening to the rustle of her clothes sliding onto the floor. Keeping his mind carefully blank, he counted off the seconds one by one. A sharp thud and a soft groan had him spinning toward the sound, reaching out just in time to catch her and keep her from falling.

"Dammit, you're weak as a kitten." He wrapped the blanket carefully around her, but couldn't help noticing the length of bare thigh that peeped through the opening in the wool, definitely female and most certainly not belonging to a child. "How old are you, Miss Winters?"

"Nineteen."

Nineteen. Good God, she really had grown up. "Old enough to have more sense. You should have let me help you." He settled her back on the bed. "When was the last time you ate?"

"I don't . . . I don't remember."

"Bloody hell." Striding toward the door, he shouted for his cabin boy, Dickey Tabor, and the gangly lad raced in from his tiny adjoining quarters.

"Yes, sir, Cap'n?"

"Fetch the lady some broth. Bring her some bread, and while you are at it, bring *me* a tankard of brandy. I suddenly feel an overwhelming need for one."

Dickey's eyes went round at the sight of the woman on the captain's wide berth. "Aye, sir. Right away, sir." He raced off toward the ladder leading down to the galley, and Marcus turned back to Brandy Winters.

"All right, now let's take a look at that leg." She lifted the blanket tentatively, exposing a slender ankle and a small, high-arched, very feminine foot. Something tightened low in his belly and Marcus cleared his throat. "Get on with it, Miss Winters. I haven't got all night."

Her pale cheeks flushed with a hint of pink. "Of course." She lifted the blanket, baring a shapely calf, and the tightness in his belly moved lower, into his groin.

Good Christ, he was getting hard for her, hard for a slip of a girl he had never given more than a moment's thought.

That wasn't quite true. He had thought of Brianne Winters a number of times throughout the years, had seen her image in his mind just days ago as they had sailed from the harbor.

And as she had said, she was no longer a child. Nor was it a child's leg she exposed. It was a woman's pretty little calf, a dimpled knee, and a very womanly thigh. His body tightened even more, and he was grateful for the heavy woolen coat that covered his unwelcome arousal.

"Where does it hurt? Ah, yes, now I see." The box had pressed painfully into her leg, bruising the skin but not quite drawing blood. She stiffened a bit as he probed at the edge of the purpling flesh, but it appeared that nothing was broken.

"I told you I was fine."

"Yes, you did, and it would seem, in this instance, you are correct. Hurts, though, I would imagine."

She glanced away. "Some."

Dickey Tabor arrived just then, along with Hamish Bass, and as they walked in, Marcus discreetly replaced the blanket, oddly reluctant for another man to see Brandy's bare legs.

"How is she?" Hamish asked.

"Nasty gash on the head. Some bruises. Nothing that won't heal in time. What about the cargo? Were you able to secure it before there was a serious problem?"

"Cargo's right as rain, Cap'n. Everything's battened down, snug as a bug in a rug. Shouldn't give us any more trouble."

"It shouldn't have been a problem in the first place. I want to know why it was." Marcus accepted the tray Dickey Tabor handed him, noting the bowl of broth and chunk of dark rye bread. Dickey set the mug of brandy down on the table beside the bed, his young eyes straying to the woman stretched out beneath the blanket.

"We gonna have to take her back, Cap'n?" the boy asked, obviously peeved by the notion.

Marcus frowned darkly. The anger he'd felt earlier bubbled up to plague him again. "There isn't time for that now. Not if we intend to stay on schedule." He turned a hard look on the girl, who bit down on her full bottom lip. "I presume your desire to see the islands has not lessened since you came aboard, Miss Winters—because the fact is you are damn well going with us."

Brandy said nothing but her faint sigh of relief sent his temper up another notch. "That will be all, gentlemen," he said to the men. "I have a few things to discuss with Miss Winters."

The men exchanged uneasy glances. "Aye, Cap'n," both of them said.

Marcus waited till the cabin door shut behind them, then turned sharply to face her. "All right, Brianne. I think it is high time we discussed exactly what it is you are doing aboard my ship. I don't know what the devil game you were playing when you decided to stow away, but—"

"I wasn't playing a game."

He arched a brow. "No? Perhaps, then, you were running

away. Considering your . . . circumstances, that might at least make some sort of sense."

"I wasn't running away."

He clamped down on a muscle in his jaw. "Then what, if I may be so bold, was the purpose of this little expedition?"

She glanced down, plucking at the folds of the woolen blanket that covered her legs. He could see her hands had begun to tremble. "It's a little hard to explain."

"Try me."

Her gaze strayed a moment, alighting briefly on the mug of broth. A curl of steam rose up and her chest expanded as she inhaled the scent. Unconsciously she wet her lips.

Marcus scowled, threw his hands into the air. "For God's sake, eat something. You need to regain your strength. We can talk again when you've finished."

Grabbing the mug of brandy from beside the bed, he downed a formidable swallow, slammed the cup back down, and stormed toward the door.

Marcus jerked it open. "Understand one thing, Miss Winters. The *Seahawk* isn't a passenger ship and you're not a guest aboard her. Stowing away was a foolish, dangerous thing to do. Before the morrow, I shall determine what punishment is appropriate for such behavior."

Marcus slammed the door behind him, his temper still raging. He climbed the ladder to the deck and when he reached it, sucked in a cold, calming breath of air. What the devil had possessed her? The last thing he needed aboard the *Seahawk* was a woman—especially one as young and lovely as Brianne Winters. Marcus silently cursed, wondering what in bloody blue blazes he would do with the chit.

And what ill wind had blown his way that she had managed to choose his ship.

CHAPTER 3

Sitting on the edge of the captain's wide bed, Brandy shivered, and not from the cold. Sweet God, she had known he would be angry. He was used to command and he had always had a formidable temper. Still, he was more furious than she had imagined. He had vowed to see her punished. Surely he wouldn't beat her!

But in truth, she wasn't really certain. It was what her father would do. *Will do,* she corrected, *the moment I set foot back inside the tavern.* She had learned to tolerate Big Jake's cruelty, was prepared to accept it as the price of her grand adventure. She hadn't expected Marcus Delaine to behave in that same ruthless manner, and a thread of disappointment filtered through her.

It doesn't matter, she told herself, sitting up a little straighter on the bed. *You're getting a chance to see the world, and whatever happens, the price will be worth it.* But she shivered again to recall the harsh look carved into the captain's features.

Her gaze shifted to the steaming bowl of broth on the tray beside the bed, but she was no longer hungry. Uncertainty formed a tight coil in her belly. Picking up the pair of breeches she had folded and placed on the chair, she pulled them on, wincing as they slid past the bruises on her leg. Her head throbbed painfully, but at least her bout of seasickness was apparently at an end.

She glanced once more at the bowl of broth. She was well enough to eat and, as the captain had said, she needed her strength. She wasn't sure when he would return and she wanted to be prepared. Reaching for the spoon, she took a taste of the broth, forcing it past her lips and into her stomach. She spooned down a bit more, broke off a chunk of dark bread, and forced it down without a problem. Apparently she had finally gotten her sea legs, as Josh Dobbs would have said.

She smiled to think of the sweet little man who had helped her on her journey. She knew he had risked the captain's ire, and vowed to find some way to repay him. She took a sip of the broth, her mind returning to her perilous episode in the hold and Marcus Delaine's valiant rescue. She'd felt safe as he'd carried her down to his cabin, safe and protected. She had always been a little bit in love with him.

It made her sad to think of the punishment he meant to deliver that would burn that small bit of love for him away.

Marcus didn't return to his cabin until almost midnight. The storm had finally abated, but the shifting cargo had crashed into the steering, jamming the mechanism, and it would have to be fixed before the ship could continue its journey.

And for some strange reason, he felt an odd reluctance to go below. The realization piqued his temper. Damn her soul, the girl was nothing but trouble. She had always been reckless, even in her younger years. She would have to be dealt with and he meant to see it done.

Determined strides carried him down the ladder. He knocked briefly, then jerked open the door without waiting for permission. He had thought that she would be sleeping, but the tray on the table had barely been touched, and she sat rigidly in the chair beside his bed. Her whole body jerked to attention the moment he opened the door.

He frowned to see that she was trembling.

"You haven't eaten. Are you still feeling ill?"

"No, I . . . I wasn't very hungry."

"Why aren't you in bed? You should be resting—I thought I made that clear. I sent word with Dickey Tabor that you would be spending the night in my cabin."

"He told me. He also said you would probably be down sometime before midnight."

"And so I am."

She stood up from her chair, dressed once more in her too-snug men's breeches. There wasn't a man alive who had ever looked so fetching in coarse brown wool. Her thick copper braid hung over one shoulder, brushing intimately against a rounded breast.

"I apologize, Captain Delaine. Not for the fact I am here, but that I've inconvenienced you by stowing away aboard your ship. I realize it was hardly the proper thing to do, but it was an opportunity I couldn't afford to pass up. And I am ready to face whatever punishment you intend to mete out for my behavior." Her chin was up, but her hands were shaking. She clasped them tightly in front of her, but each small knuckle was white with tension.

She was frightened, he suddenly realized, and trying desperately not to show it. He had threatened to see her punished. It came to him with the force of a blow that to Brianne Winters, that could only mean one thing.

"Good God, you don't think I'm going to beat you?"

Her shoulders went a little bit straighter. "Are you not?"

He felt sick to his stomach. "Of course not. Such a thing was never my intention. For years, your father has employed that particular form of punishment with little or no success. Your presence here is proof enough of that."

Some of the tension eased from her shoulders, but still she stood rigid. "What, then?"

Marcus stared at her, torn between anger and pity. "Why did you run away?"

"I told you—I'm not running away. I'm going on a voyage. I'm traveling to a place I've never seen, someplace new and exciting—a place beyond the walls of the White Horse Tavern."

He mulled that over. It was difficult not to be sympathetic, yet it galled him that she had involved him in her reckless adventure. "Why did you pick the *Seahawk*? There were a hundred ships in the harbor. Why is it my misfortune that you have chosen mine?''

She flushed a little, her cheeks turning to rose against the coppery hue of her hair. ''Because *Seahawk*'s journey to the Bahamas was a short one. And though I knew it would be dangerous for a woman traveling alone, I trusted that you would keep me safe.''

''And yet you believed that I would beat you.''

She shrugged her shoulders and glanced away. ''I suppose, in my heart, I had hoped that you would not.''

He felt an odd little tug at his insides. ''You trusted me to keep you safe—is that not what you just said?''

''Yes.''

''And so I shall. You realize, Miss Winters your reputation is in tatters and has been since the moment you stole aboard a ship with a crew of fifty men.''

''I work in a tavern, Captain. I don't have a reputation.''

True, though it didn't seem quite fair. ''All right, since we are agreed on that point, for the balance of the voyage you'll be staying in here. Dickey Tabor will bunk with Hamish Bass and you will occupy his quarters. They adjoin mine through that curtain over there.'' He pointed in that direction. ''It's the only place I can be certain that you will be safe.'' He shifted, started walking. ''Your accommodations will hardly be luxurious, but until your return to Charleston, they will simply have to do.''

''I am grateful, Captain, for whatever you can spare. In regard to the matter of my passage, I have saved a little money. I had hoped—''

He stopped and turned. ''I told you, Miss Winters, the *Seahawk* isn't a passenger ship. The people on board work for their keep, and so will you.''

Her shoulders went a little bit straighter. ''I don't mind working. I would prefer to have something to do.''

''Then by all means you shall. As soon as you feel well enough, you'll work in the galley with our ship's cook, Mr. Lamb. In the meantime, whenever you are not at labor, you will remain in here.''

"In here? You mean inside the cabin?"

"That is exactly what I mean. You won't leave this room unless Mr. Bass or Mr. Lamb goes with you. You won't return without one of them accompanying you."

"You don't mean I can't go up on deck?"

"That is what I said and that is what I meant."

"But that is ridiculous. I haven't gone to all of this trouble just to stay locked up in here."

"You will—unless you wish to find yourself at the mercy of fifty woman-hungry men." She paled a bit. "Don't misunderstand me, Miss Winters. There are good men aboard the *Seahawk,* but as with any other vessel, there are men who are somewhat disreputable. Where a woman is concerned, there is no way to predict what they might do."

"I was raised in a tavern. I can take care of myself."

Marcus arched a brow. "Can you? And just how good a job have you done on this trip so far?"

She flushed again, but she said no more and, for the moment, neither did he.

"It's getting late," he finally told her. "I suggest you retire to your quarters and get some sleep. The men expect to eat early. You'll be awakened well before sunup. If you are feeling well enough, you can begin your duties then."

"I'm sure I'll be fine." He watched her turn and walk to the curtain, her round little bottom moving with womanly grace beneath her woolen trousers. Heat moved through him, settled low in his groin.

Good God, she would be sharing his quarters, sleeping in the tiny room just a few feet away. For years he had told himself she was too young, a child barely out of the schoolroom. He had watched her slender body ripen from girl to woman, had tried to ignore his growing attraction, but in truth, it had mushroomed each time he saw her. With her fiery hair and high, lush breasts, Brianne Winters was surely a temptation.

The voyage to Bermuda might be a short one for Brandy, but to Marcus it would seem like years.

* * *

Brandy snuggled into her narrow berth with a soft smile on her lips. Marcus had been angry—furious, in fact—but he had not been cruel. He wasn't like her father, not at all.

A sweet feeling of warmth stole through her as it always did when she thought of Marcus Delaine. As uncertain as her meeting with him had been, she couldn't help thinking how handsome he looked, his navy blue tailcoat perfectly fitted across his broad shoulders, his thick black hair curling just over his collar.

True, she had been fearful of the course he might take, but in the end he had been more than fair.

Except for the part about staying in the cabin.

But there would be time to address that issue later. For now she was happy just to be aboard, to be safe and warm and bound for adventure. Stripping off her clothes, she pulled on the cabin boy's night rail, left for her use, pulled back the woolen blanket, and climbed into bed. Though her head still throbbed, it wasn't pain but excitement that made it impossible to sleep. Tomorrow she would begin her journey in earnest. Brandy could hardly wait.

Marcus knelt beside Hamish Bass in the hold of the *Seahawk.* He picked up a broken length of wooden ricking, turned it over in the light of the whale-oil lantern the first mate held, and examined the notch cut in the wood that might have been the work of a knife or saw blade, and marks on the side that could have been the blows of a hammer.

"This piece has been weakened, just like a good deal of the rest. If Dobbs hadn't been down here when the cargo started shifting, instead of just a banged-up steering mechanism the uneven weight distribution might have capsized the ship."

Hamish Bass looked uneasy. "If didn't know better, I'd think we was sailin' under a curse."

"If we are, it's a man-made curse. Someone's out to cause us trouble. It's either a member of the crew or a man outside who has hired someone to do this. Either way, we've got to find out who it is."

"Aye, that we do."

"And we have to make sure it doesn't happen again."

Hamish scratched his heavy gray beard. "It won't be easy. No reason to suspect anyone in particular. No one's been actin' strange. Aside from this, nothin's happened out of the ordinary. Could be anyone."

Marcus ran a long dark finger over the broken piece of ricking, examining the odd cut in the wood. "Dammit, why are they doing this? What are they trying to prove?"

"Beats me, Cap'n. If we could figure that out, we'd prob'ly be able to figure who it is."

Hamish was right about that. Someone was out to cause trouble for Hawksmoor Shipping. But why? Who was behind the attacks? And what did he mean to accomplish? God, he wished he knew.

"I want the watches doubled. If anyone sees anything that doesn't look quite right, he's to report it to you or to me."

"Aye, sir, I'll see to it meself."

Marcus just nodded. He was worried, and that was for certain. Along with the lives of the nearly fifty crewmen in his care, now there was also the life of one small woman.

Brandy slept, though she hadn't thought she would. No one awakened her as she had expected, and it was late in the morning when her eyes snapped open, the sun shining in through a tiny window, one along a row at the rear of the ship that continued into the captain's portion of the cabin. She jerked upright, then groaned at the sudden sharp pain that careened through her head.

Swinging her legs to the edge of the cabin boy's narrow berth, she waited for a moment until the pounding began to ease. Moving slowly, she came to her feet and made her way to the porcelain pitcher on the table, the only furniture besides the bed and the chamber pot beneath it in the room.

Brandy poured water into the basin and washed her face, grateful to discover that as long as she didn't move too quickly, she felt passably normal. When she finished her hasty toilette, she pulled on her clothes and stuck her head through the narrow, curtained doorway.

Captain Delaine was long gone, of course, and she felt a bit guilty that she wasn't up and working just as he was. Determined to find him, or at least find the galley and Mr. Lamb, she pulled open the door and stepped out into the passage.

A light at the end led her to the ladder leading up. She had nearly reached the top when she glanced up to see a pair of shiny black boots. They encased long, muscular legs in tight black breeches. Narrow hips and an equally narrow waist fanned out to shoulders as wide as the ladder. Marcus Delaine scowled down at her, his smooth black brows drawn together in the middle of his forehead.

"May I ask what it is you are doing out here, Miss Winters?" The chill in his voice was as frosty as her name. "I believe I told you you weren't to leave the cabin."

"I—I . . ." She took a step backward down the ladder, then another. "I was looking for you, actually. I'm ready to go to work. I thought if I could find either you or the galley, I could begin my duties."

He scowled for a moment more, digesting that bit of news. "Come here." She took a breath and started back up the ladder, stopping at the top just a few feet in front of him. Dark eyes, a deep midnight blue, skimmed over her from top to bottom and something swirled in the pit of her stomach. "You're certain you feel well enough to work? Your head isn't hurting?"

"Only just a little. Not enough for concern. I'm sorry I overslept. If someone would have awakened me—"

"You were sleeping the sleep of the dead. Apparently your time in the hold took its toll. The sleep must have helped. The color has returned to your cheeks."

She smiled warmly. "I told you I am fit and ready to earn my passage."

"Very well. I shall take you to the galley. Mr. Lamb will tell you what to do." He walked beside her several paces, then stopped and turned, frowning darkly again. "I don't suppose you brought any other sort of apparel. Those breeches are hardly proper for a woman." When his eyes lit on her bottom, the heat burned up her neck and into her face.

"I had to find a way to board the ship. Dressed as a man, no one paid the slightest bit of attention."

Marcus looked askance at that, as if he thought it highly unlikely she could ever pass for a man. Instead he said, "I suppose there is nothing we can do, at least not until we reach the islands."

"Actually, I did bring a few other clothes. I was going to fetch them once I was up and about. If you could ask Mr. Dobbs to bring up my bundle from wherever it may have landed during the chaos below, I would certainly be grateful."

His expression changed, hardened. "I'll see that your clothes are brought up, but it won't be Dobbs who'll be bringing them. Thanks to your foolishness, Mr. Dobbs will be spending the balance of the voyage confined in the hold."

"What!"

"That is correct. You forced him to disobey my command in order to do your bidding. Aboard a ship, that is an error that can result in the most dire consequences. It's an act that cannot go unpunished. Dobbs knows it, the crew knows it, and now so do you."

"But that isn't fair! Mr. Dobbs was only being kind. I begged him to help me. I . . . I tricked him into doing it. If anyone is to blame, it is me."

"I'll not argue with you on that score. Unfortunately, you are not part of my crew and Dobbs is. He knew the penalty for his actions when he decided to keep your presence a secret. The results could have been even more disastrous than they were."

"But . . . but . . ."

"The subject is closed, Miss Winters. Now if, as you have said, you are feeling up to it, let us proceed to the galley."

She opened her mouth to say something more, but the captain had already started walking, long strides that made her run to catch up. When she did, she reached out and caught his arm. "The hold of this ship is damp and cold and crawling with vermin. What you are doing to Mr. Dobbs is barbaric."

A muscle jerked in his cheek. ''Barbaric, is it? You didn't think it was barbaric when Dobbs chose to leave you down there the better part of a week.''

''That was different. I asked him not to tell you.''

''Yes, you did, and Dobbs chose to defer to your wishes instead of obeying my orders.''

''It . . . it still isn't fair.''

He turned and his blue-black eyes pierced her. ''Life is rarely fair, Miss Winters. But in this case, I would say that justice is well served. Mr. Dobbs is confined to the hold for disobeying orders. You are confined to my cabin. In future, perhaps neither of you will make the same mistake again.''

He turned and started walking, and though she seethed inside at his treatment of poor Mr. Dobbs, it was obvious there was nothing she could say to change his mind.

She walked in silence as they crossed the deck and stopped at the door of the deckhouse that served as galley, but along the way half a dozen sailors turned to watch them pass. Men began to whisper. She could feel their eyes on her, hear their low, ribald laughter. Ahead of her, Marcus's broad shoulders grew more and more rigid. He turned at the door to the galley.

''Perhaps this isn't a good idea after all. Perhaps you should simply remain in my cabin.''

''No!'' She nearly shrieked it. ''I—I mean, please, Captain Delaine. I've a skirt and blouse in my bundle. As soon as it is retrieved, I can change into more appropriate clothing.''

He made a stiff nod of his head. ''All right. Perhaps that will accomplish our purpose.''

They stepped inside the galley, which sat on the main deck in a small building off by itself. It was positioned, she knew, to protect the ship from possible fires. Marcus turned to the cook, a short, tubby little man with a bulbous red nose and fat pink earlobes. Brandy thought he looked a bit like an elf.

''Miss Winters, this is Mr. Lamb. Cyrus, Miss Winters will be working for you for the balance of the voyage. She'll be happy to do whatever it is you tell her.''

''Please . . . my name is Brandy.''

''Brandy?'' The name came out with a hint of a brogue.

She thought that perhaps she had seen him in the tavern a couple of times, but she wasn't sure. "Well, now, and what kind of name for a lass would that be?"

She smiled into a face that looked warm and friendly. "Brianne is my real name. Apparently when I was a child I was a bit of a terror and my father gave me sips of brandy to help put me to sleep. I must have acquired a taste for it. It wound up being my name."

One busy brow pulled down. "And do ye still carry a cravin' for the devil's brew?"

She grinned. "I confess I still enjoy the taste. But I rarely drink even a glass of sherry and I assure you, Mr. Lamb, I am not a drunkard."

He laughed, a rollicking, happy sound. "Well, good enough, then. No doubt we'll get on just fine."

Marcus strode to the doorway. "Now that we've dealt with Miss Winters's drinking preferences, I shall leave the two of you to your work."

"Aye, Cap'n." The stout little man winked at her and grinned. "White beans and ham hocks tonight. They're always a favorite. Mayhap Miss Brandy will bake us up some bread."

"I believe I could do that." She smiled and the little man smiled back. When she glanced at the door, she saw Marcus watching, an odd look on his face.

It slid away and he scowled. "I'll expect you to see her safely back to my quarters when you're finished."

Cyrus Lamb's mouth went a little bit thin. "That I'll do, Cap'n. Ya needn't fear. The lass will be returned to ya safe and sound."

Neither man said more, nor did she, but she wondered what meaning lay beneath their last exchange.

As Marcus had known it would, word traveled like wildfire through the ship. A woman stowaway had been found and she was staying in the captain's cabin. Though he had never brought a woman aboard and had always been discreet in his affairs, none of the men seemed surprised he had placed the girl under his care.

And they assumed—to a man—he was receiving her favors in return for his protection.

He grumbled a phrase he hoped no one heard. He would let them think what they wished. It would help to keep her safe, though in truth, aside from locking her in, there was no way to protect her completely. *Seahawk*'s days in port had been few, and the men had scarcely had time to assuage their sexual appetites. And Brianne was undoubtedly a temptation.

Many of them knew her from the tavern. They had watched her at work, bending to wipe up the tables, her hips wriggling seductively. She had enchanted them with her sweetly feminine smiles while her breasts strained deliciously against the front of her peasant blouse. They had hungered for her then as they hungered for her now.

In truth, he could hardly blame them. Marcus sighed and shook his head. Grumbling at the unwanted hand fate had dealt him, he continued along the deck to check the progress of repairs on the steering.

Brandy dragged a huge metal spoon through the thick batch of ham hocks and beans that was cooking on the old iron stove. Steam rose up all around her. It was hot and damp in the galley, even with the narrow door open and a faint breeze whispering in. Perspiration trickled between her breasts, and though the ship was no longer under way, it was difficult to work with the shifting, rolling motion of the sea beneath the hull.

Blowing a stray lock of hair out of her eyes, she grabbed a towel and reached into the big iron stove to pull out another loaf of bread. It was difficult work, cooking for a crew the size of the *Seahawk*'s, as hard as any work she'd ever done. But it was a job she'd do—and gladly—for a chance to see a bit of the world.

And Cyrus Lamb's good humor lightened the tasks she undertook. ''Well, now, lass, what are ya thinkin' of the *Seahawk* so far?''

Brandy smiled. "She looks to be a fine vessel, indeed, Mr. Lamb, though I did hear the captain say there was some problem with the steering. I gather that's the reason we're no longer under sail. Do you think it will take long to repair?"

He wiped his hands on the rag stuffed into the pocket of his brown leather apron. "Not long. The lads will have her shipshape and canvas flyin' in no time at all."

She set the hot tray of bread on a black wrought-iron trivet on the table. "I wish I could see more of her, but the captain is determined to keep me locked away. Hopefully in time—"

" 'Tis best, lass, ya do as the cap'n tells ya and stay away from the men. A pretty little thing the likes of you would have 'em fightin' over ya like dogs over a bone."

She flushed a bit, embarrassed to think it might be true, and changed the subject. "They are certainly well fed." The smell of ham hocks, beans, and baking bread filled the galley. "I rather thought sailors ate weevily hardtack and gruel three times a day."

"Not while Cyrus Lamb is ship's cook. Course, now, on a long voyage, there's times they eat gruel and molasses and are glad enough ta get it, once the fresh meat's gone. This trip, food and water ain't much of a problem."

Brandy pondered that. "Is there water enough for a bath, do you think? I could certainly use one."

"Aye. I would guess there is . . . if ya talk sweet enough to the cap'n."

Sweet enough. Thinking of Joshua Dobbs held captive in the dank, dark hold, she would rather have hit him over the head. She dragged the big spoon through the bean pot again, then rapped it against the side a little harder than she meant to. She set the spoon aside and began attacking the clutter in the galley.

Cyrus Lamb set a big dirty pot on the dry sink, poured boiling sea water into it along with some harsh lye soap, and began to scrub. "It's frownin' ya are, lass. Do ya mind the work so much, then?"

"No! I don't mind the work at all." She smiled. "And you're quite good company, Mr. Lamb."

"Then what is it has ya frownin'?"

She set an empty tray down on a heavy wooden table. "It's Joshua Dobbs. The captain has confined him to the hold and it's my fault he's there. He's such a sweet little man. It just isn't fair."

" 'Tis more than fair, lass. 'Tis a standin' order to report the presence of anyone aboard who doesn't belong. Josh knew it when he decided to keep his silence. Cap'n had to see him punished or he'd have trouble with the rest of the crew. Josh's lucky 'tis only time in the hold and short rations, and not somethin' a whole lot worse."

Short rations? Poor Mr. Dobbs. Brandy said nothing more, but her temper remained on edge. Perhaps Marcus had no choice in what he'd done and in a way she could understand his position. Still, it was her fault and she couldn't simply ignore it.

They worked throughout the day, cooking and cleaning, then starting all over again. With nearly fifty men to feed, the task was never-ending. The cabin boy, Dickey Tabor, arrived to serve the meals while Brandy remained out of sight in the galley, then afterward the three of them sat down to eat. Dickey eyed her suspiciously, as if she had usurped his place with the captain when she had taken his bed. She tried to draw him out, hoping they could be friends, but he remained surly, and she finally gave up trying.

From time to time, men in the crew would appear in the galley on one errand or another. Hamish Bass came in several times. A good-looking young blond sailor named Brigham Butler appeared, having suffered a gash on his forearm from his work on the topsail high up in the rigging. Cyrus tended it and sent him on his way, but Brandy didn't miss the roguish smile and lengthy perusal he gave her before he headed out the door.

A tough-looking bald-headed sailor named Jillian Sharpe came in, carting a barrel of salted herring up from the hold.

Cyrus grumbled his thanks and quickly shooed the big man out the door.

And Dandelion made her first appearance.

"She knows better than to come beggin' for food," Cyrus scolded, picking up the mottled calico tabby who was the ship's cat. "She's to be mousin', workin' for her food like the rest of the crew." But his hands were gentle as he carried the cat to the door and gave her a light shove out onto the deck. Dandelion lifted her chin and meowed once in disapproval before she sidled away.

All in all, it was an exciting, taxing day. By nightfall, Brandy was exhausted, but she was used to hard work and she would get used to this.

And there was something important she had to do.

Chapter 4

It seemed hours before supper was finally over, the plates and pots scrubbed and readied for the following day. By the time Brandy was ready to leave the galley, she had a square of linen filled with bread and meat hidden beneath her shirt and she had devised a plan she believed would carry her safely below.

There was nothing she could do to get poor Mr. Dobbs out of the hold, but she could certainly see he had something decent to eat.

It was well after dark by the time she left the deckhouse, a sturdy breeze rolling the ship back and forth as it lolled heavy-hulled in the water. As the captain commanded, Cyrus Lamb walked her back to her cabin.

''Cap'n'll be down soon, I'm thinkin'.'' His gaze slid off toward the floorboards, his pink earlobes turning a slightly darker shade of red. ''Isn't many a man could stay long away from a lass with your charms. 'Tis safe ya'll be, once he's here. Good night to ya, lass.''

Brandy flushed, too, realizing how it must look to the cook and the rest of the crew for her to be sharing the captain's cabin. Marcus had warned her, but there was really nothing she could do.

''Good night, Cyrus.'' She closed the door behind her and leaned against it. The captain would be down, and soon, but not because of her charms. Simply because he slept there. If Cyrus Lamb thought Marcus Delaine had the slightest interest in her, he was sorely mistaken. The knowledge was oddly depressing.

With a weary sigh, she turned her attention to the matter at hand, one of far more importance than Marcus Delaine's taste in women. Josh Dobbs was alone in the hold with barely enough to eat and she was determined to help him. Spying her meager bundle of clothes, retrieved from below and sitting on the captain's wide berth, she hurried over and untied it.

As she had hoped, her woolen cap sat atop the items she had brought. She dragged it on over her braid to hide the bright sheen of her hair and hurried back to the door, pressing an ear against it, listening as Cyrus Lamb's footsteps faded. Then she lifted the latch, stepped outside, and started down the passage, the cook's prediction of Marcus's arrival echoing in her ears.

The captain would be down, and soon. By the time he arrived, she had to be back inside the cabin.

Brandy set to work, careful to stay in the shadows and avoid any member of the crew. The corridors were dark and dimly lit by heavy brass whale-oil lamps. A soft noise echoed behind her and a feathery chill slipped down her spine. She held her breath, straining to hear, but the sound had long faded and she heard nothing more.

She continued down the passage, her eyes searching the darkness. As she descended the ladder, she shrugged off a sense of foreboding and prayed the feeling of being watched was merely her imagination.

Brandy awoke, jarred for a moment by her unfamiliar surroundings, then she relaxed against the pillow. After a rocky start, last night's mission had been a success. It had taken a while to find her way along the darkened corridors, but eventually she had found the area in the bottom of the hold where Joshua Dobbs was imprisoned. It was a tiny, airless chamber that smelled of tar and pitch, with only a narrow slot in the door to pass through food and water.

Still, against Dobbs's protests, she was able to slip him the bread and meat she had brought and make her way back to the captain's cabin just seconds before his arrival.

With no time to change out of her shirt and breeches, she had huddled beneath the blanket feigning sleep, listening to his movements as he undressed and moved around the room. Once she had heard him approach the doorway and her breath caught, but he merely lifted the curtain, satisfied himself that she was abed, and let the curtain fall back into place. It seemed hours before he fell asleep and she could safely undress, climb beneath the covers, and fall asleep.

She was tired this morning, though her headache was finally gone, and she felt her lack of sleep was worth it. At least Josh Dobbs had a decent meal to sustain him, and her conscience felt considerably better. Better still, when she climbed from her narrow berth to investigate the sounds coming from the cabin next door, she found the captain busily directing Dickey Tabor and one of the crewmen to place a tub filled with steaming hot water in the corner.

Marcus smiled at the look on her face. "We've plenty of rainwater after the storm. Cyrus mentioned you might like a bath. I'm sorry I didn't think of it sooner. At any rate, there is the water. Use it before it gets cold."

"Yes . . . yes, I will. Thank you, Captain Delaine."

He turned to leave and her gaze followed his graceful strides as it always seemed to, his long frame so tall he had to duck to step through the door out into the corridor. The moment he and the men were gone, she hurriedly stripped off her clothes, tossed the rumpled, dirty breeches and badly soiled shirt across a ladder-backed chair, and approached the tub. Her bundle was sitting on a small table beside it. Brandy unbraided her hair and brushed out the tangles with the bristle brush she had thought to bring along, then stepped into the water.

With a sigh of pleasure, she sank down, leaning against the back of the warm copper tub for long, contented moments. Reaching for the soap Dickey Tabor had set out for her use, she began to scrub her hair.

A small fire burned in the little iron stove in the corner of the cabin. Once she was finished with the bath, she dried the long heavy strands and hurriedly dressed for work in the simple dark brown skirt and white cotton blouse she had rolled up in the satchel. The other dress, the best she owned, a high-waisted pale mint green muslin, she hung up in her tiny cabin, hoping the damp sea air would smooth out the wrinkles before the ship reached its destination.

It wasn't long before a brisk knock sounded at the door—Hamish Bass or Cyrus Lamb come to fetch her up to the galley. As she walked over to open it, she caught a glimpse of herself in the small oval silver-speckled mirror on Dickey Tabor's wall. Freshly washed, her hair was a bright, glistening copper, long and thick and tied back with a length of brown velvet ribbon. Her blouse was clean and, though it wasn't cut low, it outlined the fullness of her bosom and nipped in sharply at the waist.

She looked feminine and womanly, even if the clothes were simple and scarcely new. She couldn't help wondering if Marcus would notice the change and if he would approve.

Unfortunately, Brandy didn't see the captain at all that day. Hamish Bass walked her up to the galley in the morning, and at the end of the evening Cyrus Lamb walked her back to the cabin. She sighed to think, after the long hours of difficult labor, she no longer looked as fresh and appealing as she had that morning, yet the womanly air remained. If only Marcus would see her that way.

Each day, as she was escorted to work, an occasional sailor gave her the eye, but her protectors made it clear she was off limits even for a moment of conversation. It wasn't the way she had imagined the voyage would be, and she frowned at the amount of time she had been cooped up since she had boarded the ship in Charleston.

At least her nightly forays granted her a breath of fresh air. She looked forward to the moment she would cross the windswept deck each night and peer for as long as she dared out at the shiny silver sliver of moon and the black, endless sea.

"Cap'n'll be joinin' ya soon," the elfin little cook said. "Good night to ya, lass."

"Good night, Cyrus." She flashed him a last bright smile and tried to hide her impatience for him to leave. The instant the door clicked shut, she raced to her tiny cabin, grabbed her woolen cap, and pulled it on over her hair, hiding its bright color against the darkness. Her heart was pounding, beating a wild tattoo as it did each night she attempted her risky endeavor.

Brandy dragged in a steadying breath, checked the passage to be certain it was clear, stepped outside the cabin, and made her way toward the hold.

By now she knew the way, and it didn't take long to reach the tiny cell-like enclosure where Josh Dobbs was imprisoned. He came to his feet at her approach and peered through the slit in the door.

"I told you before, miss. You shouldn't be here. Cap'n'll be mad at us both, he finds out you come."

"The captain isn't going to find out, and if by some chance he did, it is hardly your fault I shoved food through the hole in your door."

The dim light of a lantern sitting on the rough plank floor slanted out through the opening, and in the yellow rays she could see Josh grin, deep lines fanning out at the corners of his eyes.

"Can't say it don't taste good. Them ham hocks was mighty fine and so was that slab of salt pork you brung last night. And you surely do bake some fine bread, Miss Brandy."

"Tonight I've got stewed chicken." Amazingly, she had discovered the *Seahawk* traveled with a pigsty on deck, as well as a chicken coop, which provided the men with poultry but not eggs, since the hens immediately stopped laying the moment they felt the shifting deck beneath them. Even so, fresh meat usually ran out long before they reached port. Fortunately, this trip was short and meat was still abundant.

"I hope you brung me some more of that good bread."

Her lips curved into a smile. "As a matter of fact, I did." He took the tray she shoved through the narrow slit and handed her the one from last night he had hidden beneath his straw pallet. "I'll see you again on the morrow." She tossed him a quick farewell wave, then turned and headed toward the ladder that led back up on deck.

As usual, she needed to hurry. The hold was three levels deep and she had to be careful that she wasn't seen. She hurried her pace a little faster. God forbid Marcus arrived at the cabin before she could get there.

She had just reached the top of the ladder to the level above and started toward the next set of stairs when she heard a faint sound behind her. She paused to listen, her heart tapping out a warning.

She told herself there was nothing to fear, that it was simply rats in the hold, but a chill moved over her skin and the feeling of being watched returned with a vengeance, pricking her senses like a pungent smell.

She glanced around, straining to see into the darkness. Nothing. But her steps became more hurried and a bit unsteady as she headed toward the next set of stairs.

Jilly Sharpe flattened his powerful frame against the damp wooden hull of the ship. He was a big man, thick across the shoulders, bull-necked, with a hard-muscled torso. It was Jilly's second voyage aboard the *Seahawk.* Before that he'd been aboard a merchantman called the *Windsong* based out of Boston. He'd had trouble with the captain, who called him belligerent and said his attitude was "disgraceful."

Jilly didn't care what the bloody bastard said. He was tired of the fools aboard the *Windsong* and glad enough for the chance at another berth. Of course, he'd already had a run-in with Delaine, for pinching a portion of that little mealy-mouthed cabin boy's ration of salt pork. He'd warned the little worm to keep quiet, but the boy hadn't listened. Instead, he'd run squealing to the captain, and Delaine had stepped in. He'd given Jilly extra duty—and a warning that the next time he tried it, the consequences would be far worse.

Since then, Jilly had left the boy alone. But he hadn't forgotten. Once a man crossed Jilly Sharpe, Jilly didn't forget.

Dickey Tabor's time would come. For now he had other, more important matters to attend.

The light sound of feminine footsteps echoed from the shadows. He squinted into the darkness of the passage and he smiled.

Marcus stood in the wheelhouse next to his whiskered first mate. "Steering feels solid and steady. The lads did a fine job of mending."

"Aye, they did, Cap'n. It'll please 'em to hear ye said so."

The door to the wheelhouse was open and a cool night breeze blew in. Marcus filled his nostrils with the scent of the sea, felt the soft mist dampen his skin. The rigging clattered and clanked, a vibrant melody to his ears. Only the rhythmic forward momentum of the ship, the shifting and straining of the hull beneath the sails, were missing, the final players in an opera of the sea that had brought him contentment for the past ten years.

"The repairs are completed. She appears to be fit and ready. It's time we made way. Give the order to hoist the sea anchor, Hamish." The anchor was a length of canvas fashioned to steady the ship while they worked to fix the steering. "Raise the foreyard. Hoist the spars and get the studding sails aloft. If we're lucky, we'll catch a good stiff wind off the keys and be able to make up for some of the time we've lost."

"Aye, Cap'n." Hamish grinned, his mouth a fat pink hole in his dense gray beard. " 'Twill be good to feel her movin' sleek and swift again, 'stead o' wallowin' like a tub in the water." Marcus nodded briefly, and Hamish began relaying his orders.

"You want me to take the wheel now, Cap'n?"

Marcus nodded once more. "It's been a long day, Hamish. I look forward to a good night's sleep." His friend's expression said he wasn't so sure about that, not with the comely little baggage who had lately been sharing his cabin. Marcus sighed to think of it, recalling as he made his way below how difficult it had been these past few nights to fall asleep.

He prayed tonight he was tired enough her presence would not matter.

The ship shuddered a little as the sails were hauled up and the *Seahawk* tacked toward a new course. Marcus barely felt it. He was thinking of Brandy Winters, hoping she would follow the pattern she had established and already be fast asleep. When he reached his cabin, he wearily opened the door, glanced around, and breathed a sigh of relief. The girl had retired and he was more than grateful.

He listened for a moment but heard no movement in the tiny room next door. A quick glance behind the curtain to assure himself that she was safely abed, and he'd be able to get some sleep.

Marcus lifted the flap and stared into the darkness. It took a moment for his eyes to adjust, to convince his mind what he was seeing was actually real. The bunk was unmade. The little room was empty. His mouth thinned into a line of fury at the same moment his heart kicked in with a surge of fear.

Brianne Winters was not in her quarters, nor anywhere else in his cabin. Marcus swore, his hands balled tight with anger. When he found her this time, perhaps he really would beat her!

Brandy struggled frantically, clawing at the rough, blunt fingers clamped over her mouth. A brawny chest pressed into her back and a thick, muscular forearm tightened like a vise around her waist, making it hard to breathe. She kicked out behind her, her brown leather shoe connecting hard with his shin, but her attacker only laughed.

"You're a fiery little baggage. Makes a man hard just thinkin' of all that buckin' and thrashin' you'll be doin' beneath him."

A fresh shot of fear rolled through her and a whimper crawled up from her throat. The sound died behind his hand and for that she was grateful. She didn't want him to see her fear, to know the terror building inside her. Instinctively, she knew it was exactly what he wanted.

Her eyes rolled wildly, madly searching her surroundings for something or someone who might save her. She was one level down from the open deck, deep enough in the hold that it was dark and dank, and rows of crates and boxes formed the perfect place for him to accomplish his purpose. He must have planned it that way, for he was plunging deeper into the shadows, dragging her backward, lifting her half off the ground with an ease she found appalling.

She tried to scream, but the words were muffled by a thick, callused hand and the effort was useless. She swung a fist backward, whacked him hard across the face, then raked her nails down his cheek. A hissing sound slid past his lips and he spun her around, gripping her throat before she could make even a squeak.

''You'll pay for that, gel. And I'm warnin' you—one more trick like that, I'll take my knife to your pretty face. I'll carve you up in little pieces.'' He shook her. ''You hear me, gel?''

She nodded and her eyes slid closed in an effort to hide her fear. In the dim light of a whale-oil lamp hanging on the wall, she could finally make out his face. She had seen him in the galley, delivering supplies. She even remembered his name. Jillian Sharpe. Jilly, Cyrus Lamb had called him.

''You're thinkin' that you know me. Well, it ain't gonna matter. You ain't tellin' Delaine nothin' of what went on. You been spreadin' your legs for him. Now you'll be spreadin' 'em for me. Whisper a word of it, and I'll cut out your pretty little heart.''

With that he dragged her onto a pallet piled high with bags of flour and came down heavily atop her. He was a big man, widely muscled through the chest and shoulders. His hand was rough as he ran it along her legs and began to shove up her skirts. He smelled of sweat and tobacco, and terror slid through her in thick, mind-numbing waves.

Sweet God, was there no one around who could help her? She thought of Marcus and prayed with all her might that he would finish his tasks and return to the cabin to find her missing. Even if he did, by the time he discovered where she was, it might very well be too late.

The heavy man on top of her settled himself more deeply between her legs. He gathered her wrists into one wide palm, dragged her arms above her head, then pressed his foul, suffocating mouth over hers to silence any attempt to scream. Brandy struggled wildly, trying to shrink away from the hand moving intimately over her breast, crudely massaging her nipple. He worked the buttons on his fly, then slid a hand beneath the hip he had bared to grasp her bottom and pull her against him.

Tears burned her eyes even as she renewed her struggles to break away, trying to bite him, trying to twist free, knowing that in moments he would be thrusting his hardness inside her. In the back of her mind she thought she heard noises, but surely it was only wishful thinking.

After that, things seemed to happen all at once, and yet each instant seemed to take forever. Two men appeared out of the shadows, one of them fair and blond and coming up the ladder from below, the other dark and tall, racing toward her from the ladder leading down from the deck.

The blond man reached her first, the sailor named Brig Butler, she dazedly recalled. His hand clamped over Jilly Sharpe's thick shoulder. He jerked hard, dragged the man away, and the fight was on.

"You bloody bastard! What kind of animal are you?" Butler swung a solid blow that slammed Jilly Sharpe against the wall. He was up and on his feet, charging into the sailor's midsection, knocking him sprawling against the hull. Several more blows were exchanged. More men appeared, shouting and running, grabbing the two sailors and trying to drag them apart.

Then Marcus Delaine's deep voice cracked like a whip across the shadowy darkness. "Stand where you are! All of you!" He crossed the last few feet to the men, his glance straying only once in her direction. "Get them out of here. Take Sharpe below to join Dobbs—I'll deal with him on the morrow. Escort Mr. Butler to his quarters. I'll speak to him a little later."

He turned then and started striding to where she huddled

against the wall, shaking all over. Brandy thought she had never seen such a look of barely contained fury on another human's face. He stopped just inches in front of her.

"Are you hurt?" The words were clipped and sharp with anger.

"No, I . . . no . . ." Slowly she came to her feet, bracing herself against the hull for fear her shaking legs would not hold her.

The captain gave her a swift appraisal, assuring himself her words were true, and saw that her clothes were back in place, though her wool cap had come off and the ribbon had been torn from her hair, leaving it in matted tumbled waves around her shoulders.

A muscle jerked in his cheek. Anger made his voice deep and harsh. "I believe I told you not to leave my cabin." She tried not to flinch as he reached toward her, his long dark fingers biting into her arm. Hauling her to his side, he urged her roughly toward the ladder.

He said nothing as they climbed the stairs, nothing as they crossed the deck and made their way along the passage to his cabin. Even as the door closed with a solid thud behind him, he made no effort to speak.

Her heart beat like a battering ram. It was obvious how hard he was fighting for control, and a hard knot balled in her stomach.

He drew in a steadying breath, let it out slowly. "What were you doing down in the hold?" The icy chill in his words cut right through her. She trembled faintly, wishing she could tell him, knowing she could not.

"I'm . . . I am grateful to you, Captain, for coming when you did . . . you and Mr. Butler. If you had arrived a moment later—"

He gripped her shoulders and dragged her closer. "I asked what it was you were doing down in the hold. I want an answer."

Brandy swallowed past her fear. "I—I went exploring is all. I wasn't tired enough to fall sleep and I—I wanted to see a bit more of the ship."

He shook her, not gently. ''You're a liar—and a poor one at that. I want to know what you were doing down there, what was so important you were willing to disobey my orders.'' His mouth curved into the merest semblance of a smile. ''Meeting Mr. Butler, perhaps? Engaging in a lovers' tryst?''

''No!'' She jerked away from him. ''I wasn't meeting Butler. I don't even know him. I saw him once in the galley, and then again tonight when he came to my rescue. I was certainly not . . . not down there to meet him.''

The fire in his dark blue eyes seemed to bank a little and he turned away, pacing several times back and forth toward the tiny stove in the corner. He stopped in front of her, his eyes hard once more.

''Surely you knew the danger. I warned you about the men. I thought you understood.''

''I was being careful—at least I thought I was.''

A black brow arched up. ''You knew the danger, yet you ignored the risk. Why, I wonder? What was so important you would—'' He broke off midsentence and his eyes suddenly widened in astonishment. ''Good God, you went down to see Dobbs!''

Brandy frantically gripped his arm. ''It wasn't his fault. Please—you mustn't blame him—he begged me not to come. I wouldn't listen. It was my fault he was there. I had to find a way to help him.''

''You took him food, didn't you? And this wasn't the first time, was it?''

''It wasn't his fault! Please—you can't punish him again for something I've done!''

Marcus watched her and for a moment his hard look softened. ''Dobbs is not at risk. I can scarcely blame a hungry man for filling his belly.''

A thread of relief trickled through her. It must have shown in her face, for his features turned hard once more.

''No . . . this time it won't be Dobbs who will suffer for your folly. The man who will pay will be Jillian Sharpe. That makes two men I've had to punish because of you. I hope you are satisfied, Miss Winters.''

Her shoulders went a little bit straighter. ''I will not be blamed for Jilly Sharpe's disgusting behavior. The man deserves whatever punishment you mete out.''

''I'm glad you feel that way, since you will be required to be present at his flogging.''

The blood drained from her face. ''What?''

''I believe you heard me quite clearly. The sentence will be four dozen lashes, administered at dawn on the morrow.''

Brandy said nothing, but she swayed toward the chair and her fingers curled around the top. She thought of the way Sharpe had touched her, the things he meant to do, and suddenly she was glad he would suffer.

''After the flogging is over,'' Marcus continued, ''you will return to my cabin, where you will remain until such time as I see fit to release you.''

Brandy stiffened. ''I'm already in here far too much. What about my work in the galley? Surely you can't mean for me to stay locked up when there is work to be done.''

''That is exactly what I mean. Mr. Lamb will do what he is paid for. You will remain right here—day and night. If not for your own protection, for that of the men in my crew.''

Brandy wanted to argue, to rail at him and tell him he wasn't being fair. She wasn't the one who'd behaved like some depraved beast. Jilly Sharpe had done that. But she left the words unsaid, biting down on her bottom lip to keep them locked inside. How could everything have gone so wrong? Josh Dobbs was imprisoned in the hold. Marcus had ordered her locked away in here. She thought of Jilly Sharpe and what had almost happened and nausea rolled in her stomach.

''In the meantime,'' the captain was saying, ''I suggest you get some sleep. Dawn will come early and I believe we have both had more than enough excitement for one evening.''

She forced herself to nod. She suddenly felt so tired, almost too tired to make her feet move past the curtain into the other room. Once she did, she removed her clothes with unsteady hands, pulled on her night rail, lay down in bed, and drew the covers up to her chin.

She heard Marcus moving about, heard him leave the cabin, but even after his departure she couldn't fall asleep.

It was well after midnight when Marcus returned to his quarters for the evening. He was tired. Exhausted clear to the bone, and yet he could not sleep. Instead, he tossed and turned, and every time he closed his eyes, he saw Brianne Winters struggling against her attacker in the hold.

In the eye of his mind, he saw her as she was then, her skirts shoved clear to her waist, her pretty legs splayed, Jilly Sharpe nestled between them. One of Sharpe's big hands gripped her bare bottom, holding her against him while his mouth claimed the ripeness of her lips.

If he had ever thought of Brianne Winters as a child, the image was dashed forever. Whenever he thought of her now, he pictured her as he had seen her in the hold, her full breasts heaving, her hair an untamed cloud around her face.

He tried to sleep, but when he closed his eyes, he imagined her sprawled on her back, her hair tumbled wildly about her. But it wasn't Jilly Sharpe between her pale, shapely legs. It wasn't Sharpe whose hand cupped her bottom. It was Marcus Delaine who claimed her, Marcus who plundered a kiss from her soft, inviting lips.

The fact was, seeing her with Sharpe had destroyed the last of his illusions. In truth, he had clung to the fantasy that she was a child to keep his lust for her at bay.

The crew believed she slept in his bed. Would that it were true, he thought bitterly. Watching her working in the galley, hearing her laughter, seeing her smile—thinking of her ripe little body—he told himself she wasn't for him, that she was too young and far too innocent.

Tonight he was forced to admit the truth. Brianne Winters was a woman, not a child, and he wanted her—badly. Had, perhaps, for a good long time. In truth, he couldn't remember when a woman had lingered in his thoughts the way Brandy had since he had left her on the Charleston quay.

Perhaps it was simply knowing that he couldn't have her, that she was an innocent, not a woman of experience like the widow he saw when he was in port, or the mistress he kept in London. Whatever the reason, she appeared in his thoughts and even in his dreams.

And he felt oddly protective of her. He was glad that Brig Butler had reached Jilly Sharpe before he had, for his rage in that moment was so great the man might not have lived. From the moment he had discovered her aboard, he'd been determined to keep her safe from his men.

He glanced toward her tiny curtained chamber and wondered who was going to keep her safe from him.

Chapter 5

Through the long hours of the night, Brandy lay awake on her narrow bunk. She was so weary. More tired than she could remember. In the hazy moments before her burning eyes finally drifted closed, she heard the metallic ringing of the bells counting out the hour. Eight of them. Four o'clock in the morning.

It seemed she had slept only minutes when she was roughly shaken awake by a man's long-fingered hand. She blinked several times, saw the gray light of dawn peeking in through the single tiny window, groggily looked up to see Marcus Delaine's tall figure standing next to the bed.

Vaguely, she noticed he was wearing a fresh dark blue uniform, crisply pressed, each brass button polished to a mirror sheen.

" 'Tis time," he said gruffly. He was as handsome as ever, yet his features looked harsh, the line of his jaw etched in stone. "Get dressed. Mr. Bass will be waiting to escort you up on deck."

Her mind cleared instantly. *Jilly Sharpe. Four dozen lashes.* Dear God, how could she have forgotten? She shoved sleep-tangled hair out of her face and sat up in the bunk. "Please, can't I . . . can't I just stay here? Is it really necessary for me to—"

"Yes." Turning, he stalked away, his shoulders square, his back perfectly erect.

As he bent and ducked through the curtain leading into his cabin, Brandy shivered, her mind returning to the night before, to the feel of Jilly Sharpe's heavy weight pressing her down, his callused hands sliding over her skin, the foul taste and brutal force of his mouth over hers. Bile rose into her throat along with a hot surge of anger.

What right did Jilly Sharp have to force himself on her? What right did any man have?

The thought gave her strength. She was the one who had suffered. She would be there to watch him pay.

Hurriedly, she completed her brief morning ritual, brushed and clipped her hair back on the sides with the tortoiseshell combs that were a present from Marcus one year on her birthday, and pulled on her clothes, choosing the mint-green muslin that was the best dress she owned. Flo had helped her make it, had encouraged her to add the ruffle beneath her breast, as well as the two at the bottom of the hem. It had always seemed a bit much to Brandy, but her friend had assured her it looked exactly right.

And she did feel good in it. Whenever she wore it, she always felt pretty. The dress gave her confidence and she needed that confidence now.

Ignoring her uncertainty and the uncomfortable thudding of her heart, Brandy ducked through the curtain and opened the door leading out of the cabin. As Marcus had promised, Hamish Bass stood in the passage, his gray beard neatly trimmed, his uniform spotless, but his features looked weary and his expression was as grim as the captain's.

"Are ye ready, lass?"

She straightened her shoulders. "I'm ready." He offered his arm and she took it, clinging to it a bit more fiercely than she meant to, releasing her hold only long enough to make her way up the narrow stairs.

The wind was blowing when they reached the deck, biting through the fabric of her dress, tangling her hair. Brandy didn't notice the chill, only the row upon row of crewmen assembled around the base of the tall spruce mast, shuffling uneasily, glancing from one to the other.

Captain Delaine stood on the quarterdeck above them, his feet splayed, one hand folded behind him, the other balled into a fist. His mouth was set, his eyes darker than she had ever seen them. They touched on her briefly, then returned to the men.

As Hamish Bass urged her in his direction, other eyes skimmed over her, watching her progress, nearly fifty pairs. Brandy fought to ignore them, to keep her legs from trembling and continue walking across the deck.

Eventually she reached the captain's side and the first mate took up his position on her opposite side, leaving her standing between them. Marcus said not a word. Instead, he stared toward the ladder leading up from below, made a slight nod of his head, and three more sailors climbed up on the deck, Jillian Sharpe wedged firmly between them.

They guided him to the mast and he was stripped to the waist, leaving his massive torso bare. Sunlight glinted off the top of his shiny bald head, and his mouth formed a thin, harsh line. His eyes seemed to glitter with hatred. When they searched her out and found her standing next to the captain, they were filled with such malice, so much loathing, she shivered and unconsciously took a step away.

Marcus's hand on her waist urged her back into position, more gently than she would have expected. He nodded again and Sharpe was shoved forward toward the mast. The sailors stretched his arms above his head and bound them tightly to the huge round column.

With a sneer of derision and a last hate-filled glance, he dragged his eyes away, resting his face against the mast.

"Mr. Hopkins, you may begin whenever you are ready."

Brandy watched in silence, her heart stabbing a painful cadence up under her ribs. Ben Hopkins was the second mate aboard *Seahawk,* a man she had seen once or twice in the White Horse Tavern and again a few times in the galley. He was in his thirties, British, a congenial man whose skin wore the pocks of a childhood disease. Grim-faced, he shook out a bundle of long, knotted leather strips bound with a handle at one end.

Cat-o'-nine-tails. Brandy knew the name, a device of such torture she couldn't have imagined it in her wildest nightmares if it weren't for the sailors' stories, each told with an undisguised respect and a horrifying fear.

She tensed as the muscular seaman drew it back, heard its forbidding rustle against the deck and the snap of the deadly thongs through the air. It slapped against Jilly Sharpe's bare back and every man in the crew winced as if he felt the pain.

Brandy felt it, too, though she'd thought she would be immune. Jillian Sharpe deserved every painful stroke of the whip, yet each time the cruel lash sounded, it took all her concentration not to look away.

More blows fell, each one counted out loud. They seemed to run together and ugly welts began to appear, long thick fingers of them. Still the lash fell. The welts turned to thin lines of blood, the brown skin tearing away, exposing the raw flesh beneath. Nausea rolled through her, making her slightly dizzy. Brandy's stomach churned with such force she was certain she would disgrace herself in front of Marcus and his men.

Still the lash fell, again and again, till all she could hear was the crack and drag of leather and Jilly Sharpe's piercing screams. Four dozen lashes. It seemed like four thousand. She remembered sailors' stories of men who had received exactly that many. That number was a death sentence, she knew, delivered in what she saw now as a most brutal manner. At least Jilly Sharpe would live. But the price he would pay would be mighty.

Brandy listened to him whimper, her whole body trembling, then finally he fell into blessed unconsciousness, his head slumping forward against the mast. Still the lash continued to fall. She focused on the counting, forcing in short, burning breaths, praying it would come to an end, trying not to feel each blow like a whiplash across her conscience, accusing her of being the cause. If she hadn't gone down to the hold . . . if she had simply obeyed Marcus's orders . . .

The whip cracked again and Brandy swayed on her feet. She stared at the man bound to the mast through a hazy blur and realized she was silently weeping. She swayed again and felt Marcus's hand at her waist. He took a slight step backward, positioning himself a little behind her, allowing her to lean against him. It gave her the courage she needed, and at last the awful counting came to an end.

By the time they cut Sharpe down, she was shaking all over. His arm still firmly at her waist, Marcus placed her trembling hand on the sleeve of his navy blue coat, and turned her toward the stairs leading down from the quarter deck. For an instant, her gaze strayed toward the men, who noted the wetness on her cheeks and the paleness of her skin.

This time they wore a look of pity.

Brandy stepped through the door of the captain's cabin, and the moment she did, Marcus turned her into his arms. "It's all right, Brianne. It's over." He cradled her head against his shoulder with the palm of his hand. "It's done with and you can put this all behind you."

A soft whimper tore from her throat. Her hands pressed into his chest and the wool of his coat felt rough beneath her cheek. "Marcus . . . oh, dear God." Her eyes squeezed shut and she started crying harder, her body shaking like a leaf in the wind. "I'm sorry. I'm so sorry."

"Hush," he whispered, his hand smoothing over her hair. "You were right last night—this wasn't your fault. Jilly Sharpe has been surly and insubordinate since the moment he came aboard. He behaved like an animal. He deserved what he got, and worse."

His words settled over her like a balm and her heart felt suddenly less troubled. Marcus held her a little away to study her face, his own lined with concern. She felt his fingers along her jaw, his thumb moving gently back and forth against her skin.

Lifting her chin, he used his handkerchief to wipe the wetness from her cheeks, his eyes dark and searching, filled with sympathy and perhaps a hint of regret. For several long moments, neither of them moved. Brandy stared up at him and her heart seemed to trip and stop beating.

Marcus's gaze remained steady. Indecision and some deeper, darker emotion flicked over his face. Then slowly, almost reluctantly, he lowered his head and settled his mouth feather-lightly over hers. Oh, dear God. Soft heat unfurled, a sweet, melting sensation that drifted into her stomach and made her trembling limbs feel weaker still.

Her fingers curled into the lapels of his coat, and her head tipped back as she swayed a little toward him. She could feel his heat, the wool of his jacket, the cadence of his heart, and unconsciously she raised on tiptoe to press her mouth more firmly to his.

For a moment his body went tense, then he groaned. Hard arms came around her and he crushed her against him, deepening the kiss. He urged her lips to part and his tongue swept in to taste her more fully. Heat shimmered through her, wild, beckoning waves that made her slightly dizzy. Pleasure hot and sweet filled her senses.

She stood between the span of his legs, imprisoned by the long hard muscles in his thighs, his chest a solid wall against her breasts. His mouth was hard but somehow his lips felt soft, a perfect fit to her own. One of his hands slid into her hair. He tasted faintly of coffee, smelled of the salty sea air.

The kiss went on and on, his mouth moving softly over hers first one way and then another. Dimly she realized the thick ridge straining toward her was the stiffness of his arousal, and yet she wasn't afraid. Instead of being fearful where the hot kiss might lead, she prayed that it would go on and on and never come to an end.

It was Marcus who pulled away.

Breathing hard, he stepped back and stared down at her, a vein pulsing hard along his neck, the heat of desire still blazing in his eyes. He turned and paced away from her, raked a hand through his curly black hair.

"That shouldn't have happened. Good Christ, I can't believe it did." His eyes found hers across the room. "It was my fault entirely. Please accept my apologies."

She wanted to tell him she was glad it had happened, that for years she had dreamed what it might be like if Marcus Delaine ever kissed her. No dream could match the reality, the incredible wonder of it, and in truth she wanted it to happen again.

''There is no need for an apology,'' she said, her voice sounding frayed and slightly out of kilter. She prayed it didn't betray how badly unnerved she was. ''You gave me comfort when I needed it and I thank you for it.''

A thick black brow went up. ''Comfort?'' He smiled thinly. ''That is what it was?'' He watched her in that dark, assessing way of his, but he didn't say more, just strode to the door of the cabin and dragged it open. ''I'm sorry you had to go through that. But as I said, it is over and done. As to your stay in here, there are a number of books in my quarters. I hope they will keep you entertained. You're welcome to any you might find on my shelves.''

So her sentence was beginning. The kiss had not changed that. She forced herself to smile, to act as nonplussed as he. ''Thank you.''

''Since you haven't had time to eat, I'll send Dickey down with a tray so that you may break your fast. If there is anything else you need, just send word and I'll see that you get it.''

Brandy simply nodded. What she needed was a strong dose of fresh sea air, but obviously she wasn't going to get it. ''What . . . what will happen to Jilly Sharpe? Will he be all right?''

He nodded. ''Hamish will take care of him. In time his back will heal. He'll be put ashore at Spanish Keys, a string of small islands off Andros, the first stop we'll be making in the Bahamas.''

She watched him walk out the door, closing it firmly and sparing her not another glance. She thought of their heated kiss and felt a sharp stab of chagrin. How could a single kiss be so devastating to her and have not the slightest effect on him? Then again, why should she be surprised? Marcus Delaine had ignored her for years. Just because she had stowed away aboard his ship didn't mean things had changed.

A kiss like that meant nothing to an attractive, virile man like Marcus, a man who could have any number of women. Brandy walked over and plopped down on the bed, cursing herself for her unwanted emotions, wishing she could be as aloof and uninterested as he.

Knowing when it came to Marcus Delaine, she hadn't the slightest chance.

Marcus braced his hands on the rail, letting the wind rifle through his hair, grateful for the brisk chill in the air that cooled the hunger still heating his blood. Damn, he shouldn't have kissed her.

Perhaps it wouldn't have happened if he hadn't spent the morning fighting to keep his emotions so carefully in check. It bothered him to discipline his men, and a flogging was especially repugnant. Even when the man deserved it as much as Jilly Sharpe.

He thought back to the scene on deck. He had meant to teach Brianne a lesson. She would watch the result of her folly, her refusal to follow his orders, a lesson that in the future might protect her as well as his men. He had done it to help keep her safe.

He hadn't imagined the way she would look standing there in front of his crew, so proud, so vulnerable—so damnably courageous. Her silent tears had torn out a piece of his heart. She'd stood there trembling and he knew the will it had taken for her to remain on deck. He hated himself in that moment, cursed himself for the punishment he had inflicted upon her.

And then he had kissed her. Damn, but he shouldn't have done it. He should have dried her tears and walked away, but her pretty amber eyes had held him in thrall and her pale, trembling lips had simply been too tempting. And now that he knew their warm sweet taste, he would never be able to forget them.

Bloody hell. If he had wanted her before, he wanted her now more than ever, and though he would allow the men in his crew to believe she was his, he would not take her. He wondered if Miss Brianne Winters would see *that* situation as fair.

Hamish Bass walked up just then. Marcus forced his attention in his first mate's direction. "How is he?"

"They've taken the sogger below. Cyrus is tendin' his back. Sharpe's strong as a bull. Be back on his feet in a matter of days."

Marcus nodded. "He's a bad one. We'll put him off at Spanish Keys."

"Aye, with the girl aboard, 'twould undoubtedly be for the best."

"Do you think he's the man behind the trouble we've been having?"

"Hard to say. He mighta damaged the rickin'—for money enough, the bastard wouldn't be above it—but that don't explain the troubles ye been havin' with the rest of yer ships."

"No, it doesn't. Up until the accident with the rudder and then the ricking, I'd been telling myself it was just a series of bad luck." The torn sails aboard *Peregrine* that put them a week behind schedule and nearly cost us that timber contract, the faulty anchor on the *Raven.* "Now I'm beginning to think all of them are related. If that is the case, the man behind it is someone in a position of authority, someone with the money and power to arrange those kinds of 'accidents.' "

Hamish scratched his stiff gray beard. "It'd have to be a man with somethin' to gain."

"Exactly so."

"That timber contract woulda gone to Atlantic Limited or maybe the China Seas Company. Most likely it would have gone to Palmer Reese."

A muscle jumped in Marcus's cheek. *Palmer Reese.* He knew little of Atlantic Limited or the China Seas Company, except that their owners were fiercely competitive. Palmer Reese he had known since they were children on the Cornwall coast. Palmer was three years older, a braggart and a bully. His parents had been friends of his father's, but he and Palmer had never gotten along.

"Reese Enterprises is our biggest competitor," he said. "We've edged them out of several major shipping contracts lately. Still, I can't image even Palmer would go to such extremes."

"Maybe he would. Maybe he wouldn't. Ye never know with the likes of Palmer Reese."

Marcus said nothing more, just stared out at the water. All three shipping companies were suspect. What other enemies had he made through the course of the years? He had been thinking about it ever since they'd discovered the damaged ricking, but he was no closer to an answer than he had been before. Damn, but he wished he knew what the devil was going on.

"How's the girl?"

"She was pretty upset. She's all right now."

"She's got grit, that one."

Marcus smiled grimly. "It would certainly seem so."

"Ye want her. I can see it in your eyes whenever ye look at her." Hamish was the only man aboard who had guessed they weren't really sharing a bed, though Marcus had never said so.

He shrugged his shoulders. "I won't deny the girl is tempting. She is also young and innocent. Brianne has no future with me and it wouldn't be right to take her, then toss her aside like so much flotsam after a storm."

Hamish chuckled and scratched his woolly beard. "It don't seem fair, Cap'n. The whole blessed crew gets hard just thinkin' what goes on between the two of ye in yer cabin, and the plain truth is ye ain't touched the girl. Damn me, it don't seem fair."

Marcus felt the tug of a smile. "I'll admit, my friend, the same thought has crossed my mind on a number of occasions."

Hamish just smiled. "Mayhap afore we get back home ye'll change yer mind."

Marcus mulled that over. "For Brandy's sake, let's hope not." But it was another thought that had already crossed his mind.

Brandy rolled her head around on her shoulders, trying to work the kinks from the back of her neck. She stretched her legs out in front of her and got up from the chair where she had been curled up reading for the past three hours.

The first two days of her confinement hadn't really been all that bad. She had never had time to read, and certainly there were no books of the sort she found on the shelves in Marcus's cabin even if she had. Books of surprisingly great diversity: the poetry of William Blake, Shakespeare, Wordsworth, and Coleridge; novels of high adventure like Bunyan's *Pilgrim's Progress,* Defoe's *Robinson Crusoe,* Radcliffe's *Mysteries of Udolpho,* political treatises like the *Shrubs of Parnasssus.*

The tutor her father had provided had been given strict instructions: Brandy was there to learn the fundamentals of reading, writing, and mathematics so that she could function more usefully in the tavern. She had learned a bit of Latin, but only because Mr. Monroe, her tutor, had insisted it was necessary for even the meagerest sort of education.

Now, as she ran her fingers over the spine of a gold-embossed leather volume of a novel by Horace Walpole, *The Castle of Otranto,* she thanked God that she could read. For the first time she had learned there were worlds to be discovered between the pages of books.

Brandy stretched again, rubbing her back and rolling her shoulders. As much as she had enjoyed the hours she'd been given to peruse the captain's books, there was only so much confinement she could take. When Marcus came in tonight, she was going to plead with him to commute her sentence. Reading would be all the better with a little time spent up on deck.

He didn't appear until nearly midnight. She had filled the hours buried in the pages of several different books and she had thoroughly enjoyed the time she had spent. But nothing could take the place of wind and sun and the endless ocean vistas that spread before the *Seahawk* as it cut through the water. Nothing could compare with the exhilaration she felt watching so beautiful a ship challenging the ocean under full sail.

When Marcus came in, she was ready to confront him, to go down on bended knee if that was what it took. She heard him at the door and came up off the narrow berth, moving through the curtains into his cabin.

He turned at her approach. "You should be sleeping. Is something wrong?"

She hitched up her courage. "Actually something is wrong. I realize you had good reasons for ordering me to remain in your quarters, considering what happened with Mr. Sharpe, but I was wondering . . . hoping . . . I might convince you to allow me up on deck for a while each day—at least to catch a breath of fresh air and a glimpse of the ocean."

Marcus shook his head. "You know how I feel about that. I haven't changed my mind."

"Please, Captain Delaine. I've been reading for the past three days. I've enjoyed it—far more than I would have imagined—but I can't stay locked inside forever."

A faint smile curved his lips. "Hardly forever. We'll reach the islands in a week or so. You may go ashore once we are there."

"A week or so? I'll go completely mad in a week or so."

"That is unfortunate, for that is the way it shall be. Go to bed, Miss Winters. If we are lucky, perhaps we will each get a few hours of sleep."

Brandy clamped down on her temper. She damned Marcus Delaine for being so stubborn and herself for ever setting out on this adventure. Turning, she marched out of the room, grumbling something she wished she had the courage to say aloud.

She awakened early the following morning. Certain Marcus was already up and gone, she dressed quickly and drew back the curtain, then froze dead still in the doorway.

Across the room, Marcus stood in front of the porcelain basin on his dresser, a thick white cushion of shaving soap covering the lower portion of his face. He was naked to the waist, his tight black breeches riding low on a pair of narrow hips, course black hair arrowing down from the thick mat on his chest, disappearing inside the waistband.

Brandy just kept staring, unable to tear her eyes away from his long, muscular torso, the incredible width of his shoulders, the washboard ridges across his stomach. She had known he was strong and well built but she couldn't have guessed how beautifully sculpted his body really was, how lean and hard and incredibly male he looked without his shirt.

A dark-fingered hand drew the razor smoothly across his jaw. Oblivious to her presence, he studied his image in the small round mirror, tilted his head back, and drew the gleaming blade down the long sleek muscles of his throat. Her own throat felt suddenly tight. Her mouth went dry and unconsciously she wet her lips.

She must have made some sort of sound, for his head swung in her direction and he frowned. "I thought you were still asleep."

She tried not to stare, blinked and glanced away. "I am hardly tired. All I do is sit and read. It's a wonder I can sleep at all."

Marcus chuckled softly, wiped the last of the soap from his face. Lifting the thick leather shaving strop beside the dresser, he absently stroked the blade of his razor back and forth several times to clean and sharpen it, then set it away.

"I suppose you would rather spend the next sixteen hours working with Mr. Lamb up in the galley."

She grinned. "God, yes! If you will only just let me go up and—"

Marcus shook his head. "I've ordered you to remain below and that is what you will do."

"But—"

"The subject is closed." He reached over and plucked up his shirt, began to shrug it on over his hard brown torso. "You are willful and reckless, and you have disobeyed my orders more than once. This time you will do as I say."

Brandy sighed, trying to ignore the way the muscles flexed and moved beneath all that dark skin. Marcus turned away from her to tuck his full-sleeved white shirt into the waistband of his breeches. He had made up his mind. There was no way to dissuade him. Turning, she stepped back into her tiny airless room and let the curtain fall behind her, more disheartened than she could remember.

She didn't see the captain again that day, and by the end of the next, even with Hamish Bass stopping by for a bit of conversation and a quick game of whist, she was so restless she was pacing.

By midnight, she was determined. Marcus was going to let her out of that room—one way or another.

Marcus left the wheelhouse and descended the ladder to the passage that led to his cabin. By now, hopefully Brandy would be sleeping. He didn't want to see her, didn't like the hot surge of lust he felt whenever she was near.

Last night he'd had the damnedest time falling asleep, and this morning . . . this morning he'd gone hard the moment he had seen her standing in the doorway, staring at him with that innocently sensuous, obviously approving smile on her face.

Tonight would be different, he told himself. She had seen how useless it was to challenge him. Tonight she would be soundly asleep.

But she wasn't asleep, of course, not Brianne.

She was pacing the floor in front of the small iron stove, her hands moving restlessly, her body turning toward him the moment he stepped through the door. She didn't say a word, simply stopped pacing, and walked over to the dresser in the corner. Lifting his leather shaving strop off the peg beside the mirror, she marched over and placed it in his hands.

Marcus arched a brow. "What is this?"

"Penance." Turning, she walked over to the chest at the foot of his berth, rested her palms on the top of the box, and looked at him over her shoulder. "Go ahead. Beat me. I should rather be whipped black and blue than suffer another day of punishment in this hell you call your cabin."

His lips quirked. He couldn't help it. "You believe you are in here as a form of punishment?"

She answered him over her shoulder, "Of course. Why else would you make me suffer like this?"

He walked up behind her, admiring the saucy angle of her rump, the way the folds of her simple brown skirt outlined the sweetly rounded curves. A beating, he thought, was the last thing he wanted to give her.

"You don't believe I might think you would simply be safer in here?"

She shook her head and her bottom wriggled appealingly. "If you were with me up on deck, I would be just as safe as I am in here."

But I *wouldn't be,* he thought. Still, she had a point, and the truth was he *had* meant to punish her—at least a little. He was angry at the trouble she had caused by stowing away, and angry at himself for wanting her the way he did.

He tossed the razor strop onto the bed. "If you knew more of men, Miss Winters, you would know what a fetching picture you make posed as you are—and that beating you is hardly the notion that comes to mind."

She straightened, turned and looked up at him. She must have seen the heat in his eyes for a soft flush rose in her cheeks.

She squared her shoulders. "Tell me you will let me go up on deck. I'll work—I'll pay whatever money I have saved for my passage—I'll do anything you ask. Just don't make me stay down here another day."

She wore such a look of desperation he almost smiled. Instead he gave up a sigh of resignation. "All right, Brianne. You have managed to make me feel guilty, which is quite a difficult thing to do. I shall see that you are escorted up on deck at least once during the day and again after supper. Will that suffice?" She smiled so brightly, he felt his chest expanding.

"That would be wonderful, Captain. I shall be forever in your debt. I promise you won't be sorry."

But he was already sorry. Sorry she was there in his cabin, looking so fresh and lovely and untouched. Sorry his sense of honor wouldn't let him take her to his bed.

"It's late," he said gruffly. "Past time you were asleep."

"Yes . . . Thank you again, Captain Delaine. I look forward to the morrow. Perhaps you could show me a bit of the ship."

Marcus didn't answer. He knew what he would like to show her, but that would take place down here and not up on deck. Since that was not about to happen, he wouldn't be showing her anything at all. He would send Hamish Bass to escort her around the ship, or perhaps his second mate, Ben Hopkins.

The last thing he wanted was to spend time with Brianne Winters. He was a man of conscience, but he was only human. The more he was with her, the more likely she would wind up in his bed.

CHAPTER 6

Brandy tried to hide her disappointment the following morning when Benjamin Hopkins, second mate aboard the *Seahawk,* appeared at her door. She had so hoped that Marcus would come.

In her heart, she had known he would not. He had more important matters to attend than escorting a stowaway on a tour of his ship. In his place, Ben Hopkins shuffled nervously, a woolen stocking cap gripped in his weathered, callused hands.

"Good morning, Miss Brandy. Captain says that I should show you around the ship . . . that is . . . if it's all right with you, and if you are ready."

Brandy smiled warmly. "You may be certain, Mr. Hopkins, that I am more than ready."

He smiled then, a bit shyly, it seemed, for all his thirty-some years. "All right, then. It would certainly be my privilege."

They climbed the stairs to the deck and Brandy sucked in a deep breath of air. "You can't imagine, Mr. Hopkins, how good it feels just to feel the wind against my face, to taste this fresh sea air."

He chuckled softly. "I believe I can. I've always enjoyed being out-of-doors. That is the reason I chose a life at sea."

Gulls circled above them and the rigging clanked in the breeze. The ship rose up on a wave, then dropped into a trough as it cut through the water, sending a misty spray across the holystoned deck and dampening Brandy's face.

They started walking, slowly making a circle and returning to where they started. For the first time, she spied Marcus Delaine up on the quarterdeck and her pulse speeded up just at the sight of him.

He was staring out to sea, his dark blue eyes fixed somewhere on the horizon. He braced his log legs against the roll of the sea and clasped his hands behind him. He seemed so aloof, so alone, yet it was obvious he relished that aloneness.

She wasn't sure he had noticed her presence, since he made no move to acknowledge she was there, yet when she turned away, she felt as if he watched her, his steady gaze following them on their second lap around the deck.

They paused on their return, stopping just below where he stood, to watch a group of sailors tarring the ratlines. Mr. Hopkins explained that most of what was stationary on deck was tarred to protect it from the weather. The acrid smell rose into her nostrils, but she thought that, as harsh as it was, there was something oddly pleasant about it.

The men worked steadily, singing a lively sea chantey as their gloved hands skillfully applied the thick black substance.

> Oh, I heard the Old Man say.
> Leave her, Johnnie, leave her
> Tomorrow ye will get yer pay,
> Leave her, Johnnie, leave her,
> For the work was hard and the voyage was long
> The sea was high and the gales was strong,
> Ye may come ashore and grab yer pay,
> For it's time for us to leave her!

Brandy listened for a while, enjoying the tune and the colorful jumble of men, then Ben Hopkins led her over to where Brig Butler and several other sailors mended sail.

"Mornin', Miss Winters." The handsome blond sailor dragged the woolen cap from his head. "You're lookin' mighty pretty today."

It was the first time any of the men had been brave enough to pay her a compliment, one of the first times any of them had spoken to her at all. Apparently Brig Butler wasn't afraid of incurring the captain's wrath, as the other men seemed to be. Remembering his fearless rescue in the hold, she thought that perhaps he wasn't afraid of anything at all.

"Thank you, Mr. Butler."

He grinned roguishly, carving a dimple into his cheek. "Brig," he said. " 'Mr. Butler' sounds far too old."

Brandy found herself smiling. "All right . . . Brig. Then you must call me—"

"He will call you Miss Winters," Marcus said with brusque authority, stopping right beside her. "Whenever he has the rare occasion to speak to you at all."

"But—"

"I believe it is time you went below. I'll see you there myself, since there is some paperwork I need to attend."

She started to argue, but bit down on her tongue instead. Marcus had kept his word and allowed her up on deck. She didn't want to give him reason to change his mind. She took his arm and he led her downstairs, walked in behind her, and closed the door.

"It would be wisest, Miss Winters, if you didn't get too friendly with the crew. Brig Butler may look harmless, but in truth he's a lusty young rogue who wouldn't have a qualm about taking your innocence."

"I'm not interested in Mr. Butler except as a friend. I told you that before."

Something flickered in his eyes, something hot and urgent. For a single, hopeful instant, she thought he might be jealous. It was a foolish wish and no doubt she was wrong. Whatever it was, it was gone in a heartbeat, hidden once more behind his cool facade. "Just remember what I said."

Brandy ignored the unneccessary warning. "Thank you for allowing me to go up on deck. It is such a lovely day. I enjoyed myself very much."

Marcus merely nodded. He grumbled a phrase she didn't hear, moved behind his desk, opened a heavy set of ledgers, and set to work. Brandy settled down to the book she had been reading, one of Mrs. Radcliffe's gothic novels, and discovered that with Marcus there in the room, she didn't mind being cooped up as she had before.

In truth, it was pleasant, sitting as they were, Marcus immersed in his ledgers, she contentedly reading not far away. She thought that perhaps it would feel like this to be married, if she was lucky enough to find just the right man. The thought, striking out of nowhere, felt oddly out of place.

She didn't want marriage—at least not for years. She wanted to see things, do things. She wanted to experience life before she settled down.

Still, she couldn't help an occasional glance in Marcus's direction, couldn't help thinking how right it felt being there with him. She wondered how Marcus would feel if he knew what she was thinking.

Marcus glanced up from the ledgers he worked over. It was difficult to concentrate with Brianne in the room—nearly impossible, he conceded. He wished he could send her away, but it was by his own edict that she was there.

It still piqued his temper to remember the way she had smiled at young Butler. Forgodsake, didn't the girl have a lick of sense? Butler was a good man and a damned fine sailor. He was also a rake and a rogue, without the slightest conscience when it came to a woman, particularly one he saw as the captain's fetching little tavern wench, miles from the safety of her father and her home.

Marcus logged in several more shipping orders, then looked up again to see her sitting quietly in a chair in the corner. She wasn't fidgeting as she usually was. In fact, she appeared to be deeply immersed in her book and reading with a sort of calm contentment. Inwardly he smiled, oddly pleased by the sight.

He had felt that same pleasure earlier in the day as he had watched her strolling the deck. She was obviously enthralled by her surroundings, enamored of the sea and the crew, and bubbling with curiosity about the ship.

There was something about Brianne Winters. An inner glow. A zest for life that he had rarely seen. She seemed to overflow with it, to exude so much of it, it spilled onto those around her. Jilly Sharpe had seen it and garnered a flogging in an effort to possess it. Hamish Bass and Cyrus Lamb saw it and approved. The men in the crew sensed it and they envied him his position as the man they believed to be her lover.

Marcus watched her sitting so peacefully in his cabin and wished to God it were true.

They sailed on toward the Bahamas, Brandy's anticipation growing stronger every day. Marcus explained a little about their destination. There were nearly seven hundred islands in the chain, he said, but few were inhabited. *Seahawk* was sailing first to Black's Bay in the Spanish Keys, a small, sparsely populated chunk of land off Andros, the largest of the islands, which was south and west of New Providence, their final destination.

Though the settlers on the keys were mostly English, the place got its name from the Spaniards who had inhabited the island for a time. After dropping off supplies, the ship would head east to New Providence, where they would stop at the growing town of Naussau, the capital of the colony.

Brandy felt a ripple of excitement every time she imagined actually stepping onto foreign soil. She had never been to England, though Marcus, of course, was English, along with Ben Hopkins and many of the other sailors aboard the *Seahawk.* They had told her a number of stories and she had thought that it was a place she would surely love to visit. Perhaps the British colony would give her a glimpse of the world Marcus lived in when he wasn't at sea.

They were two days out of port, the ship running strong, a stiff wind puffing out the sails and helping to make up for lost time, when the first case of fever struck the crew.

Brandy sat reading, Dandelion curled in her lap, while Marcus recorded events in his daily log and worked on his ledgers. The first mate's arrival broke into the solace of the afternoon.

Hat in hand, Hamish Bass paced worriedly in front of the

captain's desk, his brushy gray brows drawn nearly together. "Didn't think there was much to it at first. A seaman name of Foley come down sick with it yesterday mornin'. At the time, I thought maybe he'd got a bit of a stomach disagreement, dyspepsia, ye know, or somethin' like that. Last night ol' Alf Crandall and Stumpy Jones come down with it. Been tossin' their guts—" Beneath his full gray beard, his face turned red. "Beg pardon, miss."

He cleared his throat, his eyes once more on Marcus. "None of 'em's been able to keep anythin' down, Cap'n. Their heads is hurtin' somethin' awful. Worst of it is, all three of 'em's burnin' up with fever. I don't like the look of it, sir."

Seated at his desk, Marcus frowned. "Neither do I." He glanced at Brandy, but didn't stop the first mate from speaking in front of her as she thought he might do.

"They'll quarantine us," Hamish said, "sure as 'ol Jack Frost comes in winter."

Marcus nodded, closing the heavy ledger in front of him. "Maybe not in Spanish Keys, but certainly in New Providence."

"What do you think it is?" Brandy asked, tamping down a thread of worry.

Hamish scratched his beard. "Hard to say for sure. Like as not, could be it's nothin' to worry about."

"Or it could be extremely serious," Brandy said, her fingers going still in Dandelion's soft fur. The cat must have sensed her tension, for its mottled coat stood up and Dandelion jumped down from her lap with a hiss.

"We had an outbreak of typhus fever in Charleston three years ago," Brandy said. "My father took ill with it, several of the people who work for us. I helped to nurse them. Perhaps I could take a look at the three sick men, see if that's what it is."

"No," Marcus said flatly, shoving back his chair and coming to his feet. "Whatever it is, I don't want you exposed."

"But if I looked at them—"

Marcus shook his head. "You aren't going near those men

until we know for certain what they have.'' He rounded the desk to where Hamish stood. ''Contaminated water is often the way disease is brought aboard, but we've been drinking rainwater since the storm.''

''It could also be something in the food,'' Brandy said.

''True, but we've been eating the same supplies since we left port and no one's been sick until now.''

Hamish shifted the pipe he carried from one hand to the other. Reaching into the pocket of his shirt, he pulled out a pouch of tobacco and began to stuff the bowl. ''Could be someone's done somethin' to cause it. Put somethin' in the food or drink.''

Marcus arched a brow. ''You're suggesting it could have been caused by the man responsible for the accidents we've been having?''

Hamish shrugged as if the possibility had definitely crossed his mind.

''Accidents?'' Brandy repeated. ''What are you talking about? You don't think someone would purposely do something like this?''

Marcus's gaze swung to hers. ''You remember the broken rudder that forced our return to Charleston?''

''Of course.''

''And you most certainly recall the problems we faced when the ricking broke loose and the cargo shifted. It damaged the steering and nearly got you killed.''

''But I thought that was—''

''An accident? Perhaps not. It may have been a deliberate attempt to sabotage the ship.''

Surprise widened her eyes. ''But why would anyone want to do a thing like that?''

''Money, perhaps. Competition for contracts is keen. Hawksmoor Shipping has an excellent reputation. That means we get more than our share.''

''But damaging your ship . . . deliberately making healthy men sick—''

''There's no reason to jump to conclusions. The men may have simply contracted some sort of illness. It happens, on occasion. The important thing is to get them isolated, just in case it turns out that it is, indeed, contagious.''

''Who will tend them?'' she asked.

''Mr. Lamb will be in charge. When the doctor isn't aboard, the job falls to him or to Hamish.''

Her fingers curled around the edges of the book she had been reading. ''Let me help. As I said, I know a bit about nursing. Besides, it doesn't take much skill to empty slop jars and apply damp cloths to men's brows.''

Marcus shook his head. ''A sailor's sick bay is hardly the place for an innocent young girl. *Seahawk* will take care of its own.''

Brandy started to argue, but decided against it. Only three men so far had come down with the disease. Perhaps no one else would contract it and her help would not be needed. Sweet God, she hoped so. Across the room, Marcus shrugged into his navy blue jacket and started for the door.

''I'm afraid you'll have to excuse us,'' he said. ''Hamish, I'd like to take a look at those men myself.''

''Aye, Cap'n.'' They left the cabin, leaving her alone—again. Blessed Mary, perhaps she should have argued after all. She was strong and capable—and going out of her mind with boredom. She could help those men, if Marcus would only let her.

She got her chance three days later. They were anchored off the tiny islands called Spanish Keys, not because of a quarantine but because Marcus insisted. Half the crew was down with a rampaging fever, the other half frightened to death that they would contract it, certain it was cholera or typhus fever and that many of them would wind up dead.

Determined to help, Brandy paced the floor of the cabin, awaiting Marcus's return. With so many men down sick, he was working around the clock. It was midnight when he came in, though it was obvious he didn't intend to stay.

He closed the door, cocking a brow in her direction when he saw her. ''What are you still doing up? You're beginning to make a habit of pestering me late at night and I find it quite annoying.''

She ignored the dark look in his eyes. ''Hamish says more of your men have fallen ill. I want you to let me help them.''

Marcus shook his head. ''I told you before—I don't want you sick as well. That is all that will happen if you go below and expose yourself to the disease.''

''I didn't get sick before. There is no reason to believe I will this time.''

''And there is no reason to believe you won't. We haven't lost a man yet, but we still don't know how dangerous this pestilence is.''

''Then let me help. Perhaps we can stop it before it spreads to the other men.''

Marcus raked a hand through his wavy black hair. The gesture was done with such obvious fatigue her heart went out to him. His face looked strained and a bit too thin. Faint purple smudges marked the skin beneath his eyes, and for the first time he looked uncertain.

''Hamish says the men are vomiting badly,'' Brandy pressed. ''It could be the head sickness or perhaps breakbone fever. With no surgeon aboard, Mr. Lamb could undoubtedly use my help.''

Marcus slowly shook his head. ''The foc'c'sle is hardly the place for a lady.''

''That is scarcely important. Let me go down, see if I can tell what it is. Perhaps there is something I can do.''

His eyes slid closed and a breath seeped slowly from his lungs. ''All right. First thing in the morning, we'll go below and you may examine one of the men. But you are not staying—no matter what they have.''

Brandy didn't argue. She had learned that with Marcus even a small battle won was a victory to be savored.

It was dark in the crew's quarter's in the bow of the ship, though a bright dawn sun crept over the deck above. Whale-oil lanterns sputtered from wooden pegs and the ceiling was low and confining. As they reached the bottom of the ladder, the putrid smell of illness struck her like a blow. Nausea rolled in her stomach and bile climbed the back of her throat.

Marcus's eyes swung to her face. "That's enough," he said. "You're as pale as a ghost. We're going back up on deck."

Brandy jerked away. "That is ridiculous. I'll be fine in a minute or two. I just need a moment to adjust."

He made a sound low in his throat, growled something about stubborn women. "You are certain you wish to go through with this?"

"I came to see if there is some way I can help. That is what I intend to do."

Flexing his jaw, settling a hand at her waist, he guided her toward the row upon row of berths, stacked to the ceiling with less than a foot between the man below and the one above. Breathing through her mouth, she dragged in a lungful of air and swallowed back the nausea rolling inside her.

She stopped at the first sailor's berth, Stumpy Jones, a man she had seen on deck who had one leg shorter than the other. With his cheeks sunken in and his face so exceedingly pale, he was hardly recognizable. His eyes were closed, his skin slick with sweat. Nearly unconscious with fever, he moaned softly, moving listlessly back and forth on his berth. The smell of urine and vomit was nearly overwhelming.

Cyrus Lamb walked up beside her, looking as weary as Marcus, his stout shoulders drooping with fatigue. "The lad's in a bad way. Refuses to eat, not even a bit of broth."

"What about the others?" Brandy asked. "Have they lost their appetites as well?"

He nodded. "What with their stomachs ailin', 'tisn't surprisin' that they won't eat."

"No," Brandy agreed, "but it's a definite symptom of breakbone fever."

"Maybe. Somethin' tells me it's somethin' else."

"What makes you think so?" Marcus asked.

"Can't say for sure. Just that if it was breakbone or the head sickness, by now a good percent of 'em would likely be dead." He sighed, a whispy, papery sound in the dim light of the hold. "Whatever 'tis, lass, these men are more than passable sick and I could surely use your help."

"And I am more than willing to give it."

Marcus scowled and she thought that he would refuse. "I don't like it," he said instead, his gaze sliding off to the endless sea of suffering men. "If we weren't so damnably short-handed—"

"But you are, and these men are in desperate need of attention." She rested a hand on his arm. "Let me do this, Marcus."

He looked down at the place she touched, then back to his men's pale, emaciated faces. "It doesn't appear I have much choice."

Brandy smiled and turned back to Cyrus Lamb. "Is there any chance we could get someone to carry down a cask of seawater? We could soak these men's clothes, see if we might be able to get their fevers down."

"What ya say, Cap'n?"

Marcus made a slight inclination of his head. "I'll see to it myself."

Leaving her in Cyrus's care, he strode toward the ladder, and Brandy set to work. It was an endless, grueling day, yet she relished the chance to help. When the ship's bells rang four times, signaling it was two in the morning, she said good night to Ben Hopkins, who had appeared to relieve her, eased by a sleeping Cyrus Lamb, and started up the ladder, only to be blocked by Marcus's tall frame coming down.

He paused midway, towering above her. "What the devil do you think you are doing? Are you determined to make yourself sick? I said that you could help. It never occurred to me you would stay down here half the bloody night. When did you plan on sleeping?"

Her chin hitched up. "There were things that needed to be done, and I had rested enough in your cabin to last me a good long time. Besides, no one else is getting much sleep—especially not you."

"I'm the captain. You are merely—"

"A stowaway trying to earn her passage."

A muscle leaped in Marcus's cheek. "Whatever you are, you need to get some rest. You will return with me to my cabin."

She didn't speak the obvious, that she was already headed in that direction. "As you wish, Captain Delaine."

He walked beside her across the deck and down the ladder to the passage leading to his quarters. As soon as the door was closed, he gripped her arms and turned her to face him. "And what did you think you were doing wandering about unescorted? You've seen what can happen. I thought you had learned your lesson."

She sighed wearily. Sometimes Marcus's overbearing nature was simply too much. "In case you haven't noticed, Captain, there is a dearth of escorts available at present. Which doesn't really matter since there is also a dearth of men who might pose any sort of threat. Most of them are flat on their backs in the fo'c'sle, half dead of fever."

He blinked and his hands fell away. A tired sigh whispered past his lips. "I'm sorry. I'm extremely grateful for what you are doing. I don't suppose I'm showing that gratitude very well."

Unconsciously her hand came up to his cheek. She could feel the dark stubble of his beard. "You're tired and you are worried. If you have time to be concerned for me, then I am the one who is grateful."

His gaze moved over her face. He covered her hand with his and for an instant something blazed in his eyes. Then the hand fell away and he turned and walked over to his desk. "Any sign of the fever abating?"

"Not yet, I'm afraid."

"Do you remain uncertain what it is?"

"It doesn't react quite like anything anyone has ever seen. Mr. Hopkins said that you brought fresh fruits aboard in Charleston. Perhaps there was an insect that carried disease."

"Perhaps. But we have been eating them all along without a problem. I can't imagine that is the cause."

"Then perhaps it is simply a malaise of some sort, something out of the air. If that is the case, we shall never know what it is for certain.''

He nodded, wearily began to unbutton his coat, which looked rumpled and unkempt as she had never seen it. ''I don't suppose it matters. What matters is that the men get well.''

But it remained uncertain whether or not that would happen. By now, well over half the crew was infected, though so far none of them had died. It was the only good sign in a hard-fought battle that seemed to have no end. Brandy knelt next to blond Brig Butler, the latest victim, who reached out and captured her hand.

''If you are to be my nurse, then perhaps being sick won't be so bad.''

She could feel him shaking, knew how terrible he must be feeling, but forced herself to smile. ''Some of the men have an easier time than others. You are healthy and strong—''

''Ah . . . so you noticed. I am . . . extremely pleased that you did.''

Her smile broadened. ''You are also far too bold, Mr. Butler, and far too full of yourself.'' She eased her hand away. ''Now try and get some rest. Perhaps your fever will lessen.''

He sighed tiredly and his bright blue eyes slid closed. Sweat darkened his wavy blond hair and matted it against his forehead. Still he was handsome. Handsome and charming, and she felt not the least bit attracted to him, except in the way of a friend. There was no heat, none of the turbulent emotions she felt when Marcus Delaine merely glanced in her direction.

Brandy mopped his brow with a damp cloth, then used an elbow to blot the perspiration from her own. She was tired, weary clear to the bone. And yet, under the circumstances, there was nowhere she would rather be than there, helping the *Seahawk* men.

CHAPTER 7

Marcus stood at the bottom of the ladder leading down to the fo'c'sle. Across the way, moving along the rows of berths, Brianne Winters worked to comfort his men, sponging a fevered brow, holding a man's head while he retched into a bucket what little food he'd been able to eat.

Her simple skirt and white blouse were badly wrinkled and soiled with perspiration. Strands of her bright copper hair had come loose from her braid and hung in tangled wisps around her face. She seemed not to notice. Instead her attention focused on each man as if he were the only one in the room.

Marcus felt a tightness in his chest just to watch her. Whenever she took a man's hand or simply smiled in his direction, he seemed cheered by the effort, seemed to suck in a new will to live. So far none of the men had died. He took comfort in that, and it renewed his hope that whatever malady had befallen his crew was not deadly. No new cases had been reported in the past two days. Perhaps the men were actually beginning to get well.

He wondered again if someone had somehow arranged for this to happen, but logic told him that this, at least, was merely a hazard of the life he had chosen. For years he had been lucky when it came to the health of his crew, and finally the odds had simply caught up with him.

He strode toward the woman pulling a sheet up over one sleeping sailor's form. " 'Tis past the time you were abed. I've come to see you back to my cabin." Even as he said the words, a dozen pairs of eyes swung in his direction. There was envy in their depths and though their faces looked pale, their bodies too thin and their eyes bloodshot and weary, there was also a trace of hunger.

They believed he would bed her, make love to her until he'd had his fill. If it were true, he might have felt guilty. At least he might have on another occasion. Not tonight. Tonight if she were his, he would sink himself inside her and take what he needed. He would allow himself the comfort of her tempting little body.

She turned away from the man she had been tending, crossed the few paces to his side. She looked up at him and flashed a surprisingly radiant smile.

"They're finally getting better. Mr. Foley was the first to come down sick and his fever had disappeared completely. Several others are improving as well." Her smile grew even brighter. "I believe they are all going to make it."

Relief trickled through him. He found himself smiling in return. "If they do, a good deal of the credit goes to you. Thank you for helping them, Brianne."

"I'm glad you allowed me to help."

"I shouldn't have. It was hardly your place."

Her smile slipped a little. "I have no place aboard this ship. You and I both know it. If I was able to help, then perhaps that will make up for some of the trouble my presence has caused."

He studied her face, saw the fatigue that glazed those pretty amber eyes, and thought how much she had endured these past few days. "I believe you have exonerated yourself completely."

Her mouth curved up once more. "I am pleased to hear it, Captain."

He offered her his arm. "Shall we go?"

She rested a hand on the sleeve of his coat and he could feel the warmth of her fingers. As they crossed the deck, a soft breeze fluttered loose strands of hair against his cheek. Her skirts brushed his legs and his body suddenly tightened.

An image appeared of Brianne lying naked, of her soft lips parted to return his kiss, her pale legs wrapped around him as he drove himself inside her. His shaft went hard, pressing uncomfortably against the front of his breeches, and he cursed himself for a fool.

She paused at the rail, braced her hands on the top, and gazed out at the water. "The sea is so lovely. I wondered what it would be like to be out here. I never could have imagined the vastness, the beauty. Sometimes when I think of it, I wish I didn't have to sleep, that I could come up here in the darkness and sit through the night just watching it."

He followed her line of vision out across the water. "The sea has many faces. Sometimes her beauty is gentle—she's placid and smooth as glass. Sometimes she's a temptress, a wild and dangerous vixen set on seducing a man into an icy grave. Always she is fascinating."

"You speak of the ocean as if it were a woman."

His mouth curved faintly. "I think of it that way, as a beautiful woman I have loved since I was a boy. The sea is the only woman for me."

Something flickered in her eyes, then it was gone. "What you feel is there in your face whenever you look out at the water."

"The sea is my life—the only life I've ever wanted."

She returned her gaze to the horizon, staring at the place where distant islands formed a dark, shadowy outline against the blackness that had no end. He studied the way the moonlight played over her face and thought how incredibly lovely she was, her features fine yet not frail, her lips full and gently curved.

When she turned to look up at him, time stilled, long suspended, and there seemed no choice but to kiss her. He had to feel those soft lips as he had wanted to do a thousand times since he had tasted their sweetness before. Closing the distance between them, he settled his mouth over hers, felt her stiffen a moment in surprise, then her hands crept up to his shoulders, slid gently around his neck, and she kissed him back. He could feel the rapid beating of her heart and the warmth of her small body pressing against him.

"Marcus . . ."

The whisper of his name wrenched a groan from his lips. Tightening his hold around her, he deepened the kiss, coaxing her lips apart, taking her with his tongue, sampling the fire inside the dark, sweet cavern of her mouth. He was painfully erect, throbbing with heat and need. He could feel her trembling, feel the softness of her breasts where they pillowed against his chest, feel the tightening of her nipples into hard little peaks.

His hand came up to cup one. He stroked the tip and it tightened even more. A tiny whimper slipped from Brandy's throat, the sound like tinder to flame. Blood pounded at his temples and throbbed low in his groin. He caressed a breast and wished he could tear away the fabric imprisoning the soft, creamy flesh; felt her tremble and wished she were naked and writhing beneath him.

"Marcus . . ." Her fingers slid into the hair at the nape of his neck. Her tongue touched his and another jolt of heat went sliding through him. He wanted to take her right there, to drag her down on the deck, lift her skirts, and bury himself inside her. He wanted to make love to her, to forget his weariness and lose himself in mindless pleasure.

He kissed the side of her neck, tasted the small, shell-like rim of an ear, and kissed her again, cupping her bottom and pulling her against his arousal. There was only an instant's hesitation before she melted against him, returning the kiss in full measure, her taut nipples brushing against the front of his coat, making his body harden even more. His fingers returned to the fullness of her breast, testing the weight, wanting to peel away the fabric of her blouse and caress her flesh.

A noise on deck behind them reached his ears, finally beat its way into his groggy senses. It took the full force of his will to tear his hand free of the lush weight in his palm, his mouth from the sweet fire of her lips. He straightened away and felt her sway toward him, as off balance as he had been just moments before.

"Easy, love." He steadied her within the circle of his arms, then gently set her away from him. "It's best we go below. You're weary, and this is neither the time nor the place. I apologize for taking advantage."

She opened her mouth to speak, saw the two sailors climbing the ratlines that he had seen before, flushed, and simply nodded.

Marcus dragged in a steadying breath and fought down the hot desire still pulsing through him. By the time they reached his cabin, sanity had returned. His body still ached but his mind was clear and he was once more under control.

Bloody hell! What the devil did he think he was doing? Brianne Winters was an innocent. Even if she wanted him as much as he wanted her, it wouldn't be fair to take her. Marriage was out of the question and certainly not what he wanted. His world, his dreams, all revolved around a life at sea. They didn't include Brianne Winters or any other woman.

And he couldn't simply take her, then abandon her. She was a sweet, naive young girl barely on the brink of womanhood. She deserved a husband and family, and once he took her virtue, odds were that she would never have the chance.

And there was always the possibility of getting her with child. A child needed a father, someone who would be there to guide it through the years. Marcus had no intention of being anywhere but sailing the seas.

As he had told her, the sea was his life, his love. It was all he ever wanted.

He turned to Brianne. "It's time you were abed," he said a bit too harshly. "You're tired and you need some sleep."

Confusion darkened those golden eyes. "You're angry. I'm sorry if I have somehow displeased you."

"Displeased me?" He slashed a hand through the air, frustration blackening his mood. "Bloody hell—has no one warned you what happens when a woman kisses a man the way you kissed me?"

Brandy wet her lips. "I thought . . . I thought you liked it."

"For God's sake—of course I liked it! I'm a man, aren't I? Or perhaps you still believe that no matter what you do, with me you are safe. You think you can taunt me with your luscious little body, kiss me, let me caress those lovely breasts, and I'll stand by like a bloody damned fool and not bed you. If that is what you believe, you are sorely mistaken. I warn you, Brianne—continue to flaunt yourself in front of me the way you have been and you'll find yourself flat on your back beneath me. I'll take you—make no mistake about it. I'll do as the rest of the crew believes I already have."

Brandy stared at him as if she had never seen him before, her eyes full of disbelief and perhaps a hint of fear. Guilt washed over him. It was hardly her fault. She was an untried virgin, while he had bedded more women than he cared to remember. God's blood, he should have had more sense.

"I do not flaunt myself," she said softly. Though she held her chin high, her bottom lip quivered. "And I did not kiss you. You kissed me."

The memory reappeared and Marcus stifled a groan. His body still throbbed with desire for her. His mind still roiled with images of her lush breast filling his hand. "Go to bed," he said more gently. "We shall both be better off if we pretend that tonight did not happen."

Her gaze locked with his and there was steel in them now. "You may do so if you please. As for me, I do not wish to pretend it did not happen. I wish very definitely to remember."

Shoulders straight, she turned and walked out of the room, entering her tiny quarters, letting the curtain fall back into place behind her. It danced a moment, then finally went still, and Marcus released a weary breath. He hadn't been fair to her. What happened on deck wasn't her fault, it was his. He had wanted her so badly he had simply lost control. In the future he would have to be more careful.

Remembering the look of desire in Brandy's golden eyes when he had ended the kiss, God help him, it wouldn't be easy.

Brandy lay beneath the blanket on her narrow berth, staring up at the heavy planked ceiling. Though the hours continued to creep past, she could hear Marcus moving about in the room next door, pacing the floor instead of sleeping.

She wasn't quite sure why. Perhaps their encounter had left him feeling as hot and restless as it had her, unsettled in a way she couldn't have imagined. She tried not to think of it, to forget the feel of his dark hand cupping her breast, the flood of heat that made her head spin when his fingers had grazed her nipple. Sweet God, it was sinful, the things she had allowed him to do. Her father would say she was a wanton, a harlot just like her mother.

Perhaps she was. Brandy only knew that she had wanted Marcus to touch her, wanted his kiss to go on and on, wanted to feel his hands on her body. She had wanted to touch him as well, to stroke the hard muscles beneath his shirt, to learn the shape of each solid ridge and valley. Marcus wanted to pretend it had not happened. Brandy wanted to remember.

She stared up at the planks above her head, saw a tiny spider crawl out from a crack in the wood. She watched him traversing an uncertain path, but her thoughts remained on Marcus and his passion for the sea, as if the ocean were his mistress, his one and only true love.

The sea was his life and Brandy could never be part of it. She had known that from the start and in a way she understood. Marcus didn't love her, would never love her, and yet he desired her. Tonight she had discovered just how much.

Brandy knew little of desire, but it was obviously what she felt for Marcus Delaine. In truth, she wanted him to make love to her. She wanted him to be the man who would make her fully a woman. Whether they were wed was unimportant. She didn't want marriage. She wanted to see things, go places, experience life as she never had before.

And she wanted to know passion. Marcus could show her that passion if only he would.

She sighed into the darkness, weariness finally overcoming her turbulent, whirling emotions. What to do? The question wandered vaguely in her thoughts as she drifted off to sleep. When she awakened several hours later, she still didn't have an answer.

* * *

Hamish Bass stood at the rail next to Brandy Winters. Most of the men were out of their sickbeds and back to work—thanks in good part to her—and the captain again had insisted someone be with her whenever she went up on deck.

Hamish sucked on the stem of his pipe, watching as she gazed excitedly off toward the island they were approaching. She was a fetching lass, to be sure, sweet-tongued and soft-eyed, with a ripe little body that would turn the head of any stout-blooded male. Surely it had turned the captain's.

Hamish had known Marcus Delaine since the man had sailed his first ship into Boston Harbor. The captain had always had more than his share of women, but Hamish had never seen him quite so enamored of one, and this one little more than a girl.

Not that his interest showed. Marcus was a man who guarded his emotions, as any good captain should. None but Hamish had noticed those long, heated glances beneath his lowered lids, the hungry look in his friend's dark eyes whenever they came to rest on the girl.

And there was the lass, as well. She was taken with the captain. In her younger years, she had followed him about like a worshipful puppy, begging for stories whenever he was in port. Now that she was a woman, her attraction had changed into something more, something even she didn't quite understand.

Hamish felt sorry for her. Even should the captain take her to his bed, there would be no future for her. She would simply be another of his women in another different port, one perhaps he was more fond of than the rest, but nothing more.

Even if one day he chanced to marry—which Hamish very much doubted—it wouldn't be to the likes of her, a pretty little tavern wench without an ounce of aristocratic blood. Marcus Delaine was an earl, a high and mighty nobleman. He would wed with a woman of his own class.

The facts were hard ones, to be sure. And Hamish had come to like the girl. He hated to see her hurt.

"Ye be mighty pensive, Miss Brandy. Ye've been quieter than usual of late."

Her eyes tilted up at the corners. "Have I?"

"Aye, lass, that ye have."

"I suppose I'm a bit tired, is all. I'm happy the men are well and most of them back to work. I'm excited about going into port on the morrow."

He cocked a brow. "Aye, well, I don't mean to be disappointin' ye, lass, but on this stop ye'll be stayin' aboard."

Her gaze swung to his face. "What?"

"Aye. 'Tis the cap'n's orders. Ye'll have to wait till we get to New Providence before ye'll be leavin' the ship."

"But that can't be true. Marcus—I mean Captain Delaine—has promised to take me ashore himself." She turned toward the wheelhouse, saw him striding toward them. "Isn't that right, Captain? You *are* taking me ashore on the morrow?"

The captain shook his head. "I'm afraid not, Brianne. You won't be going ashore until we reach Nassau, the capital in New Providence."

Her cheeks went bright with heat. "But you promised to take me ashore. You said I had exonerated myself. Those were your very words."

He smiled indulgently. "Staying aboard is not a punishment. The town we're off-loading supplies in isn't safe for a woman. It's little more than an outpost, not to mention the fact most of its citizens are cutthroats, pirates, and thieves. They're an unsavory lot, to be sure."

"Then why are we stopping?"

"Even pirates have to eat, and the men who run the town are paying a handsome sum for the goods we're bringing them."

Brandy stared out to sea, at the island looming larger with each passing hour. "Spanish Keys is a place I've never been, and I would like very much to see it. Surely I would be safe if I were with you."

The captain lifted her chin with his fingers. "I promised

to take you ashore and I will. As soon as we arrive at the capital."

"Aye," Hamish said, " 'Tis a pretty place, is Nassau, and far more respectable." But her mouth had gone thin and her features looked mulish. He smiled around the pipe he clamped between his teeth, wondering what she was thinking and what trouble she had in store for the captain.

Aye, she was a handful, she was. Hamish wished he were twenty years younger and she was making trouble for him.

Brandy paced the floor of Marcus's cabin. All but a skeleton crew had gone ashore, and the captain with them. Hamish Bass had been left in charge, along with Ben Hopkins, her guardians, she presumed. They were downstairs in the fo'c'sle, playing a game of cribbage. They had offered to teach her the game, but she had declined. She wasn't in the mood for cards—she wanted to visit the islands she had traveled so far to see.

Brandy knelt before the small fire in the stove and added a bit of coal. It wasn't fair that Marcus should leave her behind. For days she had been looking forward to going ashore. Now, with the men mostly gone, she had been thinking of what she might do to remedy the situation.

It was early in the evening. She still had her cabin boy's clothes rolled up in a bundle beneath the bed. Dressed as a man, she could probably sneak off the ship, take a quick look around, and get back before anyone missed her.

On the other hand, if something went wrong, if she ran into any sort of trouble, Marcus would be furious—and be proven right again.

Flinging herself down on the bed, she stared off toward the tiny window but saw only the descending darkness and nothing at all of the island. Sanity told her to do as the captain commanded and stay safely aboard the ship. Her rebellious streak said she had come this far, surely she should get to see it.

Brandy rolled onto her stomach and punched the pillow, trying to decide which voice to follow. Minutes ticked past.

A scratching noise sounded. Dandelion yowled outside the door, asking to be let in.

Brandy moved in that direction, still uncertain what she should do.

Jilly Sharpe sat with four other men at a table in the back of the Crown and Garter Tavern. It sat on a dirt street on the quay amid a cluster of ramshackle buildings across from the town's small harbor, an inlet not large enough to handle a ship the size of *Seahawk,* which was anchored just offshore.

Jilly had arrived in town aboard one of the dinghies that had carried the crew. The captain had ordered him left there on the island, to await another ship on which to earn his keep.

Jilly glared across the smoky taproom to where the crew of the *Seahawk* sat playing cards and drinking grog. Through a small doorway into another room, he could see Captain Delaine seated at a table in conversation with Garret Stone and Red Fontaine, the men who had contracted for the supplies that had been unloaded from the ship.

Jilly watched them and one of his knotty hands balled into a fist. Beneath his shirt, his back was a mass of thick dark scabs that stretched and itched and burned every time he moved. They reminded him of the flogging he had received and of his hatred of Marcus Delaine.

They reminded him of the tight little piece he'd meant to have, the captain's doxy, the girl he would take before this night was through.

Jilly almost laughed. If the captain thought it was settled between them, that he would just slink away with his tale between his legs like a bloody hound, he was in for a real surprise. Marcus Delaine had made a mistake in bringing him to Spanish Keys. Jilly had friends here, men he had known before.

And even if he didn't, for the lure of the coin stashed in the captain's cabin or the promise of tossing a pretty girl's skirts, they would join him. Adventure was the lure for men like the ones in the Crown and Garter. He leaned across the battered wooden table, speaking to a big Hungarian sailor with a cloudy blue eye he had got in a knife fight.

"Go upstairs. Tell Lola that Delaine is here. Cap'n likes a pretty piece. She can keep him distracted till we get back from the ship." She would do it, he knew, for a share of the take. Lola didn't do anything unless there was something in it for Lola.

The sailor, Janos, nodded. He grinned as he shoved back his chair and made his way up the stairs to her second-floor suite of rooms.

"You are sure there is money?" asked another of the men, Luis Estrada, a Spaniard who kept a woman there on the island.

"There's money and plenty of it. Delaine's a rich Brit from London—a bloody aristocrat. He's got money—enough for us all. And it's bound to be there in his cabin. If not, you can take your turn with the girl—soon as I've had my fill."

Luis nodded and the other two men seemed satisfied as well. They sat back in their chairs, sipping tankards of rum, watching the staircase, waiting for Lola Perez to come down to the taproom. She did so a few minutes later, her red satin skirts swishing softly around her ankles, her breasts nearly spilling from the top of her dress.

The sight made Jilly hard beneath the table, made him think of the evening ahead, of small pink nipples and a smooth round bottom that fit exactly in the palm of his hands.

Jilly went harder still. *It won't be long, my friend,* he consoled himself. *You're gonna get yours, and soon.* While Delaine was aching for a tumble with Lola Perez, he'd be swivin' that little saucebox of so hard she'd be sore for a week.

Jilly smiled with anticipation, watching the sway of Lola's hips as she made her way toward Marcus Delaine. With a jerk of his head, Jilly motioned to the others and they came to their feet.

It wouldn't take long to reach the ship. Once they did, with cutthroats like Janos and Luis, dealing with the *Seahawk*'s skeleton crew would be like swatting a handful of flies. They would find the captain's money, take it and the girl, and disappear somewhere in the islands.

There were a hundred places to hide. Delaine would never find them, and there was no one who would help him. Spanish Keys protected its own.

CHAPTER 8

Marcus watched the dark-haired woman approaching through the doors leading in from the taproom. She was tall and statuesque, with straight black hair that hung past her hips and smooth dark olive skin. She was graceful and exotic, and as out of place in the Crown and Garter as a French bawd in the House of Lords.

Through the door to the taproom he could see the men watching as she walked past, each of them craning his neck to see her more clearly, eyes hot with lust. She was the owner of the tavern, he knew, though he couldn't imagine what a woman like that was doing in a place like Spanish Keys, and he had yet to meet her. It looked as though he would meet her tonight.

She paused at the side of the table, next to where he sat, and all three men came to their feet. She flashed them a sensual smile. "Good evening, gentlemen."

Red Fontaine, a Frenchman by birth who posed as a displaced nobleman, turned to make the formal introductions. Along with Garret Stone, he ran the island, a refuge for unsavory types like the ones in the taproom.

"Captain, may I present Miss Lola Perez, the owner of the Crown and Garter."

Marcus made a slight inclination of his head. "Good evening, Miss Perez."

"Captain Delaine arrived aboard the *Seahawk,*" Garret Stone put in. "He delivered the supplies we've been needing so badly."

She smiled, broader this time, her full red lips curving upward. ''Good evening, Captain. I've heard of you, of course. It's a pleasure to finally meet you.'' Her expression was inscrutable, aloof yet somehow seductive. All the while her jet-black eyes ran over him, traveling his tall frame from head to foot.

He returned the smile. ''The pleasure is mine, Miss Perez.'' He flashed a look at the others. ''Gentlemen, I believe our business is concluded. Perhaps Miss Perez would care to join us.''

Garret Stone spoke up. ''Unfortunately, Red and I were just leaving.'' He turned to the dark-haired woman. ''Though I'm sure Captain Delaine would enjoy some feminine company.''

He might, indeed, he thought. He was curious about Lola Perez and—after the torturous nights he had been spending with Brianne Winters just out of reach in his cabin—badly in need of a woman. If the interest he read in Lola's dark eyes was sincere, perhaps the evening might prove entertaining.

The men made their farewells and she took a seat across from him. Marcus stared at her sultry mouth, wondered at the taste of it, at the pleasure it might bring. He thought of that mouth pressed against his skin, and from out of nowhere, a memory of Brandy's soft lips trembling beneath his kiss rose into his mind.

His gaze traveled down to the swell of Lola's breasts, which were heavy and tempting, pale in contrast to the dark of her hair and eyes. Brandy's were firmer, more rounded, he thought, recalling the way her tight little nipples had strained toward his hand when he had kissed her.

He thought of making love to Lola Perez, and with the thought came a sudden, unexpected jolt of guilt.

Damnation! What the devil was he doing comparing Lola Perez to Brianne Winters—and why the hell should he feel the least bit guilty? He didn't owe Brianne his loyalty. He didn't belong to her, nor she to him. He didn't owe the girl a damnable bloody thing!

He smiled at the dark, sensuous beauty across from him.

"I know it's none of my business, and a question you have surely been asked a dozen times, but what is a woman of your obvious . . . charms doing in a place like the Crown and Garter? I should think you would prefer a city like London, or Paris, perhaps."

Lola tossed back her hair and laughed, a rich, throaty sound that made his body tighten. "I would think that is obvious, Captain—or would you prefer 'my lord'? I am told that along with being the owner of the *Seahawk* you are also an earl. The newly titled Earl of Hawksmoor, in fact, if my sources are correct."

"You are well informed, Miss Perez."

"The island is small. News travels quickly."

He smiled. "I don't believe there is a need for formality between us. Why don't you call me Marcus?"

Lola smiled, the corners of her mouth curving slowly upward. "I would like that . . . Marcus. As to why I am here in Spanish Keys, I arrived as a settler with my husband eight years ago. I was only a young girl then. Santiago died of pneumonia ten months later and I was left alone. I was desperate, nearly starving. Working here was the only choice I had."

"Losing a husband like that . . . It must have been terrible for you."

She shrugged as if it did not matter while he thought that it surely must have mattered a very great deal.

"It wasn't really so bad. In time I made enough money to buy the place. Strangely enough, I've discovered I like what I do. Over the years, I've become a wealthy woman, you see. I'm no longer at anyone's mercy. Here I'm important. I pick the men with whom I spend my time. Interesting men. Men who intrigue me. They are the only ones who share my bed." She smiled her slow, catlike smile. "You intrigue me, Marcus."

His brow arched up. He leaned back in his chair. "Do I?"

Cool onyx eyes moved over his body, came to rest on his face. "Yes, you do."

Desire pulsed through him. She was beautiful and he wanted her. In truth, he needed her. He needed a woman who could satisfy the lust for Brianne Winters that even now clashed with his desire for Lola Perez.

"Perhaps I could buy you a drink," he said.

"Perhaps I could buy you one, my lord Captain—upstairs in my suite. I'm sure we would both be more comfortable."

Marcus smiled into that knowing face. Shoving back his chair, he stood up, pulled out her chair, and helped her to her feet. As he linked her arm through his, an odd feeling crept over him, that same surge of guilt that he had felt before. It mingled with a strange reluctance. As much as his body needed relief, something held him back. He was attracted to Lola Perez, yet he felt as if something were missing.

Perhaps, he thought, it was passion. Where Brianne was fire, Lola was the image of cool sensuality, a woman of experience, undoubtedly skillful in bed. She was also calculating and self-absorbed. Her desire would be tempered with an icy control.

It occurred to him that it wasn't really Lola he wanted. Though his body responded to her dark, disturbing allure, it was Brianne Winters he wanted in his bed. He wanted to feel her fire, her innocent untamed heat. He wanted to give her pleasure and watch when she reached her peak. He wanted her and not Lola Perez, and the fact that a woman had managed to gain such a hold over him made his jaw clamp down in anger.

"Shall we go?" he said a bit more tightly than he intended, offering her his arm.

Lola eyed him a moment, then smiled her feline smile. "With pleasure, my lord."

Her lush breasts pressed against his side and heat slid into his groin. Need sank its claws into his belly. When Brianne's image arose, kissing him with such sweet abandon, a soft oath hovered on his tongue.

Damn her to hell, he thought. Tonight he would forget Brianne Winters. He would take his ease in the arms of Lola Perez.

* * *

Brandy sprawled on Marcus's berth, a book propped on her chest, Dandelion snuggled beside her, purring with contentment at the hand she stroked over the cat's furry head.

Reading to the end of the chapter, she set the book away with a disgruntled sigh. She liked to read. It was a pleasure she had never thought to enjoy. But tonight she wanted excitement. She wanted to be with Marcus in Spanish Keys. She wanted a taste of adventure.

She thought of the cabin boy's clothes in a bundle beneath her bed and yearned to put them on. Of course there was the matter of lowering another dinghy and rowing all the way to shore. No small task, yet she thought that she could accomplish it.

Brandy slammed a hand down on top of the book. It was a foolish idea, tempting though it was, one she had decided to abandon. Marcus had said it was dangerous. There was a limit to her bravado. Nor did she wish to incur his wrath again.

She would settle instead for a walk up on deck, a stroll in the faint glow of moonlight that silvered the water. At least with the men away, she had that freedom. She would savor it, she vowed, and postpone her island adventure for the day Marcus took her ashore in New Providence.

"All right, Dandy, time to go." Setting the heavy, mottled cat away, she swung her legs to the side of the bed and stood up. "You behave yourself while I'm gone and I'll get you an extra saucer of cream."

Kneeling to rub the cat's chin one last time, she started for the door leading out into the passage.

Marcus reached the top of the stairs, Lola Perez on his arm, and crossed the hall to her suite. He had just pulled open the door when young Brig Butler and a half dozen *Seahawk* crewmen came crashing into the taproom, making all kinds of unholy noise and wildly shouting his name.

"I'm up here," he called down to them, striding back over to the rail. "What the devil's going on?"

"It's Jilly Sharpe, Captain. I saw him leave the tavern a

little while ago and there was something about his movements that didn't seem quite right. Me and a couple of the men, we followed him down to the quay. There was a boat there, Captain. Sharpe and four other men—they're rowing out to the *Seahawk,* sir. God only knows what they mean to do."

A cold chill snaked down Marcus's spine. He started down the stairs without so much as a by-your-leave to Lola Perez.

"Captain?" she called after him, making him stop and turn. "Will you be back this evening?"

He shook his head. "I'm sorry, Miss Perez." An odd sensation rippled through him. It took a moment for him to realize it was relief. "Perhaps the next time I am in port." Then he was pounding down the stairs, following Brig and the others out into the night.

"We'd better hurry," Butler said. "No doubt he's gone after Miss Winters and I don't think Hamish and Ben will be enough to stop him."

Sharpe and Brianne. In his mind's eye, Marcus saw her struggling against Jilly Sharpe as clearly as he had the night it had actually occurred, and something painful jolted beneath his ribs. If he had doubted his feelings for her before, he didn't now. As they raced toward the dinghy, his heart thundered madly and fear formed a tight knot in his chest.

God, he shouldn't have left her. He'd been worried about her going ashore in a place like this. He should have stayed behind and made certain that she was safe.

"We'll need weapons," he said as they strode the wooden boardwalk. "I'm carrying a small pocket pistol but that is all. We'll need more than that if we are to deal with these men."

"We've half a dozen pistols between us," Brig said. "None of us comes to a place like this unarmed."

Marcus smiled grimly. "Good lads." They reached the dinghy and hurriedly climbed in, taking their places at the oars.

"Put your backs into it, lads!" Marcus's words rang out across the water as the crew began to pull hard for the ship. "Brianne is in danger," he told them. "I don't intend to let Sharpe hurt her again!"

With that he leaned forward, took up a pair of oars, and set to rowing with his men. Their jaws were clenched, their expressions fiercely determined. It occurred to him that as much as Brandy had helped them, perhaps they were as concerned for her safety as he. It made his chest squeeze even harder.

If Jilly Sharpe had touched her, the man was as good as dead.

Brandy pressed herself back against the wall of Marcus's cabin. Just inside the door, Jilly Sharpe and another man stood grinning.

"What's the matter, gel? Not pleased to see me?" He cocked his shiny, bald head. "Come on, now, don't be lookin' at me that way. You didn't really think I'd be lettin' you off so easy—not after what you did?"

She held a hand out in front of her as if to ward him off. "You'd better stay away from me. You were flogged for what you did before. Touch me again, there's no telling what the captain will do to you this time."

"Oh, I mean to touch you, all right. I mean to ride you hard, gel, make no mistake about it." He motioned toward Marcus's desk and the other man, a lanky sailor with coarse black hair, moved in that direction. "You find the money. I'll take care of the gel."

Brandy took another step back from Jilly Sharpe and started screaming, yelling for help as loud as she possibly could.

Jilly reached her in an instant, slammed her up against the wall, and slapped her hard across the face. "Stop that caterwaulin', ya hear? Won't do you a lick of good. There's no one to help ya. Bass and Ben Hopkins, the other three men still aboard—they've all been taken care of."

"Oh, God."

He grinned, exposing a gap between his two front teeth. Light from the whale-oil lantern made the top of his bald head glow like a beacon.

"Oh, yes," he said, "yes, indeed. Shouldn't have fooled

with Jilly Sharpe, gel. Play with the bull, you get the horn.'' He cackled at his own ugly humor and Brandy felt sick to her stomach.

Glancing past him, frantically searching for a means of escape, she jumped at the feel of his hand on her breast cupping it crudely through her blouse, and tried to jerk herself free.

Jilly pressed her back against the wall. ''Find it?'' he called over his shoulder to the lanky, black-haired, mustached man who rifled through Marcus's desk. The man jerked open the bottom drawer, lifted out a heavy pouch of coins, and grinned.

''It is here, my friend, just as you said.''

''Didn't I tell you? Not bad for a few minutes' work.'' He started laughing again and when he did, Brandy jerked free and bolted for the door. Sharpe was on her in an instant, knocking her down and forcing her arms up painfully behind her.

''You always did have grit, gel.''

Brandy struggled against the length of rope he jerked from his pocket and bound around her wrists. He tied her ankles, loosened the scarf tied around his thick neck, and used it to gag her. Hauling her roughly to her feet, he bent and tossed her over one of his wide shoulders.

Fear and the rag in her mouth made her throat go dry. Her lungs constricted and for a moment it was nearly impossible to breathe. Thoughts of what Jilly Sharpe meant to do made her heart batter madly against her ribs.

Oh, dear God. She had wanted an adventure. She had never meant for it to end like this! Jouncing against his heavy muscled shoulder, the blood rushing into her head, Brandy closed her eyes and sent up a fervent prayer, one for her herself, one for the men in the crew that Sharpe had somehow dealt with.

When they reached the deck, three more tough-looking sailors joined them—and nowhere a sign of the *Seahawk* crew.

''I see ya got the wench,'' one of them said. ''Did ya get the money, too?''

''Aye, that we did,'' Sharpe said. One of his big hands squeezed her bottom, and she swore a muffled curse she had learned in the tavern, but of course he couldn't hear. ''We'll have a good time tonight, boys—that I promise.''

Brandy's stomach rolled with fear. A wave of nausea made her forehead break out in a sweat and her bones jarred uncomfortably with every step he took.

It didn't take long to reach the starboard side of the ship. From her upside down position, she caught a glimpse of the water below, saw the dinghy the men had rowed out in.

''Luis—you and Janos go down first. I'll hand the gel down to you.''

A big sailor nodded. She noticed he had only one good eye. Reaching for the line that led down to the boat, he had just started over the side when a harsh voice cracked through the air and he froze, one leg suspended above the rail.

''Stand where you are!'' Marcus stood at the front of his men, his long legs splayed, the wind ruffling his curly black hair. The sound of pistols cocking split the cool night air. ''No man makes a move if he wants to live.''

Brandy's eyes slid closed. She thought she had never been so glad to see anyone in her life. Jilly Sharpe adjusted her roughly against his shoulder, but he didn't put her down.

''You want the gel—you'd better put those pistols down. Ain't that right, boys?''

The other four men stood transfixed, hands hovering over the weapons stuffed into the waistbands of their breeches, but none of them reached for one.

''Put the girl down, Sharpe,'' Marcus commanded. ''You're a dead man if you don't.''

''Got it all figured, eh, Cap'n? You just march in here givin' orders like I'm still one of your lackeys and I'm gonna do what you say. You really think I'm gonna just hand her over after what you done?''

Peering around Sharpe's shoulder, she could see Marcus's

face, see the murderous set of his features. "I said put her down. I'm not going to say it again."

Brandy held her breath. She could feel the tension in Jilly Sharpe's big body. Very slightly, an inch at a time, he moved backward toward the rail. Marcus extended the gun in his hand. Six other *Seahawk* crewmen pointed pistols at the rest of Sharpe's men.

Instead of being afraid, Jilly Sharpe grinned. "Here's the way it is, Cap'n. You shoot me, the girl goes over the side. Bound up like she is, she'll sink like a soddin' stone. She'll be shark bait for sure, and you the one to blame."

An icy chill ran through her. Dear sweet God! For the first time she realized Jilly Sharpe stood close enough to the rail that she was suspended above the water.

"You want the gel alive, you let us get into that boat down there and leave. We take her as far as the shore—just for protection—and once we're there we turn her loose. You can come and get her and no one gets hurt."

Brandy's mouth felt so dry she couldn't swallow. Across the way, straining to see from her upside down position, she watched Marcus's face go pale. Surely he wouldn't let them take her. Sharpe would never let her go—he meant to see her punished. He was lying. Dear God, surely Marcus knew he wouldn't keep his word! She was desperate to warn him. But it was insane even to move.

"You want a deal, Sharpe? Put the girl down and I'll let you and your men go free. If I find out the rest of my crew has been left unharmed, you can row back to the island and none of us will follow."

Sharpe stared at Marcus. Defiantly he fondled her bottom and she tried to twist away, swearing again behind gag.

"You want me to put her down? All right, Cap'n—down she goes." His shoulder jerked up and she heard Marcus cry out in rage. Then she was falling. Gunshots cracked across the deck. Terror shot into her heart. She tried to suck in a breath the instant before she hit the water but the gag in her mouth made it impossible to get enough air.

The cold water jolted her, stung her bare arms, face, and

throat, then closed over her head. Sweet Mary, trussed as she was, she would drown for sure! Panic made her frantic. She tore at her bonds, struggled to loose her hands and feet, but the ropes held tight. Her full skirts wrapped around her, dragging her down like an anchor, sending a fresh jolt of fear shooting through her.

She tried to struggle upward, to somehow reach the surface. Her long hair floated like a heavy copper curtain around her, then rose upward as she continued to descend. Her lungs burned. She strained to hold her breath a little longer, to stave off death for as long as she could. Her chest was on fire. Sweet God, she had to breathe!

She tried to see through the murky black water, praying that someone would save her. Where was Marcus? Was he trying to reach her?

Would he remember her once she was gone?

She tried to imagine his face but the image grew fuzzy and began to fade. Her lungs felt like hot coals burning inside her and the urge to breathe became impossible to ignore. Her chest heaved. Water rushed into her mouth.

She was dying. Just like Jilly Sharpe had said.

Marcus dove deeper, pushing himself past the limits of his endurance, knowing he was putting his life at risk, that he could very well die in these same dark waters with Brianne. His lungs were on fire, burning with the need for air, and still he swam down, farther into the black void below.

Kicking his feet, digging with all his strength, he fought his way down, into the cold dark sea. In the eye of his mind he could see her, there, just out of his reach in the inky blackness. She was there—he knew it—if he could only find her.

His hands groped madly, searching the water, knowing in his heart it was too late, knowing she was gone and that he could not save her. The air in his lungs felt like fire. He had to breathe. He had to return to the surface. And yet he made one last, reckless effort, kicking with his feet, his hand slicing wildly through the water, searching, seeking, desperately hoping. . . .

He felt it then, the silky strands he knew were her hair, grabbed a fistful, and dragged her toward him. Kicking his legs with all his strength, he surged upward, determined now, willing himself to reach the surface, praying to God that both of them would live.

It seemed so far. Too far. He knew he'd never make it. Then the shadowy light of a lantern hanging from the side of the ship dug its way into the murky gloom. It renewed his strength and then someone was there in the water beside him, shoving Brianne toward the surface, pushing them both toward the light.

Several more men appeared in the water. Hands dragged them upward. His head broke the surface and sweet cool air rushed into his burning lungs. Brig Butler floated beside him, helping to hold him up. Brianne's limp figure was already being hauled out of the water.

"Can you make it, Captain?" Brig asked.

Marcus saw Brianne's body being lifted over the rail and managed to nod. With the help of some of his men, he climbed the rope ladder to the top and hoisted himself over the rail.

The sight that greeted him was enough to make his blood run as cold as the icy sea. Three men shot and bleeding—one of them a *Seahawk* crewman. Jilly Sharpe dead and another man dying, frothy blood spewing from his lungs.

And Brianne Winters, unbound at last but unconscious, her small limp body draped face-down over a barrel rolled onto its side. Two men worked over her, pressing down on her shoulders, rolling the barrel back and forth, fighting desperately to revive her.

It was obvious that she wasn't breathing.

Marcus's heart beat dully as he stumbled to her side. His insides felt leaden, his chest hurt with every indrawn breath, and yet he was determined.

He had hauled her from the very throat of death—he refused to let her die now.

He came up behind her and the other men stepped away,

their eyes cast down, a trail of tears clinging to one man's cheek.

Marcus ignored them, ignored what those tears meant. She wasn't going to die. He wouldn't let her. Instead he knelt and began to work over her, pressing his hands into her back, rolling the keg back and forth, trying to force air into her lungs. It was all they knew to do. Sometimes it worked. More often it didn't.

"Brianne, can you hear me?" The words came out scratchy and hoarse. "Don't you dare die, do you hear? I am the captain of this vessel and that is an order. Damn you—breathe!"

He pressed down with all his strength, willing her to drag in a lungful of air, but her body remained limp and unresponsive.

"Breathe, damn you!" He pressed down hard, his gut knotted with sick fear, rolling her back and forth over the barrel. "You're going to live, dammit! Do as I say!" He pressed again with all his strength and for the first time since he had known her, Brianne actually obeyed. She coughed up a great geyser of water and started sucking air into her lungs. Marcus closed his eyes, felt an odd sharp sting behind them, and allowed sweet relief to trickle through him. She was breathing at last. Brianne was going to live.

As soon as she stopped coughing and started to breathe evenly again, he turned her over on the barrel, bent, and scooped her up into his arms. With her head against his shoulder, he started for his cabin.

He had just reached the ladder when Hamish stepped into his path. "How's the lass?"

"Half drowned, but otherwise she'll be all right. What happened to the men?"

Hamish shook his head. "Bastards come up over the side. Took the watch out, one by one. We never even heard 'em comin'."

"You all right?"

He rubbed the back of his head. "Damnable lump the size

of an egg. Hurts like the bloody devil. With that scum, I'm lucky I'm still alive."

"What about the others?"

"Some scrapes and bruises, some bad lumps, but none of them fatal. They fought well, they did, but none were a match for Jilly Sharpe and that passel of cutthroats what come with him."

"You did the best you could. One of our men took a lead ball in the shoulder. Cyrus is looking after him."

"What'll we do with Sharpe's men?"

Marcus worked a muscle in his jaw. "Put the bastards ashore—all of them. As soon as you're finished, hoist the sails and let's make way. I've had more than enough of Spanish Keys."

Hamish nodded, his gray brows pulled together. "Aye, Cap'n. I was hopin' ye'd say that."

Marcus started again for the ladder. Feeling Brandy stir, he tightened his hold, carrying her down the stairs and along the dimly lit passage. Her head nestled into his shoulder and he thought how small she felt—and how close he had come to losing her.

An image of Jilly Sharpe rose up, his head canted sideways in a spreading pool of blood. He didn't regret for a moment that he had been the man to pull the trigger.

Marcus opened the door to his cabin and stepped inside. A chair was overturned, papers and books strewn all over the floor. Signs of Brianne's struggle were apparent everywhere he looked and Marcus felt a jolt of satisfaction.

He felt her stir, her body beginning to shake in his arms. Her eyes were heavy-lidded, but they were open and she was looking up at him. Carefully, he set her on her feet beside the bed, steadied her against him, and began to strip away her soggy clothes.

"Marcus?"

He didn't bother to stop. Her skin felt icy cold and her movements were stiff and jerky. "I'm right here, love. We're going to get you warm and out of those wet clothes." He took off her shoes and stockings, unfastened the tabs on the waistband of her skirt and the single white petticoat beneath, and shoved them down over her hips.

"You saved my life," she said softly, drawing his attention to her face. "I was dying. I couldn't see you, but somehow I knew you were there in the water. I didn't think you would reach me but you did."

He wrapped her in his arms, pressed her tightly against his chest. "I wasn't about to let you die. I'm the captain of the ship. I was my duty to protect you." He smiled into her still-damp hair. "Besides, you haven't yet seen New Providence."

Brianne looked up at him, gave him a soft, grateful smile, and Marcus had to force himself to pull away. He determinedly went back to work, drawing the ties on her cotton blouse, beginning to shove it off her shoulders. Brandy caught his fingers, wordlessly asking the question.

"It's all right. I've seen a woman naked before. I only want to help you."

She swayed a little and started to tremble even harder. Glancing away, her cheeks softly flushed, she nodded, and he eased the wet blouse from her shoulders. Her chemise was all that remained. Marcus peeled it away with businesslike movements, trying not to stare at her breasts, not to notice how full, pink-tipped, and lovely they were. Fighting the lure of the damp curls gleaming like fire at the juncture of her legs.

He forced his gaze away and lifted her into his arms, drew back the blanket, and settled her beneath the covers. Turning, he moved away from the bed and began to strip off his own wet clothes, all but his boots, which he had jerked off in the water when they began to weigh him down.

"Marcus?"

He kept his back to her. Naked, he reached for a dressing gown and pulled it on, then turned to face her. "What is it, love?"

"I was wondering if . . ." She hauled in a shaky breath, looked at him again. "Every time I close my eyes, I see him in my mind. I hear him laughing as the water sucks me down. I don't want to think of him. I don't want to remember him ever again. Will you hold me, Marcus? Please?''

He knew he shouldn't. He couldn't trust himself where she was concerned. But she looked so lost, so vulnerable. She still sounded so frightened.

And she had nearly died.

Marcus settled himself on the edge of the bed and reached for her, easing her into his arms. She felt so small snuggled against him, so small, and yet he could feel her womanly curves. The blanket slipped down to her waist. The feel of her naked breasts pressing into his chest made his body begin to grow hard, to rise up beneath the soft, slick silk of his navy blue dressing gown.

Damn, but he wanted her. Knowing how close he had come to losing her only made him want her more. He had to get away from her before it was too late.

And yet he could not force himself to leave.

Chapter 9

Brandy clung to Marcus's neck. He smelled of seawater and his black curly hair felt smooth and damp beneath her fingers.

If she closed her eyes, she could remember him standing there naked, his back turned toward her, hard muscle moving beneath his sun-dark skin. Lean ridges flexed across his shoulders, rippled the length of his long, sinewy legs. She could see his tight round buttocks as he had stripped off his wet black breeches.

Sweet Lord, he was beautiful, so dark and powerfully built, so incredibly male. Even the scars she had seen, one across his thigh, the other slashing into his hip, could not mar the perfection of his body.

She had wanted to reach out and touch him, ached to have him hold her as he was doing now. Her fingers slid over the blue silk of his dressing gown, smoothing the lapels, feeling his muscles tighten. She could see, framed by the V in front, the dense black hair on his chest. Even through the silk, it lightly abraded her nipples.

A soft ache arose. Heat fanned out through her limbs, sank lower, into the pit of her stomach. What would he do if she reached inside the robe and touched him, traced the hard bands of muscle across his chest? What would he do if she turned her head and pressed her mouth against the swift pulse beating at the base of his throat?

His hands ran gently over her back, a calming touch meant to soothe her. She realized the blanket had slipped, leaving her skin bare beneath his hands. Wherever he touched, goosebumps appeared on her flesh. Her heart was racing, pounding a mad tattoo, and suddenly it was as difficult to breathe as it had been beneath the water. Her head was spinning. She felt as if she were drowning again.

"Brianne?" He tipped her chin with his hand and she looked into those penetrating, deep blue eyes. "If I don't leave, soon I won't be able to."

She moistened her lips, felt them trembling. "Please don't go. I want you to stay here with me."

His dark gaze pierced her. "Do you know what you are saying? Do you know what will happen if I stay?"

She swallowed, forced down her nervousness. She knew exactly what would happen if he remained, and it was exactly what she wanted. "I know."

A low sound came from his throat. His mouth came down hard over hers, not soft and sweet but hot and ravishing, making his intentions clear. It was a deep, almost savage kiss, one of fierce possession. He was breathing hard, his gaze burning hot, when he broke away.

"Are you certain this is what you want? You know the life I lead. You know nothing can ever come of this. We'll have no future—nothing but these few days together."

"I know. I don't care. Make love to me, Marcus. Teach me how to be a woman."

His arms tightened around her. He kissed her again, more gently this time, tasting her deeply, thoroughly, slanting his mouth over hers, molding their lips perfectly together. With expert skill, he sampled and coaxed, his kisses soft and seeking and wildly seductive. He took her deeply with his tongue, and she felt as if she had stepped off the end of a pier. She was dizzy all over again, her heart drumming madly in her ears.

"Marcus . . ." She kissed him with the same hot urgency, her tongue touching his, hesitant at first, then with more and more confidence.

Marcus groaned and the blanket fell away beneath his hands. He stripped off his dressing gown and the dark blue silk slipped off the bed, pooling in a forgotten heap on the floor. He kissed her, cupped her breasts, plucked the ends into tiny buds with his fingers. The pad of his thumb felt rough against the tip, which throbbed and swelled into his hand. Lowering his head, he took the heavy weight into his mouth.

A sound escaped from Brandy's throat, a soft, urgent whimper. Scorching heat burned through her. A smoldering fire sprang to life in her blood. Hard hands stroked her body, skimming along her skin, smoothing over her breasts and belly, teasing and caressing, sliding along the indentations of her spine, moving over her hips. Easing her backward, he pressed her down in the feather mattress and she could feel his hardness, the hot, thick, rigid length of him, the pulsing fullness that was larger than she had imagined.

Marcus kissed her again, fierce burning kisses that made her nipples ache and the place between her legs throb and burn. His dark head moved down. He laved her nipple with his tongue, circled the tip, then sucked in the rounded fullness. Brandy arched upward at the heat sweeping through her, at the pleasure that flared out into her limbs. Her fingers dug into his shoulders. Solid muscle bunched as she pressed her lips against his hot, dark skin.

With his hands and his mouth, he caressed her, his fingers moving down her body, pausing for a moment at her navel, then sliding lower. They sifted through the thatch of copper curls at the base of her thighs, gently eased her legs apart, slipped between the damp folds of her sex, and a long dark finger slid inside her.

Brandy moaned, her body straining upward toward his hand.

For a moment the hand went still. "Don't be frightened. I'm not going to hurt you."

"I'm not . . . frightened."

With tender care, he stroked her, gently at first, then more deeply. Pleasure, sweet and fierce, shot through her, making her shudder with need. He tested the slickness, stretching her, preparing her to accept him.

"You're ready for me," he whispered, kissing the side of

her neck. "You're trembling all over. You want me to come inside you."

She wanted something, anything to ease the sweet ache she didn't quite understand. "Yes . . . oh, God, yes, Marcus, please."

He came up over her in a single motion, his eyes dark blue and piercing. The planes of his face looked harsh in the moonlight slicing in through the row of windows above his bed. His nostrils flared and a look of burning desire rose into his features.

"You're mine," he said. "You always have been." And then he took her, driving himself in hard and deep. Brandy cried out as a sharp pain sliced through her, and Marcus went still.

She could feel him shaking, feel the tension in his long lean body as he fought to remain in control. His hand came up to her cheek. "I'm sorry. I tried to go slow, but I . . . Are you all right?"

She gave him an uncertain smile, her body stretched and oddly filled, aching a little, but still somehow wanting. "I think so."

He started to move, gently at first, and she realized she *was* all right. The pain was receding, the heat returning, shimmering over her skin, making her nipples peak and her stomach muscles tighten. He was moving faster now, driving harder, stroking deeper.

"I want you," he said, his jaw clamped tight. "God, I have to have you."

Unconsciously, her legs opened wider, taking him deeper still. She felt filled with him and on fire. Clutching his shoulders, she ground her hips against his, arching upward with each of his thrusts. Marcus pounded into her again and again, and with each of his driving strokes, something tightened inside her.

She was clinging to a precipice, hanging on and afraid to let go, yet desperately wanting to.

"Let it come," he softly coaxed. "Give yourself up to it. Do it for me."

Something fierce tore free inside her. It shimmered for a moment just out of reach, then washed over her in deep penetrating waves. She was drowning all over again, immersed in heat and incredible pleasure. She cried out as the sweet tide rippled through her, fierce and raw, amazing in its strength, unlike anything she had ever known.

"Marcus!" she cried, but he didn't seem to hear her. His body had gone rigid, his jaw tightly clamped, his head thrown back, the black hair bunching in soft waves at the nape of his neck. He drove into her a few more times, then went still, holding himself above her as he reached his own release.

Several seconds passed before he slumped against her, resting his dark head next to her cheek.

Lying beneath him, she felt limp and sweetly sated, her body slightly battered and still tingling with pleasure. She was truly a woman now, she thought, no longer a girl. She had given herself to Marcus Delaine, wholly and completely. And she was glad.

In truth, she was in love with him. She couldn't remember a time when she hadn't been. She knew she always would be. She tried not to think what her life would be like once he returned her home. The thought made her sad and in this moment she didn't want sadness.

He eased himself off her, curled her into the circle of his arms, pulled the sheet up over them against the chill. "I'm sorry if I hurt you. The first time there is no other way."

She snuggled against his shoulder. "I'm fine. Thank you, Marcus."

A smooth black brow arched up. "What for?"

"Making me a woman at last. I thought I was before but I was wrong. I wasn't a woman until now. Not until this very moment."

His hand came up to her face, smoothed back her hair. It curled damply around his fingers. "You're a woman, Brianne. Never doubt it. I assure you, from this night forward, I never will."

A different sort of pleasure, sweet and warm, washed through her. She pressed her cheek against his shoulder, felt the heat of him, the incredible strength. Her eyes fixed on the mat of curly black hair on his chest. She trailed a finger over the hard ridges and valleys, circled a flat copper nipple, and felt a faint tremor run through his long lean frame.

''Now that I am a woman,'' she said with her newly acquired sense of confidence, ''I believe I should like to learn more of men. I wish to see you, Marcus—all of you.''

A sleek black brow arched up. He chuckled, a rumble in his chest. Drawing back the sheet, he allowed her to examine him, taking in the flat plane below his rib cage, the line of thick black hair that arrowed past his waist and pooled around the heavy weight of his sex. It rested softly in a nest of damp black curls, but the instant she reached in that direction, the fleshy ridge began to thicken.

Brandy jerked her hand away and Marcus chuckled again.

''The problem with being a woman,'' he said in his resonant voice, ''is the effect it has on a man. Particularly this man.'' Dragging her beneath him, he rolled on top of her, pressing her into the soft feather mattress. Brandy gasped as his hardness slid inside her. ''You've a good deal to learn yet, sweeting.'' He dropped soft kisses on the side of her mouth. ''The night is still young. If you are feeling up to it, perhaps we should continue your education.''

The hot sensations began almost at once, whispery little pulses that tugged at her insides. ''Yes . . .'' she breathed, already beginning to move. ''Yes, we should, indeed.'' Sliding her arms around his neck, she kissed him. As Marcus had said, the night was yet young. There were hours until the morrow.

Tomorrow, she thought with a sudden pang. Tomorrow there would be consequences for what she had done. Brandy shuddered at the notion. Giving herself up to Marcus's kiss, she found herself wishing tomorrow would never come.

CHAPTER 10

Palmer Reese worked over the ledgers sitting open on his wide mahogany desk. Besides the heavy leather-bound volume, an expensive crystal inkwell and matching sand shaker sat next to a silver-trimmed tortoiseshell pen with a snowy ostrich-plume quill.

A forest-green leather ink blotter protected the polished surface of his desk, and a small oval frame held an ivory scrimshaw of his most prized possession, his flagship of the line, the *Fairwind.*

Aside from those things, the desktop was empty and rubbed to a glossy sheen, each item sitting precisely in its place, as did each of the items in his immaculately clean, pristinely cared for office/warehouse on the embankment across from the London docks.

Palmer looked out the window, down at the tall row of masts bobbing along the quay. For a moment, all he saw was his reflection, a man with wavy dark brown hair and a handsome face, a well-built man, though in the past few years, with the money he had made, the expensive food and drink, he had turned a little fleshy.

His eyes finally pierced the glass and he saw the ships more clearly. *Fairwind* was still at sea, but the *Windsong* was in port, her holds being loaded with cargo for another voyage. Unfortunately when she sailed, her hull would not be nearly as full as it should be. They had lost their contract with Savannah Trading for the shipping of cotton and rice, a contract he'd had for years.

A nerve jumped in his cheek. He needed that cargo—deserved it. Instead it had gone to Hawksmoor Shipping, more of his profit siphoned away, and all because of Marcus Delaine.

Palmer scoffed. The Earl of Hawksmoor and his bloody aristocratic pedigree. It made Palmer's blood boil to think of it. Just because the man had inherited a title and wealth didn't mean he was better than anyone else, that he deserved the shipping contract Palmer had worked so hard to keep.

The fact he'd run into a few little problems while he was dealing with the company shouldn't have mattered. A few late arrivals, a few lost kegs and crates. Every shipper had his problems now and again. He smiled grimly. Even Marcus Delaine.

A knock sounded at the door. "You may enter," he called out, glancing up to see Stuart Washburn, vice president of Reese Enterprises, step into the office.

"I've news I thought you'd be pleased to hear." Stuart was a thin man, tall and gaunt, with sharp pointed features and slightly sallow skin.

Palmer's brow went up. "And what news might that be?"

"*Peregrine* has just limped into port." He smiled, his thin lips barely curving. "It seems she's had trouble with her anchor—some sort of faulty release, I gather. Seems to have caused her a good deal of trouble."

Palmer's own lips curved. "What a pity."

"Isn't it, though? Apparently she has returned with most of her cargo."

"That ought to make the shippers extremely unhappy."

"I'm sure we'll hear them screaming all the way to the docks."

"Perhaps we should offer to help them out, contract for part of the goods so at least some portion will remain on schedule."

Stuart placed a pile of papers, bills of lading he had brought, on top of Palmer's desk. "As a matter of fact, that is exactly what I was thinking. They need help and we are just the ones to give it to them. I'll see to the matter myself."

Palmer didn't say more and neither did Stuart, but both of them wore smiles of satisfaction.

Hamish Bass watched his friend leaning against the rail. The captain's jaw was set, his eyes intent. A course wind ruffled his hair. The captain didn't notice. His thoughts were miles away and Hamish believed he knew exactly where they dwelled.

"Good mornin' to ye, Cap'n."

He looked up, for the first time aware of the first mate's presence. "Good morning, my friend."

"Ye've the look of a man far away with his thoughts. 'Tis the lass, I be thinkin'."

"Aye, that it is."

"Ye've taken her to ye bed." Marcus frowned, but Hamish ignored him. "I've known ye too long and too well, lad. I know 'twas never yer intention. I think it were a fact afore it ever happened."

Marcus didn't answer, just raked a hand through his black, wind-tossed hair.

"So . . . now that ye've had her, is yer cravin' for her gone? Can ye set her away and leave her be?"

A muscle leaped in the captain's lean cheek. "I thought perhaps I could. In truth, I want her more than ever." He sighed, the sound lost in the wind sweeping over the deck. "I've always been a man of moderation, Hamish, even when it came to women. I took one to my bed when I felt the need. It never went much further than that. This time it's different. I can't remember ever feeling such uncontrollable lust."

Hamish nodded sagely. " 'Tis the fire in her, I'll wager. Ye can see it in her eyes, hear it in her voice. She feels a grand passion for life—like a hot blaze, it is, burnin' deep inside her. That kind of fire in a woman seeps into a man's blood."

Marcus's fingers dug into the rail. "I don't like it—I'll tell you that. I don't like it a bloody damn bit."

"Ye'll be takin' her back home soon enough. Keep yer wits about ye until then, ye'll be all right."

The captain gave him the edge of a smile. "How is it you know so much about women, Hamish?"

"Fifty years of stayin' out of their clutches. Man learns to be cagey, learns where the real dangers lay. Stay away from the fire, lad. Else ye might wind up gettin' burned."

Setting the stem of his pipe between his teeth, Hamish turned and walked away, thinking of his friend, thinking of the girl the captain had taken to his bed. Lass like that one—she was a danger to any man.

Hamish wondered, if he had met a woman like that when he was the captain's age, would he have continued to run as he had for all of these years?

Brandy didn't see Marcus all the next day. That night she was sure he would come, that he would invite her into his bed and they would make wild, passionate love, but when he returned, it was so late she was already sleeping.

The following day was much the same, just a few simple words before he left to go on deck, then listening for his footfalls in the darkness when he returned late to his cabin and finally fell asleep, alone in his big bed.

Something was wrong, she knew, but she wasn't sure what it was. Even when they reached New Providence and he took her ashore as he had promised, he remained carefully aloof. Brandy was worried, uncertain what she might have done to displease him. She wanted to ask him but she was afraid.

Fortunately, as the day slipped past, a bright, golden sun overhead, lovely white sand beaches, warm spring breezes, incredibly clear blue skies and equally clear blue water, it was impossible not to enjoy herself. Eventually even Marcus began to relax, watching her excitement with a gentle, indulgent smile, renting a small black phaeton to drive her around the island.

The town itself was small and impossibly quaint. Most of the buildings were Georgian in design, made of wood or fashioned of stone. Many were hip-roofed with lovely open verandas, the windows covered by louvered wooden shutters.

Outside the small town itself, some of the houses were

roofed with thatch, but Marcus explained that because of the danger of fire, people were no longer allowed to use such materials in the city. Earlier they had parked the phaeton near the center of town and walked through the square near the wharf. On Bay Street, the main street of the capital, handsome public buildings were being constructed and vendors lined the walk across from where boats were docked.

"It's charming, Marcus, yet there is an exciting hum of activity."

His gaze followed the workmen hammering on the building across the way. "I have always been partial to Nassau. I've been shipping goods here for the past six years and I've yet to grow tired of the place."

They passed along a line of vendors in front of a covered market. Inside, tradesmen sold vegetables and fruits, conch and fish. Brandy wrinkled her nose at the pungent smells even as her eyes darted with undisguised excitement from one sight to another.

They walked between the rows of stalls: straw weavers, shell merchants, woodcarvers. At one of the booths, she paused, her interest caught by a display of brightly embroidered shawls. Smiling, Marcus draped a length of forest-green silk around her shoulders, the delicate fringe hanging well past her waist.

"Is this one to your liking?"

"It's lovely."

He smiled. "Then it is yours."

"Are . . . are you certain?" Her fingers trembled as they smoothed the richly embroidered fabric. "It must be very expensive."

"It's only a small gift, Brianne. I would be pleased if you would accept it."

She did so with genuine pleasure. "It's beautiful, Marcus. I have never owned anything nearly so lovely."

His smile slid away, replaced by a frown. Reaching down, he gently tilted her chin up. "You should have dozens of beautiful things. Perhaps one day you will."

Brandy glanced away. "Mostly I just want to see new

places, to learn about life, as we are doing today."

They walked on down the street, passing a spot called Vendue House, an arcaded, open building where an auction was being held. Slaves, she saw, feeling an unwarranted chill. Black-skinned men and women shuffled forward, their dark heads drooping, their shoulders bowed as if they carried the weight of the world.

"I didn't think Englishmen kept slaves," she said.

"Only in some of the colonies."

"I probably shouldn't say this, since I am from the South, but I have never agreed with the notion that one man should own another." That one man should bend another to his will, she thought. It came far too close to the life she was living at the White Horse Tavern.

"It's not a sentiment I adhere to, either, yet for now it seems to be a fact of life."

Brandy didn't say more. It was too perfect a day to dwell on the unpleasantries of human nature. She would have plenty of time for that once she returned home.

"Are you hungry?"

"Now that you mention it, I'm starving." They picnicked on the beach, drank wine and coconut milk. It was a wonderful day, a day of laughter and excitement, a day worth every hardship she'd been forced to endure on the trip. By the time they returned to the *Seahawk* just before sunset, she was filled with pleasant memories and a warm feeling of contentment. Pausing for a moment at the rail, she turned to look back at the island.

"It's so lovely," she said, studying the distant white cottages surrounded by trees and hedges. "Does it look anything at all like England?"

"There are sections of Nassau that have the same sort of homes you might find back home. We have thatched roofs in the country, just as they do here."

She smiled wistfully. "I would love to see it. I have thought of going there many times. Perhaps one day I will."

Marcus turned to look at her. Something moved across his

features and his jaw seemed to tighten. "I won't be there if you do. Most likely I'll be at sea."

Her bright smile faded. She hardly needed a reminder. "I'm certain you will. On the subject of your life, you have made yourself perfectly clear." She smoothed back a long auburn curl that had come loose from the ringlets she had fashioned atop her head. "I, however, want no more restraints. If I wish to go to England, I shall. If I wish to go anywhere at all, I shall find a way to get there."

Marcus scowled. "You and your foolish dreams. A woman is meant to marry, to give her husband sons. When the time comes, that is what you will do."

Brandy arched a brow. "That is what you think? Do you think I would have made love to you if I meant to marry and settle down?"

His eyes seemed to darken. "You are telling me you do not intend to wed—that you would be content as some man's mistress?"

She tossed her head. "I don't know. Perhaps that is all I wish to be. If I were in London—"

He gripped her arm. "If you were in London, you'd be nothing but a pretty little bauble on some man's arm. You would be at the mercy of your protector, completely his to command. You would have little of your precious freedom. In truth, your life would be just slightly better than it is at the White Horse Tavern."

Brandy jerked free of his hold. "Once I've returned to Charleston, what I do will be none of your concern. If I wish to live as some man's mistress . . ."

Her words died away at the hard look on his face. Brandy gasped as Marcus scooped her up in his arms.

"What do you think you're doing?"

He didn't answer, just crossed the deck on those long legs of his, descended the ladder to the passage leading down to his cabin, opened the door, and strode in, kicking it closed behind him.

"You wish to be some man's mistress?" He let go of her legs and she slid the length of his body. "Perhaps you have forgotten, sweeting—you already are.'' With that he captured her mouth in a punishing kiss. She could feel his anger, his temper, the fury he barely contained.

She could feel his hardness pressing against her and, as angry as she was, her body infused with heat. His hard mouth plundered, fierce and wildly determined, and her insides began to quiver. He ravished her with his tongue, cupping the back of her head to hold her still for his greedy assault.

His hands came up to her breasts and he massaged them roughly through the gown, his fingers determindedly pebbling the ends. She whimpered as he cupped her bottom, dragging her more solidly against him, yet somehow maneuvering her backward till she pressed against the wall.

Then he was lifting her skirts, his hands sliding up her thighs, smoothing over her skin, teasing her with expert skill. He must have felt her trembling, for he parted the folds of her sex and began to stroke her. She was wet, she realized, her body throbbing with heat. The angry clash between them hadn't lessened her desire for him. Sweet God, the power of his fury only seemed to heighten her growing need.

Marcus kissed her and Brandy moaned at the hot, hard feel of his mouth over hers. All day she had been watching him, laughing with him. Wanting him. Each night she had ached for him. She had missed his touch, missed his kiss. Now she was on fire for him.

Her fingers curled into the lapels of his coat. Beneath her skirt, his hand moved between her legs, caressing her flesh, preparing her to accept him, while the other popped the buttons at the front of his breeches. Then his rigid length was probing, finding entrance, and plunging deep inside.

Brandy gasped at the pulsing fullness, at the sharp pleasure spiraling through her limbs. She could feel the tension in his body, the fierce, driving need, but the moment he was buried inside her completely, he stopped.

With a sigh, his head tipped forward to rest against hers. ''God, I'm sorry. I don't know how this happened. I just couldn't seem to help myself. Whenever I'm near you, I can't seem to—''

Brandy dragged his mouth down to hers for a hot, needy kiss. "Don't stop," she pleaded. "God in heaven, Marcus, please don't stop."

Marcus blinked, then he groaned. He kissed her hard, his hands tightened on her bottom, lifting her up, and he began to thrust wildly inside her. He raised her legs and wrapped them around his waist, bunching her green muslin gown, pounding into her again and again. All the while, Brandy kissed him, twining her arms around his neck, the pins long gone from her hair, the heavy curls sliding down around her shoulders.

"God's blood, you drive me insane," he whispered, taking her mouth in another greedy kiss, sending little tongues of heat licking into her stomach.

In minutes, she reached a crashing release and Marcus followed. For long moments there was only the sound of their breathing and the thunderous roar of Brandy's heart.

With great care, Marcus eased her legs from around his waist and set her gently on her feet, then stepped away to adjust his clothes. Across the room, her eyes found his but he glanced away, and it occurred to her that he was embarrassed. Surely not, she thought. Surely she was mistaken.

Marcus cleared his throat, his shoulders oddly rigid. "I realize you are new to all of this. I hope . . . I hope I didn't hurt you." He glanced toward the row of windows. "I assure you, I am not usually so . . . I am not generally so . . ."

Brandy closed the distance between them, pressed her fingers against his lips. "I liked what we did, Marcus. Do not apologize for giving us both so much pleasure."

Penetrating midnight eyes locked on her face. Something hot flickered in their depths, then it was gone. A corner of his mouth edged up. "Once again, you surprise me. Perhaps this passage home will be even more interesting than I had imagined."

Color crept into her cheeks. "Perhaps it shall, Captain Delaine."

Chapter 11

In the end, Marcus's words proved true. In the days that followed, the weather held and the seas were fair. The captain's duties lessened, leaving him a good deal of time to spend in his cabin.

Brandy joined him in his wide featherbed and they made wildly passionate love. It was a glorious time, more wondrous than she could have imagined. But the journey was a brief one. Two weeks, she discovered, was a very short time when a woman was in love and the man she loved would be sailing off without her.

They never spoke of that, or talked at all of the future. There was no future for them, she knew, and so she pretended the future did not exist.

But of course it did, and once it arrived she stood grimly at the rail of the *Seahawk* staring off toward the horizon, seeing the familiar lines of the Charleston Harbor, the tall church spires that formed a distinctive outline of the city.

Marcus walked up beside her, settling an arm casually around her waist. "Well, we are almost there."

"Yes . . . so I see."

"Are you glad to be returned?"

She glanced up at him. "You must know that I am not."

He said nothing for a while, just followed her gaze to the elegant homes and single houses of Charleston, their piazzas and magnificent gardens still no more than tiny dots on the distant shoreline.

"I won't be staying in the city long, I'm afraid. *Seahawk*

is already under contract for a return shipment of goods to England.''

Her hands began to tremble. She reached over and took hold of the rail. ''How . . . how long will you be gone?''

''Quite some time, I'm afraid. From England, we're bound for the Orient. In truth, Brianne, it could be more than a year before my return.''

A hard lump rose in her throat. She had thought to wait for him, see him from time to time in the months ahead. But a year or more. It seemed like forever. Perhaps he had planned it that way.

''I suppose our parting will truly be good-bye, then.''

''You know what my life is like. We both knew this day would come.''

''Yes . . .'' She had known, but she had pretended it would not happen.

Standing beside her, Marcus unbuttoned his navy blue jacket and pulled a small leather pouch from his waistcoat. Brandy heard the jingle of coins, and her spine went a little bit rigid.

''I want you to take this.'' He pressed the pouch into her hand, along with a folded-up slip of paper. ''You can use it to give yourself a start somewhere else, if that is truly your wish. My address in Cornwall is written on the paper. If you should ever need anything—anything at all—send word to me through my brother Rexland at Hawksmoor House. He'll know how to find me.''

Brandy felt the hot sting of tears. He was leaving. It was really going to happen and there was nothing she could do to stop it. The paper shook between her fingers. She slid it into the pocket of her simple brown skirt, but handed back the pouch of coins.

''I won't take your money, Marcus. What happened between us . . . I didn't do it for money. I won't cheapen it by taking your money now.''

His mouth went a little bit thin. ''I am giving you this as a friend who wishes to help you secure a future. And because there might be . . . consequences . . . resulting from the time we've spent together. Take the money, Brianne. It is the least I can do.''

He held out the pouch, but Brandy shook her head. ''I won't take it, Marcus.''

''Dammit, woman—what will you do if you discover that you are with child? I want you to take this and promise me you will write to my brother should you find that you carry my babe.''

Brandy wet her lips, which had suddenly begun to tremble. What if Marcus was right? What if even now she carried his child? Instead of fear, the thought brought a sudden rush of joy she hadn't expected. If only it were true! And yet, deep in her heart, she was certain it was not. If she carried his babe, she wouldn't feel this terrible emptiness that turned her insides to lead.

His hands settled firmly on her shoulders. ''Promise me, Brianne. I couldn't bear to think you carried my child and there was no one who could help you.''

Brandy glanced away. ''If there is a child, I promise I will write to your brother, but I won't take your coin. My loving was a gift. All I had to give. Please, Marcus—accept it as it was meant.''

For long silent moments he just stood there. Then he sighed and shoved the pouch of coins back into the pocket of his coat.

''You'll be returning to the tavern. You'll have to face your father, and he can be fearsome. I'm going with you.''

Brandy shook her head. ''I appreciate your concern, but your presence would only make things worse. I hope by now my father's ire will have lessened. Even if it hasn't, I'm not the same person I was when I left. I won't let him bully me again.''

A corner of his mouth curved up. ''I am glad to hear it, and no, you are definitely not the same. You're stronger now. I believe you will do with your life whatever it is you wish.''

What she wished at the moment was to spent the next fifty years with Marcus Delaine. That they were not suited to wed did not matter. Nothing mattered but being with him, and that she could not do.

Brandy stared out across the water. She would never look at a ship again without thinking of him. She would never look at the sea without remembering what it had been like to lie in his arms. She loved him, deeply and forever. She would always love him, whether he was with her or a thousand miles away.

As the ship sailed the final distance into the harbor, he left her and returned to his duties. She didn't see him again until *Seahawk* reached the dock, not until the vessel was secure in its berth and the gangway had been lowered.

As Brandy stood ready to depart, Dandelion clutched in her arms, purring, rubbing her furry head against Brandy's cheek, Marcus appeared in front of her.

"Saying good-bye to an old friend?"

"A dear one, if not so old. I'm going to miss her."

"I'm sure she'll miss you as well." Gently lifting the cat from her arms, he settled the animal carefully back on deck. Dandelion yowled a soft farewell, then raced toward the ladder leading below.

Another man approached. Brandy recognized the short, rotund figure of Cyrus Lamb. He reached out and took her hand, squeezed it gently. "Take care of yerself, lass. From the sound of it, 'twill be a goodly length of time till our paths will be crossin' again. 'Tis for certain we're all gonna miss ya."

Brandy felt the quick burn of tears. "Thank you, Cyrus. I'll miss you all as well. Say good-bye to the others for me, will you?"

"Aye, lass, that I will."

Marcus smiled at her gently. "I believe it is time we went ashore." When Brandy nodded, he rested her hand on the sleeve of his coat and led her across the gangway onto the dock, pausing near the end. "You're certain you don't want me to go with you to the tavern?"

Brandy forced herself to smile. "I'll be fine."

"We'll be in port for at least several days, so I won't say good-bye until later."

Days, she thought. Just a few more days and her love would be gone. She brushed a tear discreetly from the corner of her eye, forced the edges of her mouth to turn up.

"All right. We'll save good-bye until then. Will you be staying at the Pines?"

He cocked a brow.

"Is that not where you usually stay when you are in town?"

"Yes, it is. I am merely surprised you would know."

Her eyes met his. "I know a good deal about you, Marcus. I know about the widow you see, as well. I pray if you need comfort while you are in port, you will no longer turn to her."

His mouth quirked, his elegant lips curving up in a smile. "I assure you, my love, you have left me in little need of comfort for quite some time."

Brandy smiled, surprised that she could when her heart hurt so badly. "Perhaps you will stop into the tavern later on this eve."

"I'll be busy for a while, but there is a chance I'll be able to find the time."

Brandy just nodded. They shared no kiss good-bye. Those days were ended. At his last brief nod of encouragement, she turned and walked off toward the tavern. Her chest felt leaden. Her insides were tied into knots, yet Marcus seemed unconcerned. She meant little to him, she knew, not much more than a pleasant diversion. In a few days' time, he would return to the sea and all too soon he would forget her.

It made a hard lump swell in her throat, made a soft ache throb deep beneath her breastbone. *You have to forget him,* she vowed, knowing she never would. Still, she had meant what she had said—she was a different person now, stronger than she was before, and sooner or later she would get over him.

She glanced down at the simple brown skirt and blouse she wore. Soon she would don the stomacher that thrust up her breasts and a skirt that showed her ankles, the uniform of the White Horse Tavern. Soon she would face her old life again.

I'll find a way out, she vowed, *without Marcus's money. I'll make a new life for myself.* But not yet. For now she needed time to mend her broken heart and decide what she should do. She had hoped by the time she returned she would know the answer, but she did not.

Brandy glanced ahead, past a spotted dog gnawing on a bone and two small, ragamuffin boys playing hopscotch in an alley. The tavern lay ahead, dimly lit behind the windows, the doors open, beckoning sailors within. Turning her attention to the coming confrontation with her father, she squared her shoulders, her resolve still strong even if her stomach was a little bit queasy.

The boardwalk creaked beneath her feet as she walked down the block toward the big red sign hanging above the thick-walled building. When she reached the heavy oak door that led inside, she looked back at the *Seahawk* one last time.

She was surprised to see Marcus's tall frame silhouetted at the end of the gangway, his dark gaze still following her movements even as she stepped inside the White Horse Tavern.

Marcus returned to the deck of the *Seahawk* while his crew completed the last tasks necessary to secure the ship and prepare it for reloading on the morrow. Water casks needed to be refilled, the larder restocked, new line brought aboard, and minor repairs begun.

There was much left to do, yet all he could think of was Brianne. She had refused the money he had offered and now was returned to the White Horse Tavern.

What would Big Jake say when he saw her? What would he believe of her unexpected departure? More importantly, what would he do?

The more Marcus thought about it, the more uneasy he became. Dammit, he should have gone with her, whether she wanted him to or not.

When Hamish Bass appeared on the quarterdeck, his steps

more a swagger than a walk, Marcus intercepted him. "Something's come up. I've an errand to run. I'm sure I won't be long. Keep an eye on the ship until my return."

"Aye, Cap'n." Hamish dragged the pipe from between his teeth and smiled in that knowing way of his. "I been worried about the lass meself. Jake Winters is a hard man and not a forgivin' one."

Marcus only nodded. Hamish always seemed to know his thoughts. He was not wrong this time. Turning toward the dock, Marcus made his way along the quay until he reached the tavern. The taproom entertained a handful of sailors, but it was not yet crowded. His eyes scanned the smoky interior, but he saw no sign of Brianne.

Instead, he recognized the dark-haired serving maid who also worked in the tavern. She bent over a table in the corner, serving a round of drinks to a couple of half-drunk seamen, but her eyes kept straying toward the door leading out behind the tavern—and she looked decidedly concerned.

An uneasy shiver ran through him. Marcus started in the woman's direction.

"Excuse me, Miss . . ." He worked to remember her name, but with his thoughts on Brianne, for the moment it escaped him.

"It's just Flo, Captain Delaine, but I am surely glad to see you." She glanced worriedly toward the door. "Big Jake just came in. When he saw Brandy, well, he just went a little bit crazy."

Marcus's whole body went stiff. "Where are they?"

Flo took his arm and led him to the door at the rear of the tavern. With every step, Marcus's stomach tightened into a harder knot.

"He dragged her out to the stables. He was callin' her terrible names, wantin' to know the truth of where she'd been. He was in a fit of temper like nothin' I've seen. You gotta help her, Captain, before Big Jake does something awful to her."

Marcus didn't wait for more. He tore through the door like a man shot out of a cannon, racing across the yard toward the stables at the rear. In a tack room down at the end, he could hear Big Jake shouting, and his heart plunged into his stomach.

"I'm gonna beat the livin' daylights outta ye, girl. I'm gonna whup ye like I never done before!"

"Get away from me!" Brianne warned. "I'm not going to let you beat me. I'm not a child—I'm a woman. And I'm not afraid of you anymore."

Big Jake growled low in his throat. "By God, girl, you'd better be afraid!" Marcus heard the sound of leather slapping flesh and rage urged his legs even faster. When he reached the tack room, he jerked open the battered wooden door, and the smell of musty hay and old leather assaulted him. Brianne faced her father from the corner, an arm held up to shield her face. A long red welt ran from her elbow to her shoulder.

"Stop it, Jake!" Marcus grabbed the razor strop, jerked it from the man's big hands. "Brianne's right. She's a woman, not a child. What she does is her business, not yours. It's time you accepted the fact."

Her eyes swung toward Marcus. Relief shone for a moment, then Big Jake's hand whipped hard across her face. "Ye been with him, ain't ye? That's where ye were? Run off with the likes of Delaine. Yer just like yer ma—nothin' but a no-good little whore."

Brandy made an odd little sound of pain, and Marcus wanted to kill Jake Winters. It took every ounce of his control not to wrap his hands around the man's beefy neck and squeeze the life from his overblown frame.

"You're a fool, Jake Winters," he said, the words harsh with the anger he felt. "You don't realize what a prize you have."

Jake spat on the dirt floor of the tack room. "A prize, is she? But ye won't be marryin' her, will ye? Ye'll leave her belly swollen, but ye won't be takin' her to wife."

Marcus's hand unconsciously fisted. "What I do is none of your concern. What happens is between the two of us. But I'll tell you one thing, Jake Winters. If you ever lay a hand on your daughter again, I swear on everything I hold dear, I'll come back here and I'll kill you."

Big Jake straightened, his eyes hard with the remnants of his anger, but the fight had gone out of him. He released the pent-up breath he had been holding. "Get in there and get to work," he said to Brianne. "Long as ye live under me roof, ye'll do as I say."

Brianne hesitated only a moment, then made her way past him, her head held high, her shoulders straight. She paused at the door and turned. "I'll work for you, Father, but I won't destroy myself for this damnable place the way I did before. I'll do my share, but I won't take your abuse. From now on, I'll live my life the way I see fit and if you don't like it, I'll be more than happy to leave."

Jake said nothing, but he clamped down hard on his jaw. He needed Brianne and both of them knew it. She had practically run the place since she was ten years old. Stalking past her out of the tack room, he strode off toward the tavern. He slammed the door behind him as he marched inside.

Marcus turned to Brianne. "Are you all right?" She nodded, but when he opened his arms she went into them and he could feel her trembling.

"You stood up to him," he said softly against her ear. "You made him take notice and you didn't back down an inch."

She looked up at him and for the first time she smiled. "I stood up to him. I did, didn't I?"

"I'm proud of you." He pressed a kiss on her forehead, holding her tightly against him. He tried not to think how good she felt and how empty his arms would feel without her. "You're going to be all right, you know. Whatever you decide to do, you're going to be all right."

A soft, sad smile played over her lips. "Yes . . . I suppose I'll be all right. But the truth is, Marcus Delaine, I'm going to miss you."

An unexpected tightness coiled inside him. His throat felt swollen and suddenly it was hard to speak. When he did, the words came out thick and gruff.

"I'm going to miss you, too, love." Until that moment, holding her as he was, inhaling the scent of her hair and feeling the warmth of her body, he hadn't realized just how much.

Four days later, the *Seahawk* sailed out of Charleston Harbor, and Captain Marcus Delaine, Earl of Hawksmoor, sailed out of Brandy's life.

She stood on the dock that morning, as final preparations for departure were made and the last of the crew returned to the ship, all but Marcus, who still stood beside her. An icy wind swept down from the north, tangling the long copper hair she'd left loose around her shoulders the way Marcus liked it, and molding her skirts against her legs. She wore the lovely green shawl he had bought for her in the islands, but it wasn't nearly warm enough. The harsh breeze sliced through the light fabric, raising goose bumps on her skin and chilling her all the way to the heart.

Or perhaps it was simply Marcus's departure, knowing once he boarded his ship, she might never see him again.

"It's time to go," he said softly, cutting into the silence, the words stirring an emptiness deep inside her.

She looked up into his face. "I know."

"I won't soon forget you, Brianne."

Brandy swallowed past the hard lump in her throat. "In time you'll come back. You'll return to Charleston as you always have."

He only shook his head. "You mustn't wait, Brandy. You must think of yourself and your future. Take what you want from life. Do what you want—as I intend to do."

She glanced away. He wouldn't wait for her. He was making that perfectly clear. And waiting for him would do no good, not when it was apparent how little she meant to him, when it was certain she had no part in his future.

"I know you're right. That is exactly what I must do." But it didn't make the parting any easier. And it didn't make her love him any less.

"I'll always remember the days we've shared, Brianne,"

he said. "You gave me a gift I shall always treasure." His face looked solemn, almost grave. "I have a gift for you in return." Reaching inside the pocket of his waistcoat, he extracted a small silver box and placed it in her hand. "Open it."

Brandy did so, her fingers slightly shaking. Lying on a bed of deep red velvet sat a small, exquisitely fashioned silver locket.

"I got it several years ago in Spain. I never knew exactly why I bought it. Now I know I bought it for you."

Brandy blinked and a drop of wetness began to trickle down her cheek. Bending her head, she let Marcus fasten the chain around her neck, the locket cool against the skin at the base of her throat. Her fingers ran over the beautifully etched silver on the front of the locket.

"Thank you," she whispered. "I'll cherish it always." She wondered if, once he was gone, he would think of her at all. If he would recall with the least fond memory the passionate hours they had spent making love. She would have been sure he would not if it hadn't been for a single last touch, a final brief moment when his long dark fingers caressed her cheek and she felt him tremble.

"I hope you find whatever it is you are seeking," he said softly, gruffly. "I hope that you will be happy."

Brandy fought back tears. "I wish the same for you, Marcus."

He only nodded. Bending his head, he brushed her lips with a kiss, but even as he bade his final farewell, his mind seemed to drift away, as if he had already returned to sea, to his ship and his next great adventure. He turned and started walking, his long legs moving purposefully up the gangway. He paused at the top, stopped and looked back at her one last time, a long, slow, penetrating glance that could have meant a dozen different things. Brandy wanted to believe he was forming a memory of her to carry with him.

As she would always carry a memory of him with her.

* * *

Two months came and went. Brandy couldn't have guessed how difficult those two months would be. No day passed that she didn't think of him. No day passed that she didn't miss him. She was desperately in love with him and the fact that he was gone from her life didn't seem to matter in the least.

There were times she wished she had never stowed away aboard his ship, but in that regard, at least some good had come from her grand adventure. The uneasy truce she had reached with her father remained in force. As she had hoped, he had discovered her worth while she was gone. In truth, he needed her to help him run the tavern.

And perhaps he was just a little afraid of Marcus Delaine.

Whatever the reason, from the day of her return, he treated her with at least the same accord he reserved for the rest of his employees. Not much to say of a father's regard for his daughter, but better than he'd treated her before. The hours she worked now were shorter, which gave her a little time to herself. Time, unfortunately, that was usually spent thinking of Marcus Delaine.

"God, Flo, I miss him so much." They were sitting in Brandy's small attic bedchamber, Brianne in her night rail, Flo still wearing her serving maid's clothes.

"I tried to warn you," her friend said. "I knew you were headin' for trouble when you came up with your crazy scheme to stow away."

Brandy fiddled with the end of her long copper braid. "Perhaps it was crazy. It was something I just had to do." She looked into her best friend's face. "I'm in love with him, Flo. I think I've been in love with him my whole life."

The dark-haired woman sighed and leaned back in her chair. "It's a woman's lot, I think, to love a man even when he doesn't love her in return."

"Is that the way it is with you and Willie? You love him but he doesn't love you?"

"In the beginning it was. I was just eighteen when I met him. He was blond and fair. I thought he was the handsomest man I'd ever seen." Flo stared off in the distance, as if she could see him as he was then. "He was the son of a preacher and I was already workin' in the tavern. He wanted to make love to me, but he told me right off he couldn't marry me. His father would never approve. I loved him, anyway. I gave him what he wanted."

"What happened after that?"

"His father insisted he marry a girl from the church. Willie did what his father wanted. Six months later he came back to me. He was miserable. The girl was a conniving little witch who didn't care a whit about him. She was as cold as an icicle in bed. He needed me, he said. And I surely needed him. We've been seein' each other ever since, the better part of eight years. Not often, you know, and never here in the tavern. But I believe he's come to love me. And I know I'll always love him."

Brandy didn't say more. Flo's story was simply too sad. It made her think of Marcus and she felt like crying all over again. She didn't notice when her friend left the bedchamber, only heard the soft click of the door closing behind her. If anyone understood her misery, it was Flo.

Perhaps the reason her friend left her alone was so she could grieve in peace.

CHAPTER 12

Marcus stood at the rail of the *Seahawk*, staring out at the water. Whitecaps broke over the surface and a stiff, cold wind pushed the sails. They cracked and snapped as if they battled with an unseen force, and in a way they did. In the end they were the victors, harnessing the wind, if only briefly.

Marcus and his crew were two weeks gone from England, the beginning of a voyage that would carry the ship into the China Seas. Marcus had never been to the mystical East before. He had been wanting to go for years, should have been looking forward to the trip, been eager to reach so distant a port—and he was.

It was one of the things he loved about his life at sea, the places he went, the exotic people he met on each journey. And yet there was a difference this time, something subtle, a feeling he couldn't define. He only knew in the past few months the lure of far-off places seemed to have lost its once-brilliant sheen.

"Ye've been standin' there awhile, starin' out at the water. Is it the lass again, that's weighin' on yer mind?"

Marcus almost smiled. Hamish was uncanny. "It's strange the way she slides into my thoughts at the oddest times. I can't help worrying if she is all right."

Hamish stroked his heavy gray beard. "If ye've left her with a . . . problem, yer brother will see to it. He's a good lad, one who doesn't shirk his duties."

Marcus shook his head. "Rex is overburdened as it is. On top of the earldom he is managing for me, he has recently come into an inheritance of his own. Sometimes I wonder how he does it.''

''Still, he'll see to her, as ye have told him to.''

''Yes, I suppose there is nothing to worry about. If she carries my babe, she'll be well provided for.'' But the thought did not sit well with him, Brianne round with his child and he not there if she should need him. It was an odd thought, since he had never considered such matters before.

''The lads still talk about her, ye know. I think they were all a bit in love with her.''

Marcus did smile then. ''There was something about her, wasn't there, Hamish? Sort of a goodness, I think. She liked people and they liked her. She would loved to have seen the East.''

Hamish eyed him shrewdly. ''Perhaps ye should have brought her along.''

He only shook his head. ''A woman has no place on board a ship. You know that as well as I. Besides, assuming the deed is not already accomplished, sooner or later I would have gotten her with child.''

The older man chuckled, sort of a wheezy sound. ''Aye, there's no doubt of that. Not with that one's fiery nature. And ye could hardly make a tavern wench into the Countess of Hawksmoor, could ye?''

Brianne's image appeared in his mind as she was that first night he had found her aboard his ship, in the full-sleeved shirt and tight-fitting breeches of a lad. ''No, I suppose she would hardly fit the part. Besides, I don't want a wife. I don't want to be trapped into the same boring existence as my brother and the rest of the British aristocracy.''

''Aye, that I know. 'Twould never do for the likes of ye, Cap'n. Yer meant for the sea and always will be.''

It was true. Marcus had accepted the fact long ago and he was happy with the life he had chosen. But there were days like this one when he missed the sweet scent of a woman, missed the soft feel of her skin and the touch of her hands on his body. There were times he missed hearing her gentle laughter, missed the sparkle of excitement in her lovely golden eyes.

In truth there was only one woman that he had ever missed. He wondered how long it would take him to forget Brianne Winters.

Brandy walked along the quay, staring off toward the water. A blue sea lapped peacefully against the hulls of a dozen ships. In the distance, a single sail edged the horizon. Overhead a pair of gulls dipped and swooped with the breeze.

Brandy watched them with longing, remembering the days she had seen them from the windswept deck of the *Seahawk,* guarding the memories of the tall dark man who had stood beside her. It had become her habit to go down to the sea each week. Somehow it made her feel closer to the man she had loved and lost.

She knew the sailors talked about it, the way she watched and waited, as if her lover would return, his great ship carrying him back to her from over the horizon. It was no secret what had happened aboard the *Seahawk.* There were no secrets when the ship held a crew of nearly fifty men.

Oddly, instead of condemning her, the men seemed to view her with an odd sort of respect, awed that she could love a man so deeply. It was as if they wished they could be so lucky a man, that they might find a woman in a port somewhere who would love them as she loved Marcus Delaine.

Her father grumbled about it, calling her ten kinds of a fool. But the fact she didn't carry the captain's babe seemed to pacify him somewhat. Their uneasy truce remained. She had not wavered in her determination to lead her own life and maybe he even felt a grudging admiration.

Which was why, perhaps, the shock was far greater when a sailor burst through the door of the taproom shouting that Big Jake Winters was dead.

Seahawk continued its eastward journey, each day blending into the next. Instead of fading from his mind, more and more often Marcus found his thoughts returning to the woman who had shared his cabin. At times, it was as if the ghost of her remained.

Damnation! During the day, his mind strayed from his duties. He could see her smiling as she worked in the steamy galley or bent over one of the crew who had fallen ill with the fever. When the men sang a lusty sea chantey, he could hear her laughter. At night he dreamed of her naked and writhing beneath him, his shaft sheathed warmly inside her. Night after night, he awakened hard and aching with desire for her, his body drenched in perspiration.

Even the trouble he'd found waiting in London, more problems with Hawksmoor Shipping—cargo delays, damage to the *Peregrine* that had cost them an important contract—even that could not cast her completely from his thoughts.

Nor the storm that even now lashed the ship. It had risen out of nowhere, the wind whipping fiercely against the sails, the deck pitching violently beneath him. As he barked a new set of orders and the men fell to the tasks, Brianne seemed to be there beside him.

At times he hated her for the spell she had somehow cast over him.

The ship dipped into a trough, timbers creaked, and a huge wave crashed over the bow. "Close reef the topsail!" he shouted. "Reef the foresail!" The men raced to obey his command, and the ship shuddered with their efforts. "Look to the mainsail!" he shouted. "Make sure she's three-reefed and well secured!" As the gale continued to build, he ordered the topsail furled and an hour later took in the foresail. Still she was lying down to her taffrails, water gushing into her scuppers, and driving very fast.

"I don't like the look of it," Hamish said as he walked into the wheelhouse. "Storm's a bad one. Bad as any nor'easter what ever howled up out Hades."

"*Seahawk* will hold. Her hull is sound and her sails are strong. She'll come through without a problem."

But Hamish still looked worried, his thick gray brows drawn down over tired blue eyes, his curved pipe long dead, resting limply between his callused fingers.

Four more hours passed but the storm did not lessen. *Seahawk* plunged from one trough into the next, rising high on a giant wave, then crashing into the seemingly bottomless pit on the opposite side. All the while her weary crew battled ceaselessly to keep her on course.

Standing at the base of the huge spruce mast, his heavy oiled slicker battered by dense sheets of rain, Marcus peered into the relentless gale, his sharp gaze following the violent whitecapped sea. Off the starboard side a wall of water rose up out of nowhere and the big ship lurched sideways. From somewhere through the storm, he thought he heard the loud, splintering crack of wood, and alarm tore through him.

"Look out above, Captain!" Brig Butler's young voice cut through the shriek of the wind, and he jerked his head skyward, spotting the danger, but it was already too late.

Marcus felt the crushing weight of the crossarm like the blow of a sledge against his body.

"Captain!" Brig Butler raced toward him as Marcus went down, pinned to the deck beneath a tangle of sail and line and the wet, slick weight of the heavy wood.

Pain shot through his body, so fierce he thought he might be sick. His head felt as if it had been split open and his bones felt crushed. The last thing he saw was Hamish Bass's pale, frightened face as the older man bent over him, wildly shouting orders, gently stroking his forehead, and softly calling his name.

Big Jake's death hung over the White Horse Tavern like the pall of smoke that usually rose above the tables. Two weeks had passed since the fatal accident that had crushed him beneath the wheels of a runaway dray, a huge, fully laden freight wagon that had slammed into everything in its path and killed Big Jake almost instantly.

Two weeks. That was the length of time it had taken Brandy to accept the reality of her father's passing. Until then, she had existed in a fog of numbness. It wasn't grief, she told herself. How could she possibly grieve for a father who never loved her?

And yet she felt something. A pain she couldn't quite name. Perhaps she sorrowed for the family they could have been, or the love they had never shared. Whatever it was, she worked from dusk until well after midnight, carrying on her duties in a strange state of semi-awareness.

Flo was a rock of support, helping her get through the burial with its simple graveside service, helping her cope with the day-to-day activities of running the tavern without the man whose thundering presence had reached into every crevice and corner.

"At least I won't starve," Brandy said to Flo as they counted the night's take of money. "The place makes more than I ever dreamed."

Flo's black brows drew into a frown. "It surely seems to." She shook her head. "All those years that miserly father of yours never gave you a cent. He could have at least seen you had decent clothes, but no—he was too damnable cheap to take care of his own daughter."

Brandy looked up from counting the till. "You know, Flo, I've been thinking. If Big Jake was making so much money, what did he do with it? He surely didn't spend it. At least, if he did, I never saw where it went."

It was three days later that Brandy finally found out. The day her father's solicitor arrived with a small leather satchel that contained his final will.

"My father had a will?" Brandy said to the man, dismayed.

"He did. Does that really seem so strange?" James Nolan was a slight man with thinning blond hair and tiny spectacles that circled small brown eyes. "I shall endeavor to relay the contents . . . if there is a place we might find a bit of privacy."

"Of course." Brandy glanced to where Flo stood near the doorway, uncertain what to think. "But I would like my friend to come along."

The little man nodded and Brandy motioned for Flo to join them. Together the group made its way into a small chamber off the taproom that was used for private meetings. It was spartan, with only a scarred oval table and ten battered chairs, but the walls were freshly painted and the windows newly washed. It smelled of the lye soap they had used to scrub the floors.

It was in that small, nondescript room Brandy discovered not only did she own the White Horse Tavern, but something a lot more important.

"Your father invested very wisely," the little man told her, once they were seated at the oval table. "He saved every penny, except for the sums he lent out. He was very careful who his borrowers were, and his shrewdness earned him a substantial return. In a word, Miss Winters, your future is extremely secure. As a matter of fact, you are a very wealthy woman."

Brandy just sat there, unable to believe what she had heard. Her head was spinning. She was afraid if she stood up, her legs would not hold her. "My father had a fortune and he left it all to me?"

"He had no other heir, my dear. And he was quite specific about it. I believe, Miss Winters, in his own way, your father cared a great deal about you."

Brandy didn't believe that. Or perhaps in some way he did care. Big Jake wasn't a man who knew how to show his affection—if indeed he possessed such a thing. Whatever the truth, Brandy no longer cared. That day, thanks to Big Jake's untimely death, she received the first and only gift he had ever given her, a gift she had wanted for most of her life—freedom from the White Horse Tavern.

"What will you do, Miss Winters?" James Nolan refolded the document he had just read and shoved it back into his leather satchel.

Brandy sat up straighter, her mind still reeling from the shock of her good fortune even as resolve spread though her. Finally, she was able to stand. "Sell the damnable place. I never want to see it again." Impossible as it was to believe, she was a wealthy woman. She didn't have to face another miserable day at the White Horse Tavern. She didn't have to suffer the brutal memories it held, the awful memories of a painful childhood.

She glanced over at Flo, the woman who had stood by her through thick and thin. "Or better yet, I shall deed it to my friend." Brandy grinned. "From now on, Flo, consider yourself the owner of the White Horse Tavern."

Flo's hand shook as it rose unconsciously to her throat. "But I couldn't possibly accept—"

"It's yours, Flo. For years you've been like a sister to me. Take it. Do with it whatever it is you wish."

"But what will you do?"

"Leave here. Go someplace new. Find out what the world is all about."

"But where? Where will you go?"

Brandy pondered that. It was hardly an easy decision. She would have to consider carefully, give it a good deal of thought. She wasn't in a hurry. She had her freedom and now she could do as she wished. Unbidden, Marcus's image came to mind. Brandy firmly pushed it away. He had made it clear she had no place in his life and she had accepted the fact, difficult as it was. Marcus was gone and she didn't know where. Even if she did know—it was the one place in the world that she could not go.

Hamish Bass stood in the open door of the captain's bedchamber in his fancy London town house, his brown felt hat clutched in his gnarled, weathered hands. Hamish stared down at them, feeling as if they belonged to somebody else. He noticed that they trembled.

Across the room, Marcus Delaine, captain of the *Seahawk*, lay in the middle of a big four-poster bed, broken and hurting, his body ravaged, his face turned toward the wall. Hamish closed his eyes against a wave of sadness that sat like a crushing weight upon his chest. He had come to see the captain every day since the ship had been forced to return to London, since an army of doctors had been called in to examine him and confirm that his legs were badly broken, that his back was injured as well.

That Marcus Delaine would never walk again.

"He's sleeping now, Hamish." The captain's brother Rexland had come to the city as soon as he got word of what had happened. He was a good man, loyal and hardworking. The boy had stayed at his brother's side since the moment he had arrived, but it hadn't done a lick of good.

"Aye," Hamish said, "sleepin'. Maybe the rest will do him some good." But Hamish didn't believe it. The captain wasn't really asleep, he knew, he was hiding from the truth of what had happened, unable to accept the terrible fact that he was now a cripple.

"I'll tell him you were here," his brother said softly.

"Aye. Tell him I'll stop by again on the morrow."

Rex nodded, a younger, softer version of his brother. "What of the ship, Hamish? He'll want to know what you've found out about the accident. He'll want to know if there was any indication of foul play."

Hamish had been asked the question before, had been silently asking it himself every day since the damnable crossarm went down. "None so far, but we've only just begun the repairs. The storm did a passel of damage. We had to saw off the mainmast at the deck line when she split and the crossarm come down. There was damage to the hull and we took on a good bit of water. 'Twill take a bit of time to know for certain, but so far there's no sign it was tampered with. We'll keep lookin'—real close-like—I promise ye."

Rex nodded. "Thank you." Neither man said more. There was nothing more to say.

Hamish left the town house and headed toward the dock, turning the collar of his woolen coat up against the sudden brisk wind that blew in off the Thames. Unsteady footsteps carried him toward the ship, the only place he truly felt at home. *Seahawk* was in dry dock for God only knew how long, but eventually the damage would be repaired. The ship would be ready to sail again, heading to faraway places.

This time, her captain would not be going with her.

Hamish fought down the piercing sadness that rose in his chest at the thought.

* * *

Marcus leaned back against the tufted leather seat of the Hawksmoor traveling coach as it passed through the last few miles of Cornwall countryside on its way to his home on the cliffs.

They were traveling along the coast, over the rocky soil that marked the area around the small seaport village of Tintagel, Marcus alone in the carriage while the servants who tended him rode up on top with the coachman, grateful, he was certain, for the respite, if only for a while, from the unpleasant task of tending their master's needs.

His eyes slid closed against the wave of pain that crashed down on top of him whenever he thought of the life he now lived. The anguish tearing through him, he knew, had nothing to do with the pain in his broken, useless limbs. He clenched his jaw in an effort to force it away, hardened his heart to the agony of knowing he was less than a man, nothing more than a useless cripple.

Something burned at the back of his eyes. He blinked and clenched his fists and the burning went away. From the waist down he felt nothing. If only the rest of him could be numb as well. Instead, he felt suffocated, his chest crushed by so much pain and regret he could scarcely breathe. He was so stricken with grief and ravaged by heartache he had lost the will to look beyond the next hour and certainly not the next day.

And always there was the anger. He lashed out with it, hurting those around him, knowing he should accept what had happened but completely unable to.

On top of it all was the doubt. The nagging suspicion that someone had done something to the ship, that someone had somehow damaged the mast and caused the accident that had unmanned him.

Again and again on the long journey from London, he had replayed that last fateful day aboard the ship. If only he had noticed the fault in the mast. If only the crossarm had splintered ten seconds later. If only his thoughts had been focused more clearly he might have been able to step out of the way.

But none of those things had happened and now he sat there in the carriage, little more than a shell of the man he had been. He thought of the future with disgust and longed to be free of it completely. Perhaps if he had the courage, he would find a way to make this terrible nightmare end.

The coach rumbled along, coming to a halt at last in front of the huge stone mansion on the cliffs. Hawksmoor House. Fifty bedchambers, ten drawing rooms, a state dining room, libraries and studies, endless halls and corridors. The house was more than three hundred years old. Thanks to his ancestors, it was a magnificent mix of age and warmth that should have been daunting but wasn't.

He had loved the place as a boy, yet as he'd gotten older and accepted the fact it would never be his, he had turned that love in another direction, to the sea that surrounded it, encompassing a life that fulfilled his every dream. That dream was lost forever, just like the use of his legs.

The door of the carriage swung open and his manservant, Frederick Peterbrook, a large heavyset man who had been with the family for years, began to help him down. Big hands found his useless legs, turned them into the doorway, reached up to pluck him out as if he were a babe.

Heat rushed into Marcus's face and he had to look away. Embarrassment and humiliation warred with pain and rage. He wanted to shout at the man, to command that he leave him in peace, but he needed to get into the house and there was no other way.

Instead, as the big man settled him into a waiting chair and together with a footman carried him inside, he bit down on his anger. He stifled the fury that threatened to erupt, scalding everything and everyone in its path. Instead, he simply turned into himself, burying his pain, burying his rage.

Becoming some other, different man who could live with the awful shame.

Weeks passed, one after another, and still Brandy had reached no decision. Now that she had her freedom, she found herself waiting, searching for a sign that would tell her what she should do.

It arrived just a few days later. The day that Brig Butler, crewman of the *Seahawk,* shoved through the doors of the taproom, tall and blond and fair. Spotting her the moment he came in, he strode toward her with obvious purpose and seeing him, Brandy went dead still.

Brig had sailed from Charleston aboard the *Seahawk.* For a single wild, heart-stopping moment, she thought that Marcus had returned. Then she noticed the tense, worried expression on Brig's handsome face and she knew in a painful instant that it wasn't the truth.

"Mr. Butler." She tried to smile but the look in his eyes kept her from it. "I . . . I'm surprised to see you here. Surely the *Seahawk—*"

He only shook his head. "I arrived here aboard the *Snow Goose,* another Hawksmoor ship. The *Seahawk* is presently in England."

"England? I thought they were headed for the Orient."

Brig cleared his throat, his face drawn and tight, his expression decidedly uneasy. It made her own unease build. "There was a storm," he said, "a very bad one. *Seahawk* was severely damaged. We were forced to return to London for repairs." His eyes, usually a clear, sparkling blue, seemed dulled by an unreadable haze. "There was an accident, Miss Winters. A very bad accident."

Brandy swallowed. Her legs had started to tremble. "An accident?" she repeated, a tight little quiver in her voice. "What . . . what sort of accident?"

Brig took her hand. "Why don't we sit down? It's been a long while since we've spoken. Perhaps we could find a quiet place to talk."

Her insides started shaking. The look on Brig's face said that something was terribly wrong. "Tell me, Brig. Tell me what has happened."

The blond man glanced away, dragged in a breath that helped to compose him. "We were two weeks out of London when a storm blew in, practically out of nowhere. As I said, it was a bad one. *Seahawk* was holding her own. We had faith in Captain Delaine and none of us were overly concerned. Then a big wave hit the ship and suddenly it lurched sideways. The mast splintered. The captain was injured when the crossarm came down. That is the reason I came here. I thought you would want to know."

"Marcus . . . Marcus was injured?" Her head was spinning, her chest gone suddenly tight. Surely she had misunderstood. Brig eased her down into a chair and this time she didn't resist him. He seated himself in a wooden chair beside her and once more took her hand.

"I'm sorry, Brandy. He's been hurt very badly, I'm afraid. Both of his legs were broken. His spine was . . . damaged."

The last of the color bled from her cheeks. "His spine?"

"Yes."

"And he . . . he sent you here to tell me?"

Brig shook his head. "No. He hasn't the faintest notion I am here. I came because I knew the way you felt about him—all of us did. We could see it in your eyes whenever you looked at him. And even though he never allowed it to show, we knew how fond he was of you. Captain Delaine is in trouble, Brandy. I came because I thought you might be able to help him."

Brandy couldn't speak. Her throat had closed up and tears burned the backs of her eyes. They welled for an instant then began to slide down her cheeks. She swallowed hard, worked to force the words past her lips, which suddenly felt stiff and numb. "There is . . . there is more, isn't there?"

Brig released a long, uneven breath. "He can't walk, Brandy. After the accident, we returned to England and he was taken to his home in Cornwall. From the day he discovered he would have to leave the ship, that he would never be able to sail as her captain again, he's been like a living dead man. I went to see him—a group of us did, Mr. Bass and some of the *Seahawk* crew. He lives in a fancy house on the cliffs above the ocean, but he never goes outside. He just sits there all day long staring out at the water."

"Oh, dear God." She closed her eyes, and she could see him, sitting there all alone.

"His brother has tried to help him. There were a number of physicians in London, more that went out to the house."

"And none of them were able to do anything for him?"

"I don't know for sure. I only know I couldn't stand to see him that way. Marcus was a friend of my father's—he never told you that, did he?"

"No . . . he never did."

"My father is a merchant, a very successful one. I'm his only son. The last thing he wanted was for me to run off to sea. Captain Delaine spoke to him, somehow he made him understand how important this was. I looked up to him—all of us did. We couldn't stand by and do nothing."

Brandy blinked and more tears rolled down her cheeks. "I have to go to him. I have to get to him as quickly as I can."

Brig Butler squeezed her hand. "I hoped . . . prayed you would say that. I've saved a little money. The rest of the crew put in as well. Together there's enough for your passage." He dug into his pocket, but Brandy caught his hand.

"I don't need money, Brig—not anymore. My father passed away several weeks ago. It seems he left me very well settled. I have money enough to do anything I wish. I intended to leave here. I just didn't know where I would go." She brushed at the wetness on her cheeks. "Now I do."

"It won't be easy," Brig warned. "He saw us just that once. Now they say he won't let anyone in. Only his brother and the servants who tend him."

Brandy sat up a little straighter. "I assure you, Mr. Butler, once I am there, he will let me in—one way or another."

Brig Butler smiled for the very first time. He slid back his chair and came to his feet. "I'm sorry to be the bearer of such bad news, but sooner or later you would have found out, and, well . . . all of us thought . . . the crew, that is . . . we thought one of us should be here when you did."

Brandy stood up, too. Her chest ached unbearably. The lump in her throat made it nearly impossible to speak. Rising on tiptoe, she pressed a trembling kiss against his cheek.

"Thank you for coming, Brig. You'll never know how much this means to me."

Gently he smiled down at her. "Perhaps I do. I only hope that one day I am lucky enough to find a woman who will care for me the way you do Captain Delaine."

CHAPTER 13

Rexland Delaine closed the door to the Oceanview drawing room, leaving his older brother walled inside. The place was Marcus's chosen domain, a gilt and mirrored chamber at the rear of the house with views out over the water that seemed to stretch forever. The room had been his brother's favorite since he was a boy.

Rex wondered if now, forever locked in his chair, Marcus even saw the incredible beauty that beckoned beyond the windows.

Rex thought of his brother, of the difficult hours he had spent in his presence, and the muscles in his jaw went tense. He raked a hand through his wavy black hair, leaving it a bit disheveled.

God's blood, what a morning.

Though Rex and Marcus had been born of different mothers, they looked a good deal alike. Rex was a little bit shorter, his features less harsh, his eyes a lighter shade of blue. But his hair was the same slightly curly black and his skin would have been as dark if he had spent as many hours in the sun.

The youngest of the three Delaine brothers, Rex was the one with the easiest disposition, the charming one, though lately his considerable charm seemed to have escaped him. Marcus was the cause. He had always been the difficult brother, arrogant and driven, determined to succeed on his own, unwilling to bend in any way to their father's demands. Rather the black sheep of the family.

Rex almost smiled. Now that their older brother, Geoffrey,

was dead, Marcus was the Earl of Hawksmoor. He had never wanted the title, shunned it even now. Ironically, of the three Delaine sons, it was Marcus who came closest to their father's authoritative personality.

Rex's smile slid away. A powerful, commanding figure his brother had always been. Now he was demanding as well, brooding, inconsiderate, and impossible to handle. Rex knew he was hurting, that he felt his life was over.

In truth, Rex believed his brother wished the accident had killed him, instead of leaving him what Marcus called "a hopeless cripple."

Rex leaned back against the closed door of the drawing room, trying to gather his strength. He was tired. So damnably, utterly weary. When he wasn't managing Hawksmoor lands and holdings, he was working on his own estates, part of a recent, quite sizable inheritance from his maternal grandfather. Now the business of Hawksmoor Shipping had fallen into his hands as well. It seemed he worked from dawn until dusk and still there wasn't time to get all of it done.

And there was this constant worry for Marcus. His brother was drowning in despair, eaten up with hopelessness and defeat. Hour after hour, he simply sat in front of the window, staring out at the water, longing for the life he'd once had. God's blood, if only there were some way he could help him.

Rex dragged in a steadying breath and shoved away from the door. Worrying wouldn't help. In truth, he didn't have time to worry—he had too bloody much to do.

Vowing to get some of it done, he strode down the corridor, making his way toward the study and the pile of paperwork that awaited. A commotion at the front door caught his attention as he neared the foyer, some sort of argument involving whoever had the misfortune to appear on the opposite side.

The butler, Milton Giles, stood firmly blocking the entrance, and clearly he wasn't pleased.

Rex strode forward. "What is it, Giles? Is there some sort of problem?"

"I'm afraid, sir, there is."

"What, if I may ask, is the nature of this problem?"

In answer, the tall, gaunt butler merely swung open the door. Rex's brow shot up at the small red-haired woman standing on the wide stone steps outside.

"The lady has come to see his lordship. I have informed her he is not receiving callers, but she refuses to leave."

Rex's eyes skimmed over the woman's petite figure. She was attired in an expensive traveling dress, the shade a bit too bright a green. Though the silk faille was well cut and obviously costly, there seemed to be a few too many ruffles across the bodice and a garish-looking row flared out at the hem. The bonnet she wore over her bright copper hair sat at a jaunty angle, yet there seemed to be a few too many flowers around the brim.

"May I help you?" Rex asked, for the first time seeing past the baubles to the lovely face and shapely figure of the woman on the porch. "Miss . . . ?"

"My name is Brianne Winters. I've come to see Captain Delaine. He is also the Earl of Hawksmoor. I believe this is where he lives."

The name rang an instant bell. Rex felt the pull of a smile. He knew who this lady was. His brother had told him a good deal about her before he'd departed on his ill-fated voyage. "It is indeed where his lordship resides. Do come in, Miss Winters. I'm Rexland Delaine, Marcus's brother."

She didn't hide her relief. Apparently she knew who he was as well. "It is a very great pleasure to meet you, Mr. . . . or is it my lord?"

"It's simply mister, I'm afraid."

She smiled at that. "It is a pleasure, Mr. Delaine. Your brother spoke of you quite fondly."

"As he did you, Miss Winters."

She seemed surprised at that. "He did?"

"It was some time back . . . but yes, as a matter of fact, he did."

She seemed pleased and even more relieved. "I have traveled quite some distance to see him. I won't leave until I do."

His brow arched up. His brother had said she was quite a

spirited woman. Apparently it was the truth. "Am I to presume you have heard about the accident?"

"Yes. One of the men from the *Seahawk* brought me the news. That is the reason I'm here."

He eyed her a moment more. She carefully took his measure as well, then her gaze flicked away to her surroundings. Her hands were shaking, he saw, as her eyes took in the huge domed ceiling with its heavy crystal chandelier, the black and white marble floors beneath her green kid slippers. There was no doubt that she was nervous, yet she also looked determined.

"All right, since you appear quite set in your purpose, perhaps we should go into the drawing room where we may be private."

Big golden brown eyes, slightly tilted upward, swung back to his face. "As you wish, sir."

She was lovely in the extreme, he now saw, hardly in need of the ruffles and baubles that only disguised her beauty, however briefly. Her breasts were high and full, exposed modestly but enticingly above the top of her high-waisted pea-green gown. Her ankles were trim, her neck slender and perfectly arched, her skin as smooth as cream. Marcus had said that he'd wanted her quite badly. Rex could well see why.

He led her down the hall to the White Drawing Room, a chamber done in ivory and gold with high molded ceilings and ornate gilt mirrors on the walls. A pink marble hearth sat at each end of the room, and fresh-cut flowers bloomed from silver vases.

Standing beside him, Miss Winters surveyed her surroundings, and she couldn't disguise her wonder, or her approval.

Not that she seemed inclined to try.

"It's lovely." She studied the room again, one of Rex's favorites in the house. "From the outside . . . fashioned as it is from all those great blocks of stone, the house looks cold and uninviting, but inside . . . inside, it is beautiful, and it isn't cold at all." She smiled then, a soft, sincere, unaffected smile, and he knew in an instant that his brother had felt far more for this girl than the lust that he had admitted.

"I'm glad," she said, "that Marcus had a place like this to come home to."

He noted the way she said his brother's name, with an odd sort of longing, and a funny thread of hope sprang to life inside him.

"You realize my brother has been very gravely injured. If you came here expecting to find the same man you knew aboard the *Seahawk,* you are bound to be sadly disappointed."

Her eyes leaped to his and her face went suddenly pale. "Are you saying that . . . that something has happened to his mind as well as his body?"

Rex shook his head. "No, no, of course not. His legs are useless, that is all. His mind is as sharp as ever."

She breathed a sigh of relief and for an instant her eyes slid closed. When she looked back at him, her shoulders seemed a little bit straighter. "Then he is exactly the same man he was."

Rex couldn't help an inward feeling of approval. Still, it wasn't completely true. "Inside, perhaps he is. On the surface, he is different. He believes his life is over. There are times I believe he wishes he were dead."

The girl looked away, but not before he caught the slight sheen of tears. She blinked furiously, then scrubbed away a drop of moisture that ran down her cheek. Straightening her small shoulders, she swung her eyes back to his face. "That is a ridiculous way to feel and I intend to tell him so. Please . . . you must let me see him."

A corner of his mouth curved up. "Somehow I don't believe I could stop you even if I wanted to."

She tried to smile, but he could see how worried she was.

"Normally, I would inform him that he has a visitor. But if I do . . ."

"If you do, he might refuse to see me."

"Exactly so."

"Then we will surprise him. We will simply give him no choice."

Rex grinned. "Rather the way you did before, Miss Winters, when you stowed away aboard his ship?''

A hint of color rushed into her cheeks. Her lips were full and well shaped and they curved up now at the edges. ''Very much like that, sir. Very much like that, indeed.''

Brandy followed Rexland Delaine back out into the hall, walking along the gleaming marble floors to the patter of their echoing footsteps. Her legs were shaking, her knees knocking together beneath her skirts with every move.

She was out of her element in the beautiful house, a magnificent structure beyond anything she had ever seen. It had taken every ounce of her will to walk down the imposing tree-lined drive and up those intimidating wide stone steps. But Marcus was the reason she had come and no pile of stone, no matter how artfully put together, was going to keep her from him.

They continued down the hall and Brandy paused beside a narrow, marble-topped table to remove her hat and gloves. Though she knew little of the social graces, she was certain it was not the thing to do when a lady went calling, but she didn't really like the bonnet that Flo had helped her choose, and she wanted Marcus to see past her newly fashioned garments to the person she was before—the tavern maid he had left on the dock in Charleston.

''Ready?'' his brother asked, not questioning her odd behavior, as if perhaps he understood. Already she liked this youngest Delaine. He was handsome and gracious, a softer, less forceful version of Marcus, and instinctively she believed that he loved his older brother very much.

And he was worried about him. Extremely worried.

''As ready as I'm ever going to be.'' Which meant, of course, she wasn't ready at all. In fact, she was shaking inside, her fear and uncertainty building every second. She was desperate to see him again, ached for the suffering he had endured.

When Rex Delaine stopped outside the door to another of the mansion's many drawing rooms, Brandy took a long, courage-building breath. What would Marcus say when he saw her? Would he be happy that she had come? Or angry that she had taken it upon herself to interfere in his life again?

"Shall we go in, Miss Winters?" Rex asked.

She steeled herself and nodded, prepared at last to face Marcus. The moment the door swung wide, she discovered she wasn't prepared at all, not when she stepped into the room and the man in the straight-backed chair turned his dark head away from the window and stared in her direction.

For an instant she swayed on her feet and only the subtle pressure of Rex Delaine's hand on her arm kept her from falling. Instead of the tall, unbearably handsome man she had loved, a thin, hollow-eyed, gaunt-faced man stared back at her, his features drawn into a hawklike parody of the arrogant, dynamic man he had been before.

His cheekbones were razor-sharp, his cheeks pale and sunken in, his black hair overly long and decidedly unkempt. He wore no coat, and his frilled shirt was rumpled in a way he would never have allowed before.

And yet in an instant she saw past his ravaged state. He was Marcus and he was hurting.

It was all she could do not to run to him, to wrap her arms around him and hold him tightly against her. She wanted to comfort him, to mend his injured body and heal his tortured soul.

"Marcus . . ." she whispered. Ignoring the thunder of her heart and her trembling limbs, she started toward him, sure he hadn't yet realized who she was. The narrowing of those piercing dark blue eyes, the tic that started in his cheek, told her he knew exactly who she was, and that he was wildly, furiously angry.

"Bloody hell, Rex—what have you done!" His harsh words cracked across the distance between them, halting Brandy where she stood. "If you are responsible for bringing this woman here, I swear I will never forgive you."

Brandy swallowed. She closed her eyes a moment, willing herself not to turn and run. Brig had warned her. Rexland had warned her. She had known it wouldn't be easy.

She forced a stiffness into her trembling limbs. "Your

brother had nothing to do with my coming. I only just arrived. We met for the first time a mere few moments ago."

Angry color seeped under his pale skin, making him look more like the man he was before. "I don't know why you are here and I don't care. I want you out of here."

A sharp pain slid through her. Hurt and grief all at once. Ruthlessly, she tamped it down. "I heard what happened. I came because I care about you. Because I was worried about you."

He scoffed at that. "There is hardly a reason to worry. My legs, such as they are, have mended. I am simply unable to walk. Your presence here isn't going to change that. Now that you have satisfied your curiosity, please be on your way."

Mixed with the pity, Brandy felt a tiny spurt of anger. "That is what you believe? That I have traveled thousands of miles out of simple curiosity? You think now that I have seen you, I will simply go away?"

"You will do exactly as I tell you."

Her chin went up. "I am sorry, my lord Captain. I am no longer at your command. The fact is, I have rented a cottage here in Tintagel, just down the road from this estate. For the next several months, that is where I intend to remain."

Marcus's face turned a mottled shade of red. "Are you insane? Can't you see that you are not welcome? You will leave this house at once and you will not be allowed to return again."

With a casual air she did not feel, she turned to his younger brother, praying she had read him correctly, that she could count on him to help her. "Marcus appears to be somewhat overwrought, I'm afraid. I shall leave him to recover himself. On the morrow, I shall return, if that is acceptable to you."

Rex Delaine merely smiled. "I shall look forward to seeing you again, Miss Winters."

"Bloody hell!" Marcus's voice rang across the room. The tea service sitting beside him went crashing to the floor.

Brandy smiled sweetly. "I hope you will be feeling a bit

less ill-tempered by then, Lord Hawksmoor. It really doesn't suit you."

Marcus swore foully, slammed his fist against the arm of the chair, and whirled away to stare back out the window. It took all of her courage to simply turn away, to follow his brother out of the room and wait while he quietly closed the door.

She was shaking all over, her stomach rolling with nausea, swaying on her feet. She wanted to simply sit down and weep, but she knew that she could not. Instead she forced some stiffness into her legs, made her lips curve up in a smile.

"Well, considering the circumstances, I don't think that went too badly."

Rex Delaine's expression changed from grim resignation to astonishment. His lips twitched, then suddenly he burst out laughing. When he finally brought himself under control, he wiped tears of amusement from his face. "I believe, Miss Winters, we are going to get along just fine."

Brandy actually smiled. In that moment, she knew without doubt that she had an ally. And if she was lucky, perhaps even a friend.

Sitting in his straight-backed chair, Marcus ground his jaw. His hand balled into a fist and he slammed it down on his numb, unfeeling limbs. How dare she have the gall to barge into his life again! How dare she! If he could have paced the floor, he would have. Instead he sat in his chair with his insides churning, silently calling her every vile name he could think of.

The last person in the world he wanted to see was Brianne Winters. The last person in the world he wanted to see him as he was now, a broken, defeated shell of a man, was Brianne Winters. God, how could his brother have let her in?

He thought of those moments again, wishing he could strangle Rex Delaine, wishing he could blot the look of pity he had seen on Brianne's pretty face. It hadn't lasted long, only an instant, but it was there just the same, and he would never forget it.

"Your lordship?" A footman nervously poked his head through the drawing room doors.

"What do you want?" Marcus snapped. "I told you I wasn't to be disturbed."

"You haven't eaten all day, my lord. Your brother thought perhaps—"

"If I want something to eat, I'll ring for a tray. Now get out and leave me in peace."

"Y-yes, my lord. Of course, my lord."

The door closed swiftly, leaving him alone once more. Marcus turned to stare back out the window. Sitting as it was on top of a Cornwall cliff, the house commanded a view of the sea that was unsurpassed. Today the ocean was a dark midnight blue that extended unbroken as far as the horizon. The sky was still clear, but clouds had begun drifting in. The sun was fading, disappearing behind a wall of incoming fog. Beneath it the sea remained calm, unlike Marcus, who still sat there fuming.

Most days he watched the sea with longing, his mind on his ship, on the days he had spent striding the deck, days he would never know again.

It tore him apart to think of it and yet he could not stop. Day after day, he sat in the drawing room, consumed by the loss he felt, consumed by his need for the life he had loved, the voyages he would no longer make, the ship that would never again sail under his command.

As he had this day and the day before and the day before that, Marcus stared out at the building swells, heard the piercing screech of a gray and white gull rising over the water. Then a distant sail passed by just over the horizon, a sight that earlier in the day would have tightened his stomach into a desperate knot of grief.

Now he was so angry he barely noticed the scene that would have haunted him for the balance of the day.

Instead all he saw in the huge pane of glass was the face of the woman who had appeared like a specter out of his past. The only things in front of him were the golden brown eyes and fiery copper hair of Brianne Winters.

* * *

Brandy couldn't sleep. Every time she closed her eyes, she saw Marcus's haggard, weary face, saw the dull glaze of pain in his eyes, saw the terrible defeat.

He was drowning in sorrow and grief. He couldn't look past the things he had lost to the reasons he had yet to live. Life was so precious and it could be sweet. Dear God, she had to help him!

By the time morning arrived, she was exhausted. Her muscles groaned with fatigue and a dull ache throbbed in her temples. Still, she forced her legs to the side of the bed, lifted a leaden arm to ring for her maid, Sally Dunston, and began to ready herself for the day.

"I brought you some chocolate and cakes," Sally said, setting the tray on a small carved table near the dresser. She had dark brown hair, was slender of build, shy, and a little withdrawn, but she was sweet and attentive, and Brandy had needed a companion to accompany her to England, since it was hardly acceptable for a young lady to travel alone.

In the beginning, she had hoped that Flo would go with her, but that was a futile wish.

"I'm not like you, Brandy. Charleston is my home and I haven't the least desire to leave. Besides, Will is here and he needs me."

"*I* need you," Brandy had argued. "This thing with Will can never work out. If you went away, perhaps you would find someone else."

Flo smiled sadly. "I told you—for me there is no one else."

Brandy didn't argue. Instead, she simply hugged her, wished Florence well with the tavern, made her friend promise to write, or at least find someone to do it for her since she hadn't the skill, then hired Sally to go with her instead and set off on her journey to England.

It hadn't been easy, just two women on their own, but at least she hadn't gotten seasick as she had before, and eventually the ship had arrived in London. Marcus had given her his brother's address in Cornwall before he'd left Charleston.

She made her way there from the city, had been fortunate to find a small, well-cared-for cottage on a parcel that bordered the earl's huge estate, and moved herself in.

Now, as she tied the ribbon of her narrow-brimmed bonnet beneath her chin and smoothed the long purple plumes, she thought of the defeated man she had found in the drawing room, and knew if there was any way at all she could help him, the trouble she had gone to would be worth it.

"Shall I expect you home for supper, Miss Brandy?"

"I imagine so. The captain will hardly be glad to see me and I'm not sure how much of his abuse I am prepared to handle all at once."

Sally smiled sweetly. "You'll bring him around. I know you will."

Brandy returned the smile. "Let's hope so, Sally." She prayed the girl was right, but in her heart, she wasn't so sure.

Marcus fidgeted in his chair before the hearth in his massive bedchamber. He had never thought to stay in the ornate room, would have preferred to occupy his smaller, less elaborate bedchamber down the hall, but now he was the Earl of Hawksmoor, and the servants would be aghast at the thought he might do otherwise than reside in the master's suite.

He had rarely noticed the furnishings when his father and mother had lived in this part of the house. Now he knew every wrinkle in the gold brocade counterpane, every fold in the burgundy velvet bed hangings, as well as those in the draperies at the window.

The room was elegant in the extreme, yet Marcus saw it as a velvet-lined prison. He sat there now, waiting for his valet to finish helping his dress, needing the man's assistance to do even the simplest tasks. Fortunately, Frederick was a large man, capable and loyal. He had been adamant in his insistence that he be the one to care for the master of the house.

Marcus inwardly cringed. Like a child, he thought. Dependent on the people around him, no longer able to take care of himself. Unconsciously, he reached down to rub his useless legs. In his darkest imaginings, he never would have dreamed his life would come to this.

His life. Silently, he spat the words. He had no life, none at all. He never would again. He fidgeted in the chair, waiting for Frederick to return with fresh garments. He had worn the same clothes for the last two days simply to be perverse, to countermand the feeling that he was somehow at the mercy of Frederick and the rest of the servants. Today he couldn't bear the thought of putting on those same soiled, wrinkled clothes again.

Marcus glanced at the ormolu clock on the mantel. It was already ten o'clock in the morning. It took so much time these days, just to dress and prepare for the day ahead. He hated each one, couldn't bear to see the rising of the sun, to know another useless day awaited him.

He wished he could simply lie down one night and fall into a deep, undisturbed sleep, a sleep so complete that he would never awaken. He glanced again at the clock.

Perhaps, if he was lucky, she would not come.

He wished it. Sweet Lord, how he wished it. And yet . . . and yet . . . God, she had been beautiful. Even in her overdone gown, she was the loveliest woman he had ever seen. He despised her for it, despised her for making him remember how beautiful she had looked lying naked in his bed, her pretty golden eyes moving with wonder over his body.

Even now, he could remember the way it had felt to kiss her, to be inside her, to make love to her as he never would again. He wanted to weep with the reminder of another part of himself he had lost. He wouldn't do that, of course. He would steel himself against the urge, as he had done from the moment he had awakened in his cabin aboard the ship and discovered he was unable to move his legs.

Then he'd held at least a small thread of hope that he would recover. Now he had none. Not when his legs were dead weights merely attached to his torso. Not when his greatest efforts could not move a single solitary muscle.

It was over and he knew it, had accepted it.

Now *she* was here to taunt him with the knowledge and

make him wish more than ever that he was still a man. His hand squeezed into a fist. Perhaps, after the welcome she had received, she would not come.

The notion settled over him, an even heavier weight than his unless legs.

He turned and barked a command, and Frederick came hurrying into the room. "I want you to cut my hair. It is exceedingly long and bothersome. I wish for you to trim it at once."

Frederick stared at him in amazement, then quickly gathered his wits. "Yes, my lord. Of course. I should have seen to it sooner."

His valet didn't remind him he had tried on numerous occasions to make the earl appear more presentable, but Marcus had refused.

To hell with him, Marcus thought. *It's none of his concern.* But in truth, he was a bit amazed himself. He had no reason to care about his appearance, so why the devil . . . ? He let the thought trail off, refusing to consider the cause of his change of heart, settled himself against the chair, and waited for Frederick to return with the scissors.

Brandy left the cottage just before noon to make the short walk to Hawksmoor House. When she arrived, she was surprised to find Rexland Delaine standing in the entry almost as if he had been waiting.

He invited her in with a smile that seemed to hold a hint of relief. "I wasn't sure . . . after the way my brother behaved . . . I though you might not return."

"I've traveled a goodly distance. A few harsh words are hardly enough to turn me away."

Rex nodded, looking even more relieved. "You said that you were staying nearby."

"That is correct. I have taken a lease on the Hammond cottage. It borders your estate on the western side."

"Yes, I am familiar with the place. I hope you're comfortable there."

"I'm there with my maid, a cook, and a chambermaid.

The view is lovely and the cottage is charming. We are all of us quite comfortable.''

Rexland cleared his throat, looking a little uneasy. He glanced around to be sure that they were alone. ''I realize it is none of my affair, but when my brother spoke of you, I got the impression you were . . . He implied that you might, perhaps, be in need of financial assistance. If money is any sort of problem—''

''I appreciate your concern, Mr. Delaine, but I'm no longer in the same situation. My father passed away a few months back. He left me very well settled. In truth, I inherited a very large sum.''

He smiled quite broadly. ''Then I shall not worry, and should my brother be concerned I will set his mind to rest as well.''

She nodded, though if yesterday was any indication, she doubted that Marcus would have the least concern. She glanced down the hall toward the drawing room he had occupied the day before. ''How is he?''

Rex Delaine shook his head. ''About the same—brooding and difficult. At least he had something to eat this morning. He usually eats barely enough to subsist.'' He smiled. ''I think you made him so mad he worked up an appetite.''

Brandy sighed. ''He certainly wasn't happy to see me.''

''I suppose on the surface it would seem so. After you left, he raged at me for nearly an hour, demanding I bar you from the door.''

Brandy groaned.

''Believe it or not, I happen to think that's a very good sign.''

An eyebrow went up. ''How could you possibly think the fact your brother loathes the sight of me could in any way be a good sign?''

Rex grinned. ''Because, my dear Miss Winters, that is the most emotion he has shown about anything since he learned that he couldn't walk.''

Brandy wasn't sure she agreed with his assessment, but it didn't really matter. She had come there to help him and she meant to find a way. She only prayed that he would let her.

''Shall we beard the lion, Miss Winters?''

She smiled. ''Waiting won't make it any easier.'' Rex offered his arm and they started down the hall. Even knowing the reception she would receive, she found herself longing to see him.

CHAPTER 14

Marcus felt like pacing. It was a habit he had never thought about before. Now that he was confined to this bloody damned chair, he missed even the smallest things that he had been able to do.

He glanced toward the door of the drawing room for perhaps the hundredth time since his arrival.

More and more he was certain that she would not come.

And why the devil should she? He had told her in no uncertain terms that she wasn't welcome, and he had meant every word.

A knock at the door interrupted his mental tirade. Rex swung it open without waiting for his permission. Marcus stiffened at the sight of the small copper-haired figure who marched in, dressed in an elaborate lavender gown. He loathed the god-awful thing on sight, and the silly little purple plumes that danced on her bonnet. He would have preferred her in her simple skirt and blouse, or even in those damnable breeches.

''I told you not to come.''

Her chin went up with the swift determination he had seen a dozen times. ''Yes, you did. And I told you I was no longer yours to order about.'' As if she ever were, he thought glumly.

''I've a bit of work to attend in my study,'' Rex said. I believe I shall leave you two to visit for a while.''

Marcus turned the brunt of his formidable temper on his brother. ''I am the Earl of Hawksmoor and lord of this house.

I command you to remove this woman at once.''

Rex just grinned. ''Sorry, did you say something, brother? I don't believe I heard what it was.'' Gingerly he stepped out of the room and closed the door, leaving them alone.

Anger worked a muscle in Marcus's jaw. His eyes swung to hers, pinning her with the same dark look he had used to command his men. Another woman would have withered beneath that fierce glare. Not Brianne Winters.

Her gaze met his, ran slowly over his face. It felt like a soft caress, warm and oddly disturbing. ''Are you not in the least glad to see me, Marcus? Once we were friends. Has your accident somehow changed that?''

He allowed his gaze to travel down her body, noting again the expensive clothes. Where had she gotten them? he suddenly wondered, and a spark of something very like jealousy slid along his deadened spine.

''It is obvious that at least some things have indeed changed. Those clothes, for example. Since you are no longer my mistress, I assume some other man is seeing to your welfare.''

Color rushed into her cheeks. Her chin hiked up a notch. ''I bought these clothes myself. My father passed away and, believe it or not, he left me a good deal of money. I'm a wealthy woman, Marcus. I'm no longer at any man's mercy, not even yours.''

He scoffed at that. ''You were hardly at my mercy. I don't believe there was a time you obeyed even one of my commands.''

She smiled at that, her lips curling prettily. God, she was lovely.

''I always obeyed your commands, Captain—as long as I agreed with them.''

His mouth edged into the faintest of smiles. It felt odd on his face and he wiped it away. ''What do you expect to accomplish by forcing your unwanted presence upon me?''

She considered that a moment, a line creasing her forehead. He wondered if she noticed he had trimmed his hair and suddenly wished he hadn't.

"I'm not certain yet. Perhaps I merely wish you to know that I'm still your friend."

Something bitter rose inside him. Something dark and perverse. "Were I not bound to this chair, my love, I'd prove we were far more than friends. I'd take you, as I did before. I'd ride you long and hard and you would soon learn what it is I need from you—and friendship is the least of it."

She blushed furiously but held her ground. "If that were all you needed, Marcus, I would gladly give it. For now, I believe there are other comforts you need far more. Perhaps I'll find a way to give you that instead."

Marcus said nothing. He had barely heard her reply. Instead, his mind was suddenly filled with images of Brianne naked. He could see her as she was the last time they had made love, her hair a fiery curtain across his pillow, her breasts high and melon-round, her nipples hard and straining against his hand.

Lust, an emotion he never thought to feel again, washed over him in a towering wave. "I want you to leave," he said hoarsely, desperately. "If you are truly my friend, you will go away and never come back here again."

Brianne said nothing for the longest time. Slowly, she walked toward him. He stiffened as she bent forward and pressed a soft kiss on his lips.

"For now, my lord, I will do as you say. But I'll be back on the morrow. And the day after that and the day after that, until you are truly healed."

"I'll never be healed, Brianne. Your coming here will not change that."

Brianne didn't answer, but her eyes held such tender emotions he had to glance away. In silence, she crossed the room, leaving him alone as he had wished. Even as the door closed quietly behind her, he could see her face as she had bent over him, taste her soft kiss on his lips.

His eyes slid closed on a surge of pain. In the last few months, he had learned to hold the pain at bay. Now it rose up with wicked force, slashing at his insides, taunting him, threatening to destroy him.

Please, he silently prayed, *make her go away.*

But even as he thought these words, another, even more fervent plea rose inside him.

Please, God, let her stay.

Brandy made her way down the hall, brushing the tears from her cheeks. She hurt for him. God, she hurt for him so much. Instead of heading for the door in the entry that led outside, she turned in the opposite direction, determined to search out his brother, wherever he might be. Surprisingly, the butler—Giles, he was called—gave her no argument, simply escorted her down a long, marble-floored hall to Rex's study.

The younger Delaine beckoned her in, rising from where he sat behind a polished rosewood desk, crossing the room and stopping just in front of her.

"So . . . you are still here. I thought by now he might have sent you running."

"He certainly gave it his best."

He smiled. "Already you've survived far longer than I would have imagined, though you do look a little bit pale. Why don't we sit down?"

Brandy nodded. "Thank you."

Rex seated her on a deep brown leather sofa then rang for tea. In moments, a footman appeared with a lovely gold-trimmed porcelain teapot and two matching cups perched on an exquisite silver tray. She thought that perhaps on such an occasion the woman should pour but the notion was daunting and she didn't know for sure. Rex took over the task himself, saving her the embarrassment of having to ask.

He handed her the teacup, adding just a bit of cream and sugar in the English way. She had discovered she liked it very much.

"How did it go?" he asked. "If the way your hands are trembling is any indication, I would have to guess my brother was as stubborn today as he was the last time you were here."

"Marcus is a very proud man. Help isn't easy for him to accept, not from me or anyone else." She took a sip of her tea, then set it with a nervous rattle back in its gold-rimmed saucer. "He looked a little better. But perhaps yesterday we simply caught him unawares."

Rex shook his head. "I don't think so. He might not admit it, but I think the improvement in his appearance is due to the fact that you have appeared."

Brandy smiled softly. "I noticed he has trimmed his hair."

His mouth tipped up at the corner. "Thank God for that. Poor Peterbrook has been after him for weeks." His lips were shaped very much like Marcus's, she saw, firm and beautifully carved. Brandy felt a pang of longing.

"His eyes looked brighter," she said, "and there seemed a bit more color in his cheeks."

Rex chuckled. "That is because you make him so angry. It's good for him, I think."

Brandy took another sip of tea, noting the interesting flavor. She'd never drank tea that tasted like the petals of a flower. "I didn't ask you before, but I would very much like to know what the doctors have to say about his condition."

Rex's broad shoulders seemed to sag. Wearily he shook his head. *He is nearly as tired as his brother,* she thought, noting the slight purple shadows beneath his light blue eyes. It occurred to her that Marcus's accident had taken its toll upon this Delaine as well.

"He's had doctors by the score," Rex said. "When I first arrived in London, a number of physicians had already been brought in. Since our return to Hawksmoor House, some of the most renowned doctors in England have been here to examine him."

"What did they say?"

Rex took a long sip of his tea, setting it very deliberately down in front of him. "Mostly, their opinions were the same—damage to the spinal cord that cannot be repaired. The certainty he will never walk again."

The words made a hard knot tighten in the pit of her stomach. " 'Mostly,' you said. Were some of a different opinion?"

"One man only, a doctor from London. He was younger, less experienced, but also less close-minded. He was the last man to examine him. Dr. Merriwether thought that perhaps there was a chance Marcus's injury was not of a permanent nature. You see, my brother's accident did not cause a paralysis of his . . . He remains in control of his bodily functions."

Brandy flushed, but did not look away. "Then perhaps there is some hope."

"Dr. Merriweather thought that if Marcus were willing to make the effort, he might be able to stimulate the muscles that move his legs. The doctor believes there may be a chance, remote though it is, that Marcus would be able to walk again. My brother, of course, did not believe him."

"Why not?"

"Because five other very good doctors told him the man was a fool. They said it was better to accept the truth of what had happened and learn to live with it than to dwell on false hope and spend his life trying to achieve something he could not."

Brandy pondered that. She tried to view the situation as Marcus would, to imagine what it might feel like to have your hopes raised, to think there might be a way to return to the life you once loved, and then to miserably fail. Still, she couldn't quite force herself to ignore this one small bit of encouragement.

"I realize you barely know me. You haven't the slightest reason to listen to my opinion or give it any sort of credence, and yet I am hoping you will."

"Marcus spoke highly of you. You have traveled thousands of miles because you care a good deal about him. That is reason enough for me to listen to whatever it is you have to say."

"Then I ask that you bring that young doctor back to Hawksmoor House to examine Marcus again."

Rex shook his head. "I wish I could, I truly do. If I actually believed there was any credence at all to his theory, I wouldn't waste a moment bringing him here. Unfortunately, I am unwilling to take the chance. If my brother became convinced he could regain the use of his legs and then failed, I'm afraid this time it would destroy him."

Brandy set her cup and saucer aside and rose from her chair, crossing the Oriental carpet to the tall mullioned window. The study, paneled in sumptuous dark wood, faced the front of the house, looking out on the winding gravel drive to the road leading into the village. Today the sun beat down on the trees along the drive and glinted off the water in the fountain at the entrance.

"Perhaps you're right," she said, her eyes on a small spotted thrush that perched on the branch of a tree. "Perhaps it isn't worth the risk." At least not yet. Not while Marcus's health was still so fragile, so uncertain. First he would have to heal, not only his body but his soul. He would have to learn to see the beauty of life, see that whether he could walk or not was unimportant.

"Will you return again tomorrow?" Rex asked, joining her at the window.

Brandy turned to face him. "As long as he needs me, I'll come."

Rex smiled. "My brother may not believe it, but in some ways, he's a very lucky man."

Brandy smiled, liking Rex Delaine more and more.

She left the big stone mansion and went back to the cottage but, as she had promised, day after day she returned. At first Marcus remained surly, lashing out at her, saying cruel things simply to hurt her.

Like the day she arrived in her pink sateen tunic dress with its bright green underskirt. It had short puffy sleeves, a high ruched collar, and tiny tucks across the bodice. Marcus hated it on sight.

"I see you have returned in another of your god-awful dresses."

Startled and stricken, her eyes swung to his face. "You . . . you do not like the way I am dressed?"

He grunted. "Pink and garish green? Hardly. With your bright coloring, you look like a little peahen who has borrowed the peacock's feathers."

A small, involuntary sound slipped from her throat. When she finally found her voice, it came out weak and uneven.

"B-but I paid a fortune for these gowns. They came from a very expensive dressmaker in Charleston. She assured me . . . sh-she said that they were the height of fashion."

He must have noticed how pale she had grown, for some of the bitterness in his voice seemed to fade. "I am certain they are. Perhaps on another woman they would look quite presentable. On you they are completely and utterly wrong."

Tears threatened. None of his other taunts had been able to make her cry. Now here she was, whimpering like a fool because he didn't like her clothes. "I thought you would be pleased," she said softly, "that you would be happy to see I could dress as well as any other woman. I thought that—" She broke off then, unable to finish.

"You thought what?"

She forced some stiffness into her backbone. "That instead of a tavern wench, perhaps you would see me as a lady."

Something moved across his features, regret for his words or perhaps something else. "There was a time I saw you as a child," he said softly. "On the ship, I saw you as a woman. Always I have seen you as a lady."

Her throat felt tight. Perhaps that was so, but it wasn't quite the same. Brandy turned away, hurt still pouring through her. "If you will excuse me, my lord. I believe I am not feeling very well." She started for the door, wishing she could run, forcing her feet to move more slowly.

"They are fools, the lot of them," he said gruffly as she walked away. "You don't need acres of lace and a forest of bows. You're far too lovely to hide behind an ocean of ruffles. You were the most beautiful woman I'd ever seen in your simple tavern maid's clothes."

Brandy stopped midway to the door. Her heart was hammering, trying to pound its way through her ribs. Slowly she turned. "Do you really believe I am . . . beautiful?"

Fierce blue eyes locked on her face. "My legs are dead. I am not. I can still appreciate a woman as lovely as you."

She didn't stop to think what she was doing, only flew across the room and straight into his arms, nearly knocking him out of his chair in the process. Marcus stiffened, his hands coming up as if to ward her off even as her mouth covered his in a kiss.

Marcus groaned.

"I've missed you," she whispered, pressing soft feathery kisses against the corners of his mouth. "Marcus, I've missed you so much."

For an instant time stood still. They were back aboard the *Seahawk,* standing together at the rail while a soft wind ruffled her skirts. Marcus's hands came up to frame her face. She could smell his bayberry cologne, feel the rough wool of his coat beneath her fingers. Slowly his mouth came down over hers and Brandy's eyes drifted closed. Her lips parted under his, accepting the thrust of his tongue as he deepened the kiss. It was sweet yet fierce, soft yet undeniably possessive. Brandy savored every moment. She didn't care if he could walk. She loved him. She only wanted to be with him.

She moaned deep in her throat, tasted the inside of his mouth with her tongue, and slid her fingers into the softly curling black hair at the nape of his neck. Something slowly shifted, altered subtly between them. Tension crept into Marcus's body and suddenly he jerked away.

Swearing foully, he untangled himself from her embrace, gripped her waist, and roughly set her from him. "Forgodsake, Brianne—what do you think you're doing? Don't you have an ounce of pity?"

His color was high, his eyes dark and snapping with anger. At the savage look on his face, Brandy's insides tightened. "What . . . what are you talking about?"

Marcus shook his head, whether in disgust at himself or her, she couldn't be sure. "God's blood—why can't you see? I'm a broken, useless, cripple. My life is over, yet when you kiss me, when you touch me that way . . ." He drew in a shuddering breath and let it out slowly. "When you touch me that way, I discover that part of me is still living. It makes me want you, Brianne. Do you have any idea what it feels like to know I can't have you? To know I am less than a man?"

"That's not true! Just because your legs don't move—"

"It isn't just my legs!" He jerked his gaze away, the muscles clamping down along his jaw. "I'm impotent, forgodsake! Do you know what that means? It means I am sitting here shaking with need for you and there is no way I can have you. I can never make love to you again. Not you or any other woman."

Brandy bit down on her trembling lips.

"I told you to go away. I begged you to leave me in peace, but you wouldn't listen. Now that you know the truth, perhaps you'll do as I say."

Brandy shook her head, feeling his torment as if it were her own. Pain slid through her in nauseating waves and the ache in her throat was nearly unbearable. "I didn't know. It never occurred to me that I . . . that you . . ." She moved away from him, off toward the window, trying to think, forcing herself simply to breathe. She closed her eyes, but tears leaked past her lashes. He was hurting, hurting so badly. Dear God, she had to help him.

The clock ticked. She dragged in a ragged breath and slowly her composure returned. Brandy walked back to the place in front of him. "I won't come near you. I'll stay away from you, if that's what you want. But I am not leaving. There are things more important than making love. We will simply have to find them."

On the arm of the chair, Marcus's hand unconsciously fisted. With a hard, dark glare, he turned away, staring past her out the window.

Brandy's heart seemed to split in two. She felt as if a thousand shards of broken glass had come slashing down on top of her. He wanted her to leave, but she couldn't bear the thought. She wanted to go to him, to tell him how much she loved him, to pull him into her arms and comfort him. The tension in his tall lean frame said that she did not dare.

Controlling an urge to weep, she crossed the room, stopping once she reached the door. "I never liked the dresses," she said softly. "I only bought them because I didn't know what else to choose and I thought that you would be pleased." She turned the silver knob and pulled it open. "Good afternoon, my lord. I will see you again on the morrow.''

Brandy left the house feeling a crushing pain—and a strange sense of elation. Marcus could not make love, but he had kissed her with unbearable longing and he had thought that she was beautiful. *Beautiful.* She clung to the word as if it were the most precious gift she had ever received.

Perhaps it was, she thought as she strode toward cottage. It certainly felt that way.

Approaching her small two-story stone house that faced the sea, she found herself smiling. ''Sally!'' she called out when she arrived, crossing the flagstone floors of the entry, stepping into the parlor beneath hand-wrought beams, stopping to warm herself in front of the timber-manteled hearth. ''Sally, are you here?''

Summer was upon them, yet on the coast there were days like this when a fire felt good inside the thick gray walls of the cottage.

The slender girl rushed down from upstairs. ''Yes, miss? I didn't hear you come in. I was busy mending some linen.''

Brandy unfastened the pink ruffled pelisse that matched her gown and tossed it onto the sofa. ''I need your help, Sally. We're going to do a little remodeling.''

''On the house?''

''No, on my clothes. We're going to go over everything I own and get rid of all those ruffles and bows.''

''But why, miss?''

''Are you telling me you like them?''

Sally flushed, color rising into her cheeks. ''Well, if you want the truth, not entirely. But it wasn't my place to say.''

''Well, I don't like them, either. Let's see what we can do to make those dresses look better.''

Sally grinned. ''All right, miss. I think I can manage that.''

Brandy smiled, but already she was imagining what Marcus would say when he saw them, hoping this time he'd be pleased. And she was wondering, deep down inside where she knew she shouldn't, if perhaps he was wrong about being able to make love.

Chapter 15

Marcus heard the sound of his brother's footfalls striding down the marble-floored hall toward the Oceanview Drawing Room. They were joined by another, lighter set, yet they were a man's and he wondered who it was.

Irritation trickled through him. He didn't want visitors. Rex knew that. And yet it was obvious someone had come to call and he would be forced to receive him. Marcus sat up a little straighter in the chair that would forever cage him, and fixed his attention on the door, his brows drawn nearly together.

Surprise lifted them a fraction. He knew the man who walked in, Richard Lockhart, youngest son of the Marquess of Halliday. Richard had spent a good deal of his childhood at Seacliff, his father's estate on the opposite side of Tintagel, and though Richard was two years younger and they were nothing at all alike, once they had been close friends.

Rex followed him in and closed the door. "A friend has just arrived. Richard has been away on the Continent. He only recently returned to England and learned of your accident. He came straightaway to see you."

This was the part Marcus hated above all else, the surprise in people's eyes when they saw how thin he had become, the pity that lingered even though they worked to hide it.

He tried to smile, but his lips were no longer used to the movement and only faintly curved. "I trust things have been better for you of late, my friend, than they have obviously been for me." He tried to sound glib, casual about what had happened, but the effort was futile and he knew that he had failed. He forced himself not to glance away.

Richard walked toward him. "I won't mince words, Marcus. I know you would loathe it if I did. I am utterly appalled by what has occurred. You have my sympathy, though I know you well enough to know you don't want it. Mostly, I simply came because I wished to see you. I have been dreadfully worried since I heard the news."

Honesty. It was a rare ingredient in a situation such as this. He found himself remembering why it was the two of them had been friends. Marcus looked into Richard's green eyes, saw concern there instead of pity, and felt an uncommon thread of relief.

"Strange . . . I believe I am actually glad to see you."

Richard relaxed at the words, and his lips curved up. He was a man of medium height and slender build with sandy brown hair and refined features, and his smile was gentle. He had always been a gentle man. Marcus remembered that about him.

"I shall be staying at Seacliff for some months," Richard said. "I have been doing some research for a book on life in Medieval England. I thought the quiet of Cornwall would be a good place to finish the final portion of the work."

Richard, always the studious one. He had wanted to be a professor, Marcus recalled, but his family had frowned on the notion, determined that he should join the clergy. Finally, grudgingly, they had accepted his interest in history and his intention to research and write about it.

"Cornwall hasn't changed," Marcus said. "The place is utterly timeless."

"You used to love it here."

Marcus felt a tightening in his chest. There was a time he had, but that was long ago. Long before he had found the sea and his true calling. He made no reply and the room fell silent. Rex cleared his throat, prepared to step into the breach, but the patter of feminine footfalls held him back. All three men turned to the door just in time to see the butler usher in Brianne Winters.

"I brought her as you wished, sir, as soon as she arrived at the house."

"Thank you, Giles." Rex turned to the woman who now stood near the door. She was gowned in a plain yellow muslin day dress, no ruffles, no flounces, no frills, her fiery hair swept into sleek, soft curls atop her head. She wore white cotton gloves but no bonnet, and she looked so achingly lovely the breath froze in Marcus's lungs.

"Good morning, Miss Winters," his brother said, pulling her gaze away from where it rested on Marcus's face. "I was hoping you would arrive in time to meet an old family friend. Lord Richard Lockhart, may I present to you Miss Brianne Winters."

For a moment, Richard just stared. When he realized what he was doing, faint color crept into his cheeks. Then he smiled with such warmth Marcus felt a thread of irritation.

"Miss Winters. It is a pleasure to meet you." He made an extravagant bow and Brandy made a slightly off-balance curtsy in return.

"And you as well, my lord."

She was nervous, he saw. She wasn't used to moving in upper-class social circles, and she wasn't quite sure what to do. Watching the heightened flush in her cheeks, he had the sudden, ridiculous urge to shield her from embarrassment. Where the absurd thought came from, he hadn't the vaguest notion. Ruthlessly, he forced it away.

In the end, he needn't have worried. Like the rest of the males she encountered, his friend took one look into those catlike amber eyes and any notion of social graces went sailing out the window. It was only too obvious that Richard was smitten.

Marcus's irritation blossomed into an unmistakable kernel of jealousy.

"The three of us practically grew up together," Rex was saying to Brianne. "Richard is the author of several texts on British history. He'll be working here in Cornwall for at least the next several months."

Brandy smiled. "That's wonderful. I'm sure Lord Hawksmoor will be delighted to have a friend so close at hand."

Richard looked at her and his smile went even brighter. Then he looked at Marcus, caught his blatant glare, and the smile slipped away. "I am certainly glad to be back," he said. "And I look forward to the company of such old friends." Richard seemed to collect himself, to put the pieces together and accept the fact that the girl was spoken for.

She wasn't, of course. It was a ridiculous notion. Marcus had no room in his life for a woman, and even if he had, there was no chance of it happening now. He glanced at Brandy, saw no particular interest in her eyes when she looked at Richard, and felt an unwelcome trickle of relief. It was insane, he knew. He should be encouraging Richard's interest. His friend might not be wealthy but neither was he a pauper. In truth, he'd be considered a very good catch.

Richard was smiling again at Brianne, but it seemed a different sort of smile, and Marcus felt another spiral of relief.

"My mother and father send their regards," Richard was saying. "Mother may be joining me in a couple of weeks. Perhaps, if Lord Hawksmoor is feeling up to it, we might all get together. I could arrange a small dinner party. We could renew our acquaintance and discuss old times."

A dinner party. *Fat chance,* Marcus silently grumbled. Just what he wanted to do, go to another man's house and let every one there see the invalid he had become.

"What do you think, Marcus?" Richard asked.

"I think I'm beginning to tire," he lied. "If you all will please excuse me . . ." Without waiting for their reply, he turned in his chair, facing away from them, and began to stare out at the water. As silence descended on the room, he almost smiled. There were some advantages to being a cripple. Being rude and overbearing apparently was one of them.

He heard the sound of footsteps as his friends escaped his presence. The doors to the drawing room closed with a thud and he leaned back in his chair. The sound of a woman's voice, tight with anger, wiped the satisfied smile off his face.

"That was incredibly rude and obnoxious. I cannot believe you would treat a friend that way."

His head snapped around. Brandy stood with her small feet splayed and her hands planted firmly on her hips. Bloody hell—would the woman never leave him in peace? "I thought I told you I was tired."

"You are not tired in the least. You are simply being obstinate."

He clamped hard on his jaw. "What did you expect me to do—sit there and encourage him? I am hardly a candidate for social occasions. I have to be carried about like a child."

"Perhaps that is the reason you are behaving like one. If I were your mother, I would put you over my knee."

The image was so absurd, Marcus actually laughed. "But you are not my mother, are you, love?"

Her pretty mouth softened, turned up at the corners. "No, I am not. I am your friend—just like Richard Lockhart."

Marcus arched a brow. "Not exactly like Richard. You, in fact, are a female. A very pretty, very appealing female. If I were still a man, I would show you exactly how different you are from Richard Lockhart."

A soft flush rose in her cheeks. "You *are* a man and you are maddening."

"And you, my sweet, are utterly irresistible. God, what I wouldn't give to be able to strip away that pretty dress and fill my hands with those beautiful breasts."

Her cheeks, already pink, brightened to a dark shade of rose. "I'm not at all certain I like this person you've become, Marcus Delaine. You taunt me with your words. Do you think I feel nothing when you speak to me that way? It makes me want you, Marcus—and we both know I am forbidden to touch you."

Surprise hit him first. She wanted him. He hadn't even considered the possibility. He wasn't the man he was—how could she possibly still feel desire for him? His eyes swept the length of her body, taking in her womanly curves, the soft rise and fall of her breasts. Remembering the way it had felt to cup them, Marcus felt a powerful surge of lust and a sudden, unexpected twinge in his groin. It was impossible. He knew that for certain. He waited, praying it would happen again, but it did not, and he realized he was mistaken.

Anger rose in the place of lust. "I don't know why you keep coming here. It can do neither of us any good. Whatever we once had is over. I'm not the man I was and you are no longer that same young girl."

"No, I am not. You made me a woman, Marcus, and for that I will always be grateful."

"You told me you are wealthy. If that is the case, you can finally do the things you've always wanted. You can travel, see the world. There is no reason for you to stay here."

"There is every reason. I'm here because of you."

He only shook his head. "Why can I not convince you?"

Brianne moved in his direction. "It's you who needs convincing. You have to learn there is more to life than striding the deck of a ship, that you still have a great deal to live for."

"The sea is my life—it always will be. Since I can never return to it, I have nothing at all to live for."

Brianne moved toward him, so close her skirt brushed his legs, but as she had promised, she didn't touch him. For an instant, he wished he could call back his hasty words.

"You're the Earl of Hawksmoor. There are people who need you, people you could help if you were willing."

"I told you—my life is the sea. That's where I belong. A ship and its crew—those are the people who need me."

"Your brother needs you. If you weren't so selfish—if you didn't spend every moment wallowing in self-pity—you would see that for yourself."

"What are you talking about? My brother is a strong, self-reliant young man."

"Yes, he is. But take a look at him, Marcus—a good, long look. Can't you see the weariness in his face? Every time I come here, your brother is working. He rarely leaves the house. You could help carry some of the burden if you only would."

Marcus shook his head. "I'm not cut out for that sort of thing. I never wanted to be an earl."

"We don't always get what we want, my lord. Sometimes God makes those decisions for us."

He glanced away, unable to meet those amber eyes that seemed to see right through him. Was he really being selfish? Was he wallowing in self-pity? Marcus had the uncomfortable feeling there might be some truth to her words. "What do you want from me? What do you want me to do?"

She smiled at him. God, she was so pretty. "Nothing much. For starters, perhaps we could go out in the garden."

"That's it? That is what you want?"

"To begin with, yes. After that, we'll have to wait and see."

It was madness to be swayed by the tenderness in her expression. His gaze traveled over the roundness of her breasts, and lust rose up again, goading him as it always did whenever she was near. If they had been aboard his ship, he would have dragged her down to his cabin and ripped away her expensive clothes. He would have taken her swiftly, buried himself inside her until this towering hunger was sated.

Instead he looked into those tilted amber eyes and thought how insane it was to do the woman's bidding.

And yet it seemed such a small request. "All right," he grudgingly agreed. "If it will make you happy, tomorrow we'll spend time in the garden."

Her smile was so bright, her eyes so full of joy, his heart expanded inside him.

"Thank you, my lord." The words, spoken so softly, with so much gratitude, sounded as if she had just been gifted with the English crown jewels.

Marcus looked away, suddenly wishing he had the power to give them to her.

Brandy returned to the cottage more hopeful than she had been since her arrival. Each day after that she returned to Hawksmoor House, staying a little longer, joining Marcus for tea in the garden, then a week later staying when Rex invited her to sup with them. Marcus grumbled each time she appeared, but each time he grumbled a little less.

By the fourth week of her stay in Tintagel, Marcus had put on most of the weight he had lost and his cheeks were no longer hollow and pale. His skin was a golden bronze, darkened again by the hours he now spent in the sun. His hair had grown a bit and curled softly over his collar. Every time she looked at him, she thought how handsome he was, every bit the virile, masculine man she had known before, and every bit as appealing.

"Will you join me today in the garden?" she asked, finding him as she usually did seated in front of the window. " 'Tis such a lovely day. The sun is out and the birds are singing."

"It's cloudy, not sunny, and if I wanted to go outside, I would be there." It was a game they played, Marcus grumbling and hard to convince, Brandy teasing him into compliance as she was doing now.

She smiled at him sweetly. "Perhaps you would do it for me."

Marcus eyed her darkly, then gave up an exaggerated sigh. "You are a shrew of the very worst sort, bullying a man who cannot defend himself."

She glanced around as if she were searching. "Where? Where is such a man? Surely you do not refer to yourself?"

Marcus chuckled softly. "Perhaps you are right. Perhaps the only person I need defending against is you."

And so it went, Marcus progressing each day, growing stronger, coming to terms with himself and his situation. He had even begun looking into the management of the estate, taking over several tasks from his brother, which helped to lighten Rex's considerable load. Brandy was grateful for each small improvement, her heart full of hope, her love for him growing with each passing day.

It was dangerous, she knew. She wouldn't be able to stay with him forever, and Marcus wasn't interested in marriage, especially now that he had lost the use of his legs. Even if he were, he was an earl. He was hardly likely to wed with a tavern maid.

And there was the darkness, the inner turmoil he carried inside him that she could never seem to reach. It was always there between them and she feared it always would be. At night she dreamed about him, but even in the dream he never held her, never kissed her. And night after night the dream always ended the same: Brandy standing alone on the dock, her whole body aching as Marcus left her and returned to sea.

Hamish Bass stepped off the mail coach in front of the Gull's Head Inn in Tintagel on the Cornwall coast. He stretched his aching muscles, weary from the long, uncomfortable journey from London.

Damn, he was getting old.

Inside the tavern, he paused long enough for a hot meal and a tankard of ale, then paid a few shillings for a ride out of town in the back of a hay wagon. With a wave of thanks, he jumped down from the wooden tailgate, slung his haversack over one shoulder, and started up the long gravel drive to Hawksmoor House.

Hamish didn't like coming to the big intimidating mansion, nor the task he had set for himself.

"Has to be done," he said aloud. "There's no avoidin' it. Cap'n'd never forgive me."

Determinedly, he walked toward the wide stone porch, his slightly bowed legs making his steps uneven. He shifted his haversack from one shoulder to the other, lifted the shiny brass knocker shaped like a hawk with its wings unfurled, and slammed it down on the carved mahogany front door.

Though he had only been to the big house on one other occasion, the butler seemed to know who he was and without a bit of fanfare, motioned for him to come in.

"I've come to see Cap'n Delaine. 'Tis important or I wouldn't be here."

"Of course, Mr. Bass. Lord Hawksmoor left a standing order some years back, should any of his crew arrive here for whatever reason they were to be brought to him in all haste. I presume that order still stands. Please come in."

"Ye have me thanks."

"I shall tell his lordship you are here. He is entertaining a visitor out in the garden."

Hamish pondered that. Entertaining a visitor? The last he'd

heard, the captain was little more'n a dead man, holed up like a mole and starin' out at the sea.

The butler, a tall thin man with short brown slicked-back hair, returned a few moments later. "If you will please follow me, I will take you to him. You may leave your bag and I shall have it put away in your room."

"There's no need a that. I can stay at the inn in the village."

"Nonsense. His lordship would be quite displeased should he discover you have journeyed so far and did not receive a decent place to stay."

Hamish said no more, though in truth he would have felt more comfortable staying somewhere else. All the fancy moldings and marble floors, the gold on the mirrors, and even the walls made him nervous. What the devil would he do if he broke something?

"Mr. Bass?"

"I'm a-comin'."

Disgruntled, he left the bag and followed the tall man down a long hall covered in fancy gold paper and out into a big formal garden that overlooked the sea.

Captain Delaine was there, sitting on a stack of pillows that had been placed on a wrought-iron bench. He was smiling, lord love it, and standing beside him was surely the cause.

At first he might not have known her in her pretty lavender dress, but he couldn't miss all that shiny copper hair. Hamish smiled at Brandy Winters, and the girl smiled in return.

"It's good to see you, Hamish," the captain said.

"Aye, as it is you, Cap'n . . . and you, too, Miss Brandy."

"Thank you, Hamish. I hope you are well."

"Right as rain, miss, to be sure."

"Brandy is visiting here in Cornwall. She lives in a cottage not far away."

Hamish nodded, pleased at the notion. "You're lookin' real pretty, Miss Brandy. I'm sure Captain Delaine is glad for the company." But when he looked in that direction, he wasn't really so sure. There was a darkness in the cap'n's eyes, pain and hunger as well. He wanted the girl, Hamish saw, and now, as it was then, he could not have her.

"I've news of the *Seahawk,* Cap'n. 'Tisn't good, I'm afraid."

The captain's broad shoulders went tense. He sat up straighter in his makeshift chair. "Get on with it, Hamish. Tell me what has happened."

"It's about the accident, sir. 'Tweren't really that, ye see. 'Twere sabotage, plain and simple." The captain's face went pale, which was noticeable since it was dark again as it was when he was at sea. "Took us months to figure it out. We nearly didn't—not until they was workin' down in the bottom of the hull. Sludge covered it for a while, but then one of the workmen seen it when the crew was muckin' out the bilge."

"What did he see, Hamish?" the captain prodded, his features no longer relaxed.

"Some of the bolts was removed from the mast where it was stepped against the hull. That's why it split. Come loose a little at a time. Got to leanin' in the storm. Someone meant for it to break, Cap'n. Coulda taken the whole blasted ship down."

The captain's hand tightened into a fist. He slammed it down on his useless legs. "I knew it. I tried to tell myself I was wrong, but deep down I knew it all along. I'll find him. I swear to God I will. If it's the last thing I do on this earth, I'll find that bastard, and when I do I'm going to kill the son of a bitch."

Miss Brandy knelt and took his hand. "I'm sorry, Marcus. So sorry."

The captain jerked away. "Leave me!" he shouted. "Both of you. Just get out and leave me alone."

Hamish didn't argue. Coming here had been the last thing he'd wanted to do. He'd known the pain his news would bring, but there was no help for it.

"It's all right, Hamish," Brandy said softly, once they had stepped back into the house. "It isn't your fault. He had to know. In time, he'll come to grips with it."

Hamish only shook his head. "Nay, lass. Not this. The

cap'n'll want revenge. He won't settle for anything less. 'Twill eat him alive, I fear.''

The girl's jaw tightened, then hiked into the air. ''No, it won't. I won't let it. I'll find a use for all that anger and hatred. I'll find a way to channel it into something else.''

Hamish reached out and stroked her hair, feeling a twinge of admiration. ''Good luck to ye, lass. If anyone can do it, 'twill be you.'' But he didn't hold much hope that she would succeed. He didn't think anyone could rid the captain of the powerful hatred he was feeling.

Not even Brandy Winters.

Stepping out into the hall, Brandy closed the door to the Oceanview Drawing Room and leaned against it. Behind the door, she heard the sound of shattering glass, then something solid crashed against the wall.

An ache rose in her chest as she thought of the bitter man on the opposite side of the door. Marcus had come so far, made so much progress. Now he was hurting again, and she was determined to do something about it. Dragging in a shaky breath, she made her way through the maze of halls and galleries, then shoved open the door to Rex Delaine's study unannounced.

''I have to see you, Rex. It's important.'' They had long since done away with the formality of mister and miss. They were comrades brought together for a common cause; each knew it, accepted it. Each appreciated the other's concern for Marcus and was grateful for the help.

Rex arched a sleek black brow and came to his feet behind the desk. ''From the flush in your cheeks and the fire in your eyes I can see that it is. Perhaps you had better close the door.''

She didn't hesitate, merely did as he suggested, then walked to his desk and stood in front of it. When Rex motioned for her to sit down, she simply shook her head.

''I can't stand it, Rex. In the three days since Hamish Bass was here, your brother's been a madman. Everything we've worked to accomplished is going to go by the wayside if we don't find a way to reach him."

Rex sighed and raked long fingers though his thick black hair. "I was afraid of this. Ever since the accident, I've been praying that was exactly what it was. I was afraid to imagine how Marcus might react if he discovered someone actually had a hand in what happened to him."

"He's behaving like a lunatic. When he isn't plotting to find the man who did it, he's ranting and raving about what he's going to do to him once he discovers who it is. He's eaten up with hatred, consumed by thoughts of revenge."

"In time, it will lessen."

"On the surface, perhaps, but not deep down inside. Revenge is all he thinks about. It's a terrible malignancy, Rex. It's more likely to destroy him than anything he has suffered thus far."

"I don't disagree. Unfortunately, I have no idea what to do about it. Before the accident, my brother was a strong, powerful man. A good deal of that strength has returned, to a great degree because of you. His drive for revenge is making him even stronger. Now he intends to use the power he wields as the Earl of Hawksmoor in any way he can to find the man who destroyed his life. Under the same set of circumstances, I would probably do the same thing."

Brandy started pacing, her pale blue skirt swirling at every turn. "When you put it that way, I can almost understand. But even if I do, that doesn't change the fact that it's the wrong thing to do." She stopped pacing and returned to the opposite side of the desk from where he had sat back down.

"I've been thinking, Rex. As you just said, Marcus is a great deal stronger than he was, not just physically, but mentally as well. I think you should bring that doctor back, the one from London who thought there was a chance he might walk again."

Rex sat forward in his chair. "Dr. Merriweather?"

"Yes."

"I told you I wouldn't do that. I haven't changed my mind."

Brandy leaned over and gripped his hands. "But you must, Rex. You have to at least pursue the possibility. You told me Dr. Merriweather thinks that if Marcus were willing to make the effort, he might be able to stimulate the muscles in his legs. I presume that effort is considerable?"

"So I gathered."

"Then what better way to channel this terrible rage that's consuming him? What better way than to give him the challenge to walk again?"

Rex said nothing for the longest time. Brandy held her breath, silently praying, wanting this chance for Marcus, unwilling to admit she wanted it for herself.

Rex closed his eyes and leaned back in his chair. For a while, with Marcus helping him run the estate, he'd looked younger, less weary. Since Hamish had arrived with his dreadful news, there were dark circles under his eyes and his face was pale.

"All right," he said at last. "I'll send for Merriweather."

Brandy made a little yip of delight, leaned over the desk, and threw her arms around his neck. "Thank you. Thank you so much."

Rex gently unwound himself and set her away. There was something in his eyes she hadn't noticed there before, but she couldn't tell what it was.

"You're welcome," he said, "but you might not want to thank me yet. Merriweather might reexamine him and conclude something altogether different this time. Or even if his opinion remains the same, Marcus may refuse."

Brandy set her jaw. "If the doctor says there is the slightest chance, I won't let him refuse."

"And if he tries and fails? What will you do then?"

Brandy's chest constricted. She couldn't bear to think of it, couldn't bear to imagine the suffering it would cause. She blinked against the unwanted sting of tears. "I'll love him, Rex, just like I always have. And somehow I'll help him get through it."

Rex Delaine said nothing more, but the turbulence had returned to his eyes. "My brother is a fool," he said softly.

"I've never thought that before, but right now I do."

Brandy didn't know what he meant and she didn't press him to find out. The darkness in his expression warned her not to.

CHAPTER 16

Sitting behind the walnut desk in the small book-lined library he now used as his study, Marcus reviewed the top sheet on the stack of papers he had been handed.

Two men sat across from him, Mickey Reynolds and Colin Kelly. Both were Bow Street runners. Tall and stout, Reynolds was a block of a man with frizzy brown hair and heavy sideburns. He had been hired when the first of the "accidents" that had plagued Hawksmoor Shipping had begun to occur. Colin Kelly, Reynolds's partner, a thinner man, more dapperly dressed, had been brought on board when the disaster had happened aboard *Seahawk* and Marcus had lost the use of his legs.

"You've done a good deal of work," Marcus said. "Your information on Atlantic Limited is extremely thorough. From what I can discern from this, you've pretty much eliminated them from the list of possible suspects."

"Yes, that was our conclusion as well, your lordship." Reynolds sat on the edge of his chair. "The company seems to be running smoothly and there doesn't appear to be anyone in authority who might be the sort to go to such extremes as to sabotage your ships."

"And the China Seas Company?"

Kelly, the Irishman, stepped in to answer that. " 'Tis sorry I am to say, milord, we aren't yet certain. The man at the top—they say he's ruthless, willin' to do anything a-tall to make money for the company. Whether or not that means puttin' a whole ship in danger o' sinkin', we don't yet know."

"You're talking about Oliver St. Simon," Marcus said, having met the man who ran the company on several different occasions.

"Aye, sir, that I am. St. Simon's the sort would sell out his own mother if he thought there'd be a profit in it."

Anger crept into Marcus's chest, making it tighten painfully. "I know St. Simon. And I agree with your assessment. What I need to know is whether or not St. Simon is the man responsible for what happened to my ship."

"We're working on it, my lord," Reynolds said. "We've been trying to make an inroad into the company. Recently, we've been able to bring a man on board who works there. Since the fellow is in a position of some authority, we're hoping he'll be able to uncover information that will settle the matter once and for all."

Marcus nodded, controlling his anger, the hatred that bubbled like a cauldron of acid inside him. It wasn't the answer he wanted, but he had known from the start it was going to take some time.

Time, he thought bitterly, was the one thing he had plenty of.

"We haven't discussed Reese Enterprises. You mention in your report that besides the China Seas Company, you find Palmer Reese—or someone in his employ—a very likely candidate."

"Aye, sir," Kelly said. "Mr. Reese is in financial straits. He's been tryin' ta keep it secret, but the word on the street is the man is in trouble and has been for a good bit o' time."

Palmer Reese. Was he capable of the kind of malice it took to destroy a company without the slightest consideration for the human losses that might be incurred in the process? He had known Palmer for years. Marcus had always thought him a weakling, a whiner, rather gutless, and certainly not the sort to engineer a campaign like this.

"Are you certain the rumors are true?"

"Not yet, sir, but we'll soon be findin' out."

Marcus pondered that, thinking that if Palmer was in financial straits he certainly didn't show it. "Is there a chance this was done by a single individual who might hold some sort of grudge, a sailor or perhaps a disgruntled employee?''

Both men shook their heads. ''The damage was too widespread,'' Reynolds said. ''It wasn't just *Seahawk,* but *Peregrine* and *Raven* as well. A man would need considerable capital to ferret out and hire the right man to handle each job.''

He had known that, of course, but he felt he'd had to ask. ''As I said, you've collected an interesting assortment of information so far. Now it's time to go forward. I want you to discover who has profited the most from Hawksmoor Shipping losses, particularly since *Seahawk* has been grounded. It's likely that all of the shippers have benefited to some degree, but it should be interesting to discover which one has gained the most. Whichever company is responsible for the sabotage—assuming that is the case—would undoubtedly have been prepared to go after the contracts we've had to give up. They would have had the most opportunity to win them.''

Reynolds shifted his large frame back in his chair. ''That is a very astute observation, my lord. We'll start working on it as soon as we arrive back in London.''

''Aye, that we will,'' Kelly put in. ''There's every chance, milord, by the time you hear from us again, we'll know exactly who your nemesis is.''

Marcus didn't say more. He ignored the ache that had risen in his back and instead rubbed his useless legs, wishing he could feel the ache there as well, instead of only numbness. An image of Palmer Reese rose into his mind. Palmer, smooth and articulate, so slick and polished he was almost greasy, Marcus used to think.

He had never liked Palmer Reese, though his father had been a friend of Palmer's father and often invited father and son to Hawksmoor House to visit.

Back then, Palmer had merely been selfish and annoying. Now Marcus wondered if Palmer was the man behind his troubles—and if one day he would be the man to kill him.

* * *

Brandy stood in the hall outside Marcus's study, watching two men, one large and stocky, the other slim and well dressed, walk out the door. They were Bow Street runners, Rex had told her, men Marcus had been paying to discover who had sabotaged his ships.

She shuddered to think of it, to recall the hatred in his eyes whenever he spoke of it, the need for vengeance that buried whatever else he felt inside.

"Are you ready?" Rex Delaine stood beside her, tall and dark and nearly as handsome as his brother. They had decided to broach the problem together, which was rather like an army of two prepared to do battle against a well-trained battalion.

"I'm rarely ready to face Marcus in one of his tirades—and there is certain to be one. Unfortunately, I haven't much choice. Not when Dr. Merriweather is sitting in the drawing room down the hall."

Rex smiled in that same warm, masculine way Marcus always used to. God, how she missed that smile.

They pushed open the door and found him bent over his desk. She wished it were Hawksmoor ledgers he poured over with such fanatical interest. Instead, it was a stack of information the runners had brought for his review, notes on possible suspects.

"I'm sorry to interrupt," Rex said, and his brother's dark head snapped up. "There is a subject we need to discuss."

Marcus cocked a bold black brow, his long fingers wrapped around a silver-inlaid, white-plumed pen. His gaze swung from Rex to Brandy and back again. "And just what subject is that?"

Rex ushered her into the room and closed the door behind them. The suspicion on Marcus's face made her heart start pounding even harder than it was already, and her legs felt rubbery and weak. She knew how stubborn he could be. She prayed with all her heart he would give himself this chance.

"We're here to discuss the subject of your recovery," Rex said.

"My recovery?" It was the last thing he'd expected to hear Rex say and he straightened, giving them his full attention. "What in blazes are you talking about?"

Brandy walked toward him, pausing midway to his desk. "Your brother and I are here in regard to a visitor who has, at our request, traveled from London to see you. Dr. Winifred Merriweather. You may recall meeting him in the city."

Marcus very carefully replaced the quill pen back in its silver holder. "I recall him quite clearly, in fact. Correct me if I'm wrong, but isn't he the same man five of England's top physicians called a bloody fool?"

Irritation made her heart beat even faster, rattling around inside her chest. "Perhaps *they* are the fools."

"Get on with it. What are the two of you trying to say?"

Rex moved closer to the desk. "We want you to let the doctor have another look at you. If Merriweather still believes there's a chance you can walk again, we want you to give it a try."

Marcus's face turned dark. "You want me to give it a try?" His fist slammed down on the top of his desk. "In the name of God, do you really believe that I haven't tried? There isn't a day that goes by I don't try with every ounce of my will to force my useless legs to make one tiny little movement. It doesn't happen. It is never going to happen! I thought you of all people understood that." He swung a hard look on Brandy. "Or has Miss Winters and her infernal optimism somehow convinced you that both of us are wrong?"

Brandy closed the short space to the front of the desk and braced her palms on the front. "I may be an optimist, Marcus, but if I am, I'm grateful for it. I realize you believe you will never walk again and perhaps you never will. But if there is a single chance, even the tiniest possibility, then you owe it to yourself to explore that chance. It would mean taking a risk, yes. You'd be exposing yourself to hopes that might never be fulfilled, but the man I knew aboard the *Seahawk* was not afraid to take risks."

"I am no longer that man."

"Aren't you? I think you are. Besides—what risk is there in simply seeing the man, listening to what he has to say?"

Marcus didn't answer. Brandy sensed the turmoil inside

him, the desperate fear fighting the terrible need.

"Speak to him, Marcus," she pleaded. "Give yourself at least that much. Rex and I will be with you. If the doctor changes his opinion, if this time he thinks it's hopeless, you can gloat over how right you were and what fools we've made of ourselves."

Marcus said nothing, but the battle inside him was plain on his face. He rubbed a hand over his eyes. "I can't . . . I don't know if . . ."

Brandy played her final card. "Those files you've been reading—the ones brought by the Bow Street runners. You're studying them because you intend to find the man responsible for your accident."

"What does that have to do with—"

"Think what you could do if you could walk."

Marcus's whole body went tense. A muscle leaped in his cheek. The hatred she had seen a dozen times stole into his features, making his face look harsh. Still, he said nothing.

Finally he nodded. "All right, I'll see him." He gave her a bitter half smile. "How can I not when you have phrased it so succinctly?"

Brandy shuddered at the bitterness in his tone. She wanted to reach out and touch him, to hold him and take away his pain.

Instead, two footmen appeared through a side door to lift his chair and he was carried into a small private drawing room down the hall. A slender, nonnondescript man in spectacles with light brown hair and mild features turned from where he had been pacing and smiled.

"Lord Hawksmoor. It is a pleasure to see you again." The young man's eyes roamed the length of Marcus's frame and brightened with approval. "You're looking very well. The sea air has been good for you."

Marcus flicked an unreadable glance at Brandy, then returned his gaze to the physician. "The sea has always been good for me." He motioned for the footmen to set his chair down near the sofa. "My brother and Miss Winters have persuaded me to submit myself to your devilish prodding and poking. If that is what you've come here to do, let's get on with it. I have more important matters to attend than humoring my friends in their fantasy.''

The doctor said nothing to that, simply nodded and walked over to his small leather satchel. He opened it and began to set out his tools.

''I'll send Frederick down to help you disrobe,'' Rex said to Marcus. ''Miss Winters and I shall wait in the Green Drawing Room until you send word that we may return.''

As they stepped out into the hall, Marcus grumbled something Brandy couldn't hear and Rex closed the door. Her palms were sweating, her heart still hammering madly. They entered the Green Room and she seated herself on a dark green brocade sofa, then waited while Rex ordered tea. He joined her a few moments later, seating himself beside her, smiling and doing his best to entertain her, but her thoughts kept drifting and she couldn't keep her mind on the conversation. Eventually he gave up and both of them lapsed into silence.

She tried not to think of Marcus, of what he must be feeling, but it was impossible. Dear God, was she doing the right thing? She had pressed him into the examination, pressed both of the brothers to take this chance. What if the doctor changed his mind? Would Marcus lose the last of his hope? Perhaps he already had, but she didn't really think so.

Every day he tried to move his legs, he had said. Hope, Brandy believed, still burned like a tiny flame inside him. If Merriweather no longer believed in Marcus's recovery, it might douse the last dying ember of that flame.

She shifted on the sofa. Tension made the inside of her mouth feel dry. ''It seems to be taking forever.''

Rex looked up from the paper he was pretending to read. ''I should rather have the fellow take a bit more time than to make the wrong pronouncement.''

Her stomach twisted, tied itself into a knot. ''Yes, yes, of course. I certainly feel that way, too.'' But it didn't make the waiting any easier. Silence descended again. She began to notice the ticking of the clock—no, there were several, she realized, a gilt one on the mantel, a black teak on a carved wooden table along the wall, a smaller, porcelain-faced clock painted with tiny blue flowers, all of them ticking at once and grating on her nerves.

The minutes stretched into more than an hour. Rex had abandoned any pretense of reading and was pacing in front of the window. Brandy fidgeted on the sofa, took a sip of her now-cold tea, then a sharp knock sounded on the drawing room door.

"Thank God." Rex strode in that direction. "No matter what the doctor says, it can't be any worse than the terrible thoughts running through my head."

That was the truth. And so together they made their way down the hall to the room where the doctor waited, pausing only an instant to gather their wits before Rex shoved open the tall, ornate doors.

Marcus sat on a sofa across the room, dressed as he was before, in dove-gray breeches, a white lawn shirt, and a navy blue tailcoat. His expression was so closed and hard she was certain the news must be bad.

Her heart wrenched. Dear God, what had she done? She wanted to help him and all she had accomplished was to cause him more pain. She swallowed so hard she was certain they could hear it. Her legs were shaking as she crossed the Oriental carpet. Knowing she shouldn't, unable to resist, she sat down on the sofa next to Marcus. He scowled, but didn't ask her to move. On impulse she reached over and caught his hand, brought it to her lips, and pressed a soft kiss in the palm.

I love you, she wanted to say. *None of this matters. I love you so much.*

Instead she dragged her eyes from his face, met his brother's worried gaze, saw the reflection of her own fears there, and forced herself to turn in the doctor's direction. She was surprised to see him smiling.

"I haven't changed my mind, if that is what both of your grim expressions are about. I am convinced, as I was before, that should Lord Hawksmoor take the proper course of action, there is a good chance he could recover the use of his legs."

"Why is it, then," Marcus ground out, "no other of a half dozen prominent physicians are in agreement with you?"

The doctor replaced an odd-looking instrument shaped like a hammer into his bag. "Perhaps they are afraid. You are a very powerful man, my lord. Should their advice prove faulty, odds are you would not look kindly upon them. In fact, your wrath could become quite unbearable."

Marcus eyed him darkly. "But you're not afraid. Why is that, Dr. Merriweather?"

The doctor placed the last of his instruments into his small leather satchel. "That is quite simple, my lord. I am young yet and not well established. I am willing to take chances other physicians are not. And I believe in myself. I am convinced there is the chance you could walk again, and if I am correct, I imagine you could be extremely grateful. Put simply—for me, the risk is worth the return."

"And what of the risk I will be taking?" Marcus said.

"You have nothing to lose and everything to gain. Unfortunately, you have nearly waited too long already. In my experience, if the patient does not begin to recover within the first six months, chances are he never will."

Rex spoke up just then. "You are saying it isn't too late? That there is yet time, if my brother were to take immediate action, for the muscles to begin to work again?"

"That is my opinion."

"And just what action are you talking about?" Marcus asked. He was reacting as he had been since the accident, hiding his vulnerability behind a wall of acid. But even as he tried to disguise it, Brandy could feel his rising hope. And one way or another, she meant to see he took the risk.

"You would need someone to work with you on a daily basis," the doctor said. "Someone to massage your legs, to help you strengthen the muscles. I recommend heated bathing of the limbs as a means of helping to relax them. We would need some equipment, of course, things to help you move about, supports you could use while you are forcing your muscles to move."

"Frederick is large enough," Rex said. "He is used to moving you around. And building whatever you require would not be a problem."

Marcus seemed to ponder that. "Yes, if I were foolish enough to agree, Frederick could help—in part. But I would not be comfortable with a man working over me in such an intimate fashion as you have described." He swung a hard look on Brandy. "For that I would require the help of someone else."

"Who?" Rex asked.

Marcus's mouth curved into smile that could only be thought of as feral. "Why, Miss Winters, of course. If she will consent to assist in my recovery, then I will agree. Otherwise I am not interested."

The doctor jerked in such surprise his spectacles slid down to the end of his nose. "Miss Winters? You would wish for the help of a woman?"

"That is absurd," Rex said. "You can hardly expect to submit a lady to the sort of intimacy your treatment would require. Her reputation would be in tatters."

His midnight eyes remained locked on her face. "The lady has reminded me on several occasions she is not in the least concerned with the matter of her reputation."

Rex stood up from his chair. "But surely you can't expect—"

"I would be willing to pay her, of course. Whatever amount she wishes. If I am going to attempt a *complete* recovery, then I believe Miss Winters's presence is essential."

Rex seemed to miss the not-so-subtle innuendo that turned Brandy's cheeks to rose. He wanted to be a man again—a whole, functioning man. And he wanted to punish her for raising his hopes when deep inside he was terrified he would fail.

Brandy lifted her chin. She had come this far; she wasn't about to let him use her refusal as a means to ignore this chance. "I don't need money. But there is something I would accept from Lord Hawksmoor in return for my help."

His brows rose a fraction, as if he had been certain she

would decline and he could escape his impending doom. "And that is . . . ?"

Brandy glanced at the doctor, who was watching the entire affair with a look of fascination. "I have a solid but basic education. I can speak properly, read and write and cipher. But I know little of the finer things. I would like to learn how to go on in Society, how to dress, how to behave, perhaps even how to dance. In short, I would like to become a lady. If you will help me do that, then I will help you."

The room fell totally silent. Rex was frowning while Marcus's eyes seemed to glitter. "There are tutors for that sort of thing. I'll have one brought here in all haste. When you're not working with me, you may spend your time with him."

"You realize, Miss Winters," the doctor put in, "your duties would require a rather personal knowledge of his lordship's body."

Brandy's cheeks went even brighter. Rex opened his mouth to speak but Brandy's look cut him off. She raised her chin a notch. "As the other two gentlemen are very well aware, I already have a personal knowledge of his lordship's body. What you're suggesting will not be a problem."

The doctors brows shot up.

"And I'm certain that you, Dr. Merriweather," Marcus put in with warning, "are the height of discretion."

The doctor made a slight sound in his throat and a stiff inclination of his head. "Of course, my lord."

It took sheer force of will for Brandy to summon a smile, since she was not at all certain what she had let herself in for. "Then we have struck a bargain, my lord. The return of your old life for my chance at a new one."

Marcus said nothing. Rex glared and shook his head. The doctor looked at his patient and smiled with satisfaction.

CHAPTER 17

The wind howled through the trees and across the rocky windswept soil. A wooden shutter, broken loose from the window of a room upstairs, banged restlessly against the stone walls. Rain poured down in dense gray sheets, slashing against the panes and rattling on the roof.

Lying in his big four-poster bed, Marcus could hear the crash of curling waves battering against the base of the cliffs, then sucking once more out to sea. The familiar sounds taunted him, dredged up painful memories, forced him backward in time to the life he had led before, the life he wanted returned to him beyond anything on this earth.

If he closed his eyes, he was there again, fighting the wind and waves from the deck of the *Seahawk,* shouting commands, watching his men bring the storm to heel, inhaling the scent of it, feeling the wetness of the rain on his face.

A harsh ache rose inside him, the pain of loss and longing like a crushing weight on his chest. Grief for the future that had been stolen away rose bitterly in his throat. God, how he missed the sea. Missed the salt spray in his face and the tilt of the deck beneath his feet. He needed it like a starving man needed nourishment, like a drowning man needed to breathe.

And now, once again, the hope of returning to the life he loved had been dangled before him, a lure he couldn't resist.

Marcus stared up at the heavy gold velvet bedhangings, his mind replaying the painful decision he had made. Merriweather had said he had nothing to risk, but it wasn't the truth. He was risking the very essence of himself, perhaps even his sanity. Marcus knew without doubt that in order to for the doctor's plan to work, he would have to accept the possibility he actually could walk again. In truth, he would have to *believe* it. If he did, his hopes would be unalterably raised.

He would expend every ounce of his energy, every effort of will he had ever possessed to accomplish that end. If he did—and he failed—he wasn't sure he could simply resign himself to spending the rest of his life as an invalid.

To have done so the first time had taken every last particle of his will.

And Brianne's unflagging efforts to make him feel whole again.

He didn't, of course, not really. But he had at least made the huge leap toward accepting what had happened as God's will and learning to live with it. Now the lure had been cast and his life was in turmoil again.

To walk again. To be whole again. With the use of his legs, he could regain all he had lost, all he'd ever been.

And there was Brianne.

He had lost her as well, though he didn't like to think of losing her in the same way he thought of losing the life he loved, or his beloved ship. It wasn't the same, he told himself. She was a woman. It could never be the same. But it hurt to see her every day. It hurt to want her until he ached with it and be fearful even to touch her.

It would hurt even more if she went away.

The thought struck out of nowhere. He didn't want to believe it, didn't want to think he had become that dependent on a woman, that he had come to need her that badly. In the eye of his mind he could see her, the soft curve of her mouth, the way it trembled when he kissed her, her fine features and fiery hair. He imagined making love to her as he had those sweet days on the *Seahawk,* and guilt trickled through him. He had used her aboard the ship. He had wanted her and he had taken her.

If he accepted the challenge the doctor proposed, he would be using her again.

A jagged branch of lightning flashed outside the window, brightening the stark Cornish landscape. A low, rolling grumble of thunder followed, echoing across the rocky soil.

Marcus listened to the thunder and thought of Brianne. God's blood, he had never meant to touch her, had done his best to resist her. He couldn't then. He couldn't now. As much as he was loath to admit it, he needed her. She gave him strength when he thought the last of his had been expended. She gave him courage when he believed that he had lost it. She nurtured him in a way he couldn't have imagined, and without her help he was certain that he would fail.

In truth, these past few weeks since Brandy had come to Hawksmoor House, in a strange way he had almost been content. Then Hamish Bass had appeared and his world had been upended even worse than it was before.

As he lay on the bed, Marcus's hand unconsciously fisted, the muscles across his chest tightening into tense iron bands. Bitterness rose like bile in his throat, and a need for vengeance so strong it made him faintly dizzy. He would do anything—anything—to find and destroy the man who had so completely destroyed his world.

Marcus thought of that nameless, faceless man and the guilt he felt at using Brianne slipped away. He needed her to make him whole. She was his best chance at succeeding. He would do what he had to do.

The doctor set his plan into motion the following day, agreeing to remain at the house until the end of the week. He would see to Brandy's instruction and help design the equipment they would need, then return each month to review Marcus's progress, or sooner if he was needed.

With a blacksmith and a cooper working in the stable, building the necessary equipment wasn't a problem: a sturdy set of parallel bars Marcus could use to pull himself along, a large wooden tub for submersing his legs, a special table for him to lie on, even a chair the cooper mounted on wheels to help move him about.

"We'll begin by working on the muscles," the doctor pronounced when the equipment was completed. ''First we'll soak the legs, then I'll show Miss Winters how to go about the proper way to massage them.''

Brandy swallowed hard and tried to ignore the warmth that rose in her cheeks. Marcus endured the matter stoically, with only the slightest tightening of his jaw. If it hadn't been for the faint flush beneath his swarthy skin, she might not have known the will it took for him to submit to such a blatant assault on his masculinity.

While servants filled the wooden tub in the room they had commandeered for their work—a pleasant chamber at the rear of the house that overlooked the ocean—Brandy busied herself straightening towels and retrieving Marcus's burgundy dressing gown. Behind a painted screen in the corner, Frederick helped him disrobe, then carried him in and lifted him into the tub. Brandy turned in time to see Marcus clamp down on his jaw and his face grow damp with beads of perspiration.

''I realize the water is hot,'' the doctor said, ''but that is necessary for complete muscle relaxation. In a minute or two, you'll get used to it.''

Marcus nodded. The water was obviously unbearable, yet he didn't complain, and Brandy felt a quick, knifing jab in the area of her heart. The doctor had warned her his recovery would not be easy, yet she couldn't stand to see him suffer.

''Try to relax,'' the doctor said. ''When it begins to cool, Frederick can lift you out and we'll start working on your legs.'' So saying, he started to leave, Frederick close behind, but when Brandy started to follow, Marcus called her back, instructing her to close the door.

''If I must sit in this infernal tub, the least you can do is keep me company.''

She tried to smile, but it came out a little wobbly. ''I would be happy to do that, my lord.'' But the truth was, talking to Marcus while he sat in a shallow bit of water that barely covered his masculine parts was more than a little unnerving. One glance at all of that smooth dark skin, at the long, strong sinews in his arms and torso, and a flush crept up her throat.

How could she have forgotten how incredibly attractive he was?

His normal weight had returned and even the months of inactivity hadn't diminished the slabs of muscle that stretched across his shoulders. Solid ridges formed bands down his stomach, and his chest was covered with black curly hair. She wanted to run her fingers through it, to feel the springy texture against her skin.

"You are staring, my love."

She jerked her eyes away, hot color flooding her cheeks. "I—I'm sorry. It's just that I had forgotten how . . ."

He cocked a sleek dark brow. "What had you forgot?"

"How . . . beautiful you are."

His eyes went from midnight blue to nearly black. They swept her from head to foot with a look of unmistakable hunger, then he glanced away. "Perhaps you were correct," he said gruffly. "Perhaps it would be better if you waited outside after all."

For the balance of the week, Brandy remained distant, listening to the doctor's instructions but not actually participating herself. The days were long and grueling. Each morning, Marcus soaked his legs, then the doctor worked over them, stretching and pulling, massaging the unused muscles. Then Marcus was lifted upright, suspended between the parallel bars, and encouraged to make his muscles move.

Each time, he failed.

"I've told you time and again," he said to the doctor as Frederick helped him back into his chair. "All this work is for nothing. No matter how hard I try, I cannot move my legs." Perspiration clung to his forehead and the muscles in his arms trembled with the effort it had taken to hold himself up. "What I don't understand is why you are so convinced I can."

Dr. Merriweather lifted Marcus's shirt and ran a pale, thin hand over the scar on his lower back. "None of us in the medical field know a great deal about injuries of the spine. I, however, have been fortunate to work quite closely with several different cases. The first I attended was that of my own brother."

"Your brother?" Brandy repeated.

"Yes. He was thrown from his horse when he was one and twenty. The resulting injury was quite similar to his lordship's." He gently prodded the scar and Marcus stiffened under his touch. "What I mean to say is the injury occurred in about the same position on the spine. That is important because the placement seems to be indicative of the severity of the damage. In my brother's case, it took a good deal of time and effort, but eventually he was able to walk again."

"And that is how you came up with the treatment you are suggesting for his lordship?" Brandy asked.

The doctor shoved his spectacles back up on his nose. "Actually, this sort of approach goes back as far as ancient times. Early Greeks and Romans wrote of the benefits of sun and water. Both exercise and massage were used by the ancient Chinese and even the Egyptians."

Marcus remained silent, simply looked over at the parallel wooden bars and clamped his jaw.

The doctor followed the direction of his gaze. "It's going to take time, my lord. You mustn't get discouraged."

But Brandy could see he had almost no faith in the doctor's plan. Perhaps, she thought, that was part of the problem.

Marcus shook his head. "I don't know. If I could feel any sort of response, any sign at all, even of the slightest nature, I might have more hope that this scheme of yours could actually work."

The doctor pondered that. Crossing the room, he opened his leather satchel and drew out a long, straight, rather fierce-looking needle. "When I examined you last week, you felt only a vague sensation, nothing you could be certain about. We've been working extensively with your muscles. Shall we try it again?"

Dragging up a chair, he bent and removed one of Marcus's shoes, then rolled down his stocking and pulled it off. His feet were slim, the toes well formed, the nails clipped short.

Brandy had never thought a man's feet could be attractive, but somehow Marcus's were.

Then the doctor shoved the pin into the bottom of his foot and a long muscle in his calf involuntarily contracted.

"Good God!" Marcus looked stunned. "I felt it. I actually felt the pin!"

"And your leg moved!" Brandy went up on her toes with excitement. "I saw it, Marcus. It actually moved!"

"Yes. . . . I didn't do it myself, of course, but it moved just the same."

The doctor smiled. "I thought that perhaps it would. There is your sign, Lord Hawksmoor. The feeling is starting to return. It might have done so sooner, if you had been given the proper stimulation. Your muscles are beginning to respond. Now the rest is up to you."

Brandy looked at Marcus. She would never forget the look on his face. It was sheer determination.

Marcus sat on the edge of the wooden table they had constructed for his use, his limp legs dangling off the side. For the tenth time that morning, he sucked in a fierce breath, concentrated with all his might, and strained to make his deadened legs move.

Sweat broke out on his forehead. The muscles in his arms and chest bulged with the effort. The tendons in his neck popped out and his back teeth ground together so hard an ache starting throbbing in his jaw.

Not so much as a whisper of motion.

He let out the deep, burning breath he had been holding. "Bloody hell! If I hadn't felt that damnable pinprick, I'd tell the lot of you to go straight to perdition."

But he had felt it, as certainly as he sat here trying futilely to move his limbs. And the hope that he might actually succeed kept him trying when time and again he failed.

Brianne rose from the chair where she had been sitting, a look of sympathy mixed with determination written across her face. "I know how hard you've been working at this, but it's far too early to quit."

He grumbled a response. No, he wasn't going to quit. At least not yet. Though he knew he was probably a fool, his hopes had been raised and he had to see this through.

And even if he wanted to quit, it was obvious Brandy wouldn't let him.

"You're almost through with this," she said. "The water in the tub is ready. Try it one more time and then we'll soak your legs."

Marcus felt the edge of a smile. Always just one more time. No matter how much effort he made—or tried to make—she demanded a little bit more. There were times he hated her for it, but mostly he admired her. She was an incredible woman, not only beautiful, but loyal and determined. He had never met another woman like her and he probably never would. He knew how fortunate he was to count her among his friends.

"Ah, my bath," he said. "I believe Dr. Merriweather has decided it would be beneficial to have the muscles worked while they are immersed in water. Is that not correct?"

Her cheeks darkened to a faint shade of rose. "Yes."

The doctor had left late yesterday afternoon to return to London. Today it was Brandy's turn to take over his care and he found himself looking forward to it. Having her touch him, massage his legs, see to his bath—it would be torture of the very worst sort, yet part of him craved that touch above all things.

Until today, with the doctor still in the house she had remained aloof and he had been glad. It allowed him to keep a tight rein on the lust she always inspired and concentrate on the tasks at hand. Not that it had done an ounce of good.

Now, however, the doctor was gone, and if he was meant to suffer the tasks the man had set for him, he might as well enjoy the intimacy those tasks required. It was foolish, he knew. He would only wind up aching for her as he had before. But seeing her every day, wanting her as he had every minute since her arrival, he was not going to deny himself a moment more—even if he couldn't make love to her as he so desperately wanted to do.

"All right, then," he said. "I shall try again and we will see if my will is stronger than the dead weights attached to my torso."

It wasn't, of course. No matter how he strained, no matter what inner language he used to command them, the muscles in his legs refused to obey, and with each of his unfulfilled efforts, a tiny speck of hope drained away.

He let out another burning breath, raked back the sweat-damp hair that had fallen over his forehead, and turned to see Brianne standing beside him. She mopped his brow with a cool, damp cloth and her fingers slid over the silk dressing gown where it rested on his shoulders. Beneath the robe his muscles tightened, and desire filtered into is belly. He thought perhaps he might have felt a faint twinge lower down.

"Next time you'll do better," she said. "I know you will." She rested her cheek against his back and he didn't push her away. He had goaded her into accepting this job, had done it as a sort of retribution. And because in his heart he didn't believe that he could succeed without her.

And in the back of his mind, he had thought that perhaps if the doctor was correct and recovery was actually possible, her presence might stimulate that part of him that was, since the accident, as dead as his useless legs.

He felt the damp cloth on his face and along the back of his neck, and her gentle touch set his pulse to pounding. When she started to pull away, he caught her wrist and drew her closer. His eyes found hers, so very gold and just slightly tilted. Cupping her chin with his fingers, he tipped her head back and captured her soft mouth in a kiss.

For a moment she went still. He could feel the warmth of her lips under his, feel the slight tremor that moved through her body. Then she closed her eyes and leaned against him, giving herself up to him as she always did. She tasted of chamomile tea and her hair smelled faintly of roses. He had forgotten how incredibly sweet she was, how her lips molded perfectly to the shape of his own. He coaxed her to open for him with subtle pressure and teasing kisses, then took her deeply with his tongue. God, it felt so good to kiss her.

Sitting as he was on the table, he was nearly a full head taller. Brianne reached up to slide her arms around his neck and a soft little mew slipped from her throat. The old fires kindled, the heat she always stirred. He didn't fight it this time, just let the hot need build inside him. He could feel her breasts where they pillowed against his chest, soft and full and incredibly arousing. His hand moved there and he cupped one, felt the delicious weight of it, teased the nipple into a hard pulsing bud.

Heat moved through him, settled low in his belly. All the while he kissed her, his tongue delving in, tasting her, remembering other kisses, remembering what it had felt like to have her naked, to be buried deep inside her. A shudder tore through him, then another. He wanted to tear off her clothes, to drag her down on the table and make mad, passionate love to her. His body, it seemed, had none of those plans.

He was limp, completely faccid, and only his mind, it seemed, was stirred nearly beyond control. With aching regret, his muscles still taut with unfulfilled need, he gently ended the kiss.

He was breathing hard and so was she.

Brianne stepped away, her eyes wide and glittering like gems. "I'm sorry, I didn't mean for that to happen, I swear. I—I just couldn't seem to stop myself."

Amusement filtered through him, tamping down the burning frustration. He cupped her cheek with his hand, traced a finger lightly along her jaw. "Neither could I," he said softly. He didn't add that the fault was entirely his or that it wouldn't be his last effort at seduction. She had come to him here at Hawksmoor House, and he needed her. He would take what he needed so badly.

Brandy smiled, her eyes still sparkling. "I had forgotten how wonderful it is to kiss you. I believe I could subsist on just your kisses alone."

He cocked a brow, his mouth edging up. "No food? No water?"

She laughed then, a light, rippling sound that did something to his insides. ''Well, perhaps enough sustenance to sustain me in between.''

As rapidly as it had come, his amusement slid away, replaced with a wariness he hadn't expected to feel. He didn't like the way she affected him, didn't want to feel the warmth she made him feel inside. He didn't want her looking at him the way she was now.

''I warn you, Brianne,'' he said, in a voice even he knew was too stern, ''you had better guard your heart. You know the man I am, the man I always will be. My ships and the sea are my life. Nothing can come of this attraction between us. Even should a miracle occur and I learn to walk again, in the end I would leave you.''

Her mouth quivered. Sadness stole into her features, dimming the gold of her eyes to the color of tarnished brass. ''I know you well, my lord. From the first, I have known the sea is your world—your one and only true love. If for a time I chance to forget, you always hasten to remind me.''

What she said was the truth, but what choice did he have? He had always tried to be honest, and yet . . . ''Knowing that, do you still wish to remain?''

She glanced off toward the window, out to the blue of the ocean beyond. Frothy whitecaps foamed on the surface and distant gulls swooped and turned in the windy currents above. Marcus watched the way she stood with her small feet splayed, her hands gripped tightly together, and found himself holding his breath, waiting for her answer, praying it would be the right one.

Slowly she turned to face him. ''We've been friends for a very long time, Marcus. In truth, more than friends.'' Her glance strayed back to the water, as if the power of the sea compelled her life as well as his own. Then her eyes found his once more. ''If returning to the sea is your wish, then . . . as your friend . . . I have no choice but to help you. I'll do everything in my power to see that your wish is fulfilled.''

Marcus said nothing. Guilt warred with need. He was using her again as he had before. At least this time she was receiving something in return. The tutor he had hired, Professor

Isaac Felton, a gangly, bone-thin man with a pointed nose and graying mouse-brown hair, had arrived late yesterday afternoon. Brianne had already started her lessons.

"If that is the case, with your permission, I'll ring for Frederick. I believe it's time for him to ready the soaking tub."

"Yes," she said softly. "But today, if you don't mind, I'll wait for you to finish before I begin work on your legs."

Marcus simply nodded. It wasn't what he had planned, but suddenly it was what he wanted, too. At the resigned, solemn look in her eyes, a tightness had crept into his chest. He didn't want to hurt her. He had never wanted that. Unfortunately, the truth was plain, and it was his duty to warn her.

The oddest part was, in some strange way, he found that he was hurting, too.

Brandy walked along the cliffs above the beach, kicking small stones out of her path with the toe of her soft kid slippers. It was growing late, the sun fanning out in watery yellows and pinks above the distant horizon.

The wind had come up, whipping her skirts and making it difficult to move over the rocky ground, but she didn't care. She needed this time alone, this time to grieve for her dreams.

Even should a miracle occur, I would leave you.

She had known it, of course, deep down inside where it didn't hurt so much, she had known. He didn't love her. He never would.

At least he hadn't lied.

A soft ache rose, throbbed beneath her heart. He didn't love her, but he needed her.

And he desired her. No matter that his body couldn't function in that way, he desired her. It wasn't enough, would never be enough, but it was all she had, all she would ever have, and she would accept it.

Brandy paused on the cliffs to watch the fiery yellow ball of sun sink slowly behind the hills. Her heart felt heavy, weighed down inside her chest. Flo had warned her of the dangers of loving a man so completely. Brandy had known the risk, yet she had plunged headlong into the abyss.

Should she back out now? Leave Hawksmoor House before the pain of loving him grew even more fierce? She knew that she could not. She had given her word, and as long as Marcus was doomed to imprisonment in his chair, she would stay. And she would pray with all her heart, use every ounce of her will to free him.

Even knowing he would leave and return to sea.

Brandy sighed as she drifted along the meandering path. At least she was gaining something for herself in the bargain, something useful, something she had always wanted. After working the afternoon with Marcus, she had spent the balance of the day in company with her new tutor, the rather odd-looking Isaac Felton, former Professor of Gentile Deportment at Lady Longmantle's School for Young Ladies.

"There is no sense wasting time," the tall, thin man had said on making her acquaintance. "I can tell by that slightly off-center curtsy that we have a good deal of ground to cover."

Brandy had flushed but raised her chin. Though she knew basic good manners and being courteous came naturally in most cases, she understood little of the finer points of etiquette, especially as it pertained to upper class British Society.

"We shall begin with formal greetings," the professor said, launching into a discussion of polite introduction, of how the person lower in rank was always presented to the one above. That was followed by a discourse on titles themselves.

"All male peers except dukes are called lords," he explained, beginning with the basics. "Dukes are referred to as His Grace. Younger sons of a duke or a marquess are addressed as lord and their first names. The earl's friend, Richard Lockhart, for example, is Lord Richard, since his father is the Marquess of Halliday. He would *not,* however, under any circumstance, be referred to as Lord Lockhart."

Heaven forbid, she thought.

"Wives of a younger son are addressed by their husband's names. If Lord Richard were to marry, his wife would be addressed as Lady Richard Lockhart, or simply Lady Richard.''

Lady Richard?

''The only time a lady is addressed by her first name is if she is the daughter of a duke, a marquess, or an earl. If you were such a young woman, for example, you would be Lady Brianne. The eldest son of a duke or marquess may receive a courtesy title, one of his father's lower titles. For instance, he might become a baron or viscount. However, unlike the Earl of Hawksmoor, neither of those titles may have an *of* in the middle. One is simply the baron this or the viscount that. Is all of that perfectly clear?''

Clear? It was as muddy as the waters of the Ashley River back home. ''I think so.'' But by the end of the session, her head was spinning. ''Good heavens, I had no idea there would be so much to remember.''

''Do not despair, my dear. It shall all become quite natural. Professor Felton is here to make certain that it does.''

Brandy forced a smile, not quite sure what to think of her odd professor, but determined to learn whatever it was he meant to teach.

She thought about him now, as the sounds of evening approached, the chirp of crickets, the hoot of a distant owl. Still walking along the path, she kicked a pebble with her shoe, then winced as the sharp edge of the stone bit into her foot. She would have to go back to the cottage before it got too dark, yet she didn't really want to face her empty room, and she was too depressed to enjoy conversing with her little brown-haired maid.

Determined to forget about Marcus and the ache that still throbbed in her heart, Brandy turned back along the cliffs toward her cottage. In the distance, she could see the towers and spires of Hawksmoor House. Through the tall mullioned windows, the yellow glow of lamps being lit flickered against the walls inside the house.

She wondered which room Marcus was in, wondered where he slept, and if, in the long, empty hours before morning, he remembered, as she did, the hot, passion-filled nights they had shared in his cabin aboard the *Seahawk*.

CHAPTER 18

A thin, late summer sun filtered down through the trees along the gravel drive leading into Hawksmoor House. Brandy made her way down the lane, climbing the wide stone stairs with brisk, efficient strides and a renewed sense of purpose.

The painful words Marcus had spoken were now safely tucked away, shoved to a place in the back of her mind where they could not hurt her. Whatever Marcus did with his life, whatever happened between them, she was his friend and she was there to help him.

Rex must have seen her coming. He was waiting in the entry to greet her, standing next to Richard Lockhart. Both men were dressed for riding, Richard in nankeen breeches and a white lawn shirt, Rex in tight black breeches and high black boots. A simple gray wool riding coat dangled over one wide shoulder, held in place by a graceful hand.

"Well, you are certainly off to an early start this morning," Rex said.

Brandy smiled. "As are you, it would seem."

Rex returned the smile and so did Richard Lockhart. "Miss Winters—it's terribly good to see you." Always excessively polite, he made an extravagant bow over her hand. "And I must say, you are looking quite radiant today."

"Thank you, my lord." She made a perfect curtsy in return, having practiced late into the evening, conquering the first of her lessons with a fervor she meant to continue.

Lord Richard apparently noticed her improvement, for his

sandy brows shot up and his lips curved faintly. Brandy felt the heat rise into her cheeks and almost wished she had stumbled.

"Richard has convinced me to break away for a day of hunting," Rex told her. "I shouldn't really go—I've a thousand things to do."

Brandy reached for his arm. "You must go, Rex. You do nothing but work from morning till night. Lord Richard is perfectly correct. You should go hunting. 'Tis certain to be good for you."

He smiled that warm smile of his. "I trust you will see to my wayward brother."

"Of course." She smiled. "Who else would be brave—or foolish—enough to try?"

His slim fingers brushed her cheek. "Only you, love, only you."

Warm affection stole through her. Rex Delaine was a kind and caring man. He was different from Marcus, but in many ways just as strong. "Do have a good time. You truly deserve it."

Rex simply nodded. Brandy watched them leave and made her way down the hall. If Lord Richard believed it indelicate for a lady to be visiting a gentleman alone, his thoughts did not register on his face. He didn't know, of course, what was really taking place inside the inner walls of Hawksmoor House, that she was working with the earl in a scandalously intimate fashion. And she was certain Rex would not tell him.

Making her way to the Oceanview Room, she was surprised to find it empty.

Giles appeared in the hall outside. "Good morning, Miss Winters. If you will please come with me. His lordship awaits your presence in the treatment salon."

Following the butler in that direction, Brandy opened the door to see Marcus sitting on the table that had been fashioned for his use, his burgundy dressing gown open nearly to the waist, perspiration slick on his brow and gleaming on the muscles across his chest. It was obvious he had already been hard at work.

Brandy took a breath, her stomach flipping over with an odd little twist. "You are certainly up and about early this morning. I thought to find you in the Oceanview Room, but you are already here and working."

He grumbled a phrase she didn't quite hear. "For all the good it has done." His gaze probed hers. "You're early as well and, I might add, looking very fetching in your pretty yellow dress."

A flush crept into her cheeks. He hadn't said so before, but apparently she had done the right thing when she had altered the dresses.

"Thank you. Actually, I was eager to get here. There are some changes I wish to make in your program."

He cocked a brow. "Changes? What sort of changes?"

Brandy walked toward him, stopping before she got too close, determined not to stare at all that lean muscle and smooth, sweat-slick skin. "I've been thinking, Marcus. Overall, I believe Dr. Merriweather's plan is a good one—working the muscles, forcing them to move as they once did. But when it comes to the effort of moving them yourself, I believe he may be starting on too large a scale."

Marcus frowned. "I'm afraid I don't see what you mean."

"You've been sitting here for days straining to move your legs. What if you simply tried to move your foot, or perhaps even a single toe?"

"I don't think that would make—"

"But you don't know for sure, and since that is so, why don't we give it a try?" Without waiting for his reply, Brandy skirted the table and moved up in front of him, taking a long, slim foot in her hands. Feeling each bone and sinew, she began to massage it, pulling the muscles in his calves, his toes, stretching them, rubbing his ankle, turning it one way and then the other. She continued her efforts, so immersed in what she was doing she didn't realize Marcus was staring.

"What is it? What's wrong?"

"I can feel your hands. I can feel them on my skin. I can hardly believe it."

"You—you can feel it when I touch you?"

"Yes. It isn't distinct, just a faint sensation, but I can actually tell where you are touching my body."

She moved her hand along his leg. "Can you feel that?"

"Yes."

Over his knee and up along the outside of his thigh beneath the silk robe. "How about now?"

"Yes. It's just a whisper against my skin, but it is definitely tactile sensation."

Brandy grinned. "Marcus, this is wonderful!"

He was smiling, actually grinning back at her. "It is, isn't it? It's incredible."

"All right, since you can feel my hand, concentrate and trace the pattern I'm making. Close your eyes and follow in your mind the path my hand is taking." She trailed her fingers down his thigh, pausing at the knee, then moving lower. "Can you feel it?"

"Yes."

Again she moved lower, over his calf, testing the long sinews there, over the round bone at his ankle. She circled it with her fingers, then moved lower, running her knuckles lightly across his toes. "Are you following?"

"Yes."

"All right, move your toes. Do it now. Don't think about it, just do it."

They moved almost at once. All of the toes on his right foot.

Marcus's eyes flew open. A look of utter incredulity made them appear wide and dark. "They moved! By God, I actually made them move!"

Brandy gave up a shriek of sheer joy. She was in his arms in a heartbeat, laughing, hugging him against her, fighting the sting of tears. "You did it, Marcus. You did it!" She looked up at him, her eyes bright and shining with excitement. "We can do this, Marcus. We can make it work. We can do it together."

His hold tightened almost painfully. A shudder rippled through his tall frame and beneath her hand, his heartbeat a cadence that told her what he was feeling. Something moved across his features, something so powerful it took her breath away. Then he was kissing her, madly, savagely, digging his fingers into her hair, knocking the pins free, tilting her head back and plundering her mouth.

All of the emotion he was feeling was there in the power of his kiss, the raw intensity of his touch. His hands were determined, holding her firmly in place, yet there was a gentleness there. And heat and need and perhaps a hint of desperation.

"Sometimes I feel so alone," he said against her cheek. "As if there isn't another soul in the world. Then you are there. Whenever the darkness threatens, always you are there."

"Marcus . . ."

He kissed her again, softly, urgently. "I need you," he whispered. "God, I need you so much."

She didn't hesitate, not even a moment, just parted the robe and began to kiss her way down his throat and across those wide, hard-muscled shoulders, nipping here, tasting there, pressing tiny moist kisses over his collarbone, down across his chest. She sucked on a flat copper nipple, ringed it with her tongue, and heard him groan. His skin was damp and salty, and the taste of him made her breasts swell and throb. She felt his fingers unbuttoning the front of her blouse, then his hands were there, kneading the roundness, tugging on the ends, making the heat sink low in her belly.

The hot lick of fire slid through her, sank into her core. Her mouth moved lower across his skin, down along the indentation of each rib, nipping the flesh over his flat stomach. She ringed his navel, parted the robe even wider, and settled herself between his legs. Cupping him gently in her palm, she bent her head to take him into her mouth.

Marcus's hand on her arm drew her gently from her purpose. Regret darkened his eyes. A tinge of embarrassment colored the skin beneath his cheek bones. "I'm not . . . I can't . . . as much as I want you, my body is unwilling to respond. I'm sorry, my love."

She pressed a finger against his lips. "Don't be sorry. You

have no reason to be sorry.'' She smiled at him softly, her face still flushed, her heart still hammering with desire. ''We've had our miracle for the day and it is more than enough.''

He surprised her with a shake of his head. ''No, not quite enough.'' Marcus kissed her again, deep, lingering, wonderfully thorough kisses.

With expert skill, he teased and nibbled and coaxed, until her body was on fire for him. She barely noticed the hand he moved beneath her skirts until she felt it gliding along the inside of her thigh. With gentle touches and a soft caress, he urged her legs apart and began to stroke her, gently at first, then with gentle purpose.

She knew she should make him stop, but the pleasure was too fierce, too powerful for the notion to fully emerge. A tremor ran through her, another and another. He slid a finger deep inside, then a second, filling her, making her body tighten and her heart knock crazily against her ribs. Deeply and smoothly, he stroked her, the sensation so intense she started to tremble. Her legs went weak while her body felt hot and tight and ready to burst.

''Marcus . . .'' she whispered, clinging to his shoulders, barely able to remain on her feet.

''Easy, love, just let it come.''

The words, spoken in husky tones thick with desire, sent her over the edge. Pleasure tore through her, sweet and wild and wonderful. She cried out his name, felt his arms tighten around her. Desire and need and love for him all rushed together, mixing with the pleasure that flooded through her in overwhelming waves.

Marcus held her as she spiraled down, whispering gentle, soothing love words, words she hadn't heard since the nights she had spent in his cabin.

''It's all right,'' he said softly. ''I've got you. I won't let you fall.'' Opening her eyes, she looked into his face.

For the fist time, she realized she was clinging to his shoulders, hanging on for dear life. Marcus's arms were bands of steel around her. Dimly, she felt him work the buttons at the front of her dress and smooth her skirt back into place. Brandy flushed with embarrassment and began to ease away.

"I didn't mean for that. . . . We shouldn't have. . . ."

"Probably not. I'm not sorry we did." His mouth curved faintly and his eyes held a glint of what looked very much like masculine triumph. She hadn't seen that expression on his face in a very long time.

While Brandy drew in several steadying breaths and fought to compose herself, Marcus pulled the bell cord hanging near his exercise table.

"I'll have Frederick fill my soaking tub. In the meantime, why don't you rest for a bit, and then we can try it again."

Brandy felt a hot rush of heat to her cheeks. If they tried *that* again, he would have to ring for Frederick to scoop her off the floor.

"That . . . that sounds like a good idea. In the meantime, perhaps I shall walk in the garden."

Marcus simply nodded, but she thought she caught that fleeting, triumphant smile again.

Palmer Reese walked along the crowded London dock, oblivious to swaggering sailors, and painted doxies, and fishermen bartering their day's catch of fish. His mind was fixed on the big, full-rigged, triple-masted ship nudging her hull against the dock, the pride of Reese Enterprises, his flagship *Fairwind.*

The largest and swiftest of his fleet, the ship had arrived in port the first of the week, and Palmer was headed for a meeting with her captain, Cain Dalton. Mounting the gangway, he crossed to the deck, a stream of laborers walking single file ahead of him, an equally long line of workers behind. Their heads were bent, their shoulders weighted down with the task of carrying cargo and supplies aboard, coal and lumber, barrels of salted herring, and casks of brandy on its way to the Indies.

Palmer smiled as he crossed to the wheelhouse in search of the captain who had worked for him for nearly ten years, ever since he had, at the youthful age of twenty-four, purchased his first ship. It wasn't a ship like this one. No, *Windrider* was a bottom-heavy old barque that wallowed through the seas like an overweight matron, nothing at all like the sleek, exquisitely designed *Fairwind.*

Palmer glanced up at the tall mast in the center of the deck. A stiff wind buffeted the rigging, which clattered and clanked above his head, and gulls perched on the crossarms supporting the tightly furled sails. The ship smelled of tar and damp canvas, not smells he was accustomed to, nor could he say he enjoyed them.

To Palmer, a ship and its cargo merely smelled of money.

"Mr. Reese!" Cole Proctor, first mate aboard the ship, a big, brawny hulk of a man, stopped him outside the wheelhouse. "Sir, Cap'n Dalton is waitin' for you in his cabin. He asked me to bring you down the minute you came aboard."

"Thank you, Mr. Proctor." The beefy man turned and led the way, his stout frame filling the corridor. Proctor knocked on the captain's door, received permission to enter, and ushered Reese inside. The first mate hesitated a moment, as if he hoped one of them would issue an invitation to join them. When that didn't happen, he closed the door, leaving the two men inside.

"It's good to see you, Cain." Reese shook the other man's hand, which was weathered and callused, his grip undeniably firm. Once-blond hair, silvered at the temples, glinted slightly in the glow of the lamp on his leather-topped desk. He was a man of medium height, but lean and able-bodied, a tough man, hard-edged, the sort Palmer liked, the sort he often found useful. "I trust the voyage was a good one."

Dalton nodded. Both men sat down around the captain's built-in leather-topped teakwood desk. "And profitable as well. Best haul we've made in the last five years."

"So I gathered. I'm pleased to say the ship will be sailing with her holds full again."

Dalton leaned back in his chair. "That is good news."

Palmer reached across the desk to the brandy decanter that sat on one corner and poured a dollop into a crystal snifter. He poured one for the man across from him and set it in front of him. "Along with the goods we've already started taking on, we've won another new contract. Manufactured goods for shipment to America."

Dalton cocked a pale brow. "Another of Delaine's former runs?"

Palmer smiled. He couldn't help it. "As a matter of fact, it is. With the *Seahawk* still out of commission, the company felt it wasn't getting the service it should. *Peregrine* was a candidate, but she's a much smaller ship and not nearly as fast as the *Fairwind*. In the end, the owners did what was most expedient and the contract is ours."

Dalton grunted. "Too bad for Hawksmoor Shipping."

"Isn't it, though." Palmer took a sip of the brandy, enjoyed the trail of fire that burned into his stomach. "In another six months, their sugar contract with Barbados Consolidated will be up. *Seahawk* will be out of dry dock by then, but without Delaine at her helm, there is every chance we'll be able to win that one, too."

"You really have it in for him, don't you?"

Palmer felt the old anger rising, seeping up through the layers of his control. How many years had he hated the Delaines? Not just Marcus, but also his brother Geoffrey, and most of all the late earl himself. But Dalton knew nothing of that, no one did. And he meant to keep it that way.

Palmer shrugged his shoulders, took a sip of his brandy. "Now, why would I have it in for him? I am simply a businessman. With Delaine out of the way, Reese Enterprises has a golden opportunity. I am merely taking advantage of that opportunity."

Dalton scoffed. "An opportunity you created. An opportunity that is making you a good deal of money. As a matter of fact, it's making you filthy rich. It only seems fair, if a man gets rich with the help of his friends, his friends ought to share in the spoils."

Palmer eyed him over the rim of his glass, and a muscle bunched in his jaw. He forced himself to relax. "You have a *job*, Dalton—one you ought to be grateful for. Especially since that job has become very lucrative, thanks to the troubles of Hawksmoor Shipping.''

Dalton took a sip of his brandy, set it back down on his desk. ''Yeah, well, I say it isn't enough. I helped you arrange those accidents. Now I want a percentage of the profits you're making because of them. If I don't get it, you may find yourself in the same kind of trouble Delaine is in.''

Palmer set his brandy snifter very carefully down on the desk. ''Are you threatening me, Dalton?''

''Maybe I am.''

Anger slithered through him. ''I wouldn't if I were you. You don't have the power to back it up.'' But Palmer did. And he had just made a decision. Cain Dalton might be a good ship's captain, but Cole Proctor could handle the job almost as well. Proctor would be grateful for the chance, and he knew nothing of what had transpired with Hawksmoor Shipping.

Palmer forced himself to smile. ''On the other hand, I suppose in a way you're right. A man like you is invaluable to a man like me. Why don't you come to my office tomorrow night . . . say, around ten o'clock? We can discuss the situation, decide how much is fair, and I'll have the papers drawn up.''

Dalton leaned back in his chair, his weathered face lined with satisfaction. ''I hoped you'd see it my way.''

Palmer shrugged, though the muscles in his shoulders felt tense. ''When a man is right, he's right.'' Shoving back his chair, he stood up and started for the door. ''Tomorrow, then? Ten o'clock?''

''I'll be there.''

But I won't be, Palmer thought. *The only meeting you're going to have is a very unpleasant rendezvous in the alley next to my office. It'll be short and sweet and you won't be walking away.*

Palmer left the captain's cabin, crossed the deck, and headed down the gangway with quick purposeful steps. He needed to get back to his office. He had matters of importance to arrange.

* * *

Brandy worked with Marcus every day for the next three weeks. It was one thing to move his toes. It was another thing entirely to be able to move his legs. Not that he wasn't making progress.

"I know how difficult this is," Brandy told him, standing next to where he hung by his arms between the long wooden parallel bars, his feet resting like so much dead weight on the polished oak floor. "But you're doing very well, all in all. We knew it wouldn't be easy."

"Damn legs feel like they weigh a thousand pounds," Marcus grumbled.

"At least you can feel them." She moved between the bars, took hold of his ankle, massaged the weary muscles. "Move it again."

He struggled, strained, sweat popped out on his forehead. Slowly, by minuscule degrees, the ankle moved and the foot dragged forward.

"Very good. Now the other one."

Marcus drew in a fortifying breath, steeled himself, gathered his strength, moved the other ankle, and the foot slid slowly forward. "At this rate," he growled, "I shall be a doddering old man by the time I am able to walk again."

Brandy laughed. "I hardly think you will be that old, my lord. Your progress is increasing at a faster rate every day. Dr. Merriweather is going to be ecstatic."

The doctor had arrived just that morning, though they hadn't seen him yet. A light knock at the door announced his impending arrival. Marcus gave permission for him to enter and Giles ushered the slim, brown-haired man into the room.

"I'm sorry, but I couldn't help overhearing, and actually, Dr. Merriweather is beyond ecstatic." Walking toward them, the physician's youthful face split into a smile. "I came as soon as I received your message." He studied Marcus from head to foot, noting the lines the perspiration on his forehead, the way the muscles in his forearms still bulged with the strain of his latest effort. "The letter I received said you were beginning to gain control of the movement of your legs."

''Slowly, but yes. With Miss Winters's help, I have made a good deal of progress.''

''Splendid!'' The doctor paused next to where Marcus leaned heavily on the bars. ''Why don't you show me?''

The attempt would be costly, Brandy knew. Marcus had been working all morning. He was tired now, exhausted from the effort of pressing himself so hard. Still, he gripped the bars and concentrated on moving his ankles, dragging first the left foot, then the right foot forward.

''I must say, that is extraordinary. I couldn't be more pleased. Now do what you just did again, only this time do it harder.''

Marcus shook his head. ''I'm giving it all I've got. I don't think I can push it another inch.''

The doctor knelt in front of him, examining the legs, probing and stretching the muscles. ''Perhaps that is the problem. You are pushing and not pulling. Can you feel my hand?''

''Yes. Most of the sensation has returned.''

''Good. This time don't try to lift your ankle. Pull upward from the knee. Lift your shin bone toward me.''

Marcus clamped down on his jaw. His face was slick with sweat, his whole body quivering with fatigue. The knee went up, thrusting his calf and ankle forward. It was the first time he had been able to make such a movement. It was a tremendous leap and Marcus knew it. He grinned and his gaze flashed to Brandy's, sharing another sweet moment of triumph.

The muscles in his legs were shaking violently by the time he had both feet once more beneath him, and she worried for a moment that his arms might not continue to hold him up. Fortunately, Dr. Merriweather realized the extent of his fatigue and summoned Marcus's valet. Frederick moved him to the table so the doctor could continue his examination and Brandy left them alone.

Half an hour later, she was invited to return.

''His lordship has worked very hard this morning,'' Merriweather said, dropping several instruments back in his leather satchel and snapping the latch. ''He's in fine physical condition, and as I said, his progress is remarkable. However, his treatment must continue. The usual massage should be performed and as you know I prefer it done while his legs are submerged."

"As you wish," Brandy said, unwilling to glance at Marcus. It was one thing to assume such intimate tasks when they were alone, another altogether to do so when the doctor was present. To her relief, once Frederick had filled the soaking tub and Marcus was immersed, the doctor left them alone, retiring to his rooms upstairs to unpack and refresh himself after his arduous journey.

Brandy knelt on the floor beside the tub. "I'm so happy for you, Marcus. It won't be long until you're completely back on your feet."

Instead of smiling, Marcus frowned. "I hope you're right."

"Of course I'm right."

"Merriweather can't guarantee it, you know. He says the degree of recovery differs with each individual case."

"You'll succeed," Brandy said firmly. "I know you will."

Marcus cupped her face with his hand. "And if I fail?"

Something close to fear jolted through her. She couldn't bear the thought that he might fail—it would simply be too painful. "If you fail, we'll deal with it together. For now, that isn't an option. At present, all we're going to think about is doing what it takes to get you back on your feet."

But Marcus couldn't stop himself from worrying. There was so much at risk, so much he had to lose. Leaning his head back against the rim of the tub, he closed his eyes and let the heat of the water soak away his fatigue. He had grown more accustomed to the burning temperatures the doctor prescribed. Strangely enough, he had actually begun to enjoy these moments in the tub. As he enjoyed the feel of Brianne's small hands working the muscles of his legs.

She smoothed them, stretched them, kneaded them. She turned them, extended them, deeply massaged them. Every caress went right through him, every touch made a tiny thread of heat slip into his groin. He lusted for her, wanted her beyond anything he had experienced. Yet his body refused to respond.

He hated himself for it. Hated the way it made him feel. When her hand accidentally brushed between his thighs, he felt a slight twinge low in his belly but nothing more. Angry at himself and embarrassed, he caught her wrist.

"That's enough," he snapped. "I grow weary of your ministrations. Leave me for a while."

"I didn't hurt you?"

God, yes, he hurt, but not in the way she meant. It hurt to want her and not be able to have her. It hurt to be less than a man. "No . . . you didn't hurt me. I simply wish to be left alone."

She frowned at his gruffness, but acquiesced and quietly slipped away. Marcus watched her leave, a weary sigh of frustration sliding past his lips as she closed the door. Without her there, the room seemed suddenly dimmer, as if the sun had slipped behind a cloud. In the wake of her departure, some of his energy seemed to have drained away and before the water had cooled he found himself wishing that she would return.

He rang for his valet instead. He had promised her time with her tutor. He might not be the man he once was, but he was still a man who kept his word.

CHAPTER 19

The fragile, sweet strains of a harpsichord floated across the ornate Green Drawing Room.

"All right," the professor said, smiling down at Brandy from his considerable height, made to appear even taller by the thinness of his legs in the snug striped breeches he wore. "We'll start with a country dance."

The housekeeper, Mrs. Findlay, a plump, well-groomed woman in her fifties, a former governess who was better educated than most women of her station, smiled at them from her seat in front of the harpsichord.

Professor Felton smiled at Brandy. "Ready?"

Standing in the professor's thin shadow, she discovered she was suddenly nervous. Still, she swallowed with a bit of difficulty and nodded.

"Relax," he said, noticing the way her fingers bit into the waist of her gown. "Try to enjoy yourself. You have done exceedingly well with the rest of your lessons. You will have no problem with this."

She smiled and felt a little less tense. She practiced the steps several times with the professor, then turned to see Rex Delaine standing in the open door.

"Mind if I join you?"

"Not a'tall," the professor said. "The more, the merrier, especially when it comes to dancing."

Rex moved farther into the room, his gaze bright with approval. "Miss Winters appears to be quite an apt pupil."

"Yes. Indeed she is."

''Perhaps she should try a new partner.''

''Splendid notion, yes, yes, indeed.''

As Rex walked toward her, the professor smiled and stepped away, and her nervousness returned.

''Shall we try a quadrille?'' the professor suggested, moving toward the woman seated at the harpsichord.

''I should prefer to dance the waltz,'' Rex said. ''I realize it is still a bit scandalous, but sooner or later I believe it will be all the rage.''

The professor's fuzzy eyebrows pulled together for a moment, then he nodded, obviously not enthused about the waltz, which even Brandy had heard was often frowned upon.

''From a distance I shall be able to observe her movements a little better.'' The professor positioned himself near the harpsichord and Brandy noticed that, unlike her gangly tutor, Mrs. Findlay was smiling.

'' 'Tis such a beautiful dance,'' she said, beginning to strike up a waltz, a soft, melodic tune that sounded a bit tinny on the harpsichord.

Rex took Brandy's hand, placed it on his shoulder, then settled a hand at her waist. ''Just let me lead and you follow. It isn't hard at all.''

She nodded, hoping she wouldn't make a fool of herself. He started off with his left foot and she stumbled, but several faltering steps later she began to get the hang of it, and she smiled. ''This is wonderful! It's like floating on air. And I don't think it's scandalous at all.''

Rex laughed. ''Neither do I.'' He was a very good dancer, his lean body moving with assurance and grace. Brandy found herself grinning, enjoying the music, enjoying the dance as she couldn't have guessed. Her gaze remained on Rex, but her thoughts had drifted to Marcus, who looked so much like him, and wistfully she thought what it might be like to dance this way with him.

A movement in the doorway caught her eye. She saw him there, a footman standing behind his chair on wheels, Marcus staring into the room, his expression carefully blank. Brandy stumbled and Rex caught her, saving her from embarrassment. Mrs. Findlay stopped the music just then.

"Don't let me disturb you," Marcus said. There was something in his voice, something cool and distant, yet a look of unmistakable pain lingered briefly in his eyes. "My brother was always a very good dancer. And you, Brianne, are quite good yourself."

"I—I am only just learning."

His dark look softened. "I suppose you've never had occasion to dance."

She ignored a soft pang of regret. "Not at the White Horse Tavern."

"Then, please, as I said, don't let me disturb you."

But Brandy shook her head. "I grow weary, trying to remember so many steps. I believe I would prefer a turn in the garden. Perhaps I could impose upon you to accompany me?"

Something flickered in those cool, dark blue eyes.

"I'm afraid I shall have to depart as well," Rex put in smoothly. "I've a good deal of work to do." With a smile and a wink at his brother, he fled the room.

"My lord?" Brandy pressed.

Marcus finally nodded. She thought that perhaps it was relief she had seen in his eyes. "As you wish."

The dining room of Hawksmoor House—gold flocked wallpaper, polished oak parquet floors, a table that seated forty—glittered with the soft light of silver candelabras. Rex had invited Brianne to join them for supper, in company with the doctor and Richard Lockhart, and the table had been extravagantly set.

Seated at the end, Marcus watched Brianne from above his gilt-rimmed goblet, amused by her sigh of pleasure as she sampled the delicious roast partridge Cook had prepared, along with salmon in lobster sauce, oysters, candied carrots and a mélange of other delights. She seemed to enjoy them all, her manners impeccable, not even the slightest hesitation at the vast array of silver spread before her.

It appeared her lessons were paying off, Marcus thought

with an unexpected feeling of disgruntlement. In a few more weeks, with Felton overseeing her every move, she would be able to conduct herself with perfect aplomb, even in the presence of royalty.

Why he found the thought annoying, he couldn't be sure.

She took a sip of wine and set the heavy crystal goblet back down on the table. "So tell us, Lord Richard, how does your writing progress?"

Richard flashed her one of his boyish, disarming smiles, and Marcus ignored a twinge of jealousy. "The project is coming along quite splendidly. I am currently working on the chapter that discusses the position of women in Medieval Society. The research has proven to be quite interesting."

"In what way?" Dr. Merriweather asked, peering intently through his wire-rimmed spectacles. "I always heard women were treated little better than slaves in those days."

Richard wiped his mouth very carefully on his white linen napkin. "In some ways, I suppose that is true. By law they were ruled from birth by the men in their families, first their fathers, then their husbands. They could own land in their own name, but their husbands had the power to dispose of it and they could not stop him. If he beat her, neither the church nor the law would interfere. They simply assumed she had done something to deserve it."

Brandy glanced away, her eyes momentarily clouding. Marcus suspected she was remembering the cruelty she had suffered at her father's hands and a tightness crept into his chest.

"Then for the most part," she said with feigned nonchalance, "things haven't really changed."

Richard's gaze swung to her face, reading at least a portion of her thoughts. An expression of sympathy came into his hazel eyes.

He cleared his throat. "Actually, women wielded a surprising amount of power in those days. They ran the estate whenever their husbands were gone, whether he was fighting a war or simply away on business. They held court, and even managed the defense of the castle, if such an act became necessary in his absence.''

Rex grinned. ''That isn't so hard to believe. Should Miss Winters have lived back then, I pity the poor man foolish enough to attack her domain.''

Richard laughed, his eyes lighting. ''Yes, I believe Miss Winters could become quite a formidable opponent if something or someone she valued were in danger.''

Brandy flushed and toyed with the stem of her goblet. She had dressed for the occasion in an elegant black and silver gown, which, aside from the gleaming silver threads of the fabric itself, was completely devoid of decoration. The very starkness of the dress against the pale hue of her skin and the shiny copper of her hair painted a portrait of stunning loveliness, and a feeling of fierce possession stole into Marcus's chest.

It was ridiculous, he knew. She scarcely belonged to him and even if he felt that way, it was a feeling that had to end. Once he was back on his feet, he would be leaving, returning to his life at sea.

Looking at Brianne, watching her smile, listening to the sound of her laughter, he prayed that day would come, and soon. In fact, the sooner, the better.

The evening ended early and Marcus ordered Brandy returned home in the Hawksmoor carriage. Merriweather stayed at the house for three more days. By the time the doctor had left to return to the city, Marcus could lift his knees—slowly, to be sure, even painfully, but each time the task was completed, he felt a new burst of hope for the future.

The movement of his legs continued to progress, but his manhood remained as dead as if he still lay flat on his back confined to his bed. It dulled his sense of accomplishment, marred his vision of the future. As far as he was concerned, even should he walk again, living as some sort of eunuch wasn't really living at all.

Certain he would fail, he'd given up any notion of making love to Brianne, yet he couldn't seem to block her from his mind. Every time she bent over him, exposing a view of those lovely milk-white breasts, every time she ran her hands over his thighs with such erotic tenderness, he got angry. He found himself lashing out at her, had begun to brood again, become surly and short-tempered. Frustration rode like a demon on his shoulders. He wanted her. God, how he wanted her.

At night he dreamed of her, awakened in a cold, slick sweat, his body on fire for her. Yet the heat in his loins could not summon an arousal. Time and again, he vowed to send her away, to get her as far from Hawksmoor House as he possibly could and end this terrible ache that constantly throbbed inside him.

Twice he had called her into his study, determined to do just that, but the soft smile she seemed to reserve just for him speared straight into his heart and any thought of making her leave flew right out the window.

In the end, he vowed to ignore her. Except when they were working, he would simply distance his thoughts, forget how enticing those lovely breasts were, how alluring those small, slender ankles. He wouldn't allow himself to remember the nights that they had made love. Unfortunately, his efforts rarely worked.

It was six days later that Marcus lay in the center of his big four-poster bed, his body tense with need, his undisciplined thoughts sliding once more to Brianne. Though he tried to block her image, he still felt the soft strength of her hands skimming over his flesh as she had worked the muscles in his legs, still suffered the burning desire for her that made his stomach clench and set his jaw on edge.

Unconsciously, his hand moved down his body to the part of him that lay flaccid and even more useless than his legs. If he actually believed he could give himself ease, he would do it, but the thought of suffering another bout of lust without fulfillment made him groan out loud with despair.

Eventually he fell asleep. Long, hot, uncomfortable hours passed, a night of erotic images of lovely rounded breasts and smiling golden eyes. Twice he awakened, his body bathed in sweat, cursing himself, cursing her.

Wanting her.

The dreams came again, Brianne naked beneath him, her small hands clutching his shoulders. He was pounding into her, taking her deeply, feeling the fierce rush of heat that swelled to crescendo in the moments just before climax. It hovered just out of reach, just beyond his grasp as it always did, leaving his body tense and aching.

Dawn filtered in through the high mullioned windows. Shafts of sunlight cut across his eyelids and forced them to open. The dream lingered, a hot mist fading into the vague horizons of his mind. Marcus swore foully, his fist slamming down on the covers, forcing them painfully against his arousal, which throbbed with a long-forgotten ache.

His gaze snapped there, to the sheet tented over his erection. For a moment, he was sure he was still asleep, still mired in his unwanted dreams. He tossed back the covers, not quite willing to believe, saw that he was hard, pulsing with the heat of desire, and once again a man. Something burned at the back of his eyes. Marcus blinked and the sharp sting went away.

He let his head fall back against the pillow and a slow smile tugged at his lips. Outside the window, morning filtered in: birds chirping in the garden, darting above the hedgerows, perching on the leafless branches of a beech tree in the corner. On the shore below the cliffs, the sound of the sea slamming against the rocks brought a second smile to his lips. How long had it been since he had lain there listening to the singing of the birds, or simply watching with pleasure as the sun rose over the water?

Marcus allowed himself a few more quiet moments, savoring the early light of morning, then rang for Frederick to help him bathe and dress. His heart felt light, his spirits the brightest they had been since the accident. For the first time in weeks, he looked forward to the day ahead.

Brandy found Marcus seated in the chair behind his desk in the small wood-paneled library he used as his study. He hadn't been in the room in days, but there he was, his dark head bent over a set of ledgers, so lost in concentration he didn't hear her approach.

Watching him at work, a gentle feeling of love trickled through her. He looked so impossibly handsome, a stray lock of shiny black hair hanging over his forehead, the carved lines of his face falling into light and dark shadow. His shirtsleeves had been rolled back, exposing the muscles in his forearms, thicker now with the hard work of moving himself about without the use of his legs.

Skirting the desk, she came up behind him, settled her hands lightly on his shoulders and felt him momentarily stiffen.

"I didn't hear you come in," he said, relaxing once more, turning his head just slightly to look into her face.

"Giles said you were working. I didn't intend to disturb you, but I simply couldn't resist." She let her fingers linger, lightly massaging the muscles that had begun to tighten once more.

Marcus sighed. "You were right about what you said. My brother has suffered enough at my selfish refusal to carry my share. I intend to rectify that problem now and in the future."

Brandy smiled. "I am glad to hear it. In truth, I don't think you'll find it so terrible a burden." Her hands moved along his neck, absently stroking, sliding into his hair. "You must have been at it awhile. Your muscles feel tight. Shall I help you relax them?" She thought he would argue, send her away. Instead he caught her wrist, brought it to his lips.

"I would like that. Very much. . . ."

Her heart started thudding. Goose bumps rose from the damp place on her wrist where his mouth had been. She helped him pull back his chair, making more room for her, then she began to knead his shoulders, his neck, the ridges of muscle across his back. She loved the feel of his hair curling around her fingers, the bands of muscle that tightened, then slowly relaxed as she worked over them.

They didn't relax today, she noted with a hint of interest. In fact, the more she touched him, the more tense he seemed to become. She thought of the sensual way his mouth had lingered on her skin, moved to the side of his chair and purposely leaned against him. Marcus might have given up on his body's response, but Brandy hadn't and she didn't intend to.

Her pale blue muslin dress was modestly cut, but a bit of cleavage rose above the bodice. Marcus's eyes came to rest there. Brandy caught the quick, hungry flare of his pupils, and her pulse kicked up.

"I believe I could be more efficient if you would allow me to unbutton your shirt." Surely he would stop her, realize her intent and demand that she leave. Marcus merely nodded.

Trying to manage her unsteady fingers, she hummed softly as she worked, pressing her breasts against his arm in a casual manner. She unfastened the buttons on his shirt, tugged it loose from his breeches, and ran her hands inside. Slabs of muscle instantly tightened. Crisp black hairs circled the tips of her fingers.

She worked on the muscles, trying to concentrate, trying to ignore the desire Marcus was supposed to feel, not her, the embarrassing dampness that had settled between her legs.

"Lock the door."

"Wh-what?" She was so involved in what she was doing, so caught up in the feel of his warm, smooth skin, she almost didn't hear him.

"I asked if you would please lock the door."

She didn't question his request. This sort of massage was above and beyond her normal range of duties, and it would be extremely embarrassing if one of the servants walked in.

Brandy crossed to the door and cranked the heavy brass latch, grateful for a moment to collect herself. She turned to find Marcus's gaze locked on her face, felt it move slowly down her body, and a jolt of heat slid into her stomach. At the open front of his shirt, the narrow white tucks stood out in stark contrast to the darkness of his skin and the fine black hair on his chest.

"Come here, Brianne." It was the voice she remembered from the ship.

She moved toward him on legs that suddenly felt wooden,

her throat going dry as she arrived beside his chair. His eyes were pools of midnight blue, fierce and commanding. They dominated her and she couldn't look away.

He caught her hand, kissed the palm, then drew it down to his lap. At the hard ridge pressing against the front of his breeches, Brandy's eyes went wide in amazement.

"You . . . you're . . ."

"Hard? Or perhaps you prefer aroused. Either will do, my love, and both are certainly true." A glint came into those nearly black eyes. "Apparently I was wrong. My legs remain, for the most part, useless, but the rest of me appears to be intact."

Brandy swallowed and wet her suddenly parched lips. "Marcus, that's . . . that's wonderful. Since that is the case, we need to—"

"Since that is the case, what I need is what you have been offering me for the past several weeks." His hand cradled her cheek, moved to the nape of her neck, and before she realized what he was about, he dragged her mouth down to his for a kiss. It was hot and fierce, impossibly sensuous. His tongue swept in, tasting her deeply, and a little whimper escaped.

Her hands were trembling. She braced them on his shoulders and leaned forward, felt his long dark fingers reach out to cup a breast. All the while, he kissed her, teasing the inside of her mouth, nibbling the corners, his tongue sliding in to take possession. He hadn't kissed her that way since they were aboard his ship. Dear God, how could she have forgotten how incredibly good it felt?

Brandy returned the kiss with eager anticipation, her tongue making erotic little forays that darted in and out. She didn't notice when he unbuttoned the back of her dress, only noticed the heat of his hands, the roughness of his palms against her skin. Desire tugged low in her belly. Heat roared into her limbs.

A soft sob slipped from her throat as he filled his hands with her breasts, testing their weight, their texture. His fingers stroked her nipples, making them ache and distend.

Shaking all over, Brandy nipped her teeth into the side of

his neck and Marcus hissed in a breath. She felt his hands beneath her skirts, felt them on the bare skin above her lace garters, and her knees nearly buckled beneath her. He stroked her thighs, parted the folds of her sex and stroked her there.

"God, you feel so good," he whispered against her ear. "You can't know how badly I want you." With that he began to pop the buttons at the front of his breeches one by one, then he was turning her back to him, lifting her up on his lap, and sliding her down on his rigid arousal.

Brandy gasped at the hardness filling her so deeply. The moment he had sheathed himself fully inside, some of the tension seemed to ease from his body and his chin came to rest on the top of her head.

"You drive me insane," he said softly. "I don't even know the man I become when I make love to you."

With her back against his chest, she could feel each of his ragged breaths, and the fierce pounding of his heart. "You're the same man you always are, Marcus. A man of strength and passion." She shifted herself on his lap, driving him more deeply inside. "And I want you, too."

Marcus made a sound low in his throat and his arms tightened around her. He was amazingly strong and he lifted her easily, setting up a rhythm that soon had her body thrumming with desire, coiling ever tighter, expanding then contracting, poised to fly away.

"I can't wait much longer," he warned on the edge of release. "It's been too long and I've wanted you too badly."

The words, spoken with such raw urgency, made the tight coil inside her snap free. In seconds, she was hurling over the edge, her body consumed with pleasure, the sweet fire burning through her like blistering flames. Trembling all over, she cried out his name, her head falling back against his shoulder.

His own release came swiftly, wildly. Marcus poured himself into her with such unrestrained fury a second towering climax shot through her. Even after the last of his passion drained away, he held her in the circle of his arms, his cheek against hers, his head resting lightly on her shoulder.

"Are you all right?" he asked gently.

She smiled. ''I am quite all right.'' Easing herself down from his lap, she straightened her skirts while Marcus buttoned the back of her dress. ''And obviously so are you.''

His mouth curved wickedly. ''So it would seem.''

She turned, cupped his lean, clean-shaven cheek with her hand. ''This proves you're getting well. You're almost there, Marcus. Soon you'll be completely yourself again.''

Marcus didn't answer and Brandy said nothing more. Soon he would be a whole, functioning man again, the man he was before—Captain Marcus Delaine.

Soon, Brandy knew, he would leave her.

A soft ache shimmered through her, destroying her languid contentment. No matter what she did, no matter how much she loved him, he would leave. Now, as she had before, Brandy was going to lose him.

CHAPTER 20

Rex Delaine walked into the small wood-paneled library his brother was using as a study. Marcus sat reviewing a tall stack of papers, bills of lading from Hawksmoor Shipping. In the past few days, his brother had been taking on more and more of the work of running the earldom: Hawksmoor House, its lands and tenants, other of the family's estates.

Rex was more than grateful. It was good for Marcus to have something useful to do, something that challenged him, as captaining his ship once had done. And he was good at it. Marcus had a natural feel for what needed doing. He was meticulous about details, and having been in command for so many years, he had a lot less trouble than Rex getting the tasks completed.

Rex smiled as he crossed the room. For the first time in years, he had time to manage his own affairs and even had a little time for himself.

Marcus glanced up from the files on Hawksmoor Shipping, his black brows pulled into a frown, the files undoubtedly the cause.

"How does it look?" Rex asked, seating himself in a comfortable leather chair on the opposite side of the desk.

Marcus shook his head. "Not good, I'm afraid. Whoever went after *Seahawk* and the rest of our ships did it with a definite purpose. We've been losing contracts steadily, one after another since the first damaged vessel limped into port."

"Any closer to finding out who's behind it?" At the cold,

hard look that slid over his brother's face, Rex almost wished he hadn't asked.

"Nothing I can prove. Word arrived just this morning, information from Reynolds and Kelly, the Bow Street runners I hired. Several companies have profited from our losses, Both Atlantic Limited and the China Seas Company." Marcus's jaw flexed. "But the man who has profited the most is Palmer Reese."

A long breath eased past Rex's lips. "I had a feeling that might be the case."

"So did I."

"It doesn't necessarily mean the man is guilty, or that he is even involved."

"No, unfortunately, it doesn't prove a thing." Marcus's hand unconsciously fisted where it lay on the top of the desk. "But more and more, I am certain he's the man who arranged for the so-called accidents that have plagued us this past year."

"Perhaps that's so, but I still can't credit his motive. Palmer's father was a lifelong friend of the family. Avery Reese and his son visited here several times a year. Forgodsake, all of us used to play together as children."

"Yes, we did. And if you remember correctly, Palmer was a conniving little worm even then, running to the elders, whining and carrying tales behind our back. You might recall that Geoffrey, you, and I received a very sound thrashing once because of him. He ran to Father, told him the three of us had gone swimming in front of the caves below the cliffs. Father had forbid it—"

"Yes, and rightly so, since it was damnably dangerous when the tides came in."

"True, but the point is, the boy was a troublemaker even as a child. And there is every chance the man is responsible for the attacks on Hawksmoor Shipping."

"You're saying the motive could simply be money."

"Exactly. If his finances were not what they seemed and he were in need of funds, he might very well be capable of executing a plan to sabotage his largest competitor. Reynolds and Kelly are doing their best to find out."

Rex said nothing. He didn't know the truth and neither did Marcus, not for sure. He prayed his brother was wrong. Palmer was, in a manner of speaking, a friend of the family, but whatever the truth, sooner or later his brother would find out. Rex shuddered to think what would happen when he did.

He was staring out to sea again, sitting before the windows in the drawing room, or in the gardens above the cliffs, his dark eyes focused nearly unblinking on the horizon.

Brandy knew what Marcus was thinking, knew the progress with his legs allowed him to dream again, to speculate on his return to sea.

Ever since the day he'd discovered he was once more able to make love, he had been making incredible headway, gaining ground by leaps and bounds. He hadn't touched her since, and Brandy knew the reason. He worried he would get her with child, a responsibility he didn't want to leave behind when he sailed away.

A soft ache slid through her. With each new dawn, Marcus attacked the problem of his recovery with a superhuman effort, able now to move both legs in a semblance of actually walking, though he still had to brace himself on the parallel bars and his steps were clumsy and faltering. With each new breakthrough, Brandy sank deeper and deeper into despair, knowing the sooner he walked, the sooner he would leave.

For the first time since her arrival, she actually tried to slow him down, suggesting they sit for a while in the garden, pretending winter was not drawing near and it was really not that cold. Or that they have one of the footmen push his chair with wheels along the path at the top of the cliffs.

Always he refused.

"I don't have time for that nonsense and neither do you. I have to exercise my legs and you should be studying with Professor Felton."

He was pressing her to learn as much as she could, pressing her as hard as he pressed himself. She knew it was because he wanted the best for her, wanted to be certain she had the chance for some sort of future, once he was no longer there.

Sitting in the parlor of her small seaside cottage, Brandy felt a tightness in her chest. Knowing he cared didn't make the hurting any less. She knew he would go—he had made no secret of it. She ached with the knowledge, but there was nothing she could do.

Time continued to pass. By the end of November, *Seahawk* had been a full month out of dry dock and back at sea—and Marcus Delaine was walking. His steps were still slightly awkward, stiff and a little bit rigid, and he was forced to use a cane, but he was able to walk nonetheless, and more and more eager to leave.

Rex must have seen it. It was there in Marcus's face every time he glanced out toward the water. And because it was plain for all to see, whenever Rex looked at Brandy, his eyes held a trace of pity.

"You know he's going to go," he said to her one morning while the two of them strolled the garden. The sea air was damp and pungent, brisk and cool upon her skin. The sound of waves crashing against the rocks drifted up from the shore below. "He won't be happy until he's back at sea."

The pain came again, swift and sharp. "I know."

"Will you return to Charleston?"

Brandy shook her head. "I don't ever want to go back to that place again."

"If you don't go back, what will you do?"

She glanced of in the distance, toward the small neat cottage above the sea, its slate roof barely visible through the trees. "I love it here in Cornwall. It's the first place I've ever been that really felt like home."

Rex arched a brow. "You're staying here in Tintagel? Personally, I should like nothing better, but are you certain it's a good idea? I would think being close to Hawksmoor House, to where you and Marcus spent so much time together, would make things even more difficult."

Her smile was a bit forlorn. "Perhaps, but I don't think

so. I like feeling close to him. Since I can't have that, living here will have to do—at least for the time being. I'm not certain what I'll do after that.''

Rex's hand, so much like his brother's, came up to touch her cheek. ''My brother is making a terrible mistake. Unfortunately, I don't think he'll be able to see it until it is far too late.''

Brandy turned away and they returned to the house through the garden. As she walked beside him along the gravel paths, the hem of her dark green bombazine skirt brushed against the topiary figure of a bear. The ivy beds were freshly tended, the winter garden being readied for the chilly months ahead. In the distance, rain clouds gathered on the horizon. Winter was nearly upon them. Lightning flashed, but it was still too far away to catch the echo of thunder.

''Cook is making sweetbreads tonight,'' Rex said, ''and my favorite dessert, gooseberry tarts. Why don't you stay to supper?''

She glanced up at him. He had invited her more and more frequently. She thought perhaps he was giving her time with Marcus, since he knew so little remained. Or perhaps he was hoping his brother would change his mind and stay.

It was a futile wish and deep down both of them knew it.

''Marcus might have other plans.''

''Marcus won't admit it, but it pleases him when you stay.''

She looked up at him. ''Do you really think so?''

''I know so. He always eats more and occasionally he even smiles. He rarely does that when you're not around.''

''He worries about his ships. He's afraid there'll be more accidents, that others may be hurt.''

''Nothing has happened since Marcus was injured. I think whoever did it is satisfied that he has succeeded. They believe my brother is out of the way for good.''

She paused on the path, turned to face him. ''But if he goes back to the *Seahawk*—''

''If he goes back, there is every likelihood the problems

will begin again. Marcus knows that. He intends to have the culprit routed by then.''

''And if he hasn't?''

''If he hasn't, he will simply have to be more careful.''

Worry jolted through her, making her throat feel raw. Unconsciously, she bit down on her bottom lip.

''You mustn't be afraid,'' Rex said gently, taking her hand and resting it on his arm as they began to walk again. ''My brother is smarter than his opponent believes. And he can be as tough as boot leather when he has to. They won't get ahead of him again.''

Perhaps not, Brandy thought, but it worried her just the same. He had nearly been killed once before. She couldn't stand the thought that something might happen to him again.

''I suppose I had better be going back in. Professor Felton will be waiting. We're supposed to discuss recent popular literature. He says the subject is nearly as good as the weather for polite conversation.''

Rex scoffed. ''And undoubtedly as boring. Why is it the least enjoyable subjects are always considered the most proper?''

Brandy laughed. ''I have no idea. Perhaps that's the reason Marcus is so determined to return to his ship—I assure you life aboard the *Seahawk* is rarely boring.''

Rex smiled softly. ''Nor would his life be boring here—if he were with you. It's a shame he's too blinded by the past and his need for revenge to see.''

Brandy made no reply, but a soft ache throbbed beneath her breastbone. *Blinded by the past and his need for revenge.* And by a love for the sea that was greater than any love he could ever feel for a woman. She knew it, accepted it. But it didn't make the hurting any less.

Dark clouds rolled in, dense, boiling layers that hung low across the evening sky. A harsh wind blew in off the sea, slamming rain-soaked branches against the stone walls of the house, forcing them rhythmically against the mullioned windows.

Brandy had worked late with Professor Felton, then, at Rex's insistence—even Marcus's—stayed to supper. Even the professor was invited and his company turned out to be surprisingly pleasant.

In the meantime, the storm continued to strengthen.

"The hour grows late," Marcus said as they finished their coffee and sweet cakes and the promised gooseberry tarts. As they had each time she had joined them, the men gallantly declined the traditional brandy and cigars, allowing her to remain in the dining room, since she was the only woman present. "I hoped the storm would abate but it hasn't. The lane will be axle-deep in mud, and Miss Winters certainly can't walk home in this gale. I'll have Mrs. Findlay prepare one of the guest rooms."

Brandy set her coffee cup down with a clatter. "But I couldn't possibly stay here. I—"

"Nonsense." Marcus shoved back his chair and stood up, leaning heavily on his cane, a gift from his brother, the silver handle fashioned in the shape of a hawk. "You're here working most of the day. A few more hours will hardly matter. In the morning, I'll have the carriage brought 'round to take you home."

Rex and the professor stood up as well, Rex smiling slightly at his brother's protective manner. "Marcus is right. You must stay the night. I'll have a footman deliver a note to your cottage so your maid won't be frantic with worry."

Brandy nodded. "Thank you." One look at Marcus and it was certain she wouldn't be leaving the mansion tonight, not if he had to haul her upstairs and tie her to the bed. The thought brought such an erotic image her cheeks went warm and she had to look away.

"Before you retire," he said, "I should like to have a word with you in private, if you don't mind."

She studied him a moment from beneath her lashes, wondering what he wanted to speak to her about. "Of course."

Professor Felton made an extravagant bow, his bony, scarecrow frame looking almost comical in the exaggerated movement. "Thank you all for a very pleasant evening. Miss

Winters, I shall see you on the morrow. Perhaps we could discuss a few new techniques for your watercolor paintings. In the afternoon, we shall endeavor to improve your French."

Marcus cocked a brow. "You are learning to speak French?"

Brandy flashed him a saucy smile. "*Oui, m'sieur le comte. Je parler Francais un petit. Y vous?*"

"Good God!" Looking utterly appalled, Marcus glared at the professor. "If I had known you were going to turn her into one of those artificial, simpering—"

"I am hardly that, my lord," Brandy snapped, her chin hiking into the air. "The fact I'm learning to speak another language has nothing to do with being artificial. I'm simply broadening my horizons—at your expense, I might add. And I am quite unashamed of taking advantage of the offer *you* proposed."

Marcus laughed. It was a good to hear the deep, unrestrained rumbling in his chest. "My apologies. It's obvious you will never be that particular sort of woman. For a moment, I was simply taken aback."

Brandy said nothing to that, but a smile tugged at her lips. Rex took his leave and the professor retired to his rooms in another part of the house. Brandy followed Marcus's halting steps into a small candlelit drawing room at the rear of the house.

"Why don't we sit down?"

There was something in his voice, something resigned and oddly disturbing. She had noticed it earlier in the evening, but convinced herself she had imagined it. Now it was there again, and this time she wasn't mistaken.

"All right." At the stern set of his features, her heart began thudding in a slow, uncomfortable rhythm. Marcus seated her on a small brocade sofa in front of the hearth where a fire burned low in the grate. Resting his cane at the side of the couch, he eased himself down beside her.

"I've been putting this off. I'm not certain why. I suppose I didn't know exactly what to say."

Something tightened inside her. "Whatever it is, it's best simply to say it and have done."

"I suppose that's so." He looked at her and she had never seen such intensity in his eyes. "I've asked you here because I wanted to thank you. It is scarcely enough, simply saying those two words. How does a man say thanks for making him whole again? For giving him back his life?" He reached for her hand, brought it to his lips. "There aren't enough thanks in the world, Brianne, for what you have so selflessly given to me."

"Marcus . . ." Her eyes filled with tears. She knew what it cost a man like Marcus Delaine to humble himself in this manner. "You don't have to thank me. Every day that I'm with you is thanks enough for me. We are friends . . . lovers. I'm happy I could give you something for the gifts you've given to me."

"Gifts? What gifts have I given you? Before the accident I was arrogant and demanding. Since then, I've been surly and overbearing and filled with self-pity. Never have you faltered in your loyalty to me. A kingdom would not be payment enough in return for your labors, a fortune in jewels would not begin to cover such a debt."

She only shook her head. "You've given me more than a kingdom, more than a fortune in jewels. You treated me like a lady when I was only a tavern maid. You stood up for me against men like Cole Proctor and Jilly Sharpe, made me feel as if I were a person of worth. You gave me my first taste of freedom in those days aboard your ship, a glimpse of life beyond my own dingy world. You valued me as a friend and, because you did, I gained the courage to stand up to my father. You made me a woman, Marcus. You taught me the sharing of pleasure. You lent me your strength when I needed it most and gave me hope for the future. Those are your gifts, Marcus, gifts I can never repay."

Marcus sat there staring. Something flickered in his eyes, which looked dark and piercing. A graceful hand came up to her cheek. "I'll never forget you, Brianne Winters. Never."

Tears burned her eyes. A harsh ache rose inside her chest. "You're leaving, aren't you?"

His hand fell away. He nodded. "*Seahawk*'s first voyage was a short one. I'll be leaving to join her the end of the week."

Pain lanced through her. It was savage, like a knife tearing through flesh and bone. The tears in her eyes began to slide down her cheeks. "I knew you would go. I hoped . . . prayed it might not be so soon."

"Brianne . . . love . . ." He reached for her, pulled her into his arms. A faint tremor ran through his long, lean frame. "If I could stay, I would. This is something I have to do. The sea is my life, Brianne. It always has been. That isn't something I can change."

Tears clung to her lashes. Marcus brushed them away with the tips of his fingers. "I knew you would go," she said. "I've always known. It isn't your fault. It's just that—" Her voice broke on this last and Marcus held her as she wept against his shoulder.

"Don't, love. Please don't cry. I can't bear it when you cry."

She shuddered, tried to pull herself together. Her throat ached. Her chest burned. Even the air seemed too hot as she forced it into her lungs.

"I never meant to hurt you," he whispered against her hair. "Please . . . forgive me."

Brandy's eyes slid closed on a fresh wave of pain. She felt close to breaking. "There is nothing to forgive. You never lied to me. I knew you would leave."

"There are times I wish I could stay . . . so many times. In my heart I know it would never work out. I would always feel the loss, the yearning for the life I was meant for."

"From the first I've known the way you were. Perhaps your sense of freedom was what attracted me to you from the start."

"You've always understood. I could see it in your eyes whenever I looked at you. There are times even I don't understand why I'm the way I am."

She looked into those blue, blue eyes, her heart squeezing hard in her chest. "Sometimes the paths we take seem to be chosen by somebody else. Perhaps God decides those things."

"Yes . . . perhaps He does."

"I'm going to miss you, Marcus."

He held her close again. "I owe you my life, Brianne. I owe you so much more."

Brandy shook her head. "You owe me nothing. A man owes nothing to his mistress."

Marcus gripped her shoulders and stared into her face. "I owe you everything! Everything! Don't you ever say a thing like that to me again!" He dragged her back into his arms and she clung to him, trying not to cry, unable to stop. She loved him so much.

She held him for long, agonizing moments, then dragged in a ragged, hiccuping breath and eased away. "I have to go up to my room. I'm tired and I—I have to . . . I have to . . . Please don't ask me to stay here any longer."

He kissed her forehead, her eyes, her nose. "I wish things could be different. I wish *I* could be different."

Brandy touched his cheek, felt the roughness of his day's growth of beard. "I wouldn't want you to be any different. I wouldn't want to change a single thing."

She forced herself up from the couch and walked away from him on legs that felt leaden. Her heart seemed dead in her chest. When she reached the door and pulled it open, she heard the soft sound of Marcus's voice.

"You knew I would return to the sea. You've always known. Why did you come here? Why did you help me when you knew that if I recovered I would leave?"

Brandy turned, saw his face, dark and ravaged in the light of the candles. Her own was wet with tears. "Because I love you, Marcus. Surely you know that. I've always loved you. I imagine I always will."

Marcus said nothing, but the muscles in his throat constricted and another tightened in his jaw. The regret on his face seemed to blossom tenfold. Brandy turned away from him and stepped out into the hall. Quietly, she closed the door.

Marcus lay in his big four-poster bed staring up at the ceiling, restless and unable to sleep. He was going away, leaving Brianne, just as he had before. It had hurt the first time. This time the pain already ate away at him and he hadn't yet left the house.

Because I love you, Marcus. I've always loved you. No one had said those words to him before, not even his mother and father. They had loved him, he knew, had shown it in their care of him, their worry, but it wasn't the same as hearing it from a woman who had come to mean so much to him.

A woman he had come to admire and hold in such deep regard. He had meant what he had said. He could never repay her for making him a whole man again. It frightened him to think what he might have become if she hadn't come to Cornwall to help him. Even if he hadn't learned to walk again, he could have made it, could have survived—because of her. Because she had forced him to see another side of life. She had forced him to live again.

In return he had hurt her, as she had known he would.

I love you, Marcus. I've always loved you. The words drove a sharp lance of pain into his heart. He owed her so much—and yet he could not stay.

The room seemed suddenly warm, the fire too hot in the grate. He dragged the nightclothes he rarely wore off over his head and tossed them to the foot of the bed. Lying naked beneath the sheet, he sighed into the darkness, knowing there was nothing he could do to change things. Not really wanting to. He was a man of the sea. Always had been. Always would be. His ships had been threatened, a part of his life stolen from him. Now he meant to return to that life, to right the wrongs that had been done him. To make the man responsible pay.

But God, he would miss her.

A noise sounded in the darkness. The latch turned on the

door. Softly, silently, Brianne slipped into the room. His chest swelled with pain.

"I had to come, Marcus. I needed to be with you—just this one last time."

The muscles in his throat went tight. God, he needed her, too. He hadn't known how much until she had stepped inside the room. He watched her walking toward him and simply drew back the covers, afraid to speak, afraid she would hear the raw need in his voice.

Perhaps she read it in his face, lit by the moonlight slanting in through the mullioned panes. Outside, the storm still raged. Lightning flashed and thunder rumbled, shaking the windows of the house. The wind howled through the trees, and the leafless branches trembled with the force.

"I'm glad you came," he said softly. "I would have come to you if you hadn't." It was the truth, he realized as he hadn't before. "I couldn't leave without telling you . . . without showing you how much I care." He reached for the tie of the soft cotton wrapper Mrs. Findlay had provided, unbuttoned the front of her plain white night rail. Her hair was loose down her back, long and gleaming like fire. He hadn't seen it that way since they had shared his cabin aboard the ship.

A bitter ache rose inside him, throbbing deep in his chest. God, she looked beautiful, so sweetly feminine, so incredibly seductive. He had never met a woman who made him feel the things he was feeling in that moment. Need, desire, joy that she was simply there. An urge to possess her, to bind her to him in a way that would last forever.

And some other, deeper emotion that he was afraid to name.

He eased the gown off her shoulders with a hand that felt suddenly shaky, watched it pool around her ankles. She stood beside the bed, naked, vulnerable, giving herself to him in that way she had since the first time they had made love.

He reached out to her, drew her to him, kissed her deeply, tenderly. Gently. Fiercely.

"Marcus . . ."

The sound of his name on her lips brought a sting to the back of his eyes. What would he do without her?

Lifting her up on the bed, he settled her astride him, watched the fall of her hair as it parted, then slipped forward to rest on her shoulders, bathing her breasts in strands of coppery silk. The nipples shown through, tight and quivering with each of her breaths.

He reached out and cupped one, stroked the tip with his thumb, watched it swell and tighten. His mouth felt dry. His heart was pounding. He looked into her eyes, saw the need, saw the love, and it moved him as nothing else ever had.

"Brianne . . ." He framed her face with his hands, brought her mouth down to his for a kiss. He savored the taste of her, the breath of her, the feel of her skin beneath his fingers. He breathed her in, inhaled her scent, absorbed the very essence of her, as if in doing so he could take a part of her with him.

He caressed her breasts, admired their beauty, held them with reverence. He tasted them that same way, filling his mouth with their weight, stroking them gently with his tongue, wanting to give her pleasure, needing to.

He kissed her again, deeply, possessively, settled his hands at her waist and lifted her up, eased her down carefully, sheathing himself inside her. A soft little whimper came from her throat and the sound of it, the feel of her gloving him so sweetly, made him groan.

Her hair drifted forward as she began to move, slowly at first, tentatively, watching him from beneath her thick dark lashes. Little by little she increased the rhythm, moving faster, taking her pleasure, giving him more than she knew. Her skin felt as soft as the petals of a rose, looked pale and flawless in the light slanting in through the window. She moved gracefully, rocking to and fro, caught up in the motion, her breathing faster, sweeping him along the road to a place of sweetness and light. His hands gripped her hips, urging her to take from him, helping her to glean that which she sought.

Her muscles went tighter, her movements faster. He met the force of her body with deep, upward thrusts, giving her what she needed, determined to see to her pleasure. Her head fell back and her breasts thrust forward. His own pleasure soared. Still, he held himself back, driving into her, watching the need in her build, feeling each of her movements, giving, giving, until her body tightened around him in sweet, nearly unbearable waves.

Her climax came swiftly, jolting him with its intensity, driving him to his own release. She found her pleasure a second time, both of them cresting together, Brianne slumping forward across his chest.

He stroked her hair and held her, his hardness still inside her. When she roused herself and tried to pull away, he simply shook his head. Easing her down beside him, he tucked her safely in the circle of his arms, holding her, knowing he would make love to her again.

In the morning she would leave him and he would let her.

It occurred to him, for the very first time, he would be the one who hurt the most when he went away.

CHAPTER 21

Brandy didn't see Marcus for the next three days. Though she continued her lessons with Professor Felton, Marcus never appeared. He was packing, making ready to leave, she knew. Every time she thought of it, her heart broke all over again.

On the fourth day, the professor announced that she had successfully completed his classes on etiquette with the very highest marks, and that he would be returning to London.

"You've been an excellent pupil, Miss Winters. I can't recall a student ever working any harder." His lips curved with satisfaction beneath his long, pointed nose. "You comport yourself with dignity and propriety. I vow, if the opportunity arose, you could converse with flawless ability in the Queen's drawing room."

She flushed at the compliments. "Thank you, Professor. You've been wonderful. I shall never forget all you've done." She went up on tiptoe to kiss his hollow cheek, feeling ridiculously close to tears. He gathered his belongings and departed the house a few minutes later, and Brandy left to return to her cottage.

The end of the week arrived. Marcus was due to leave—she refused to believe he had done so already—and still she hadn't seen him. Surely he wouldn't leave Tintagel without saying good-bye? And yet it was certainly possible. They had said their good-byes the night they'd made love in his bedchamber, a night she would never forget.

Marcus had been achingly tender. He had given her pleasure again and again, revealed a part of himself she had never seen before. She had cried in his arms, and he had held her, soothed her, made love to her again. In the morning, she had returned to her room before he had awakened and she hadn't seen him since.

Now, as she carried her embroidery to an overstuffed chair in the parlor of the cottage and sat down before the fire, she tried to tell herself it was better this way, better that he simply left without word, that it would be easier if she didn't have to watch him ride away.

She tried to concentrate on her sewing, tried to force the dark green thread to follow the lines of the pattern, but her eyes kept straying to the window, toward the distant towers of Hawksmoor House.

With a sigh of frustration, she set the embroidery aside and stood up just as a soft knock came at the door. Her heart began pounding. A glance out the smaller windows at the front of the house and she spotted the Hawksmoor carriage. The moment she dreaded had arrived.

Brandy dragged in a shaky breath and steeled herself against the pain she knew would come. She crossed the room and pulled open the door, saw Marcus standing on the porch in snug black breeches and a dove-gray coat, a graceful hand wrapped around his silver-headed cane. A slight breeze ruffled his curly black hair and his eyes looked more blue than she had ever seen them.

"Marcus . . ."

"I couldn't just go. I thought I could—that perhaps it would be better, but . . ."

A soft sob came from her throat. She was in his arms in a heartbeat, clinging to his neck, her face tilting up to his. "I prayed you would come. I prayed just as hard that you would not."

"I know. I felt the same." His arms tightened around her. He buried his face in her hair. "I wish it could be different. I wish I had the courage to stay."

Brandy glanced up at him, saw the dark smudges beneath his eyes and the weariness in his features.

His hand caressed her cheek. "I want you to know I've never felt this way about a woman. It hurts like hell to leave you. I'm lucky to have known you, Brianne."

Tears burned her eyes. She looked into his handsome, beloved face. "I would go with you," she said, knowing she shouldn't, knowing it wasn't what he wanted. "I would go wherever you wished."

He only shook his head. "I know you would. It wouldn't be right, Brianne. Not for you, or for me."

It would *be right,* she thought. *We could be happy. It wouldn't matter where we were as long as were together.* But she didn't say it. Saying it wouldn't change his mind. "Will you . . . will you write to me?"

Marcus glanced away, studying the wall above her head. He swallowed hard and nodded. "Letters are difficult to post. I'll try to send word, if that is your wish."

"Of course it's my wish. I want to be sure you're safe."

His eyes swung to hers, turbulent eyes, filled with a pain she hadn't thought to see. "And you, Brianne? What will happen to you? I told you once before, you have to do what is best for you."

Tears welled, blurred her vision. She blinked and they trickled down her cheeks. "I just need a little time. For now, I'm going to stay here." *Close to where you were.*

His eyes closed for an instant. Marcus leaned toward her, brushed his lips against her forehead. "I have to be going. It's past time I was away." But he made no move to leave, and Brandy clung to him tighter. Her throat ached. Her heart hurt unbearably.

"How long . . . how long will you be gone?"

"I'm not sure. The better part of a year, perhaps more."

A year, maybe longer. Dear God, this was truly good-bye.

His eyes held hers, troubled and turbulent. "There is always the chance you might carry my babe. If you discover that is the case, if you need anything, anything at all—"

She only shook her head. All she needed was him. It was the one thing she could not have. "I'll be fine. I can take care of myself."

Something moved across his features. "I suppose you can. I only wish . . ." He shook his head. "Nothing. My life is the sea. It always has been. It is past time I returned."

Her throat thickened and ached. She tilted her face to receive his good-bye kiss, but she couldn't have imagined the terrible pain that came with it. She couldn't have guessed the hurting would be so great she wasn't sure she could remain on her feet.

He pressed a final soft kiss against her forehead. "Take care of yourself, my love."

"And you," she whispered, leaning against the door, clinging to the edges for support. His features looked haggard as he turned away, leaning on his cane as he walked back to the carriage. Her hand trembled as she reached for the small silver locket she wore around her neck, the gift he had given her the last time they had parted. Her fingers closed over it. The edges pressed into her skin.

Marcus climbed into the coach and closed the door, motioned to the driver, and the horses leaned into their traces. All the while he watched her, his eyes fixed on her face, his features a mask of control. She watched until the vehicle rolled out of sight, watched until the sounds of the horses had long faded, and still stood there watching.

She felt like a broken doll, battered and discarded. Pain and loss swallowed her whole, seeped beneath her skin, gnawed at her until there was nothing left but an endless stream of hurting.

She stumbled into the house and closed the door, grateful no one else was there to see. Thick tears clogged her throat, and a heart-wrenching ache that went soul deep. Sinking down on the sofa, she gave in to the wracking sobs that tore through her, crying until her eyes were swollen and her nose was red, until she thought she had no more tears.

In the night, she cried again, and every day and every night for the following week. Rex came to see her, but she pretended a headache and excused herself after only a few minutes. Just the sight of him, his appearance so like his brother, made the pain unbearable again.

Richard Lockhart came to call the following week and she sat with him for a while. He came the next day and the day after that, and some of the pain began to ease.

Marcus was gone. She loved him beyond all reason. She would never love anyone else in that way. But she would survive. It was simply her nature.

On the surface, she went on with the job of living, filling her days with the simplest tasks, shopping, sewing, reading, gardening when the weather permitted, but inside she felt as though part of her had died the day that Marcus had left her. The spark of life, the flame that had burned inside her, the very essence of her being had simply gone out the day he went away.

Rex sat across from Richard Lockhart in Richard's shiny black carriage. His friend had returned last week after spending the winter months with his family in the city. He had gone to see Brianne first thing on his arrival, then come to Hawksmoor House straightaway. Richard was worried about her. And in truth, so was Rex.

"It's been months since Marcus left," Richard said, "and still she grieves for him."

Rex nodded, leaning back against the tufted red leather seat. "She isn't herself anymore. She smiles and nods and makes all the right responses, but in truth, she seems more like a puppet than the woman she was before, as though she's going through the motions but someone else is pulling the strings."

"Your brother was a fool to leave her," Richard said darkly.

"His life is the sea. It always has been."

"He could have taken her with him."

Rex shook his head. "It is simply not his way. Brianne knew that. She accepted it from the start."

"She is hurting, Rex. I think she should leave this place." Richard gazed out the window, to the stark winter landscape passing by outside the carriage. "I have spoken to my mother. She has invited Brianne for a visit."

Rex cocked a brow. "To Seacliff?"

"No. To our family home in London."

Halliday Hall, a palatial estate at the edge of the city. Even Rex had been impressed with the opulence of the marquess's mansion. "What did you tell Lady Halliday? Surely she doesn't know Brianne was . . . that she was . . ."

"Marcus's mistress?"

Rex nodded grimly. He had never thought of Brianne that way. What she felt for his brother somehow made a difference.

"My mother knows only what I've told her. That Brianne came here from America. That she is sweet and genuine, and that she has become a very dear friend." A hint of color washed into Richard's cheeks. "And she knows that I care for her greatly."

Rex straightened in surprise, his sharp gaze swinging to that of his friend. "Good Lord, man. Are you telling me you are thinking of marriage?"

Richard sat forward on the carriage seat. "Is that so hard to believe? I realize she is no longer an innocent. That was quite obvious from the way she dealt with your brother. I don't care. She is beautiful and desirable. She is kind and caring. She is perhaps the most decent woman I have ever met."

"She is also in love with my brother," Rex said gently.

Richard took a firmer hold on the brim of the tall beaver hat that rested on his lap. "Marcus doesn't want her. Brianne knows that. She needs a man who will take care of her, treat her as she deserves. We are friends already. Marriages have been based on far less than that. I am not my father's heir, so her background is of little importance. I can provide for her very well, see to her future, and . . . in time . . . I believe she might even come to love me."

Rex made no comment. The carriage wheels whirled; harness jangled and clattered. "It's too soon, you know. She isn't ready for that kind of involvement."

"I realize that. For the present, I merely wish to convince her to accept my offer and come with me to London. In another month or so, the Season will begin. I believe my mother will like her very much. I am hoping she'll be willing to introduce Brianne into Society.'' Richard's gaze sharpened on Rex. ''Will you help me?''

He wanted to and yet he felt guilty. Deep down, Rex knew, his brother cared for Brianne as he never had another woman. Perhaps he even loved her. But Marcus had made his choice. He had returned to his life at sea, and that life did not include Brianne.

''I'll help you. And I think you may be right. Staying here in Tintagel was perhaps not the wisest course. Marcus has hired a steward for the management of Hawksmoor House and the rest of his estates. I can run my own affairs just as easily from our town house in the city.'' He grinned, liking the idea more and more. ''I believe I shall go with you.''

''Splendid!'' Richard smiled, obviously delighted. ''We will simply not take no for an answer. Together, we'll present such a formidable force the lady will have to agree.''

Rex smiled. ''And if she refuses, we shall merely abduct her. One way or another, Miss Brianne Winters is going to London.''

CHAPTER 22

Brandy stood next to Richard Lockhart in the foyer of the Marquess of Halliday's lavish mansion on the outskirts of London. She could hardly believe she was there, that she had traveled with Rex and Lord Richard and the very stuffy lady's companion, Mrs. Greenwald, whom Rex had insisted accompany them.

She could hardly believe they had convinced her to come—actually more like threatened her into coming—but after her reservations had faded, and with the help of her congenial hosts, she was glad she was there.

She glanced at her surroundings, still awed by an elegance unmatched by anything she could have imagined. If Hawksmoor House was impressive, Halliday Hall was lavish beyond compare. Above her head, painted rococo ceilings arched in a majestic dome crowned by gilded angels. Busts of Roman emperors lined the walls, and a huge crystal chandelier glittered with the light of a hundred candles.

Brandy mentally shook herself, still not quite believing she was at this very moment awaiting the presence of the Marchioness of Halliday, that she had spent an entire month with Richard's family. Had, in truth, come to love them like the family she'd never had.

"There you are, my dear." Lady Halliday surged into the room on a wave of saffron silk. She was slender, blond, and beautiful, looking more like Richard's older sister than his mother. "I apologize for keeping you waiting. My husband had some last-minute''—a slight flush spread into her cheeks—''instructions he wished to discuss.''

Brandy smiled. She knew exactly the sort of instruction the lady's handsome husband had been giving her. The marquess and his wife were obviously very much in love, even after all the years they had been together. ''That's quite all right. Richard has been keeping me company.''

Lady Halliday gazed with fondness at her youngest son. ''Well, in that case, I am no longer concerned. You were in very good hands.'' She reached up and patted his freshly shaven cheek. ''Thank you for volunteering, Ritchie. The Season is practically upon us and Brianne and I are both in dire need of the proper clothes.''

Dire need? Brandy would hardly call it that. Already they had made two major forays into the world of London fashion. Grudgingly, she thanked her father for the money he had left her. Gowns suitable for the fashionable routs and receptions, house parties and balls she had attended with the marquess and marchioness were extravagantly expensive. Still, she could afford it, and she wasn't about to disgrace herself by wearing something inappropriate.

They left the house and the coach made its way through the crowded London streets. Eventually they reached the area of the city they sought, passing the elegant shops of St. James's, stopping in front of one store after another. When they arrived at Madame Rousseau's Lady's Apparel Shop, the carriage stopped again, and Richard climbed out to help them down.

''I dare say, the two of you are wearing me out,'' he said. ''I believe I shall wait for you out here in the carriage.''

His mother's fine blond brows drew together. ''Nonsense. We cannot possibly do this without you. We need your male expertise.'' She whirled toward the door leading into the shop, speaking to him over one shoulder. ''You have always had such marvelous taste.''

Richard sighed and threw up his hands, but he was smiling and Brandy thought that he was actually pleased to be pressed into going with them. For the next several hours, the women selected fabric for a dozen more new gowns and Brandy suffered the final fittings of the ones she had chosen before.

Incredibly, the marchioness finished first, perhaps because Brandy was not quite so confident in what she should choose. Seating herself on a brocade sofa next to Richard, Lady Halliday opened her painted fan and fluttered it in front of her face to cool herself in the warm interior of the shop. It was lined floor to ceiling with thick bolts of fabric, and several women worked at tables behind a curtain in the corner.

The smell of starch and dye filled the air and faintly stung Brandy's eyes. Standing on a dais in front of an elegant brocade sofa, she endured the final fitting, her gaze going to Lady Halliday, who studied with an eye of scrutiny the nearly finished gold and amber gown Brandy wore.

"What do you think, Richard? A bit of lace along the neckline just along the bust? Or perhaps we could add—"

"No," Brandy interrupted softly. "No lace. I prefer it just as it is."

"That is what you always say," Lady Halliday grumbled, surveying her from head to foot. She sighed. "Then again, perhaps in this you are correct. The simple lines somehow suit you. In an odd way, it enhances the beauty of your face and figure."

"Exactly so," Richard said softly, looking at her in that disturbing way she had noticed of late. He was a kind, generous man, and a wonderful friend. She would always be indebted to him for helping her get through the pain of losing Marcus.

Unbidden, his image came to mind, long legs splayed against the roll of the ship, handsome face bronzed by the sun, black hair windblown and curling, dark as ink against the white of his collar. She swung her gaze to Richard and forced the image away, burying it again in the recesses of her heart.

"The emerald silk is also quite lovely," Richard was saying. "Just the purest green with a hint of gold. 'Twill be perfect for the duchess's ball the end of next week."

"Indeed. An excellent choice," Lady Halliday said. She

turned to Madame Rousseau. "We'll need several items more. Do you have anything in a teal or cinnamon? With Miss Winters's coloring, those tones would do very well."

"*Oui,* my lady." The little French shopkeeper finished restacking the cast-off bolts of cloth that weren't being used. "We 'ave a number of such items. I shall bring a new selection *tout de suite.*"

Richard and Brianne looked at each other and in unison they groaned. Then both of them burst out laughing. It felt good to laugh again, to feel the lightness of it bubbling up from her throat. If it hadn't been for Richard and his family, perhaps she never would have laughed again, at least not from the heart.

She studied him from beneath her lashes. With his fine features, sandy hair, and slender build, he was definitely attractive. And his mind was attractive as well, his intelligence, his constant quest to learn. She had discovered that same desire in herself and spent pleasant hours reading the books he chose for her, then discussing with him what she had learned.

He had turned her life around, brought her out of the darkness. She owed him. Sweet God, she owed him so much. And she liked him, truly liked him.

By the time Lady Halliday had finished her shopping excursion, Brandy was exhausted. Still, it was a good sort of fatigue and she looked forward to the evening ahead. Richard was taking her to an opera. She had never been to an opera before. Just thinking about it lifted her spirits.

And Rex would be joining them. It only hurt a little now, when she looked at him and saw a glimpse of Marcus in his face.

Marcus stood behind the huge teakwood wheel of the *Seahawk,* the smooth polished spokes damp beneath his fingers. A squall had blown up out of the west, driving the ship a little off course, and a chill wind whipped his canvas slicker through the open door of the wheelhouse. The ship rolled forward and he braced himself as it dropped into a trough.

Marcus smiled to himself at the familiar groan of the heavy

timbers beneath his feet. His back was healed, his legs nearly as strong as they were before the accident. Though he still used a cane and always would, only a slight limp slowed his progress when he walked. The use of his legs had been returned, along with command of his beloved ship. He had yet to discover the culprit behind the attacks on Hawksmoor Shipping, but no new problems had arisen, at least as far as he'd been able to discern.

All in all, his life was back to normal. Except for the shipping contracts he had lost, everything he'd had before had been returned to him. Like the biblical Job, he thought. The pain he had suffered was past and all that he held dear had been gifted to him again. His life, his future, was once again his to command—

So why did he feel so empty?

''Evenin', Cap'n.''

Marcus dragged his thoughts from the unpleasant direction they had wandered and smiled. ''Good evening, Hamish.'' The older man stepped through the door to the wheelhouse, water dripping off the brim of the canvas hat he had pulled down over his ears. Strands of long gray hair clung wetly to the wrinkles on his neck.

''Storm don't look too bad, but it's hard to say for sure. Ye never can tell in this part of the world when one of them hurricanes might decide to blow.''

Marcus surveyed the flat gray clouds overhead, the dense fall of rain, and noticed a lighter gray around the edges. ''I don't think there's much chance of that, but I don't intend to take any chances. Mr. Hopkins has been ordered to reef the sails a bit more. We'll furl the topsail if she gets any worse.''

Hamish pulled the hat from his head and ran a hand through his long gray hair, slicking it back from his forehead. ''Cook's been keepin' supper for ye. Said ye haven't eaten a thing all day.''

''I was busy. Besides, I'm not hungry. I could use a cup of coffee, though.''

Hamish nodded. ''I'll see to it.'' He fidgeted a bit, didn't move toward the door. ''Ye ought to take better care of ye-self, Cap'n. Ye've lost weight since ye come aboard. Somethin's been botherin' ye. Ye ain't said, but I've a notion the both of us knows what it is.''

Marcus arched a brow. ''Do we?''

''Are ye sayin' it ain't the girl?''

Marcus shrugged. ''She was special. I cared for her a good deal. It's only natural I should miss her from time to time.''

''Aye, I suppose that's so.'' He glanced toward the door, but still didn't leave. ''Feels good to be back aboard, don't it?''

Marcus nodded, though oddly he hadn't felt nearly the euphoria he had expected. ''Very good.''

''And the China run. Ye've been wantin' to go there for years. Looks like yer finally gonna get yer chance.''

''Aye.'' But lately the thrill seemed somehow to have faded. ''It should be a profitable venture.''

''Profitable . . . aye.'' But Hamish was frowning. Perhaps he remembered that it was the lure of parts unknown, not the money, that had always enticed him before.

Marcus stared out through the rain-spattered windows of the wheelhouse. ''Storm's building a bit.''

''Aye, that it is.''

Hamish hesitated as if he wanted to say something more. Instead, he simply turned toward the door. ''Looks to be a bit meaner that we thought, and the damnable wind's as cold as the devil's brew. I'd best be fetchin' that coffee.''

Marcus's gaze followed the older man's swagger out the door. It was obvious his longtime friend was worried about him. It was foolish, ridiculous for Hamish to be concerned. So he was a little out of sorts. It was simply a matter of adjusting, getting used to being back at sea. In the end, it would all work out as he had planned. He would be happy with his life again, content as he was before.

The thought made something heavy settle in his chest. It was a feeling he had noticed before. Marcus forced himself to ignored it. Gripping the wheel, he fixed his eyes on the gray line of the horizon and thought of the journey ahead.

Instead of anticipation, he found himself counting the endless stream of days he would face before he'd be sailing home.

Brandy strolled one of the dozens of moonlit paths of Vauxhall Gardens, her hand resting gently on the sleeve of Richard's coat. "Your mother and father seem to be enjoying themselves tonight."

"Mother's always in her glory here at Vauxhall. She adores the place. She thinks it's incredibly romantic."

Brandy smiled. She could hear the orchestra playing a serenade in the distance. "Yes, I believe it is." The gardens were dense with tall trees and dark green foliage, and crisscrossed with meandering gravel paths. There were supper boxes decorated with statues and paintings, and temples and arches and pavilions. "The fireworks were wondrous."

"I'm glad you enjoyed them."

"And the music—it's really very lovely."

Richard stopped on the path and turned her to face him. "Yes, it is, but you, Brianne, are even more lovely."

Brandy flushed a little, not used to this new Richard who seemed to be paying her court. She still wasn't certain she should let him. They were, after all, hardly of the same social class. And she was no longer a virgin. But neither of those things seemed of any import to Richard, who appeared in some way to be enamored of her.

Tonight he seemed intent on pressing his suit, and she had decided to let him. She liked Richard Lockhart and she owed him. He had appeared at her door like a knight of old to save her from slowly drowning in despair. She enjoyed his company and his friendship. She would be a very fortunate woman if Richard asked her to marry.

She felt the heat of his hand over hers and noticed the faint tremor in his touch. Dressed in a dark brown tailcoat with a wide white stock, in the light of the flickering torches, he looked more and more uneasy.

"I've been wanting to speak to you," he said. "Privately, I mean. I thought tonight might provide an opportunity . . . before, that is, I went so far as to make a formal request."

Richard swallowed and cleared his throat, and her own nerves cranked up a notch.

"Yes, Richard?"

He glanced down at the toes of his shiny black shoes, his cheeks a little bit flushed, then back into her face. "What I'm trying to ask, though so far I am doing a rather poor job of it, is whether or not you would consider allowing me to pursue the matter of a marriage between us."

There it was—just as she had imagined. Richard was offering marriage, the kind of future every woman dreamed of. She told herself she was prepared for this, but now that the time had actually come, she didn't feel prepared in the least.

She dragged in a steadying breath. "I—I am flattered, of course. Even to consider such a match between us, you have paid me a tremendous honor, Richard."

"I am the one who would be honored. I should like to ask you to marry me. I won't do so tonight. I simply want to know whether or not if I did, you would consider my suit."

Brandy forced back the uncertainty that suddenly gripped her insides. Richard was a kind and generous man and a very dear friend. He had stood by her when she needed a friend very badly. In the past few months, he had become a constant in her life. She remembered how terribly lost and alone she had been when he had first appeared at the cottage. She didn't want to face that terrible loneliness ever again.

She wet her suddenly dry lips. "If . . . if you wish to pursue the matter of marriage, I would be extremely pleased, Richard."

His face broke into a grin. "Are you telling me you would say yes?"

She smiled at him softly. "You said you would not ask me tonight."

His grin went even broader. "I believe I've changed my mind."

"What about your parents? Are you certain they would approve the match?"

"They want me to be happy. They love you, Brianne. More than anything, I want to marry you. Say yes, Brianne. Say you'll be my wife."

It was suddenly hard to drag enough air into her lungs. Was marriage really what she wanted? A lifetime bound to one man? Making a home for him? Waking up beside him in the mornings? Raising his children? The answer came back with surprising force. *Yes.* She wanted a home and family. She wanted the sort of stability Lord and Lady Halliday had.

"If you are truly asking—"

He dropped down on one knee in front of her, reached up and captured her hand. "I am."

The tightness in her chest spread out into her limbs. "Then . . . yes. I should be honored to become your wife."

Richard pressed the back of her gloved hand against his lips, then slowly rose to his feet. "Thank you, Brianne. You've made me an incredibly happy man." Leaning toward her, he brushed a brief kiss on her lips.

There was no heat, no fire, only a faint, gentle warmth. It embarrassed her to discover she was disappointed.

"We'll be happy, Brianne. I promise you."

She forced herself to smile. Images of Marcus briefly surfaced, but she ruthlessly forced them away. "I'm certain we will be."

"I don't want a long engagement." He squeezed her hand. "Not unless you do, of course."

Her mouth curved only slightly. "I want whatever you want, Richard."

He bent and kissed her cheek. "Good girl. Tomorrow we'll tell my parents. As soon as it can be properly arranged, we'll be married." Richard replaced her hand on the sleeve of his jacket and began to guide her down the path in the direction they had come.

Brandy said nothing on their return to the pavilion. All she could think was that she would soon be married. As frightened as she was, with each step she took, the notion began to hold more appeal. With Richard there would be children. She would have a friend to share the pleasure of watching them grow up.

She wouldn't have to worry about the day he would leave

her. She wouldn't have to face the years ahead feeling empty and alone.

Marcus stood at the rail of the *Seahawk,* staring out at a high, windswept sea. Above his head, the sails strained to harness the force of the wind and the ship heeled toward the taffrails.

Marcus felt the chill bite through his clothes, but his mind was not on the weather. It was not on the sea, or even the ship rolling beneath his feet. Instead, his thoughts clung to the past, to days when his heart had been full, warmed by the presence of a woman.

Now those days were gone and in their place, loneliness ate at him, never let him rest. He had never been lonely at sea before, not in all the years he had sailed, not in all the ports he had gone to, not until he met Brianne.

In the months since he had left her, he had told himself a thousand times it was foolish even to think of her. She was gone from his life, gone as he had wanted. He had made it clear she had no place in his world and that she should make a life for herself without him. He had been certain this yearning for her would fade from his mind and heart.

Instead he pined for her, week after week, month after month. No matter how he tried, no matter how hard he worked, he could not forget her.

A noise up in the shrouds drew his attention to the sailors working above. Across the deck, Hamish Bass strode toward him, pulling his curved pipe from between his teeth as he approached. "We'll be comin' into Port o' Spain in a day or two, weather keeps on like this."

Marcus nodded. They were headed for the island of Trinidad in the southern West Indies. Port o' Spain was the largest harbor. "We'll be taking on cargo and fresh supplies. Shouldn't take longer than a week."

"Ye've a lady friend there, as I recall."

He arched a brow. "The schoolteacher, you mean?"

"The widow, Mrs. Reynolds, it seems to me. Golden hair and a pretty face. She always welcomes ye when yer in port."

"I haven't seen the woman in more than a year. She is probably married by now."

Hamish leaned a hip against the rail. "Then ye don't mean ta see her?"

Marcus shrugged his shoulders. He hadn't the least desire to see the woman, couldn't imagine the two of them sharing a bed as they usually did. He could scarcely remember her face.

Hamish clamped the pipe between his teeth, took a long draw and then another. "It's been months since ye sailed from home. I thought ye'd get over it. I truly believed ye would, in time."

Marcus frowned. "What the devil are you talking about?"

"The lass, my friend. Ye long for her as only a man in love can do. Ye miss her day and night. There ain't a time she ain't in yer thoughts, or somewhere close by."

He started to argue, but Hamish shook his head. "No need to deny it—it's there in yer face."

He stared back out at the water. It was the truth. He was in love with her. He'd tried to tell himself it wasn't so, but the lie no longer convinced him. "I'll get over it. In time, things will be the same as they were before." But he didn't really believe it. Not anymore.

Hamish laid a hand on his shoulder. "I'm thinkin' this time ye may be wrong. I'm thinkin' the both of us may have made a mistake."

Marcus's eyes swung to his friend. "What kind of mistake?"

"Me, thinkin' ye'd get over her, that ye weren't cut out to be a husband, to marry and settle down. You, thinkin' the sea was more important than what ye had with the woman."

Marcus shook his head. "You weren't wrong and neither was I. The sea is my home. It always has been."

"I'm thinkin' yer home is where the lass is. Ye've been different since ye came back aboard the ship. The joy's gone out of it for ye. Be honest with yerself and ye'll see it's the truth. Times change. People change. There's no shame in that."

"I'm not the sort of man to change."

"Aren't ye? I think ye would have been happy in that big house in Cornwall even as a boy if ye'd thought ye had a future there. The place is yours now, lad. It's the kind of place a man could be proud of, a place to call home."

Home. Yes, it *had* felt that way. During the time he'd been in Tintagel, he'd grown attached to the house and lands in a way he hadn't before, and oddly, he missed it. He hadn't thought he would.

"If ye go back and after a time begin to crave the sea, ye can always take her with ye."

For a moment something bright flared inside him. It was such an easy answer and yet it would never work. "It wouldn't be fair, Hamish. A woman needs roots, a home for her children."

"And ye don't need those things?"

Perhaps he did. Perhaps he had always needed them. Perhaps the sea had simply been a means of escaping the desire for something he thought he could never have. For weeks, he had missed the life he had begun to make for himself at Hawksmoor House, missed the challenge of managing his estates, of building a legacy he could pass on to his sons.

Children he had never imagined he would want.

And he had missed Brianne with a longing that ate into his very bones.

"The *Maiden* should be headin' our way. She'll be returnin' to London, once she's off-loaded her goods in Port o' Spain. Ye could go back with her. I can manage to see this old tub delivers her cargo and gets safely back to England."

Marcus felt an odd squeezing in his chest. He recognized it as hope and the intensity of the feeling nearly overwhelmed him. He had never believed he could give up the sea, but for weeks that was exactly what he had been wanting to do. The accident had somehow changed him, he realized, made him see life in a totally different manner.

"We were supposed to sail on to China. It wouldn't be right if I simply—"

"Ye'll lose her if ye wait too long."

A sharp pain jolted through him. She was his, but he would lose her. Perhaps he already had.

Hamish puffed on his pipe, then eyed him through a thick cloud of smoke. "Does it matter so much she ain't some bloody English lady?"

Marcus's hard gaze swung to his friend's weathered face. "Good God, no! I don't give a bloody damn who her father was. I never did."

Brianne's pretty face appeared in his mind, her eyes bright, her soft mouth laughing. Marcus reached for the rail, his hands tightening almost painfully around the slick wet wood. He was a man who went after what he wanted. For weeks—months—he had been lying to himself, trying to convince himself what he wanted was his old life back.

Perhaps it was the trouble brought down on Hawksmoor Shipping. Perhaps he had hoped for some sort of revenge. Perhaps he was simply afraid to leave the only life he had ever known.

Whatever the reason, the truth now stretched before him, agonizingly plain to see. The solitary life he'd once loved now left him feeling empty and alone. He wanted a new life. He wanted a home and family.

He wanted a life that included Brianne.

He glanced over at Hamish, watched the wind rifle through his friend's long gray hair. "The *Maiden,* you say?"

Hamish grinned. "Aye, Cap'n, that's what I said."

Marcus smiled, suddenly feeling lighthearted. He couldn't remember the last time he had felt that way. Then his smile slowly faded. He had been gone from England for months, had never sent even a letter. Brianne was a beautiful, desirable woman. She was intelligent and, thanks to the lessons he had paid for, could move with flawless grace through the highest circles of Society. Even his brother had been attracted to her.

What if he had already lost her?

He had behaved like a bloody damned fool. What if it was already too late?

Chapter 23

Standing beneath a glittering crystal chandelier, Brandy accepted Rex Delaine's arm and let him guide her onto the dance floor. They were attending a soiree at the Earl of Richmond's elegant town house. The Season was in full swing and an endless array of parties and balls kept her up each night into the wee hours of the morning.

"You seem to have taken to all of this rather like a duck to water," Rex said, indicating with the tilt of his head the throng of fashionably dressed ladies and gentlemen of the Ton. The music swelled and he took her gloved hand, guiding her through the steps of a quadrille. "I presume you are enjoying yourself."

Brandy smiled. "Of course I am." She was—wasn't she? She was so busy most of the time, she hadn't really had a chance to consider. "I shall always be indebted to you and Richard."

They moved forward, met again. Rex led her in a graceful turn. "You seem to have grown quite fond of him."

There it was—the opening she had been seeking for the past several days. This probably wasn't the time, but if she didn't speak up soon, word was bound to leak out, and she wanted to be the one to tell him. "Richard has asked me to marry."

A fine black brow arched up, but little surprise shown in his face. "I assume you agreed?"

"Yes. I hope you approve."

His eyes were warm on her face. "You don't need my

approval, but yes, I do indeed. You both have my heartfelt best wishes."

"Thank you."

"Richard is a good man—one of the finest. And I know he cares for you greatly."

They parted, then came back into line. "You don't think . . . you don't think I am overstepping my bounds? I am hardly his social equal."

"Perhaps not by blood. But look at you. There isn't a person in this room who doubts you belong here."

She smiled then, more sincerely this time. "I have Professor Felton to thank for that . . . and of course I shall always be indebted to your brother."

Rex glanced away and even her own gaze drifted off. They didn't say more and eventually the dance came to an end. Rex escorted her to where Richard stood beside his father, a handsome, charming man with intelligent hazel eyes very much like his son's, and blond hair slightly graying at the temples.

"You look lovely this evening, Brianne." The marquess leaned close and spoke softly in her ear. "I can't help thinking what a stunning addition to the family you will make. My son is extremely fortunate. I can hardly wait to make the announcement."

Brandy flushed. "Thank you, my lord."

Richard flashed her a tender look and smiled. He might have asked her to dance, but he had already done so several times before and, thanks to Professor Felton, she knew that until their betrothal was official it would cause gossip to do so again.

Besides, another name appeared on her card, a man she had only just been introduced to, a friend of the marquess's by the name of Palmer Reese, a wealthy shipping magnate who had mentioned he was also a friend of the Delaines.

Perhaps that was the reason she was eager for the dance. Perhaps he would know something of Marcus, might even know where he was and how he fared. She knew she shouldn't care. She hadn't heard a word from him since he had left. But then, neither had his brother. Brandy prayed that he was safe and that no more "accidents" had befallen any of his ships.

Mr. Reese appeared exactly on time for the promised dance. Dressed rather garishly in a bright green tailcoat with a pearl-studded green velvet collar, he whisked her off to the dance floor for a lively country dance. She caught sight of Rex as she walked away and wondered at the surprised look on his face. He was scowling as they started to dance, then the crowd swallowed him up and thoughts of him slid away.

She looked over at her partner, Palmer Reese. He was an attractive man with wavy, coffee-brown hair. His features were fine, if somewhat effeminate. His manners were smooth, almost overly polished. Why she took an immediate dislike to him she could not say.

She gazed up at him with a pasted-on smile. "I believe you mentioned when we met before that you were a friend of Lord Hawksmoor's."

"Yes. . . . Our families have been acquainted for quite some years. We were raised together as children." Did she imagine the sudden tic that appeared beneath one of his eyes? "Lord Halliday says you are also a friend of the Delaines."

She flushed a little. She had known this might get dicey. "My father owned property in Charleston. Captain Delaine—Lord Hawksmoor, I mean—sailed there quite often. I've known him since I was a girl."

"I see."

"You know he was injured last year, very severely, in fact."

"So I heard."

"He is quite well now, and once more back aboard his ship."

The tic became more pronounced. "He'll be gone for some time, I gather. The last I heard, *Seahawk* was carrying cargo in the Indies, then off, I believe, to China."

How could so few words drive a needle of pain into her heart? "He always wanted to see the Orient," she said softly.

Palmer eyed her with renewed interest and she worried she

had overstepped her bounds. "And what of you, Mr. Reese?" she asked a little too brightly, searching for a change of subject. "You've a sizable armada of ships of your own, I am told. Do you also sail off for ports unknown?"

A corner of his mouth edged up. "Occasionally, when there is a need, but fortunately not all that often. The sea is my business, not my penchant. I am quite content to stay right here in London as much as I can."

She laughed, let him guide her through the steps of the dance. "I quite agree," she said, simply to distract him. In truth, there was a time she had wanted adventure in her life, been desperate to travel and see the world. Since Marcus had left, those things no longer seemed important.

She banished unwanted thoughts of him. She would soon be pledged to another, had already accepted Lord Richard's proposal. He deserved her thoughts, her loyalty. She vowed as she had before, that she would be a good wife to him and a good mother to his children.

At least that was her thought when she glanced to the front of the ballroom. Brandy gasped at the sight of the tall, imposing man who stared in her direction. Marcus Delaine, Earl of Hawksmoor, stood just inside the door.

Brandy stumbled and nearly fell, her heart pounding furiously. Palmer Reese caught her arm and she found herself swaying against him. Across the room, Marcus continued to stare. A full head taller than the men who surrounded him, he was dressed in a black velvet tailcoat, the jacket perfectly fitted to his lean, broad-shouldered build. His hair shown nearly blue-black in the light of the gilded sconces. His skin was dark, his eyes even darker. They fixed on her face, his expression inscrutable, but there was something in his posture, in the hard set of his jaw. She was surprised to discover it was anger.

"I'm afraid I'm not . . . not feeling very well. If you wouldn't mind, I should like to sit out the rest of the dance."

Palmer smiled solicitously. "Perhaps we should go outside for a quick breath of air."

"No, I—" She shook her head a bit too hard, then took

a deep breath and smiled. "I would rather have something cold to drink, if you don't mind."

He bowed politely, turned, and headed off toward the punch bowl. As soon as he was out of sight, Brandy made her way toward Rex Delaine, who stood next to Lord Halliday. Rex was deep in conversation with a young blond woman Brandy had seen him with before, Lady Margaret Herring, she recalled.

She tugged on the sleeve of his coat. "I'm sorry to bother you, Rex, but I wonder if we might have a word in private?"

One look at the pale hue of her face and he swung back to the blonde. "If you will excuse me, Lady Margaret . . . ?"

"Of course." But she didn't look any too pleased.

Rex took Brandy's arm. "What is it? You look as if you've just seen a ghost."

"I think I just did. Your brother is here, Rex. Marcus just walked in."

His head jerked up. "But that's impossible. He isn't due back for at least the balance of the year." She caught his arm and turned him toward the door just as Marcus, leaning on his silver-headed cane, begin to make his way across the room.

Rex's shoulders went tense. "Bloody hell, I hope nothing's happened to his ship."

The thought hadn't even occurred to her. All she could think was Marcus had returned and she was betrothed to another man.

Lady Halliday stepped toward him as he arrived among their circle of friends. "Good heavens—I thought you had sailed off the edge of the earth, gone to China or some such place."

Marcus smiled and bowed over the woman's hand, but his eyes sought out Brianne. "The was the original idea, but there was a change of plans." She could feel their intensity and her insides churned.

"Did you have a problem?" Rex asked. "I hope nothing's happened to the *Seahawk*."

''No problems,'' Marcus said. ''At least nothing of that nature.''

She wondered what nature his problems were, but it was no longer her concern. Though he still hadn't spoken to her, his gaze remained on her face. The anger was gone, replaced by a look of warmth that sent little shivers running through her.

''Miss Winters. You're looking quite lovely. Apparently London agrees with you.''

''Thank you, my lord. And yes . . . yes, it does.'' Brandy felt Richard's presence behind her, quietly asserting his possession. She wasn't sure if she was glad he was there or annoyed that he felt so threatened.

The marquess stepped in just then. ''It's good to see you, Hawksmoor.'' He reached out to grip Marcus's hand. There was a hard cast to his features, a look of warning directed at Marcus unlike anything Brandy had seen in his face before. ''You've arrived at a very fortuitous time,'' he said pointedly. ''My son has just announced his plans to marry. We'll be making the betrothal official at a ball at Halliday Hall the end of next week. We'd be honored if you could attend.''

Marcus's eyes swung to Richard's, then flicked to Brianne. His look was filled with such burning heat she could almost feel it on her skin. He smiled at Richard, but it held little warmth. ''Congratulations, Lockhart. Am I to understand the lady in question is Miss Winters?''

Richard's gaze clashed with his. ''Yes. Brianne has consented to become my wife. I'm a very lucky man.''

Those penetrating blue eyes swung back to back her, holding her as if they caressed her. ''Yes . . .'' he said softly. ''A very lucky man.''

Brandy's legs felt suddenly unsteady. She ached to reach out and touch him, to go into his arms and feel them close around her. She loathed herself for it, but the feeling would not go away.

Dear sweet God, how could she ever have believed she was over him?

She stared at Marcus and wanted to curse him. She wanted

to lash out at him. She wanted to weep. Dear Lord, how could she be a good wife to Richard when thoughts of Marcus still tortured her mind and heart?

She could feel him watching her, an intensity in his features far beyond what she had seen in him before. Why had he come back to England? What was he doing in London?

Why couldn't he leave her in peace?

Marcus spoke to his brother, but his glance kept straying to Brianne. In a high-waisted gown of amber silk trimmed in the same gold as her eyes, she looked more beautiful than he had ever seen her.

She laughed at something Richard said, but her face was pale and there were shadows in her eyes. He wanted to chase those shadows away, wanted to hold her, to tell her how sorry he was that he had hurt her.

Marcus inwardly cursed, knowing he hadn't the right. He had lost that right when he had left her.

It was only by luck that he had found her here in London. The *Maiden* had arrived at the docks just a few hours ago. He had departed the ship, stopping at his town house to spend the night and refresh himself before continuing his journey to Cornwall.

He'd been amazed to discover that his brother was in residence at the house, though he was not at home and instead was attending the Earl of Richmond's soiree. And that Brianne Winters was a guest of Lord and Lady Halliday.

More than a guest, Marcus thought grimly. Brianne was the marquess's future daughter-in-law. Lord Richard's future wife. Not bad for a tavern maid not long off the Charleston quay, he thought bitterly, though in truth there was a time he had believed it might be good to foster a union between them. Now that it had happened, the thought made him sick to his stomach.

Too late, said a voice inside him. Just like Hamish had warned. But it wasn't too late. Not when the stakes were so high. Not when one look in those lovely golden eyes made his heart squeeze painfully and told him exactly how much he loved her. Not when he saw shadows there instead of joy.

Once she loved you, too, said the voice.

He prayed that she still did.

One thing was certain. Whatever happened, whatever she intended, Brianne Winters belonged to him. Marcus Delaine meant to have her.

Brandy fidgeted nervously. She was attending a house party at the Viscount Wembly's, in company with her usual companions, Lord Richard and his mother and father. She had been dancing all evening, pretending to enjoy herself, but in was difficult to do so when time and again she found herself glancing toward the door.

For the past three days, Marcus had appeared wherever she went. She didn't know why, or if it was merely coincidence, but his appearance kept her nerves on edge, her heart beating far too fast, and her thoughts in turmoil. Tonight the hour remained early and he hadn't yet arrived, but she had begun to watch for him, part of her praying he would not come, while a secret, hidden part of her hoped he would.

He had spoken to her each night, but each time only briefly. He was always the perfect gentlemen, yet his eyes were dark and burning as he watched her, holding her like a deer caught in the lamplight every time she looked in his direction.

He had asked her once about Palmer Reese and she had told him that she scarcely knew the man, which made the tightness in his jaw seem to ease. She wondered about their friendship, thought that perhaps some sort of conflict had arisen between them, but did not ask. She was trying very hard to forget Marcus Delaine. So far she wasn't succeeding.

Brandy wandered among the green baize tables, watching the men play whist. Richard and his father sat at a table in the corner, both of them laughing, betting modestly, mostly just enjoying the game. For a while she had stood at Richard's shoulder, and he had seemed pleased by her presence.

In a few more days, he planned to announce their betrothal.

He wanted them to marry as soon as possible and Brandy had agreed. He was such a very nice man.

She left the gaming room and wandered out onto the terrace. It was unseemly to be out there unchaperoned, but a need for fresh air and a moment alone drove her to desperate measures. She sighed as she walked toward a balustrade in the shadows that overlooked a small formal garden. Torches lit narrow gravel paths and spring flowers had bloomed: pansies and daffodils, tulips and hyacinths.

"I see you're still not overly concerned with your reputation." Marcus's deep voice spun her around. "I doubt your betrothed would be pleased to know you are out here all alone."

Her chin inched up. "I didn't know you were out here or you may be certain I would not have come."

He chuckled softly, a seductive rumble in his chest. A little tremor ran through her.

"I suppose not," he said. "More's the pity." He moved closer, till his lean frame stood only inches away. She could feel the heat of his body, smell his spicy cologne.

"Why are you following me? What do you want?"

"Do you really not know? Or are you merely pretending?"

She moistened her lips, which had suddenly gone bone-dry. "Why did you come back? Your brother said you left your ship in the Indies and returned to London by yourself."

He reached out to her, ran a long dark finger along her jaw. "Perhaps I came back for you. Perhaps I discovered that I missed you."

She only shook her head, took a step backward. "There had to be some other reason, something important you needed to do. You would never leave your ship for a woman."

Lines furrowed into his forehead. His turbulent gaze held a yearning she didn't understand. "You aren't just any woman, Brianne." He moved closer, till his leg brushed the hem of her skirt and the air seemed to thicken around them. His eyes drifted over her face, came back to rest on her mouth. "You're different, Brianne. You're not like anyone else. I should have told you that a long time ago."

She stared up at his darkly handsome face and, before she realized his intention, he bent his head and his mouth settled softly over hers. Brandy gasped, her lips parting in surprise, and Marcus's tongue swept in. His hands felt hard and strong as they drew her into the circle of his arms, pressing her the length of his body. Heat surrounded her, seemed to crawl beneath her skin.

For an instant she was his once more and the world no longer felt tilted as it had for so long, but seemed to right itself, each piece falling perfectly into place. She kissed him with all the love she'd once felt for him, with the force of all she had lost when he had left her. For a moment, the dream of a life with him glowed anew, as fresh and beautiful as it once had been.

Then she thought of Richard, thought of his kindness, his loyalty. Loving Marcus only meant more pain, more heartache, more loss. She pressed her hands against his chest and shoved him away, stepping backward several paces, her breath coming sharp and fast.

"That . . . that shouldn't have happened. It won't ever happen again. If you wish for us to remain friends, Marcus, I'd advise you to keep your hands to yourself in the future."

His gaze, hot and intense, bored into her. "I want more from you than friendship, Brianne. I always have."

Brandy shook her head, suddenly close to tears. "It's too late, Marcus. You didn't want me. You never really have. A kind and decent man has asked me to marry. Please . . . if you care for me at all, you will leave me in peace."

He looked as though he wanted to argue, but glanced away instead. His knuckles were white around the head of his cane.

Brandy turned away, fighting hard not to cry. She didn't know why he was there, but it really didn't matter. What she told him was the truth—it was too late. She didn't want to see him. She didn't want to be near him. She had finally learned to live without him and she meant to keep it that way.

Wordlessly, she walked toward the door, leaving him there on the terrace, loathing herself for what she'd allowed to happen. Guilt gnawed at her insides. How could she have betrayed Richard that way when he had been so terribly good to her?

Ignoring her trembling limbs and a sudden urge to run, she made her way back inside the house, hoping she didn't look as shaky as she felt. Lady Halliday was seated in the drawing room. She glanced up at Brandy's approach, her shrewd eyes taking in the flush in Brandy's cheeks.

"My dear, what is it? You look positively overset."

"I—I'm feeling a bit under the weather, I'm afraid. I know it's an imposition, but would you mind very much if I asked Richard to take me home?"

The marchioness stared toward the doors that Brandy had just come in through. A tall, shadowy figure stood outlined on the terrace. "I'm feeling a bit weary myself," the marchioness said. "Come. We'll tell Simon and Richard we are both ready to leave."

"Are you certain?"

Her attention strayed back to the terrace doors. "Quite certain," she said gently. "We've a good deal to do to get ready for your betrothal party. A little rest would do all of us good."

Brandy just nodded. She felt guilty and confused, and a soft ache throbbed in her heart. Richard deserved a woman who would love him wholly and completely, the way his mother loved his father. As much as Brandy cared for him, after what had happened with Marcus she wasn't certain she could ever love him that way.

Dear sweet God, if she only knew what to do.

In the Hawksmoor private box at the Theatre Royale on Catherine Street in Covent Garden, Marcus sat next to Rex and Lady Margaret Herring, the lovely blond woman Rex had been seeing for the past few weeks. Seated to Margaret's left was her mother, the Countess of Trenton. In a box across the way, he could see Brianne Winters, seated in a red velvet chair next to the man who would be her future husband.

Every time Richard touched her, every time he reached for her hand, Marcus's insides tightened.

The gilded chair next to him creaked as his brother leaned toward him. "You're in love with her, you know," Rex said softly, his pale blue eyes glinting in the light of the candles. "Why don't you just admit it?"

Marcus gazed at Brianne across the distance, hardly able to believe the lovely, incredibly poised young woman in the yellow striped gown was once a Charleston tavern maid. "She's betrothed to another man, one who is supposed to be my friend."

"Richard is my friend as well. That doesn't mean you should stand by and allow him to ruin all of your lives."

Marcus's mouth edged up at one corner. "I don't intend to."

"You don't?"

"I didn't come back to England to stand by and watch Brianne marry Richard Lockhart."

Rex frowned. "If you intend to make her your mistress again—"

"I don't."

"If you are planning to marry her and leave her for months at a time while you sail off to—"

"I haven't the slightest intention of leaving her and going back to sea. I've made that mistake already."

Rex grinned. "I didn't think you were smart enough to figure it out before it was too late."

"Thanks for the vote of confidence."

"Think nothing of it. I just hope you've also figured out how you're going to convince Brianne."

Marcus said nothing to that. He wasn't quite sure what he intended to do, only that failure was not an option. He was completely, utterly, desperately in love with Brianne Winters. One way or another, she was going to become his wife.

Marcus sat through the balance of the play, Thomas Morton's comedy *Speed the Plough,* then made his way outside. Richard had gone to retrieve the carriage. Standing on the paving stones, Lord and Lady Halliday were deep in conversation. He spotted Brianne walking toward them and stepped into her path, blocking her way.

"I have to see you, Brianne. There are things we need to discuss. I realize you would rather continue to avoid me, but that is not going to happen. When can we meet?"

Her head jerked up a little higher. He noticed her hands were trembling. "What . . . what are you talking about?"

"I am talking about speaking to you in private. Whether you believe it or not, I returned to London simply because of you. I need to talk to you. If for no other reason than the friendship we once shared, surely you will grant me that favor."

She only shook her head. "We have nothing to say to each other. You have your life. I have mine. Whatever we shared is past."

His hand came up to her cheek. In the glow of the street lamp, her smooth skin was pale, nearly devoid of color. "Are you so certain?"

Brandy swallowed and glanced away, staring off at the crowd of theatergoers milling at the front of the building. "Even if I still had feelings for you, it wouldn't matter. I've learned things about myself in the months you've been gone. I want a home, Marcus. I want children. Those are things you wouldn't be interested in. You could never be tied down that way."

"You're wrong," he said gently. "Perhaps that was true, once. It isn't true any longer."

Amber eyes came up to his face. There was pain there, he saw. He wanted to take her in his arms and drive that pain away.

"Go away, Marcus, I beg you. Go away and leave me alone." She shoved past him, pushing her way through the crowd toward the Halliday carriage. A footman bent and opened the door, and Richard helped her climb in, followed by Lady Halliday and the rest of their party. He could see the gleam of her fiery hair through the window as the carriage rolled away.

Marcus watched the vehicle round a corner and disappear

into the gray mist beyond. His chest felt tight; his heart throbbed painfully. He wished he knew the right words, knew a way to make her listen.

"Your Miss Winters is quite a delectable little morsel." Palmer Reese stood just a few feet away, casually slapping a pair of black leather gloves against the flat of his hand.

At the sight of him, Marcus went tense. "What does Miss Winters have to do with you?"

"Nothing at all, I'm sorry to say, since I find her quite intriguing. She is certainly a woman of mystery. No one seems to know much about her . . . although there has been some minor speculation that she was once your mistress."

Anger filtered through him. His dislike of Palmer Reese seemed to swell with every heartbeat. Marcus flexed a muscle in his jaw. "Is that *your* speculation, Palmer, or did you unearth that bit of slander from one of your henchmen, perhaps one of the same men you paid to sabotage my ships?"

Palmer arched a brow. "Surely you're not accusing me of any sort of wrongdoing? We've been friends since we were boys."

"Friends? I don't think so. As a matter of fact, I had a meeting today with the men I hired to investigate the problems we've been having. Several months back they compiled a list of the people who benefited most from my losses. You, Palmer, headed that list."

Palmer Reese merely smiled. "Nothing personal, Marcus. You lost the contracts. Someone else was going to get them. It was simply good business."

Marcus clamped down on an urge to hit him. "Today it was confirmed that until Hawksmoor Shipping began losing business, your company was in extremely bad financial straits."

"That doesn't prove I had anything to do with your problems."

"No, unfortunately, it doesn't. But I'm telling you now, if any other 'accidents' happen to any of my ships, I won't wait for proof. I'll come after you—personally. I'll call you out,

Reese. I could always outshoot you when we were boys. I'm an even better shot now."

Reese's jaw went tight, but his face turned a little bit pale.

"And I don't want to hear one more word against Brianne Winters. You hurt her, you're hurting me—is that understood? Either way, the result will be the same. You'll be dead and my problems will be over."

"You're insane," Reese flung at him, but Marcus didn't miss the fear that had crept into his face. More certain than ever that Palmer was the man behind the accident that had nearly cost him his legs, Marcus felt a shot of satisfaction.

With a last hard glance he walked away, leaving Palmer Reese to stare after him. The man was undoubtedly guilty, but there was no way to prove it. He recalled the meeting he'd had that morning with the Bow Street runners he had hired nearly a year ago. Reynolds and Kelly were certain Reese was the man behind Marcus's troubles. They even held a suspicion that he had done away with the man who had helped in his endeavor, Cain Dalton, former captain of the ship *Fairwind.*

Dalton had been found in an alley not far from Reese's office, his throat slit from ear to ear. Rumor was, a man had been paid quite handsomely to see the job done and Reese's name had surfaced more than once. But proof was hard to find, especially the sort the courts would be willing to accept.

There was a time Marcus had been nearly obsessed with catching the man responsible for what had happened that night aboard the *Seahawk.* Now, oddly, he simply wanted to ensure that his vessels and his men were safe. Still, the threat Marcus had made was real. If Reese tried to harm him or his ships in any way, Marcus would kill him.

Just as he would do whatever was necessary should Reese continued to malign Brianne Winters.

CHAPTER 24

Brandy had to leave. She couldn't stay in London a single day longer. She had spoken to Richard earlier that morning, pleading with him to understand and begging him to postpone the announcement of their betrothal.

"This is all simply happening too fast," she'd said. "You know how much I care for you, Richard, but I need time to think, to see things more clearly."

"It's Hawksmoor, isn't it? Until his return, you were content. You were even looking forward to our marriage."

Brandy took his hand and brushed a kiss across the smooth, well-formed knuckles. "You brought the joy back into my life, Richard. You led me out of the darkness that nearly destroyed me. For that I will always be grateful. But I need time. I want things to be right between us. I want the shadows all to be gone."

"I want to marry you, Brianne. I'd do anything for you—anything at all."

She smiled at him softly. "I know you would. I'm not asking you to wait forever. Just long enough for me to get things settled in my mind."

Richard's eyes slid closed for a moment, then he sighed. "Where will you go?"

Brandy glanced toward the windows, to a sky that was more gray than blue and tinged with a pall of soot. "Back to my cottage. Back where the air is clear and sweet and I can figure out what is best for both of us."

"I know what is best," Richard said firmly. "I can make

you happy, Brianne, if you will only let me.''

She pressed the back of his hand against her cheek. ''You and your family are the kindest, most generous people I've ever known. I don't want to hurt you or them. Give me time, Richard. I promise you, everything is going to work out.''

With a look of resignation, Richard nodded. ''I'll send word ahead. When do you wish to leave?''

''Tomorrow, if you don't mind.''

''All right. I'll see to the preparations for your journey. I'll give you a few weeks, Brianne. Then I'm coming after you and we are going to be wed.''

She hesitated only a moment, then pressed her lips to his in a soft, tender kiss. It was nothing like the hot, fierce kisses she had shared with Marcus, but then Richard Lockhart was nothing at all like Marcus Delaine. It was the reason, perhaps, she was drawn to him, the reason she intended to marry him.

Surely, once she had time to bring her turbulent emotions under control, she could accept him and the life he had promised. Surely she could put her memories of Marcus to rest.

The notion of returning to Cornwall loomed like a bright ray of sunshine slanting down through a stormy sky. Once she was home, she could find peace. All she had to do was get there.

Rex Delaine heard the front door of the town house slam open as his brother stormed in. The rap of his cane on the marble floor in the entry preceded his arrival in the drawing room.

''All right, where is she? The upstairs maid I've been paying to keep track of her says she packed and left in the Halliday traveling carriage.''

Standing next to the fireplace, Rex leaned casually against the mantel. ''Your spy didn't know where she was headed?''

''Obviously not. You, however, seem to be very well informed of the lady's movements.''

''And you think I should have pity on my older brother and help him in his time of need.''

The frown slid from between Marcus's eyes and a corner of his mouth kicked up. ''Exactly so.''

"It's going to cost you."

Marcus grumbled something beneath his breath. "How much?"

"There's a stallion I've been admiring. I saw him at Tattersall's yesterday afternoon."

"That's blackmail, you know."

"Yes, and extremely well deserved."

Marcus didn't hesitate a moment more. "All right. Consider it done."

Rex grinned. "She's gone back to Cornwall. You could have saved yourself a goodly sum of money if you'd stopped to think. Where the devil else would she go?"

Marcus merely grunted. "I was hoping that was where she was headed, but I had to be sure." He turned back toward the door, crossing the carpet with purpose and only a very slight limp. "She's run out of places to hide. She'll be in my territory once she gets back, and this time the woman is going to hear what I have to say."

"Just tell her you love her, Marcus. That's all you have to do."

Marcus turned. "Easy for you, perhaps. But even if I did that, I am not sure it would do an ounce of good."

It would certainly help, Rex thought. But perhaps his brother was right. Brianne no longer trusted him. She didn't want to risk loving him again. She didn't want to risk the pain she would suffer if Marcus left her as he had done twice before.

"Good luck, big brother."

"Thanks," he called over one wide shoulder. "I'm afraid I'm going to need it." The step-hop of his footfalls sounded as Marcus climbed the stairs to pack and ready himself to leave.

In a way, Rex envied him. He had never loved a woman, not really. Lady Margaret was beautiful and intelligent and he was attracted to her. She would make a suitable wife and he thought that perhaps it was time to think of marriage.

But he wasn't in love with her. He wasn't sure he even wanted to be. Love was painful. One look at Marcus told him that. He was in no rush to marry. He would have to give it some thought. For now he was simply glad it was his brother who faced Brianne Winters.

And Marcus was right—he would need all the help he could get.

Brandy strolled the path at the top of the windswept cliffs of Cornwall. The air was warm and moist, making her clothes cling to her skin. Below her, the sea slid up against the sand. In the distance, she could see the slate roof of the cottage and, farther along the path, the spires and towers of Hawksmoor House.

She studied their majestic beauty, ethereal in the misty shadows of the late afternoon. She knew each bold outline, could close her eyes and picture the exact placement of each mullioned window, knew the various shades of gray on the roof. It was a place that held memories, yet little by little she was accepting those memories as part of the past and pushing them away.

Each day since her arrival, she had walked these cliffs beside the house, searching her mind and heart, determined to find a place there for Richard and a future for herself. She had come to the cottage to find peace, to say good-bye to the love she felt for Marcus and ease the ache that had crept back into her heart since he had appeared in London. Each day she walked the cliffs and each day the turbulence lessened.

And now *he* had come.

To her dismay and despair, Marcus had arrived in Cornwall just that morning, and though she had not seen him, she had received a message requesting her presence at supper. The note was brief and formal, betraying little of his thoughts, all but the very last line, which simply read, *Please, Brianne, will you not come?*

She couldn't resist such a plea, and in truth, she had avoided him as long as she could. It was time things were settled between them. In the days since she had left London, she had come to the same conclusions she had reached before.

Richard Lockhart was a kind and decent man who wanted

to marry her and make her happy. She cared for him greatly, perhaps in some way even loved him, and she adored his family. Richard had offered her a place in the world where she could be loved and accepted. He offered her the promise of children, of a home where they could be a family.

Even Marcus's presence could not dissuade her, not when she knew the pain of loving him, not when she knew the kind of life she would lead. Not when she knew his home was the sea and always would be, no matter what he said.

A sigh slipped past her lips but it disappeared into the wind. An early summer storm brewed on the horizon, swollen gray clouds billowing in, churning the air as they rolled toward the shore. Brandy hoped it would rain. The spring had been drier than normal and the land needed water. She pulled the strings on her bonnet and tugged it loose, let the warm sun spill onto her face as she walked back toward the cottage.

There were several hours left until Marcus's carriage was due to pick her up for the short drive to Hawksmoor House. In the meantime, she would pen a letter to Flo as she did from time to time. She had been thinking about her friend of late, hoping all was well. She would tell her about Richard, about her plans to marry. She wondered if Flo was happy, and hoped owning the tavern had given her at least some measure of security, since it appeared she would be facing life without the help of a man.

Back at the cottage, she sat down in the parlor and composed the letter. Then, along with her little maid, Sally, she climbed the stairs to her bedchamber to choose what she should wear.

They went through gown after gown, but none seemed to suit.

"Not the pale blue—it makes me look too timid."

Sally held up another. "What about this pretty gold satin?"

Brandy shook her head. "Too seductive. It's so low-cut it fairly screams an invitation." Another half hour passed with no decision and suddenly it occurred to Brianne that she was far too concerned with what Marcus might or might not think. The notion sparked a shot of anger.

"What the devil am I doing? To hell with Marcus Delaine. Give me the emerald silk."

"I thought you didn't want anything too low-cut."

"It isn't all that low and I am not going to stand here a moment more worrying about what Marcus is going to think when he sees me in it. I don't give a fig what he thinks anymore."

But Sally merely smiled. Brandy had the oddest feeling the slender girl was conjuring images of the Earl of Hawksmoor sweeping down from the deck of his ship like some black-haired, dashing pirate to carry her away.

That was hardly the sort of thing Marcus would do and, at any rate, Brandy no longer cared. She had been in love with Marcus Delaine for years and all it had ever brought her was grief. She was no longer foolish enough to succumb to his midnight eyes and burning glances. She wasn't interested in whatever it was he had to say.

Still, by the time she had bathed and changed, her stomach was tied in knots and her hands were shaking. Had he really returned to London because of her? What could he possibly want? Why had he followed her to Cornwall?

Sweet God, she wished she knew.

Marcus was waiting in the entry when she arrived at the mansion.

"Good evening, Brianne. I'm delighted you could come." Though his words were politely formal, his eyes said he hadn't intended to give her a choice. He was dressed completely in black, except for the silver brocaded waistcoat he wore beneath his velvet-collared jacket. With his black hair and dark blue eyes, he looked unbearably handsome. It made her stomach flutter every time he glanced in her direction, and her throat felt cotton-dry.

She forced herself to smile. "Good evening, my lord. I trust your journey was not unpleasant." The mundane topic was hardly the one she wished to discuss. She wanted desperately to know why he had come to Cornwall.

"Actually, the trip was long and tedious, more so since I was eager to get here."

Of course he was eager, she told herself. He had been gone from his home for months. It was only natural that he would be eager to return. It had nothing to do with the fact she was there.

But the look in those hot dark eyes said it had everything to do with her.

"I believe Cook has supper very nearly prepared. I hope you are hungry." Long, graceful fingers wrapped around her elbow as he urged her down the long, marble-floored hall. The sleeve of his coat brushed against her breast, and a tingle ran down her spine.

"Actually, I'm starving," she said with a forced note of lightness. "I remember what a wonderful chef you have. I've been looking forward to supper ever since your note arrived." There was a bald-faced lie. She wasn't hungry at all. She could barely stand the thought of food, but she wasn't about to let him know how much his presence disturbed her.

"Have you, indeed?" A corner of his mouth quirked up. "And here I thought perhaps you would rather I had stayed in London and left you to your own devices."

Damn him! How could he always read her so clearly? "You have every right to be here, more right, certainly, than I. Hawksmoor House is your home."

Marcus didn't argue, nor add to the comment, just ushered her into a small but elegant salon at the rear of the house, a room that overlooked the sea. After he seated her at a linen-draped table lavishly set with gilt and silver and lit by flickering beeswax candles, they made polite conversation. They spoke of the weather, of his voyage to the different islands of the Indies, all of the words inconsequential, doing nothing to alleviate the butterflies swirling in her stomach, only making it more difficult to enjoy the elaborate meal.

Two tall footmen in black and silver livery served turbot in lobster sauce, medallions of veal, oysters, candied carrots, and asparagus. Candied fruits and custard appeared for dessert. Through it all, Marcus watched her, those incredible blue eyes blazing with such force there were times it was difficult to breathe. Her stomach jumped with nerves and she clutched her napkin in her lap to keep her hands from shaking. Dear God, she shouldn't have come. She had forgotten what it was like to be alone with him this way.

Marcus made a movement of his hand and the footmen appeared to remove their dishes, her food nearly untouched for all her claims of how hungry she was. Finally the task was completed and the footmen retired from the room, leaving them alone.

Marcus helped her up from her chair and they walked to the windows. She could feel his hand at her back, feel the heat of his eyes burning into her. In the distance, lightning flashed, the summer storm nearly upon them now. The sound of thunder rumbled. Torches in the garden above the cliffs flashed and shimmered in the strong, warm wind blowing in off the sea.

Brandy fought down a quaking inside that matched that of the leaves on the trees and forced herself to look into his face. "It's been a lovely evening, Marcus, but I have to be getting back home. It's beginning to rain. Soon the roads will be too muddy to traverse."

His mouth curved faintly. "You could always stay here."

Images arose of the last time she had slept at Hawksmoor House, the night she had spent in his bed. Her face flushed with warmth, and color spread down her throat and over her breasts. Marcus must have been remembering, too, for a hungry look crept into the black centers of his eyes.

The tension she was feeling kicked up a notch. "I don't . . . I don't intend to stay here." She didn't want to remember that night.

And she never wanted to forget it.

Marcus shifted his tall lean frame, moving even closer. She could feel the heat of his body, the roughness of his coat where it brushed against her skin. She could smell his spicy cologne and the male scent that belonged only to him.

He trailed a finger down her cheek and the contact made her shiver. "Are you in love with Richard?"

Brandy wet her lips, finding it difficult to speak. It was the first time he had ever referred to her upcoming betrothal. She discovered she didn't like the sound of the words on his lips.

"Richard is a good and decent man. He'll make a very fine husband."

"I asked if you were in love with him."

She swallowed, hitched up her chin. "In time, I will come to love him."

"But for the present, you are still in love with me."

She stumbled back a step, something painful stabbing into her chest. "No! I didn't . . . I didn't say that. I am not in love with you. I admit there was a time that might . . . might have been true, but not anymore."

He shrugged those wide shoulders in a gesture of nonchalance, but the tension in his body said he was hardly unconcerned. "Perhaps not. I should like to think that you are, at least a little, since I intend for us to marry."

"What!"

"If you are not in love with Lockhart, you might as well accept my suit instead of his. I'm richer and I am an earl. And I am, after all, the man who took your innocence. It's my duty to make you my wife."

She looked at him, aghast. Anger filtered through her, and hurt, and amazement. She could hardly believe she had heard him correctly. "I don't care about your money—I have money enough of my own. And your duty scarcely concerned you before. Besides, I have already accepted Richard's proposal. Our betrothal will soon be announced and—"

"Does Lockhart realize the . . . intimate nature of our relationship?"

She stiffened her spine, her heart pounding far too fast. "Richard knows the truth. He doesn't care."

"Then he is smarter than I believed." He moved closer, his gaze still locked with hers. "Though I doubt he would approve of your being here with me tonight."

No, he would not, she thought, wishing again she hadn't

come. Wishing she could leave, but not yet willing to. His mouth was mere inches away. She knew he was going to kiss her, knew she should turn and run, but her legs felt frozen in place, completely unable to move.

He cupped her face between his palms, bent his head, and brushed her lips with a feather-soft kiss. Then he settled his mouth over hers with a sureness that sent her heart skittering madly and the world spinning away. Heat shimmered through her and a deep saturating pleasure. She felt the warm, probing pressure of his tongue, sliding like silk along her bottom lip, and opened to allow him entrance.

Slow, lingering kisses, drugging kisses that numbed her mind and body. Soft and languid, they turned hot and hungry, his mouth taking possession, his strong hands pressing her more fully against him. She was conscious of his weight against her thighs and breasts and her body melted into his. His tongue slid into her mouth, stroking deeply, claiming her in a way he never had before.

A claim he no longer had the right to make.

She felt his hands on her breasts, cupping them gently, teasing her nipple through the fabric, making them ache and distend. His fingers skimmed over her flesh, moving to the back of her gown, beginning to unfasten the tiny gold buttons.

Sweet God, he was trying to seduce her! To destroy the protective wall she had so carefully constructed and enslave her heart once more. Through the foggy haze of passion, her mind screamed a silent warning. *Stop him—before you lose Richard! Do it now—before it's too late!*

Marcus deepened the kiss and her body began to tremble. Warmth seared through her. Desire sank into her bones. Then a painful image arose. She was standing on the dock and Marcus was preparing to board his ship. He was going away, leaving her behind, just as he always did. Grief lanced through her, a jagged reminder of the pain she had felt before.

With hands that shook and will forged of iron, she broke away, her breathe coming fast and hard. "No—this isn't going to happen. Get away from me, Marcus—don't touch me! Don't you dare!"

"Brianne . . . love."

Her voice was shaking. "That's why you brought me here, isn't it? So you could seduce me into betraying Richard."

"I had to discover your feelings, to know if you still cared. I had to find out the truth." He took a step toward her, his hand extended in a gesture of reassurance, but Brandy backed away.

"I won't let you do this to me, Marcus. Not again." Tears burned her eyes and her vision began to blur. "I won't let you hurt me again."

"Brianne, please, you have to listen. If you'll only—"

"No! I don't want to listen. I don't want to hear another word!" Swallowing past a thick lump of tears, she ran toward the French doors leading out into the garden. Heedless of the storm, she jerked them open and raced out into the night.

"Brianne, no! Forgodsake, come back!"

But Brandy raced on, her feet pounding through the garden toward the path along the cliffs and the safety of her cottage. Tears streamed down her cheeks, blinding her to the world rushing past. Her legs were shaking and her chest hurt with every indrawn breath. The warm rain had muddied the ground, and in minutes her slippers were soaked clear through, the hem of her gown torn and filthy. She gathered her skirts and kept on running.

She could hear Marcus calling behind her, trying to catch up, but she ran on. She had to get away, had to escape. Loving Marcus only meant more grief. Even if he married her, he would leave her. The sea was his home—it was his life and always would be.

"Brianne! Wait! Dear God, please come back before you're hurt!"

Still she kept running, until her hair had come loose and hung in soggy curls around her shoulders, until the emerald gown was soaked and clinging to her body. A jagged branch of lightning crackled above her head. Thunder followed only seconds behind it. Brandy ran on. The lights of the cottage beckoned in the distance. If only she could reach it, she would be safe.

Her foot collided with a rock and she stumbled. A stitch rose in her side, gouging between her ribs and slowing her footsteps on the path. It was narrow and muddy. A few feet ahead, a previous rain had washed a chunk of it away. She skirted the dangerous break and continued, tripped again and went sprawling, then dragged herself to her feet and started off again. She was walking now, barely conscious of where she was or where she was going. She only knew she had to escape, had to leave Marcus and the pain behind.

The cottage wasn't far. She stopped at an outcropping of rock and dragged in a steadying breath, her eyes on the yellow glow ahead. She heard the uneven thump of Marcus's footfalls on the path behind her and turned once more to flee, then screamed as he caught her wrist and hauled her into his arms.

"Sweet God, have you gone mad?" He had lost his cane along the way. He was trembling as hard as she but his hold was implacable. Brandy struggled against him, sobbing wildly, and fighting to break free.

"Let me go! You have no right to stop me. Go away and leave me alone!" Lashing out with her hands, kicking and struggling against him, she pounded her fists against his chest.

"Stop it!" Marcus commanded, tightening his hold around her. "Stop it, do you hear? Half the path is gone up ahead. Forgodsake—you could have been killed!"

Brandy stopped fighting, but her eyes remained on his face. The warm rain beat down on her forehead, ran in rivulets along her cheeks. "I won't marry you! There is nothing you can do to make me. You don't care about me. All you care about are your ships and your ocean. I won't be second to them for the rest of my life—I won't!"

He smoothed strands of wet hair back from her tear-stained cheeks. "You aren't second, Brianne, you never have been. I was just too blind to see." He tipped her trembling chin up with his fingers. "I love you, Brandy. I love you more than my ships, more than the sea. I love you beyond anything I've ever dreamed and I want more than life itself for you to marry me."

A weight seemed to crush in on her chest. Marcus loved her! For years she had prayed it would happen. Now, though it thrilled her heart, her mind said it no longer mattered.

She brushed at the tears, her eyes full of sadness. "You love the sea, Marcus. I could never be enough for you. Even if we married, sooner or later you would leave me."

He only shook his head. Curly black hair clung in slick, wet strands to his forehead. His clothes were soaked clear through and covered with mud. "You're wrong, Brianne. I love you and I'm not going to leave you. Not now, not ever—I swear it. I need you, Brandy. I don't want to live without you."

A swell of emotion rolled through her. He loved her—she could see it in the depths of his eyes. And there was no doubt she loved him. Wildly, passionately, and forever. As much as she had tried to fight it, she loved him still.

"Marcus . . ."

"Please . . . say you'll marry me."

She dragged in a shuddering breath. It was insane. It would bring her nothing but pain, yet part of her wanted it even more than he. "How could we possibly marry? You're the Earl of Hawksmoor. I'm nothing but a tavern maid."

He smiled at her with such tenderness something sweet tore open inside her. "You're the bravest, most passionate woman I have ever known. You're sunlight in the darkest of shadows. You're joy in sadness. You're my life and my love and I want to be with you always."

Brandy leaned against him, her heart aching at the beautiful words. She knew that he meant them and that he believed they were true. She only wished she could believe them, too.

"I love you, Marcus. I always have."

Marcus kissed her then, a fierce, burning, passionate kiss that left her breathless and wild with yearning.

"I need you so much, Brianne. More than you could ever imagine. Will you marry me?"

She rested her palm against the hard, strong line of his jaw. Raindrops washed down his cheeks and over her hand. Marcus needed her, and she loved him. No matter what happened, she couldn't deny him. "If you're certain . . . if you really believe this is what you want, I'll marry you."

His eyes slid closed and he dragged her into his arms, pressing his cheek against the top of her head. "Thank God." Then he was kissing her again, sinking down to his knees in the wet warm soil, and pulling her down beside him. The fire she'd felt before flared instantly to life. God, it had been so long and she had missed him so badly.

Easing her backward, heedless of the muddy earth, Marcus came up over her and began to shove up her skirts.

"I have to have you," he whispered, kissing her neck and shoulders, planting small soft kisses across the tops of her breasts. "I have to know you're mine. I've thought of nothing else for months."

"Marcus . . ." Desire surged through her. Her skin tingled beneath his mouth and turned her blood to liquid flame. She felt his fingers at the front of her gown, felt the fabric ripping apart, felt his hands on her breasts, molding them to the shape of his palms, stroking the tips into hardness with his thumb.

She was wet and ready, on fire for him. One of his hands worked the buttons at the front of his breeches. Brandy moaned as he freed himself, found her core, then sank himself inside her, filling her completely with a single hard thrust. For a moment he paused, his tall frame poised above her as if he savored the moment, then he was kissing her again, ravaging her mouth, his hands kneading her breasts.

Fierce, deep strokes carried her higher and higher. Brandy clung to his neck, her body arching upward, taking him deeper still. The sweet moment of climax burst over them at nearly the same instant. She heard him cry her name and love for him welled up inside her.

The rain had turned to mist, the storm moving on. The rumble of thunder grew distant, allowing her to hear the ragged beating of his heart.

"I love you," Marcus said, brushing wet hair back from her cheek. "I was a fool to leave you."

"I love you, Marcus. I love you so much." It felt good to speak the words, to accept the truth she had denied for so long. Only a single doubt remained, just a tiny thread of fear that she might be making a mistake. Brandy looked into his handsome, beloved face, and told herself she was doing the right thing.

But the doubt refused to fade.

Chapter 25

They were married by special license in a small parish church in Tintagel. Brandy barely recalled the vicar's words, only remembered Marcus's strong, clear voice as he had vowed to love, honor, and cherish her for all the days of their lives.

Two days later, word was sent to Richard, a brief note from Marcus, and a lengthy missive from her, begging his forgiveness and asking that they remain friends:

> *I love him, Richard,* the message said. *It wouldn't have been fair to you if we had married. You deserve a woman who will love you with all her heart, not simply the broken pieces.*

Brandy prayed he would understand and one day he would forgive her.

Meanwhile, the days and nights with Marcus were everything she'd ever dreamed. They spent endless hours walking in the garden or along the cliffs, speaking of the future, making passionate love. He spoke with excitement of his plans for the future, talked of Thomas Coke and his agricultural successes, as well as Lord Townsend's notions of crop rotation, which Marcus intended to implement there in Cornwall.

"Your plans sound wonderful, Marcus."

"The ideas aren't mine, but I intend to make them so. I've several other estates with substantially more acreage and far better soil. These new techniques should work even better there."

It pleased her to hear the eagerness in his voice when he spoke of the future. It kept that single tiny doubt at bay and encouraged her to trust him as she once had.

Still, when she saw him staring out at the water, gazing off toward the horizon, she couldn't help wondering what it was that he was thinking.

Palmer Reese stepped lightly off the gangway onto the deck of the *Fairwind.* The ship was in port for a couple of days, then she'd be making short runs up and down the coast, staying close to home for the next month or so. Palmer had arranged her schedule that way. He had plans that would make him even more money and the *Fairwind* was an essential part of that plan.

"Mr. Reese, sir, 'tis good to be 'avin' ye aboard." The first mate, a swaggering, bowlegged seaman named Jigs Marlin, with stringy blond hair and eyes that were slightly devoid of sincerity, came striding toward him. "Cap'n Proctor has been waitin' for ye below. I'll take ye down to 'is cabin."

Palmer raised a hand. "No need for that. I know the way. I'm sure you have work that needs to be done."

Marlin scowled at the reminder and the slight disapproval in Palmer's voice. "As ye wish, sir." He ambled off to resume his duties and Palmer started forward, ignoring the curious stares of the crewmen, making his way toward the ladder leading down to the captain's quarters.

Cole Proctor was waiting, dragging open the door at Palmer's first light rap, giving him a big, gap-toothed grin and motioning him inside.

"I got your message. Woulda been happy to come to your office." He was a big, beefy man, not nearly as intelligent as Cain Dalton, but capable enough at captaining the ship. And not nearly so much trouble.

"I'm certain you would have," Palmer said, ignoring the seat Proctor offered, making his way instead to the carved wooden sideboard to pour himself a brandy. "I wanted to take a look at the ship, see what sort of shape she was in.''

Proctor beamed. ''She's in fine shape, Mr. Reese. Fit as a fiddle. I keep these soggers workin' day and night. Ain't no shirkin' goin' on 'round here.''

''That's very good,'' Reese said, filling his glass, then taking a sip. ''I have plans for the *Fairwind* and I need her in prime condition. In the meantime, you'll be making short hauls to nearby ports, here and on the Continent. I want you to use the time working with the crew to increase the ship's overall speed.''

Interest flickered in Cole Proctor's eyes. ''You got somethin' in mind, Mr. Reese? Somethin' you might be wantin to tell me?''

''I'll tell you when the time comes. In the meantime, suffice it to say I want the *Fairwind* to be the fastest full-rigged ship on the water. You make certain she is and there'll be a good deal of money in it for you and a bonus for your crew.''

Proctor grinned. ''Leave it to me, sir. I'll take care of everything.''

''You'd better—if you want to continue as captain of this ship.''

Proctor's grin slid away. Palmer downed the rest of his brandy and set the glass down on the sideboard. ''As I said, I came to take a look at her. Shall we go?''

''Aye, sir, whatever you say.''

Palmer ignored the hostile note that had crept into Proctor's voice. Now that the man knew the stakes, he was far more likely to get the job done.

And it was imperative he did. Reese's jaw tightened with determination as he ducked his head and stepped out into the passage.

Marcus sat in the large, book-lined office that had formerly been his brother's study. Now that he had undertaken the formidable job of managing the vast Hawksmoor holdings, he needed the space, and Rex, grateful to be free of the burden, had gladly obliged.

The warm months of summer had passed since his marriage, days of contentment unlike anything he could have imagined. He had never expected to find so much joy in being married. Or to discover the sort of love that made his chest go tight simply watching his wife cross a room. When she gave him that special smile she reserved just for him, he felt like the luckiest man in the world. The sound of her laughter could stir his body and make him hard, make him want her even if they had just made love. Thoughts of her lingered in his mind until he forgot what he was doing, or even what he was about to say.

At times it was embarrassing.

Like earlier in the morning when Rex had arrived in his study to find him staring like a lovesick fool out the window, watching Brianne at work in the garden.

''Still head over heels, I see.'' Rex strode toward him grinning. ''Sometimes I envy you, Marcus. Then again, sometimes I thank my lucky stars it's you and not me.''

Warmth crept into the back of his neck. He cleared his throat and motioned for his brother to take a seat on the sofa across from him. Rex had arrived from London earlier that morning. Other than a moment of greeting, this was the first time they'd had a chance to speak.

Rex sat down and Marcus seated himself in the tufted leather chair behind his desk. ''It's good to see you, little brother. How are things in London these days?''

''Pretty much the same as when you left. Richard has started to recover. Lately, he's been seeing a young woman named Marybeth Winston. He seems to be smitten already, and she is definitely interested in him. I think in time he'll forgive you for stealing Brianne away.''

Marcus made a sound low in his throat. ''I did him a favor,'' he said gruffly. ''He never could have handled her.''

''Perhaps not the woman she is since your return. She wasn't the same without you, Marcus. She was only a shadow of the woman you see out that window. I'm glad you came back. I'm glad for both of you.''

Marcus stared out at the garden. Brianne was playing with a yellow tabby cat who looked a bit like Dandelion, laughing at the creature's antics as it attacked a dried leaf on the path at her feet. She had found the animal injured in the stables and taken it under her care. The cat now slept in the house, far too often at the foot of his bed. "I'm a lucky man, Rex, and believe me I know it."

Pulling an envelope from the pocket of his waistcoat, Rex leaned forward in his chair. "There was a reason I came to see you."

Marcus's gaze sharpened. "Other than brotherly love? I wondered if perhaps there might be."

Rex reached over and dropped the envelope on top of the desk. "These arrived at Hawksmoor Shipping's London office the end of the week. Papers from Reynolds and Kelly. I read them—I thought they might be important. After I saw what was in them, I thought it best I brought them here in person."

Marcus paused in the act of opening the envelope, his gaze darting back to his brother's face. He didn't miss the somber expression that had crept over his features. Returning to the task at hand, he drew out a thick sheaf of papers and began to read.

First a letter from Mickey Reynolds, detailing the contents of the envelope, which included several parchment documents along with parish records from a small church in Hounslow, just a few miles outside of London. He knew the town. When he remembered it was the place Palmer Reese had been born, he began to read the letter with a renewed sense of purpose.

His fingers felt brittle by the time he had finished. He leaned back in his chair, released the pent-up breath he had been holding.

"Good God, I can hardly believe this."

"Neither could I, but obviously it's the truth. Aside from the birth documents, there are trust fund records from the Bank of London. Father had been placing bank drafts in Avery Reese's account for nearly thirty years."

Up until the day he died. The flow of money had ended then, perhaps by oversight. Knowing Palmer as his father must have, more likely by design. "Guilt money, I suspect,"

Marcus said. "Father wasn't willing to claim the child as his son, but he wouldn't abandon him completely."

"That sounds like the earl, though it's still hard to accept. Palmer Reese is our brother."

"Half-brother," Marcus corrected bitterly.

"As am I," Rex softly reminded him.

"My father loved your mother. That's hardly the same as this. According to these papers, Avery Reese's sister, Rachael Stowe, was a pretty young widow with a sordid reputation. When she died in childbirth, Avery took Palmer to raise as his son."

"And not out of sheer benevolence, if I'm correctly reading between the lines." Rex shifted his position on the sofa. "Father paid for Palmer's education, even for the house he was raised in."

"The earl was already married when Palmer was born, but the boy was still his oldest son. If Father had claimed him, he would have been heir to the Hawksmoor fortune."

Rex's features hardened. " 'Vengenance is mine, sayeth the Lord.' I say it's a damn good motive for the attacks against Hawksmoor Shipping."

"Palmer was always resentful of us. Now I understand why."

"He thought he should have been the one to inherit the title and fortune."

"Apparently so. Combined with the financial problems he was facing—along with the money he has made since the 'accidents'—I'd say he's had every motive. Unfortunately, these documents still aren't proof enough for the courts."

"So what do we do about it?" Rex asked.

Marcus rubbed his chin with the tips of his fingers. "I'm not sure. But I'm certainly not going to stand by and let him get away with it."

Rex just smiled. "I never thought you would, big brother."

Brandy stood at the window of the drawing room. Through the garden behind the house, she could see Marcus walking along the cliffs, his eyes focused on the distant sails of a ship barely visible against the blue horizon.

A tiny ray of worry filtered through her. Was that longing she saw on his face when he stared out to sea? What was he thinking? Feeling?

Brandy knew what *she* was feeling. She was more in love with him than ever. But in the weeks since they had wed, the worry had refused to disappear, the tiny nagging fear that sooner or later he would leave her.

She saw him turn and head back toward the house. Perhaps he was thinking of Palmer Reese, of the news Rex had brought from London three days ago. Reese was Marcus's illegitimate half-brother and obviously the man behind the attacks on Hawksmoor Shipping, the man who had nearly cost him the use of his legs.

What would Marcus do about it? The question had rolled through her mind a thousand times since he had told her of his discovery. With a sigh, she left the drawing room and went in search of him. When she reached the entry, she saw him in conversation with the butler, who had apparently intercepted a message. Rex also walked up just then.

"It's from Tom Darton, my manager at Hawksmoor Shipping," Marcus said, leading the way toward his study. Brandy followed the two men in.

"What does it say?" Rex asked.

"It's in regard to the upcoming Consolidated Sugar contract. They're Hawksmoor Shipping's most valuable customer. Tom is worried about losing the contract."

"That would certainly pose a problem," Rex said. "Especially after so many other setbacks this past year."

Marcus nodded, his eyes still fixed on the paper. "Tom says Consolidated has decided to do things a little bit differently this year."

"Differently how?" Brandy asked.

"They're going to hold a contest for the bid renewal. It's not unheard of, though they've never done it that way before. They're going to award the contract to the company whose ship makes the fastest time from London to their sugar milling operation in Barbados."

Brandy felt a sinking in the pit of her stomach. Unconsciously her hands formed into fists against her skirt. "Does that mean the *Seahawk* will have to compete?"

"Of course." Both men answered at the same time, two sets of blue eyes swinging toward her.

"I suppose Palmer Reese will also be competing."

"Palmer's been wanting that contract for years," Marcus answered. "He'll do his damnedest to get it."

"Unfortunately, with the bid going out this way," Rex put in, "he'll have a damned good shot at it. The *Fairwind* is one of the fastest ships on the water."

The sinking feeling mushroomed to a cold feeling of dread. Her eyes remained on Marcus. "I imagine Consolidated Sugar will be expecting you to captain the *Seahawk.*"

For the first time, he seemed to sense where her thoughts were leading. He must have noticed how pale she had grown, for he tossed the letter onto the top of the desk, turned, and strode toward her.

Reaching out, he took her hand. "Tom suggested I go, yes. Thanks to Palmer Reese, Hawksmoor Shipping no longer earns the money it once did. We can't afford to lose that contract."

Brandy swallowed past the tight knot in her throat but words seemed to escape her.

Marcus caught her shoulders and turned her to face him. "You aren't thinking this means I'm going back to sea?"

"Are you not? It sounds that way to me."

"This is a single voyage. I realize I'll be gone for a couple of months, but I have no choice. Hamish can't handle this—at least not nearly as well as I can. I have to go, Brianne. Surely you can see that."

She could see it, all right. Only too clearly. He was leaving again, returning to his life at sea—as she had always feared he would. And the worst part was, he was perfectly right in wanting to go.

"I understand why you have to do this, Marcus. I know

how hard you've worked to build Hawksmoor Shipping. I know how you feel about the company and the people who work for you. I simply want to go with you."

Marcus's eyes widened in surprise. He clamped his jaw and shook his head, as she had known he would. "You know I can't do that."

"Why not? I'd love to see Barbados and—"

"It's out of the question. There is every chance Reese will attempt to do as he has before and create some sort of problem. I won't put you in that kind of danger."

She wasn't surprised, yet a soft ache rose in her chest. She wanted to argue, to convince him to take her along. But deep down she had known this would happen. Her heart had known, but her mind had refused to listen.

Tears burned the backs of her eyes. She turned away so that Marcus wouldn't see.

"I wish you luck," she said to him softly. "I have no doubt you'll win." Forcing her legs to move, she walked away.

Marcus stared at her small, retreating figure, a knot building in his stomach. "I thought she would understand."

Rex's gaze remained on the door even after she was gone. "I think she does. She knows you have to go. She also knows you promised not to leave her and return to sea, and now you are breaking your word."

Irritation trickled through him. "I don't believe this—not you, too. What do you expect me to do? If I let Hamish captain the *Seahawk,* there is every chance we'll lose that contract to Palmer Reese. If that happens, Hawksmoore Shipping might as well close its doors. A lot of good people will lose their jobs, to say nothing of the fact that Palmer Reese will succeed in doing exactly what he set out to do—ruin Hawksmoor Shipping and get some sort of twisted revenge against our father."

Rex raked a hand through his hair. "I can't tell you what to do. Perhaps, if you give her some time, she'll be able to accept your leaving."

Marcus's hand slammed down on the desk. "I'm not leaving, dammit! I'm doing a job I have no choice but to do. As soon as I'm finished I'll be back, and that will be the end of it.''

For a long while Rex said nothing, but it was obvious he had his doubts. Apparently Brianne did, too. The clock on the mantel ticked into the silence. ''When will you be going?''

Marcus sighed. ''As soon as I can arrange it. Fortunately, *Seahawk* is due back in port sometime next week. After that, I'll need at least another week to get her ready.''

''I imagine this is Palmer's idea. He's always bragged the *Fairwind* is the fastest ship of its size on the water. I wonder how he arranged it.''

Marcus glanced to the door, thinking of Brianne and hating Palmer Reese more than ever. ''God only knows. One thing is certain—he inherited Father's glib tongue.''

Rex laughed. ''Father could talk a nun out of her habit. Perhaps that is how he got himself into trouble with the young widow Stowe.''

Marcus smiled faintly. ''Perhaps it is. Whatever the truth, I certainly rue the day he slipped into the pretty widow's bed.''

For Brandy, the next days passed in a haze of disturbing emotions. Part of her understood completely why Marcus had to leave.

He has no choice, that voice said. *His company is depending on him. The people who work for him are depending on him. There is nothing else he can do.*

Unfortunately, a second voice reminded her he refused to take her with him. It was the same voice that whispered how much he loved the sea, how he thought of it as his mistress. How he loved it more than he ever could a woman.

It was the voice that warned that once he returned to the life he loved, he would do so again and again, always leaving her behind to endure a lonely life without him.

The days crept past. Since his decision to leave, Marcus had been solicitious, telling her again and again how much he loved her. At the same time, he had been oddly distant, his mind on Palmer Reese and the confrontation ahead. Last night he had made love to her with incredible tenderness. She thought that perhaps he sensed how hard this was for her, how worried she was about the future.

Saturday, the day of his leaving, arrived all too soon. Marcus was packed, the carriage ready for its journey to London. Rex had left two days earlier, returning to the city to begin the needed preparations.

Now it was time for Marcus to join him, and Brandy's stomach clenched with dread. She told herself to accept what she had known from the start, what she could not change, what she had known she would face when she had agreed to marry him. But it wasn't an easy thing to do.

He came into the bedchamber walking purposely, the cane so much a part of him now it no longer distracted from his graceful movements but seemed to enhance them, adding to his masculine appeal. For an instant her heart twisted up inside her. Dragging in a steadying breath, she forced herself under control. He had to go. He had no other choice, and deep down she had always known he would return to sea.

"Are you ready?" she asked, summoning a shaky smile.

Marcus nodded. "My bags are loaded. The carriage awaits out in front." He sighed and raked a hand through his hair. "I wish I didn't have to leave you."

Her smile faltered, faded away altogether. "So do I," she said softly.

"If it weren't for the danger, I would take you with me."

She glanced away, blinking fiercely. "You never cared much for a woman on board your ship. I'm sure that hasn't changed."

Marcus reached out and caught her chin, forced her to look at him. "That isn't true—not anymore. It is simply that I want you safe."

Brandy drew away, moved off toward the window. "Sometimes being safe isn't the most important thing."

Marcus approached behind her. She could hear the rustle

of his jacket as he drew near. "You don't believe I *want* to go?"

"You've always loved the sea, Marcus. Of course you want to go."

He turned her to face him, drew her into his arms, cradling her against his chest. "It's imperative I regain this contract. I'm going because I have to. I love you, Brianne. I'll be back as quickly as I can."

Brandy just nodded. He had to go, and yet her heart felt leaden. She could feel the crisp starch of his shirtfront against her cheek, smell the clean, masculine fragrance of his skin, and for an instant her careful control threatened to crumble.

He released his hold and a feeling of emptiness washed over her. "I'll miss you, Marcus," she said softly, looking into his dear, handsome face. "Please be careful."

Bending his head, he kissed her and Brandy kissed him back, loving him in that moment more than she ever had before, terrified she was losing him, that the pull of the sea would simply be too strong.

"I'll be back as soon as I can." A last hard kiss and was gone, his footfalls echoing like a death knell as he made his way down the hall and out of her life again.

Marcus had almost reached the carriage before the nagging at the back of his head became a clanging hammer of warning. He thought of the journey ahead, imagined the long, lonely weeks he would be spending at sea. He thought of Brianne and how much he had missed her before, how close he had come to losing her, and his insides twisted up inside him.

He had told her the truth—he didn't want to leave her. But the risk of taking her along was simply too great.

Sometimes being safe isn't the most important thing.

Marcus paused at the bottom of the front porch stairs. Surely she didn't think he was returning to sea for good? That this was simply the beginning of a life she would have no part in? And yet there was something in her eyes, something of longing and loss. He had begged her to marry him, had promised her he would not leave her, that his life at sea was over. And it was.

But in truth, part of him wanted to go back to sea, wanted to feel the deck of the *Seahawk* beneath his feet—at least for a while.

Marcus drew in a shuddering breath. In a way Brianne was right. He loved the sea and always would, but he loved his wife far more. He didn't want to lose her—not for any reason. He remembered only too clearly what his life had been like without her.

Marcus felt a soul-deep chill. There was danger on this voyage, to be sure, but Brandy was the strongest, bravest woman he had ever known, and if he was careful, he could find a way to protect her. Leaving her behind, he suddenly saw, severing the bond of trust they had only begun to rebuild, was an even greater risk—one that could destroy them both.

Marcus turned at the bottom of the steps and started back into the house, his heart pounding almost painfully inside his chest. He strode down the carpeted hall toward the elaborate suite he shared with Brianne, opened the door, and stepped into the room.

She was sitting in a chair in front of the window, her back to the door, staring out at the water. Though she wasn't making a sound, her shoulders shook as she sat there silently weeping. She turned as he walked in, jumped up from the chair, and hastily brushed the tears from her cheeks. Marcus's heart twisted hard inside him, his long stride halting just inside the door.

"Marcus . . . ?" Her cheeks were still damp, her golden eyes desolate and filled with pain. A swell of emotion streaked through him, made his fingers shake where they clutched the head of his cane.

"Brianne . . . love. I'm sorry."

"Marcus . . . what is it? What's happened? Did you forgot something?"

His throat closed up. He wanted to hold her, to take away the darkness in her eyes. God, how could he have been such a fool? He swallowed past the lump in his throat and smiled at her gently.

"No, love. I remembered something. I remembered that you were more important to me than any contract, any race, any thoughts of revenge. I remembered how I felt when I lost you, how desperate I was when I thought you might marry someone else. Suddenly I realized what a fool I've been."

Brianne said nothing, but her hand reached down to grip the arm of the chair. Her golden eyes clung to his face. "I don't. . . . I don't understand."

"I made you a promise before we were married. I asked you to trust me. If I leave here without you, I'm breaking my promise and destroying that trust."

Her bottom lip trembled. "Are you saying that you're taking me with you?"

"Now and anytime you want to go. I won't leave you again, Brianne. I promised you that and I meant it. I hope you can forgive me for forgetting what's important."

"Marcus . . ." She took a single step toward him and Marcus caught her up in his arms.

"God, Brianne." She clung to his neck and he thought nothing had ever felt so wonderfully, incredibly good. He kissed her, desperately, thoroughly, and Brandy kissed him back. "Pack your things," he said softly. "You're going to see Barbados. And we have a race to win."

The sweet sound of laughter bubbled up from her throat. Such a beautiful sound, he thought, more certain than ever he had done the right thing.

"We *will* win, Marcus." She tossed back her cloud of copper hair. "Against the two of us, Palmer Reese doesn't stand a chance."

Marcus just smiled. Reese didn't stand a chance and neither did he. Brandy Winters had won the contest for his heart long ago, in the days she had changed from girl to woman at the White Horse Tavern.

CHAPTER 26

The London docks seethed with activity. The street in front of the quay bustled with freight wagons, carriages, and horses, the jangle of harness and the shouts of men at work. Drunken sailors, doxies, merchants, and dockworkers all crowded into each other as they made their way along the cobbled street.

Leaning against the rail of the *Seahawk,* Hamish Bass absently watched their progress. Like rats in a maze, he thought with a shake of his gray-haired head, already looking forward to returning to his life at sea. More often his gaze fixed on the work going on aboard the *Seahawk.* The ship had been in port almost a week. The day after their arrival, the captain had appeared on deck carrving the news of Consolidated Sugar and the race they would have to win in order for the powerful sugar company to renew its shipping contract.

Hamish smiled, glad to have the cap'n back aboard. If anyone could win against the *Fairwind*—which wouldn't be an easy task—it would be Marcus Delaine.

Hamish's smile curled into a full-fledgd grin. The captain's arrival hadn't surprised him, though the appearance of his new wife was a mite unexpected. Brandy Winters Delaine, Lady Hawksmoor, had come aboard with a look of excitement and a smile for the men in the crew. She had made herself useful right away, going to work down in the galley with Cyrus Lamb to help feed the small group of men who remained aboard, though the captain had grumbled it weren't dignified for a lady to be doin' such a thing.

The lass had merely smiled. Then she had up and kissed

him, right there in front of the men. She said she'd go crazy if he left her below all those weeks in his cabin with naught to do but read.

The captain had given in, of course. He was a different, happier man than he was the last time Hamish had seen him. Hamish chuckled to think the captain had surely done the right thing in marryin' the lass and bringin' her with him.

Hamish turned at the sound of footfalls, saw young Brig Butler walking toward him.

"Mr. Bass—have you seen Captain Delaine?" Brig had returned to England some months back and was working for his father, trying his hand at becoming a merchant. But the lad had heard about the race and he was determined to come along.

"We've got a problem, sir. We need to find the captain right away." Blond and fair, Butler strode the deck as if he were the owner instead of a lowly seaman. Odd thing was, Hamish liked that about him. He was capable and he knew it. The lad was becoming quite a man.

"Are you two looking for me?" Marcus stepped out from behind the wheelhouse, Brandy right beside him. "What is it, Mr. Butler?"

A commotion on deck interrupted his reply. "Stop him! Stop that man before he gets away!" Three sailors exploded up the ladder, chasing a big, beefy sailor who tore across the deck. "Don't let him escape!"

As the man raced past, Marcus stuck his foot out and the heavy man went sprawling. In seconds, Brig Butler had him pinned to the deck, a muscled forearm locked around the stout man's throat.

"Set him on his feet," Marcus commanded, and Brig hoisted him up, shoving one of the man's arms up behind his back, forearm still wrapped around the man's powerful neck.

"Tell him, Deeks," Brig demanded. "Tell the captain what you were doing down in the hold."

Deeks wildly shook his head. "Nothin'! I weren't doin' nothin' but workin' on the timbers like I was 'ired for."

"He was usin' a chisel on the gear wheels, Cap'n Delaine,'' one of the sailors said. ''He was weakening the wood so's eventually it would break.''

Marcus pinned him with a hard, dark glare, taking the chisel and turning it over in his hands. ''Amazing, isn't it? What a little tool like this will do. Weaken the gear wheels, ship loses its stearing. If it had happened during a storm, *Seahawk* might have capsized. Were you trying to sink us, Mr. Deeks, or merely slow us down?''

''I don't know what yer talkin'—''

Brig cranked hard on the arm behind Deeks's back. ''How's your memory now, Deeks?''

''I wasn't tryin' to sink ya,'' he panted. ''Just slow ya down, make sure ya weren't the first man to Barbados.'' He was breathing hard, clawing at the arm around his throat.

''You worked on the *Seahawk* before, as I recall.'' Marcus slapped the chisel against his palm. ''While you were at it, I imagine you've done other jobs like this. You caused some of the accidents we had, didn't you?''

Deeks's eyes darted frantically around, searching for a means of escape. Brig forced the man's arm up a painful inch.

''Didn't you?''

Slowly, he nodded.

''Who hired you?''

When Deeks didn't speak up, Brig clamped down on his throat. ''Palmer Reese,'' he croaked out. ''Sometime back, 'e come to me shop, offered me more money than a man could make in a year. '' 'E knew I'd been workin' for ye. 'E wanted me to weaken the rudder.''

''Go on,'' Marcus prodded.

''Last night 'e came again. 'E knew I was workin' on the *Seahawk,* like before. 'E told me about the race and asked me if I could find a way to slow ya down so as 'e could be sure to win. That's all it was, I swear it. Just a way to slow ya down so's 'e could win.''

''Hamish, fetch me some rope to tie him up. Mr. Deeks and I are going to pay a little visit on my old friend Palmer Reese.''

Brianne clutched his arm. "Don't you think we should let the authorities handle this? Why don't we send for a watchman?"

Marcus worked a muscle in his jaw. "In due course, love. First I want to talk to Reese."

"But wouldn't it be better if—"

"No."

Brianne's chin hiked up. "All right—if you won't listen to reason, then I'm going with you."

"You're not going anywhere. You're staying right here."

"But—"

"For once in your life, do as I tell you, Brianne." Her face turned red and her lips went thin, but she didn't argue, just turned and stalked away.

Marcus's gaze followed her progress and he fought down a hint of amusement. "Hamish, you keep an eye on things while I'm gone. Mr. Butler—give me half an hour's head start, then go to the magistrate's office. Bring them to Reese's building on the embankment." Marcus took a hard grip on the stocky man's bound arms. "As for you, Deeks, I'm afraid you'll have to come with me."

Brandy twisted the fabric of her skirt and peered worriedly out the window of the hackney carriage she had hired on the quay where *Seahawk* was docked. It didn't take long to reach her destination. As soon as the conveyance drew to a halt, she stepped down, handed the man several shillings, crossed the cobblestone street, and stood in front of the door to the office of Reese Enterprises.

Getting there had been easier than she'd imagined. Hamish had been busy shouting orders. Brig was working below. She'd simply skirted the men, descended the gangway to the dock, and hailed a passing hack.

Marcus had only been gone a few minutes before she had left, yet her worry continued to build. She should have convinced him to go to the authorities. She could only imagine what Palmer Reese might do when Marcus confronted him with the beefy Mr. Deeks. Or, for that matter, what Deeks might do.

Brandy stiffened her spine and shoved open the heavy wooden doors. She had known where Reese Enterprises was. She had passed the three-story brick building every time they'd left or returned to the ship. It was cool inside now. A small area set aside for clerical work filled one corner, but no one was there. Through the thick oak timbers above her head, she could hear men's voices coming from the second floor, Marcus's husky baritone and Palmer's smoother, more genteel tones. Deeks was whining and Reese began threatening, his voice louder now.

Brandy's heart started thudding. For months she had played the dutiful wife, obeying her husband's wishes. This time his safety overrode his commands. At least she could go for help if it looked as if it were needed.

Quietly she climbed the stairs, hoping they wouldn't creak and give her away, then crept down the hall. The voices grew louder. Something shattered against a wall and Brandy's heart slammed hard. She pressed her back against the cool white plaster and eased closer, straining to hear the men's words, wishing she had brought a watchman with her, as she very nearly had done.

It was too late for that now. She moved closer, turned the knob, and eased the door open a crack. Through the narrow slit, she could see Marcus standing next to Deeks, whose florid features were suffused with angry color. A few feet away, Palmer Reese stood rigid, his eyes burning with a wild sort of light and fixed unwaveringly on Marcus's face. Instead of the fear she had expected to see, there was an odd smile on his face.

"So . . . aside from what Mr. Deeks has told you . . ." Reese said. "I gather you have finally unearthed the matter of our kinship."

"If you want to call it that. Personally, I prefer to ignore it."

Palmer shrugged his shoulders, though his expression was hardly nonchalant. "So did your brother Geoffrey."

Marcus's eyes went wide. "Geoffrey knew you were Father's by-blow?"

Reese stiffened at the term. "He didn't discover we were brothers until just before he died. Not until the day of the accident."

The color leeched from beneath Marcus's swarthy cheeks. "You're not saying you had something to do with his death?"

Again the faint lifting of the shoulders. "I should have been the heir. If Geoffrey had to die, it was the Earl of Hawksmoor's fault."

"Good God—you arranged the accident on the bridge! You paid someone to weaken the timbers, just as you paid Deeks to sabotage my ship!"

"And quite a good job I did, too. I must admit to discovering a knack for such things. It isn't as easy as it might seem."

Unconsciously Marcus stepped toward him, his hands shaking as they balled into fists. "You murdered my brother. You very nearly killed me. Now, by God, I'm going to kill you!"

Chaos erupted in the room. Marcus lunged for Reese and Deeks bolted for the door. The instant the burly Deeks moved between the other two men, Reese jerked a pistol from the pocket of his coat and whirled toward Marcus, the weapon pointed straight at his heart. Brandy screamed as the weight of Marcus's body crashed into Palmer Reese and sent the gun flying, landing, then spinning across the floor to slam against the door just a few inches away from where she stood.

Brandy reached though the opening and snatched it up, aiming the heavy weapon with a shaky hand at the burly man racing for the door.

"You had better go back inside, Mr. Deeks. I don't think my husband is through with you yet." Deeks stepped backward, his hands still tied behind him, and Brandy followed him in. It was the first time she had ever been glad she was raised at the White Horse Tavern.

Across the room, Marcus was pounding away at Palmer

Reese. Palmer's nose dripped blood. His shirtfront gleamed with a spray of crimson. Perspiration-slick brown hair hung limply over his forehead. Marcus hit him again, smashing the back of his head against the floor, and Palmer's eyes slid closed.

Marcus raised a fist to hit him again.

"Don't do it, Marcus. He isn't worth it. Besides, wouldn't you rather see him hang?"

Marcus's fist shook with the effort of will it took to pull the punch. His chest was heaving, his breath coming fast. "The bloody whoreson killed my brother."

"I know," Brandy said gently.

For the first time in minutes, Marcus seemed to realize where he was and what was going on in the room around him. The haze of anger appeared to lift and he glanced to where Brandy stood in front of Deeks, the pistol steady now, pointed at the man's barrel chest.

With an exhausted sigh, Marcus heaved himself up off Reese's body and came to his feet. He bent and retrieved his cane and had just started in her direction when Brandy caught the flash of silver in Reese's hand.

"Marcus!" Swinging the pistol away from Deeks, she aimed at Reese and pulled the trigger. The painful blast rang in her ears, the vicious recoil tearing the gun from her fingers. For a moment, the grisly scene seemed frozen in time, Deeks and Marcus staring, their eyes wide with shock, blood oozing from the front of Reese's waistcoat just to the right of the silver buttons.

Dragging himself up on an elbow, Reese looked down at the pumping stream of red as if he couldn't believe what he was seeing, then he fell back on the carpet and his eyes slid closed. A final breath whispered past his lips.

"He—he had a gun, Marcus. It—it's there in his hand." Marcus pulled his eyes away from Brandy and knelt at the dead man's side. He pulled the small pocket pistol from his pale, limp fingers.

"Palmer was always a man of surprises." Marcus's attention swung to Deeks, who glanced longingly toward the door.

"I wouldn't do that if I were you. Brig Butler is on his way here now with the authorities. By the time you reach the bottom of the stairs, there'll be watchmen all over the street."

The burly man's shoulders sagged in defeat. His head hung forward as he sank down in a straight-backed wooden chair. Crossing the room to Brandy's side, Marcus eased her into his arms.

"It's all right, love. It's over."

Her body started to tremble. Brandy leaned against him, fighting to hold back tears. "He would have killed you, Marcus."

Marcus kissed the top of her head. "I think that's what he's wanted all along. I imagine if he had succeeded, Rex very well might have been his next victim."

She released a shaky breath. "I've never killed a man before."

Marcus tightened his hold around her. "You saved my life, Brianne. I was worried about putting you in danger on this voyage. As it's turned out, if you hadn't come along, I would very likely be dead."

Brandy slid her arms around his neck and he held her tightly against him. A door opened on the street below and she could hear the thunder of footfalls racing up the stairs.

"I believe Brig has arrived with reinforcements."

Relief slid through her. "Thank God."

A few seconds later, the door swung open and Brig walked in. As watchmen swarmed around Deeks and the dead man, Marcus led Brandy downstairs.

"They'll want some sort of statement from each of us. I should think you would rather do it down here."

Brandy nodded, grateful to be away from the sordid scene upstairs. Standing next to Marcus, she leaned against him, tilting her head back against his shoulder to look up at him.

"After what's happened, I imagine Consolidated Sugar will be certain to renew your contract."

He nodded. "Yes, I imagine they will."

"I suppose that means the race is off, that you won't have to beat the *Fairwind.*"

He smiled with an unmistakable trace of disappointment. "It won't be necessary now. Once the story of what's happened comes out, Reese Enterprises will be out of business."

"I can't say I am sorry about that, but I was thinking . . . wondering . . . do you think there is any chance we could still go Barbados?"

Marcus's dark eyes crinkled at the corners and a rumble of laughter rose up from deep in his chest. "Ah, Lady Hawksmoor, you are a treasure." He grinned. "If Barbados is your wish, how could I possibly deny you?"

Brandy laughed. "I love you, Marcus."

"I love you, Brianne—more than the sea, for as long as there is a sea and beyond."

Brandy went up on her toes and kissed him. There was no more doubt, no more fear. Marcus loved her and he would never leave her. They had found their home in each other and, wherever they were, as long as they were together, their hearts would be at peace.

Author's Note

Some of you may have had a vague feeling of recognition when you read this story. The idea for it came from a song popular in the seventies about a tavern maid and the sailor she loved, a man she could never have because his life would always be the sea.

Brandy was the name of the song, and I had always thought it one of the most romantic I'd ever heard. But typically, as a writer of Romance fiction, I wanted it to have a happy ending. What would it take, I wondered, to make a man realize that love for a woman could be even more important than his love of the sea?

Over the years I came up with the story of Brandy Winters and Marcus Delaine. I hope you enjoyed it, and whenever you hear the song you'll remember their story has a happy ending.

On a last note, for those of you who enjoyed NOTHING BUT VELVET, I hope you'll watch for Lucien's story, SILK AND STEEL, coming soon from St. Martin's Paperbacks.

Best wishes and good reading,
Kat

NS599

Survey

TELL US WHAT YOU THINK AND YOU COULD WIN

A YEAR OF ROMANCE!

(That's 12 books!)

Fill out the survey below, send it back to us, and you'll be eligible to win a year's worth of romance novels. That's one book a month for a year—from St. Martin's Paperbacks.

Name ____

Street Address ____________________________________

City, State, Zip Code _______________________________

Email address _____________________________________

1. How many romance books have you bought in the last year?
   (Check one.)
   __0-3
   __4-7
   __8-12
   __13-20
   __20 or more

2. Where do you MOST often buy books? *(limit to two choices)*
   __Independent bookstore
   __Chain stores *(Please specify)*
      __Barnes and Noble
      __B. Dalton
      __Books-a-Million
      __Borders
      __Crown
      __Lauriat's
      __Media Play
      __Waldenbooks
   __Supermarket
   __Department store *(Please specify)*
      __Caldor
      __Target
      __Kmart
      __Walmart
   __Pharmacy/Drug store
   __Warehouse Club
   __Airport

3. Which of the following promotions would MOST influence your decision to purchase a ROMANCE paperback? *(Check one.)*
   __Discount coupon

__Free preview of the first chapter
__Second book at half price
__Contribution to charity
__Sweepstakes or contest

4. Which promotions would LEAST influence your decision to purchase a ROMANCE book? (Check one.)
   __Discount coupon
   __Free preview of the first chapter
   __Second book at half price
   __Contribution to charity
   __Sweepstakes or contest

5. When a new ROMANCE paperback is released, what is MOST influential in your finding out about the book and in helping you to decide to buy the book? (Check one.)
   __TV advertisement
   __Radio advertisement
   __Print advertising in newspaper or magazine
   __Book review in newspaper or magazine
   __Author interview in newspaper or magazine
   __Author interview on radio
   __Author appearance on TV
   __Personal appearance by author at bookstore
   __In-store publicity (poster, flyer, floor display, etc.)
   __Online promotion (author feature, banner advertising, giveaway)
   __Word of Mouth
   __Other (please specify)______________________________

6. Have you ever purchased a book online?
   __Yes
   __No

7. Have you visited our website?
   __Yes
   __No

8. Would you visit our website in the future to find out about new releases or author interviews?
   __Yes
   __No

9. What publication do you read most?
   __Newspapers *(check one)*
      __*USA Today*
      __*New York Times*
      __Your local newspaper
   __Magazines *(check one)*

__*People*
__*Entertainment Weekly*
__Women's magazine *(Please specify:________________)*
__*Romantic Times*
__Romance newsletters

10. What type of TV program do you watch most? *(Check one.)*
    __Morning News Programs (ie. "Today Show")
    (Please specify:________________)
    __Afternoon Talk Shows (ie. "Oprah")
    (Please specify: ________________)
    __All news (such as CNN)
    __Soap operas *(Please specify: ________________)*
    __Lifetime cable station
    __E! cable station
    __Evening magazine programs (ie. "Entertainment Tonight")
    (Please specify: ________________)
    __Your local news

11. What radio stations do you listen to most? *(Check one.)*
    __Talk Radio
    __Easy Listening/Classical
    __Top 40
    __Country
    __Rock
    __Lite rock/Adult contemporary
    __CBS radio network
    __National Public Radio
    __WESTWOOD ONE radio network

12. What time of day do you listen to the radio MOST?
    __6am-10am
    __10am-noon
    __Noon-4pm
    __4pm-7pm
    __7pm-10pm
    __10pm-midnight
    __Midnight-6am

13. Would you like to receive email announcing new releases and special promotions?
    __Yes
    __No

14. Would you like to receive postcards announcing new releases and special promotions?
    __Yes
    __No

15. Who is your favorite romance author? ____________________

WIN A YEAR OF ROMANCE FROM SMP

(That's 12 Books!)

No Purchase Necessary

OFFICIAL RULES

1. To Enter: Complete the Official Entry Form and Survey and mail it to: Win a Year of Romance from SMP Sweepstakes, c/o St. Martin's Paperbacks, 175 Fifth Avenue, Suite 1615, New York, NY 10010-7848, Attention JP. For a copy of the Official Entry Form and Survey, send a self-addressed, stamped envelope to: Entry Form/Survey, c/o St. Martin's Paperbacks at the address stated above. Entries with the completed surveys must be received by February 1, 2000 (February 22, 2000 for entry forms requested by mail). Limit one entry per person. No mechanically reproduced or illegible entries accepted. Not responsible for lost, misdirected, mutilated or late entries.

2. Random Drawing. Winner will be determined in a random drawing to be held on or about March 1, 2000 from all eligible entries received. Odds of winning depend on the number of eligible entries received. Potential winner will be notified by mail on or about March 22, 2000 and will be asked to execute and return an Affidavit of Eligibility/Release/Prize Acceptance Form within fourteen (14) days of attempted notification. Non-compliance within this time may result in disqualification and the selection of an alternate winner. Return of any prize/prize notification as undeliverable will result in disqualification and an alternate winner will be selected.

3. Prize and approximate Retail Value: Winner will receive a copy of a different romance novel each month from April 2000 through March 2001. Approximate retail value $84.00 (U.S. dollars).

4. Eligibility. Open to U.S. and Canadian residents (excluding residents of the province of Quebec) who are 18 at the time of entry. Employees of St. Martin's and its parent, affiliates and subsidiaries, its and their directors, officers and agents, and their immediate families or those living in the same household, are ineligible to enter. Potential Canadian winners will be required to correctly answer a time-limited arithmetic skill question by mail. Void in Puerto Rico and wherever else prohibited by law.

5. General Conditions: Winner is responsible for all federal, state and local taxes. No substitution or cash redemption of prize permitted by winner. Prize is not transferable. Acceptance of prize constitutes permission to use the winner's name, photograph and likeness for purposes of advertising and promotion without additional compensation or permission, unless prohibited by law.

6. All entries become the property of sponsor, and will not be returned. By participating in this sweepstakes, entrants agree to be bound by these official rules and the decision of the judges, which are final in all respects.

7. For the name of the winner, available after March 22, 2000, send by May 1, 2000 a stamped, self-addressed envelope to Winner's List, Win a Year of Romance from SMP Sweepstakes, St. Martin's Paperbacks, 175 Fifth Avenue, Suite 1615, New York, NY 10010-7848, Attention JP.